BLOOD

SWEAT

AND

FEARS

ALSO BY EMMA SALISBURY

THE DS COUPLAND DETECTIVE SERIES:
FRAGILE CORD (Book One)
A PLACE OF SAFETY (Book Two)
ONE BAD TURN (Book Three)
ABSENT (Book Four)
FLESH AND BLOOD (Book Five)
STICKS AND STONES (Book Six)
WHEN DARKNESS FALLS Book Seven)
MADE TO BE BROKEN (Book Eight)

THE DAVY JOHNSON EDINBURGH GANGLAND SERIES:
TRUTH LIES WAITING (Book One)
THE SILENCE BEFORE THE SCREAM (Book Two)

Blood Sweat and Fears

Emma Salisbury

Copyright

Copyright © 2023 Emma Salisbury
All rights reserved.

No part of this publication may be reproduced or transmitted in any form or by any means without permission of the author.

All the characters in this book are fictitious and any resemblance to actual persons living or dead is purely coincidental. Although real place names and agencies and support services are referred to in this book the storyline relating to them is completely fictitious.

Cover design by Jane Dixon-Smith
Interior design by Coinlea Services

*In loving memory of Anne Rowarth
I stand on the shoulders of the sister who
marched before me.
Love ya sis.*

ACKNOWLEDGEMENTS

My thanks to those without whom Blood Sweat and Fears wouldn't have made it this far include ex-Police Officer Stuart McGuire, who served with Greater Manchester Police for 16 years before resigning at Sergeant rank, for his time and guidance on police procedures as well as his beady eye for detail. Lin White at Coinlea Services for pointing out embarrassing errors. Sally Howorth and Sue Barnett – for weeding out the howlers. To Lynn Osborne who continues to keep me right.

Thanks also to my amazing readers, without whom all of this would be without purpose. As a thank you, several readers who subscribe to my author newsletter were selected to have characters named after them in the book. I had to create a character specially for one of them - Alfie, a Black and Tan Dachshund. I hope that everyone enjoys what I've done with them!

To my wonderful family for accepting me without question. To Stephen, for the bottle of fizz on a Friday regardless of the progress I've made.

BLOOD SWEAT AND FEARS

OPERATION MAPLE TASKFORCE MEMBER DIRECTORY

Commander Peter Howorth	Overall command of operation. Based with SENET (Sexual Exploitation National Enquiry Team), Europol, National Crime Agency. Promoted to Chief Superintendent during his time at GMP's Child Sexual Exploitation and Public Protection Units.
Superintendent Tony Romain	Senior Investigating Officer responsible for day-to-day operations and assimilating intelligence. On secondment from the Met's Art Crime Unit, specialising in high end art and antique theft. Previously a protection officer assigned to the Royalty Protection Squad, SO14.
Detective Superintendent Lara Cole	General oversight of Operation Maple. Attached to the Organised Crime Unit at Nexus House.

DCI Amjid Akram	Investigation of financial irregularities. Based with Economic and Cyber Crime, City of London Police (Previously with the National Crime Agency)
DCI Shane Swain	Core investigation team. Seconded from TITAN, North West Organised Crime Unit Previous Secondment: Europol
DI Joe Edwards	Core investigation team. Specialist officer in 'Lawfare', where facts are withheld from the public through 'Super injunctions'. Previously involved in the investigation into phone hacking by the press.
DI Benjamin Taylor	Core investigation team. CHIS handler (Covert Human Intelligence Source) with the South East Regional Crime Unit. Previous secondment: Europol
DS Kevin Coupland	Core investigation team. Seconded from Murder Investigation Team, Salford Precinct station.
DC Noah Rainey	Digital Forensic Unit
DC Jared Ozin	Digital Forensic Unit

ADDITIONAL PERSONNEL

UCO 592　　　　　　　　Undercover officer
(AKA Jay O'Neill)
DS Catherine Arnott　　　Organised Crime Unit, The Met
DI Melvin Jones　　　　　British Transport Police

PROLOGUE

NOW

By the time the first squad car arrived two paramedics were already working on the victim. A crowd had formed around them despite the piss wet drizzle that soaked everyone to the skin. Screamers, pointers, folk who thought it was their civic duty to stand and gawp.

Two uniformed officers clambered out of the car, barking at the crowd to disperse, let the emergency services get on with their job.

'At least the poor bastard hasn't got far to go,' one onlooker muttered as they moved on, nodding in the direction of Salford Royal Hospital across the road, its main entrance illuminated against the dark sky.

'Fucking joyriders,' muttered another, 'locking 'em up isn't enough…'

'Did you see what happened?' one of the officers demanded, glancing at his colleague who was speaking to a woman in a quilted jacket, zipped up against the cold. The woman was crying and shaking her head, presumably in answer to the same question.

'I didn't need to see it to work out what's happened,' the onlooker replied. 'They're always racing along this stretch of road. You take your life into your hands just crossing to go to the bus stop. The number of times I've called you lot out, but no one bothers turning up…'

The crackle of radio static as Control informed them more units were on their way.

'All a bit bloody late now…' the man chimed.

Two more paramedics ran over from the hospital. One immediately joined his colleagues; the other waved his arms at the crowd whilst shouting at the officers to help give them some bloody room. A second squad car pulled into a parking bay beyond the bus stop; the officers in this car were older, heavier round the middle. Within minutes the crowd had been sent packing, the area taped off and the details of the witness who'd called it in taken down and passed onto a detective who emerged from an unmarked car. The older PCs tugged at their Kevlar vests as they eyed the rookies, as if to say 'That's how you do it.'

The detective, a tall, black man with an athletic build, eyed the uniformed officer nearest to him. 'How long have they been working on the victim?'

The officer shrugged without thinking. Found himself squirming under the detective's gaze.

'Twenty minutes,' said one of the rookies. 'They were going full pelt when we got here. Witness claims the car mounted the pavement at speed. She didn't stand a chance of getting out of the way.'

'Did they get a look at the driver?'

The officer gave him a look. 'If white shifty-looking male narrows it down then your luck's in.'

DS Chris Ashcroft knew there was no such thing as luck. Certainly not enough of the good kind anyway. He watched the paramedics lift the victim onto a stretcher, caught the eye of one he'd seen on other shouts, where the outcome could swing either way. Where a gasp of air was the difference between murder or attempted murder.

The paramedic shook his head. Some were just

impossible to call. 'They'll take bloody good care of her,' he said, nodding towards the hospital's accident and emergency entrance.

Ashcroft watched as a dozen medical personnel in different coloured scrubs rushed through the automatic doors heading in their direction. He stepped towards the stretchered victim.

'She's one of ours,' the paramedic explained, indicating the hospital logo on the victim's tunic, just visible beneath her jacket. A c-spine collar had been placed around her neck. An oxygen mask covered her nose and mouth. The medics swarmed around the stretcher like angry wasps, manoeuvring it towards the entrance to A and E.

Amid the shouts as the paramedics handed over their charge, Ashcroft bent to retrieve a plastic ID badge that had fallen to the ground as the victim was moved. More staff had gathered on the hospital's forecourt. This group was silent, straining to hear the list of injuries suffered by one of their own. Ashcroft glanced down at the badge as he followed the stretcher. His mouth ran dry when he caught sight of the photograph. 'Jesus, fuck,' he muttered.

'She's a nurse in the neo-natal unit,' the paramedic added once the handover was complete. They'd reached the double doors leading to resus. Staff had gathered in the corridor outside it.

A male nurse blocked Ashcroft's path when he tried to enter. 'Authorised personnel only,' he choked out, before turning his back on him.

His services no longer required, the paramedic steered Ashcroft to the waiting area.

Ashcroft's chest thumped as he shifted his gaze once more to the name below the photograph, hoping to

Christ he'd mis-read it. The breath caught in his throat.

'She's married to one of your lot, isn't she?' the paramedic said.

Ashcroft jerked his head up and down as he pocketed Lynn Coupland's ID badge. Swiped at the sweat forming on his brow.

THREE MONTHS EARLIER

SEPTEMBER

CHAPTER ONE

There'd been the obligatory piss up. The back room of The Volunteer Arms had been commandeered by Salford Precinct's rank and file. Some came to wish him well, others to check the grumpy twat in the murder syndicate really was leaving.

The announcement of his transfer had been met with suspicion. An elaborate April first hoax, only April had been and gone long since.

'I always thought the only way you'd leave the team was feet first,' DC Turnbull confided when the decibel level in the bar had dropped enough that conversations were possible.

Word had spread that DCI Mallender and Chief Superintendent Curtis had put money behind the bar. Off-duty officers binge-drank their way through the drinks menu with all the gusto of a student during freshers week.

'No offence like,' Turnbull added when DS Kevin Coupland eyeballed him.

'None taken,' Coupland drawled, the drink making him mellow. Plenty more would have bet on him being carted off by Professional Standards, he didn't wonder. Ironic really, given the circumstances. There were those who wondered whether the grand send-off from the powers-that-be was to hide a demotion. After all, who in their right mind would choose to work for Greater

Manchester Police's Organised Crime Unit? But his rank hadn't changed, so it was a sideways move at best, for longer hours and even greater risk. It didn't add up.

Coupland understood the reason he'd been sworn to silence. Why he'd had to sign the Official Secrets Act. Apart from him, the Chief Super and DCI Mallender were the only people in the room who knew what he was really doing. That he'd joined a taskforce whose sole aim was to take down the Dutchman, an elusive scumbag who traded in human trafficking and online sex abuse.

Coupland recalled when the idea had first been put to him by an ex-colleague, DI Alex Moreton, whose words still rang in his ears:

'Every Chief Constable in the country has been instructed to reduce gender-based violence. It's come from the Government but this time it isn't political rhetoric. We need to gain maximum traction. Collaborating with other forces to dismantle the networks abusing women and girls has to be a priority.' She'd paused, giving her words time to sink in. 'I could put a word in, Kevin, if you wanted. Get you seconded to the operational team.'

The wheels in motion had moved smoothly for once. His transfer rubberstamped before he'd had a chance to talk himself out of it, though Lynn had made a sterling effort.

She'd taken the news about his secondment hard, with trepidation if the truth be told. *These are hard core criminals prepared to kill to protect their network*, she'd reminded him. *What was it about danger that attracted him so?*

But then he'd explained about the culture the taskforce was trying to eradicate. A culture where women and girls were portrayed online as nothing more than playthings, watched by millions of men all too keen to tap in their credit card numbers. Change had to start somewhere, and this was as good a place to start as any.

After a while they'd stopped talking about it. Coupland knew enough to know that this wasn't acceptance on her part by any stretch of the imagination. She wasn't happy with his choice, but she knew better than to talk him out of it. Instead, an uneasy peace had settled between them.

He felt the Chief Super's gaze sweep over him, making him turn to look in the senior officer's direction. Chief Superintendent Curtis. A man who carried his newfound greatness with ease. As though he knew that he was fulfilling a pre-determined destiny. Coupland, the polar opposite, preferred not to think too far ahead. Looking forward felt to him like tempting fate. He preferred to live in the here and now, to see no more than the six feet in front of him.

There was something odd about the way Curtis looked at him, and when he excused himself from the group he was talking to and made his way towards Coupland he broke eye contact just for a moment. What now? Coupland wondered. Had the powers-that-be decided that they couldn't justify his involvement in the task force after all? Negativity came second nature to him, an outlook that served him well. Besides, he was too long in the tooth to change now. He forced a smile on his face when Curtis came to a stop in front of him.

'Look, Kevin, there's something I need to tell you.'

Coupland eyed him steadily. 'Go on then,' he said, readying himself.

'There's been a bit of a development,' Curtis began, his eyes making contact with DCI Mallender across the room as though this speech had been rehearsed and the

DCI was on standby in case Coupland acted up. Coupland waited.

'There's no easy way to say this,' Curtis began again.

'I can see that,' said Coupland.

'I'm afraid Kieran Tunny was released today.' He paused, adding: 'On a technicality,' as though that would soften the blow.

Coupland blinked. He tilted his head to one side as though he couldn't quite hear what had been said, but he'd heard it alright. Of all the accusations that could be levelled at Chief Superintendent Curtis, poor enunciation wasn't one of them.

Coupland barked out a laugh. 'This is a wind-up, right?' He looked round to see if the others were in on the joke, yet none of the officers drinking their body weight in beer paid them any attention.

He turned his full beam stare on Curtis. 'What technicality? The case against him was watertight. I was the one that submitted it to the CPS. There wasn't a T crossed or an I dotted that I didn't oversee first. I checked everything in triplicate. The bastard was found guilty of conspiracy to murder. It was him who gave the order for James McMahon to be executed. We've even got a transcript of the text he sent giving the command, for Christ's sake.'

A few looks thrown in his direction made Coupland realise that he was ranting, that he hadn't drawn breath in over a minute and that the Chief Super was looking more than a little uncomfortable.

Kieran Tunny was a notorious crime boss who held Salford in the palm of his hand. Stints in jail were no threat to men like him and it showed in the way he settled disputes. Even so, he was skilled at covering his tracks, staying one step removed from any conviction. This had been different. An instruction to kill that could be traced directly to Tunny.

Coupland's features had twisted into a scowl but he reshaped them to neutral to show he meant no harm.

Curtis acknowledged his effort with a nod. 'Kevin, I don't need to tell you that your work on the case was exemplary. I'm afraid it was forensics who dropped the ball. The lab contracted to gather samples at the crime scene has been under investigation following a complaint from another force. It appears they have been the subject of a full-blown review. His Majesty's Inspectors found a lack of standardisation in their approach, and their scientific interpretation was inconsistent.'

Coupland's brow creased. 'You lost me at review, sir, what are you trying to say?'

'There have been instances of contamination, where extraneous material was introduced into the analysis.'

Coupland's features returned to their natural frown. 'Nope. Sorry, you're going to have to try again. An "O" level in woodwork only gets you so far.'

The Chief Super's nod was hesitant, as though uncertain whether Coupland was serious or not. He tried again, using words that didn't contain quite so many syllables. 'The lab is being investigated for contamination-related issues. DNA recovered from our crime scene was detected on a swab taken from an entirely different case that was being analysed in the same facility.'

In a money saving exercise in 2012, the government's Forensic Science Service had been closed down, services sub-contracted to private firms or carried out in police labs. The tendering system had resulted in a high turnover of providers, with work constantly changing hands and a consequent increase in quality failures together with a loss of skills. Another own goal by the men in suits.

'The convictions that resulted following McMahon's murder are considered to be unsafe.'

'You mean Sean Bell, the gobshite who mowed him down, has been released too?'

'Yes. It was his release that prompted Tunny's lawyer to appeal. You can't be guilty of conspiracy to murder if the person you are supposed to have conspired with has their conviction quashed.'

Coupland kept his scowl in place, unconvinced. 'How do we know Tunny didn't nobble somebody on the inside? I wouldn't put it past him.'

Curtis eyed him shrewdly. 'Remember Hanlon's Razor – one should never attribute to malice something that can be adequately explained by neglect.'

That did nothing to make Coupland feel any better. 'Fucksake!' he spat, slamming his pint glass down on the countertop.

'The regulator was duty bound to inform all parties concerned. The appeal against Tunny's conviction was heard at the High Court this morning. Lord Justice Hamilton questioned the credibility of any of the lab's findings relating to the investigation. He overturned the conviction and ordered Tunny's immediate release.'

All that hard graft to make sure the case was watertight, and it was an external agency that dropped the ball. Coupland had a glare that stopped most men in their tracks. He tried not to use it on others in the job but right now his brain refused to play ball, Curtis getting the full force of his death stare.

'I've made my feelings clear to the Chief Constable,' Curtis assured him. 'The government needs to do a U-turn on the way forensics is handled, otherwise we're pissing into the proverbial.'

Coupland tried to read the Chief Super's face as he spoke. Given this was his last day with the division he wasn't sure why he was telling him. An obligation to be the bearer of bad news, perhaps? Or an attempt to get him to stay. The wheels were too far in motion for that to happen. Barring acts of God, he was heading to the Organised Crime Unit whether Tunny was behind bars or not.

When pressed to make a speech, Curtis managed to string several words together about Coupland without using the word belligerent or referring to the time he'd been suspended.

DCI Mallender spoke up next, announcing there had been a whip round before presenting him with a thermos flask and multi-pack of M&S boxers. 'For all those nights you'll be spending on surveillance,' Turnbull quipped, in case he hadn't understood the joke. The story that had been concocted, to explain his secondment, was that he was joining the OCG Unit at Nexus House, the serious and organised crime hub for Greater Manchester Police. The news had ruffled the team's feathers at first. Such was the rivalry between both units it was like a life-long United fan changing their allegiance to City. Krispy glanced over at him with all the bewilderment of a puppy returned to the rescue centre by its new owners.

'It's only a secondment, kiddo,' said Coupland with a pang, resisting the urge to pat the junior DC's head. 'I'll be back before you know it.'

'It's gonna be weird though, Sarge, especially since we're not allowed to contact you.'

'I can't have distractions while I'm focusing on my new post,' Coupland said firmly. 'Besides, it won't help DS Ashcroft if you lot keep running to me every time his back's turned.'

Krispy didn't look convinced.

Coupland clasped his hands in front of his chest. 'Mummy and Daddy love you very much, we just need some time apart, that's all.'

Ashcroft, who'd only caught the tail end of the conversation, narrowed his eyes. 'Can I just check who's Mum?' he asked.

'If you need to ask the question then you already know the answer,' Coupland volleyed, enjoying the banter. Truth was they were already sidestepping each other. Trying out their new positions for size. It was only right that Ashcroft would want to flex his muscles his own way, didn't need Coupland breathing down his neck.

'You've made your choice,' Ashcroft had said, 'you can't ride two horses with one backside, even if one is a white charger.'

There'd been a couple of occasions, once news of his transfer had been made public, that Coupland had been tempted to come clean with him. But the powers-that-be had made it clear there could be no leaks. He'd answered the team's puzzled questions as best as he could, aware of the look Ashcroft sent him whenever he thought he wasn't watching.

'I'll be back before you know it,' he said, unaware that the chain of events, the high-speed train with his name on the destination, had already been set in motion.

*

Tonto's reception class uniform was hung up behind his bedroom door ready for the morning. For the last few weeks they'd made a point of mentioning school every day to normalise it. They'd tried to make it sound like fun, telling him about the new friends he'd make, the children from nursery who would be moving up with him.

Staring at the little blue sweatshirt and grey shorts his grandson would wear for the first time tomorrow, Coupland wondered where the hell the years had gone. One minute it was Amy standing on the front doorstep, Lynn taking her photograph to record her first day at school, the ritual continuing every new school year thereafter. Tomorrow it would be Tonto's turn to be preened and turned out for inspection, stray locks of hair tucked into place, remnants of breakfast wiped away with spittle and the cuff of a sleeve.

Amy was apprehensive. She worried how he would manage without her paving the way. Explaining his mood swings. Playing down his tantrums. Acting as an interpreter between him and the world around him. His nursery report had described him as *Full of beans, boisterous, high spirited.*

'When do those descriptions change to *disruptive*, Dad?' she'd asked him, after finding out the teacher had described other kids as *considerate, cooperative, thoughtful.*

'He'll be fine, Ames, stop worrying. It's reception class not sixth form.' Coupland tried to deflect her anxiety but only up to a point. They'd need to keep a watchful eye. The knack of getting through school intact was learning to play by the rules, both in and out of the classroom. Not to be so much of a loner you got picked on by the other kids, or so popular you never had to try hard. It was a minefield.

Tonto, on hearing Coupland's footsteps in his room, came charging out of the bathroom clutching his toothbrush. It was impossible for him to walk anywhere. To exercise caution. To consider the dangers around him. It was full pelt or nothing. He scrambled downstairs. Clambered up the monkey bars in the park. Sprinted into the road if they weren't quick enough.

He was wearing his Batman pyjamas, which he wore so often the colours were starting to fade. 'It's time for my bedtime story, Grumpy,' he said, settling himself down on his bed.

Coupland made a point of eyeing the toothbrush in his grandson's hand.

'Oops, I forgot,' Tonto said, giggling, scrambling off the bed and into the bathroom to put it away. In the blink of an eye he was back, cross-legged on the bed looking up at Coupland expectantly. The time he spent with his other granny, Karen Underwood, hadn't caused any noticeable waves so far. Still early days, granted. She'd be biding her time until her probation period was over if she had any sense, Coupland reckoned, then checked himself. There'd been no remnants of Tonto's father in the family home she still occupied, albeit alone since her divorce. Coupland himself had driven the boy over for his first visit. He'd carried out reconnaissance on all the rooms while Karen made tea. There was no shrine to Vinny. No newspaper cuttings glued to the spare room wall. When Coupland had eventually joined her in the kitchen, they'd smiled at each other, albeit for very different reasons.

Tonto sidled closer, placed his hand on Coupland's

knee. 'Big day tomorrow, Grumpy,' he said, solemn eyes looking up at him.

'I know, kiddo. Are you excited?'

A flash of irritation flitted across his grandson's face. 'Not me, silly! You! Mummy said you start your new job tomorrow.'

'I do.'

'Is that why Grandma made you buy new clothes?'

'Nothing gets past you, kiddo.'

'So, are you excited?'

'I suppose.'

'You'll make new friends.'

Coupland's nod was slow. 'It's possible,' he agreed.

'Just don't thump anyone at breaktime.'

'Keep your voice down!' Coupland hissed, putting a finger to his lips. 'I gave you that piece of advice on the QT.' Though it would serve him well if he followed his own advice from time to time.

'You can borrow one of my pencils if you like,' Tonto offered.

Coupland's chest swelled. 'You keep them, draw your mam a nice picture she can put on the wall. Is that a deal?'

'Deal,' said Tonto, his eyelids starting to droop.

Coupland suppressed a smile. He picked up a book from Tonto's bedside table and began to read.

*

He hadn't so much given up smoking, rather he'd agreed not to smoke at home, which was something else entirely. He'd been relegated to smoking in the garden for as long as he'd been married. He'd thought naively that even with Tonto on the scene things would remain the same. That was before the boy had seen fit to start imitating him, stomping round the garden with a pen in his mouth, removing it with stubby fingers to blow imaginary rings of smoke into the air.

'Kids copy what they see, Dad,' Amy had rebuked him.

'So how come you never smoked?' Coupland challenged, only to feel the red laser dot of Lynn's contempt burn into his forehead. So, he'd agreed not to smoke anywhere near the premises, and never, absolutely never, in the car.

'I don't know why you don't just pack it in,' Lynn had said, and he'd smiled like a maths professor explaining a really difficult equation.

'It'll make me walk more,' he'd said instead, as though the answer was that obvious. After all, his GP still wittered on about his step count. Not quite the answer Lynn was looking for, but in Coupland's eyes it was a compromise.

He'd taken to walking the length of his street and back while he enjoyed his last cigarette of the night. He felt like a night watchman, doing the rounds of the premises he was guarding, checking all was well. He wasn't the only person pacing the wrong side of midnight. He nodded at a man with bloodshot eyes and unkempt hair, rubbing the back of a newborn strapped into a sling around his middle. *That's the easy bit, mate*, he felt like saying, knowing fine well he'd get no thanks for sharing *that* pearl of wisdom.

At the end of the road he turned, lighting up a second cigarette for the return journey. He passed a teenage girl he recognised snogging the face off a boy at her garden gate. Coupland cleared his throat loudly as he passed them. Startled, the couple sprang apart. 'Don't you have a paper-round to be getting up for in a couple of hours?' he said to the boy, whose pimply face under the streetlight had turned crimson.

Above them, a bedroom window opened and a man with hair sticking up eyeballed his daughter before bellowing: 'IN. NOW!' He jerked his thumb towards the interior of the house in case directions were required.

'I'll see you tomorrow,' the girl whispered before hurrying inside.

Coupland waited until she'd closed the door behind her. 'I'm guessing she meant you not me,' he said, clocking spotty's grin. 'Now jog on before I do you for loitering.'

Satisfied, Coupland smoked his cigarette down to the filter, stubbed it out then dropped it into a nearby bin before calling it a night.

CHAPTER TWO

He'd been told to report to Detective Superintendent Lara Cole on arrival at Nexus House, the serious and organised crime hub for Greater Manchester Police. Unlike his old station that backed onto Salford shopping precinct, Nexus House was a large, purpose-built modern office block in Tameside. Home to several police specialist units including economic and cold case units, it was now the shared hub for Operation Maple.

It was also where Coupland's old colleague, DI Alex Moreton, was based. She hadn't replied to his earlier text informing her he was on his way in, and when he'd asked after her while collecting his new ID badge at reception he was told she was in conference. Oh, how the mighty love their meetings.

He was escorted to the corridor outside Superintendent Cole's office and told to wait. The chairs arranged in a single line outside her office looked marginally more comfortable than the moulded plastic variety on the ground floor, but he preferred to stand. He was surprised to feel knots tightening in his stomach. Nerves, most likely. He walked up and down the corridor, to keep them at bay.

Coupland was long enough in the tooth to know the back story of many of the officers he came into contact with on a daily basis. Whether drowning their sorrows over a pint on residential training courses or joint working when he'd picked up a shout on another station's territory. Moving to this task force afforded him no such luxury. Plucked from around the UK, the assortment of officers he'd be working with were strangers to him. There'd be an opportunity to meet and greet at today's induction, granted, though he was more interested in what their colleagues would say about them out of earshot than the spin they'd use to introduce themselves during this morning's show and tell.

Tonto was right to be concerned. The first day in a new job was the equivalent of your first day at school, and first impressions mattered. As long as he didn't bite anyone or pull their hair, he should be OK.

At precisely the time Coupland was due to meet with the detective superintendent, the door to the office opened and a woman wearing a tailored trouser suit beckoned him inside. Her handshake was firm and purposeful. 'Take a seat,' she told him, gesturing to the chair in front of her desk.

He waited for her to return to her own chair and sit down before he lowered himself into the seat indicated. He could do courteous when needed.

Detective Superintendent Lara Cole leaned back in her chair and studied him. Coupland took the opportunity to do the same. She had short, cropped hair, feathered around her face, a hint of grey showing through blonde highlights. She wore plain studs in her ears. A simple pendant hung in the V of her white blouse. Someone who didn't rock the boat, Coupland thought. Or someone trying to give that impression. In an institution where balls continued to be the preferred genitalia as far as the senior rank and file were concerned, he wasn't fooled by her demure appearance. In order to get as far as she had she'd have had to grow a pair of her own, or have them transplanted after surgically removing her opponent's. Time would tell which camp she fell into.

'You come highly recommended, DS Coupland,' she said, appraising him with cool eyes. 'By that I mean that there's nothing in your career history that shows how you fit the team profile. You're here on the say-so of others.'

Coupland held her gaze. He'd been expecting this, though not perhaps while the seat beneath him was still cold. 'This job is ten per cent knowledge and ninety per cent experience, and for that there's no shortcut, Ma'am. I've seen first-hand what the Dutchman is capable of. I've even eye-balled him. I'm not sure how many of my new colleagues will be able to say that.' Now wasn't the time to admit he'd been some distance away when he crossed paths with him. That at the time he hadn't realised that was who it had been. If he'd known, if he'd had some *fucking* iota… maybe they wouldn't be sitting here. He squirmed in his seat as though the thought made him uncomfortable.

The skin around her eyes softened. 'I also heard you like to stand your ground. That's good. In fact it's vital. There are a lot of egos in the room next door. You're going to be introduced to many officers today who will query your place alongside them. How you respond will influence how they interact with you for the rest of your time here.'

'Appreciate the heads up, Ma'am.'

'You're ready for this, though?'

Coupland cocked his head to one side. 'I don't get you, Ma'am.'

'What we're about to do will suck the life blood out of each and every one of us. If we're doing our jobs properly, that is. You'll eat, sleep and shit the job. I'll expect nothing less. But be warned. We'll be treading on toes unused to being challenged. People with influence who'll cry we're being overzealous when we get too close. Think of a case that's made you unpopular. Someone to be derided.'

Coupland leaned back in his chair, stumped. Buggered if he could think of just one. 'Feels like you've described my career history, Ma'am,' he admitted.

Cole nodded. 'Very well. Just be aware there will be no ticker tape parade when this is over. Assuming that we are successful, of course. Even that can't be taken for granted at this stage.'

Coupland understood as much. Despite outcry to the contrary, the public didn't really have a clue about this kind of crime. The extent of it. The horror of the abuse and murders went without saying. What they didn't fully compute was that the perpetrators walked among them. They weren't demons. Not in the conventional sense. No horns or forked tails. No balaclavas or 'Hate' tattoos across their foreheads. No chequered criminal history or first name terms with the local constabulary for the wrong reasons. They weren't loners. There was no vulnerability to be taken advantage of. It didn't enter anyone's minds that the most prolific offenders of this crime did the school run, made small talk at the checkout, were chatty and caring one minute, distinguishable from the rest of society solely by the rules they broke the next.

'Of course what we really need to do to put the kybosh on this crime is to recondition the public's mindset,' said Cole.

Coupland wondered what she had in mind. Locker room posters training men how to masturbate responsibly? Ethical porn. *Please check the age of the person you're jerking off to on screen.* As tag lines went he'd heard better.

'Surely that's a job for the politicians,' he said, thinking there were enough wankers sitting in the House of Commons.

'You'd think so, wouldn't you?' She made a wafting motion with her hands. 'Politicians are like serial shaggers. They promise you the earth while scanning the room for their next bit of action.'

It took a great deal of willpower for Coupland to stop his eyebrows shooting into his hairline. He'd never heard Chief Superintendent Curtis be so direct about anything. He wondered if she was like this with her peers, or had she cranked it up because he was a lower rank, wanting to appeal to a much simpler outlook?

She caught his expression and smiled. 'Pay no attention to me, DS Coupland. It's easy to get caught up in what life would be like in a perfect world. That's never going to happen, though, right?'

Not the pep talk he was expecting, he conceded, though he kept that morsel to himself. 'We'd be out of a job if it was,' he said diplomatically.

'I hope you've got a good support base around you,' she commented, moving the conversation on. 'One that tolerates mood swings while you keep them in the dark.'

Not for the first time, Coupland gave thanks for Lynn's unwavering patience.

The cases Coupland had dealt with over the years had hardened him. But not enough. Sometimes the darkness leaked out uninvited: a flashback of a child's shattered body while putting Tonto to bed. In his job it was a fine line between letting something that might never happen hold you back, and being reckless. If truth be told he had trodden the reckless path more times than he'd admit to. Sometimes there were no other choices.

'These are the cases you'll never discuss, apart from with a counsellor. You'll be given full access to mental health support during your secondment,' she added. 'In your own time of course.'

There was a file on her side of the desk with his name on. His personnel file, he suspected. It was thicker than most, but then his run-ins with Professional Standards were bound to leave a paper trail. Going by the size of it, he was single-handedly responsible for decimating several rain forests. If he thought she was going to rake over any of it he was mistaken. Lifting it in her hand as though feeling the weight of it, she opened a desk drawer and dropped the file in before slamming it shut. A smile pulled at her mouth when she looked back at him. 'Come on,' she said, pushing herself out of her chair. She moved round towards the door. 'I'm not interested in all that getting to know about your private life crap. Let's take you into the lions' den.'

*

It was agreed the first major team briefing would take place in the conference suite. A spacious meeting room on the same floor as Lara Cole's office. It was big enough to be rented out at weekends for wedding receptions,

Coupland reckoned, as long as the happy couple's relatives weren't fazed by personnel moving around the building in stab-proof vests and balaclavas. Then again, he'd raided nuptials in certain quarters of Salford where that was the dress code.

The room was set out theatre style, with hardbacked chairs set up in rows along the centre of the room, all facing one way. A lectern had been placed at the front of a low stage, a projector screen mounted on the wall behind it. Two dozen detectives gathered at the entrance to the room, where large tables had been placed against a wall serving tea, coffee and an assortment of pastries that would have had Coupland's old team elbowing each other out of the way to get to. Small groups had already formed as attendees clustered around the refreshments sizing each other up.

There was a buzz to the room. Laughter. The odd pat on the back. For all intents and purposes it resembled a meeting of the local chamber of commerce rather than a task force assembled to dismantle a network of sexual predators.

When Coupland walked in alongside Lara Cole every person turned in their direction, as though they were cattle rustlers entering a saloon bar in the Wild West.

'DI Coupland, welcome!' A man with a head shaped like a bullet stepped forward, arm outstretched to shake Coupland's hand.

'It's DS, not DI,' Coupland said resolutely. Either the new suit Lynn had made him buy especially for the occasion made him look better than he was, or the guy knew his rank and was just being a twat.

'No matter,' said Bullet Head. 'There's no standing on

ceremony here.'

Only the very senior ranks said things like that. The lower ranks would never get away with it. Even then everyone knew it was one of those things said but never meant. Like saying sorry when you interrupted someone speaking.

Bullet Head swept his arm wide as though dancing girls and a marching band were about to appear, rather than a bored-looking catering assistant replacing empty vacuum flasks of coffee. 'Welcome to Operation Maple,' he boomed. The name Maple had been chosen due to its strength and hardness, although Coupland preferred to think of it as the wood the Dutchman's coffin would be made from. Some criminals didn't deserve a trial.

Coupland stretched his mouth into a smile. Tried to think of something DI Moreton, or DS Ashcroft for that matter, would say. 'I'm very pleased to be here,' he said, hoping he didn't sound like a jaded actor plugging their next film on The One Show.

Bullet Head beamed. 'Excellent! We have a huge task ahead of us, but with all the experience and energy in the room I'm confident we will achieve our mission. Now, please excuse me,' he said, stepping away from the group before heading towards the front of the room, a minion on either side of him. The chattering groups took this as a cue to sit down.

'Who is that?' Coupland asked Cole.

'Commander Howorth, he's the one running the whole show,' she replied, moving swiftly to secure a chair on the front row without waiting to see if Coupland would follow. Coupland took his time. Not wanting it to look as though he'd deliberately chosen a chair at the back of the room, but moving in that direction nonetheless, lingering on the edges of a couple of groups before bagging a chair at the back. Once seated, he ran his gaze over the sloped shoulders, fat necks and bald spots of the officers ahead of him, his attention settling on Bullet Head who was now standing behind the lectern.

Commander Howorth bellowed a welcome, gesturing to empty seats at the front for those not fast enough on their feet to secure seats further back. The fifty or so people gathered studied the relevant pages in the case folders that had been put together and placed on every chair.

Coupland flicked through his copy. The front of the file served as a directory of the taskforce members. Beneath each name, a photograph and list of their credentials. There were at least a dozen PHDs in the room, several law degrees and a couple of Masters in Criminology, although where Coupland came from that was just another name for gangster. Two attendees had diplomas in psychology.

Coupland skim read until he found the entry against his own name. *DS Kevin Coupland,* seconded from *Salford Precinct Murder Investigation Team,* it stated simply. Whoever had compiled it hadn't even bothered uploading his photograph. He wondered if his Certificate of Attendance for the Diversity in the Workforce course he'd attended a couple of years back would have counted. Even his Woodwork 'O' level would have filled some of the blank space beneath his name.

Coupland flicked over the page to read the commander's biography. Peter Howorth. Based with the Sexual Exploitation National Enquiry Team, or SENET for short, he'd spent two years seconded to Europol – the EU law enforcement agency. Prior to that, a ten-year stint at the National Crime Agency. He was promoted to Chief Superintendent during his time at GMP's Public Protection Unit. The guy knew his stuff.

Coupland looked up as the commander's voice boomed from the lectern. 'You are all part of a task force assembled to identify and remove the Dutchman and his cohort from society.' A quick glance at his minions who were stationed at a side table with a laptop and the silhouette of a man was transmitted onto the screen behind him, a large question mark at its centre. 'For the uninitiated among you, meet the rich paedophile's Mr Fixit, so called because he rubs shoulders with the cream of society, and by cream I don't just mean super rich. We're talking powerful. Titled. These people have connections your regular crime lords can only dream about.'

Another glance at his minions and the on-screen silhouette was replaced by the silhouette of a group of people, a map of the UK in the background.

'In order to "service" his sick clients, he runs a team of operatives known as Passmen. They're called Passmen because they're able to pass all the criminal record checks. For all intents and purposes, they're as clean as a whistle. They remain dormant for most of the time, similar to terrorist sleepers. Then on the Dutchman's command they abduct a victim for whichever rich client is in town, disposing of them afterwards. Everything that happens in between is recorded and uploaded onto the dark web – with the perpetrators' identities protected at all times. They've got away with it for so long due to the Dutchman's connections. He represents the gateway to politicians, judges, lords… people with status and enough powerful friends to make scandal disappear. This is where the real money is in the exploitation industry.'

The Commander's gaze travelled over several rows before he spoke next. 'He has remained elusive, because of his high-profile network. In order to bring him in we need to isolate him from those protecting him, which means striking at the very core of our establishment. Politicians, financiers, high ranking members of the criminal justice system, celebrities. People with influence, who have used their status to help him evade capture.

'To date our resources have been limited. We simply haven't had the money to go after the big hitters. In terms of his "Passmen", collectively, the police service is data rich but information poor. Scattered across many IT systems, multiple records have existed for the same suspect. Because of this, his criminal network has been able to run rings round us.'

At least he was telling it like it was, thought Coupland. Police numbers had been cut and digital forensic units were buckling under the weight of the sheer volume of computers, mobile phones and other electronic media requiring analysis in this type of crime. As a result, police forces across the UK had to be selective in who and what they investigated, concentrating on images distributed over messaging apps like WhatsApp. Coupland still couldn't get to grips with how those participating in these networks normalised this crime. The shorthand they used as they engaged in depraved conversations glorifying and inciting vile acts. The problem just kept getting bigger. Before the digital age, social norms were able to repress a person's urges to seek out such material; the Internet offered no such condemnation. If anything, it offered reassurance, where not only was the urge accepted, but encouraged.

'I know what's going through your mind. It's all very well putting in the hard yards, but until the courts back us up we've just created another revolving door.'

Deterrents were in place, but they weren't being used by the courts. Even though a single offence of downloading images carried a maximum sentence of 10 years, it was more common that a first-time offender pleading guilty wouldn't receive a custodial sentence. Possession of a category A image – the most serious type – received 12 months' custody, which would often be suspended, or substituted for a community order. All this, and yet everybody knew how offences like this escalated over time.

'Which is why it's vital we catch those at the top of the chain, so we can deprive those subscribing to these vile sites from getting their hands on this material.' Addiction was creative. There was nothing to say that perverts deprived of their fix wouldn't find it another way, find other networks that offered the so-called stimulation they needed, but they had to start somewhere.

'Thanks to the Met's use of analytics,' the Commander continued, nodding in the direction of a man on the front row, 'we are able to mine text, audio and video data to help us predict where the Dutchman will turn up next.'

Must be about the only thing the Met had got right in recent months, Coupland thought, given they'd been placed into special measures in relation, amongst other failings, to their backlog of child abuse referrals. A situation Greater Manchester Police had recently found itself in. It wasn't all down to poor leadership, Coupland acknowledged. Part of the reason given for the failures was the number of young and inexperienced police recruits brought in as part of the national drive to replace thousands of officers cut during austerity measures. Got to love those ministers, thought Coupland.

A series of statistical and data trends replaced the silhouettes on screen. It was too much for Coupland's addled brain. Instead of scrutinising bar charts and scatter diagrams, his mind projected the sickening video images he'd seen while he and Ashcroft had collaborated with the Public Protection Unit during an investigation into missing teenage girls.

The images had been uploaded onto Utopia, the sick site on the dark web run by the Dutchman. Utopia specialised in every perversion, masquerading in the name of entertainment. Each victim suffered every kind of abuse, right up until some keyboard monster paid an additional premium to watch them be snuffed out on screen.

Coupland dropped his gaze to the file on his lap. The taskforce's mission statement followed the list of delegates and their biographies. The number one priority was to determine the identity of the Dutchman. Despite being the linchpin in a sexual exploitation network that stretched across Europe, he had somehow managed to retain his anonymity. Traditional methods of tracking and tracing your common or garden fugitive had so far failed. The brilliance of this monster was that he operated in plain sight, fully able to cover his tracks whichever way he moved. Well-connected in every sense of the word. Not bad for someone who legend had it had spent six years in a Dutch prison.

Commander Howorth introduced three civilian

members of staff who were sitting a couple of rows in front of Coupland, sweeping an arm towards them like a magician introducing his lovely assistants. It was their job to index every statement taken, and every suspect profile created, and then enter them onto the HOLMES2 – Home Office Large Major Enquiry System – database. It was a thankless task, noticed only when a ball was dropped.

A brief nod of his head before the Commander turned his attention to two fresh-faced officers on the front row. He raised his hands to instruct them to get to their feet.

'I want to personally introduce you to Noah,' stated the Commander, extending his hand towards a mixed-race DC with dark wavy hair flattened to his scalp as though he'd slept overnight with a beanie hat on, 'and Jared…' whose mousy hair had been scraped back into a ponytail. The Commander beamed as though introducing his gifted offspring.

Unsure what to do next, Noah and Jared half turned to stare at the congregation behind them. Both were well over six feet, stooped, as though lacking self-confidence, or spent all day sitting hunched over computers. In the absence of knowing what else to do they took a mini bow before dropping back into their seats. Like Coupland, the suits they wore looked as though they had been bought specially for the occasion. He suspected they'd be more at home in baggy jeans and gaming hoodies. Coupland placed them at no more than late twenties, not long enough in the job for it to get the better of them. It didn't seem right to expose them to this level of depravity so early in their careers.

'…together, Noah and Jared make up our dedicated

Digital Forensics Unit,' added the Commander.

There were more introductions. More headline statistics.

The Home Office figures regarding Child Sexual Exploitation made grim reading. Throughout the UK five hundred arrests were made per month in an effort to combat online sexual exploitation. Statistics from the National Crime Agency showed that approximately 150,000 accounts registered across the most harmful sexual abuse web sites were believed to be registered in the UK.

Coupland already knew that online child abuse drew a British audience of 80,000 people, equal to the UK's entire prison population. Figures like that made him wonder if the right people were currently incarcerated.

Any good public speaker knew the importance of reading the room. The vital signs to check for: whether the eyes of the people in the front row were still open or had taken on a glazed expression, or those sitting in seats further back had slipped out their phones. It gave the speaker an opportunity to change tack. Up the ante a little, invite a bit of audience participation. The problem with the police service was that the person standing at the front of the room didn't need to bring the audience round to their way of thinking. They weren't exactly preaching to the choir, more *telling* them what to sing. There'd be no 'Praise the Lord' and hand waving either. For all intents and purposes, to those assembled, Commander Howorth *was* God.

Coupland couldn't be certain whether his face was looking as uninspired as he was feeling, but when the Commander's gaze fell on him for a smattering of seconds he announced it was time for a comfort break, inviting everyone to reconvene in twenty minutes. More than enough time for a satisfactory bowel movement, should anyone need it. Or, more importantly for Coupland, a cigarette in the car park if he sprinted to the lift and hot-footed it through reception downstairs.

Once in the car park he slipped his phone out to check for messages, then remembered there wouldn't be any relating to work, this being his first day in the unit. He was about to return it to his pocket when it vibrated in his hand, notifying him of an incoming text. He tapped in his passcode. Tapped onto an unopened message from Amy. She'd sent him the doorstep photo of Tonto in his school get-up. An imp in a uniform one size too big for him and shoes that made his feet look like boats. Coupland tried to think of a reply that conveyed how he felt. Settled on a thumbs up sign and an emoji face sticking out its tongue.

He'd no sooner breathed out his first lungful of smoke into the air when he heard footsteps approach him from behind. 'You're a hard man to keep up with, DS Coupland,' said a voice he'd heard a lot of that morning.

Coupland felt a pang of disappointment when he turned to see the Commander approaching him. 'Fancied a bit of fresh air,' he replied, biting back the words, *on my own*. The Commander pulled a packet of cigarettes from his dress tunic along with an expensive looking lighter, the kind that came from a jeweller, usually with an engraved message from a loved one. He took out a cigarette and lit it, returning the pack to his pocket. 'I couldn't help notice you looked a little bored, detective sergeant, as if there was somewhere else you'd rather be,' he said before drawing down his first lungful of nicotine. At least this time he'd remembered his rank.

Coupland shook his head, blowing smoke through the side of his mouth as he formulated an answer that was a tad more palatable than a straightforward 'yes.' 'Not bored, sir, just keen to get going. As you are aware, the Dutchman temporarily moved his operation to Salford two years ago. I had the dubious pleasure of acquainting myself with one of his passmen during a murder enquiry which exposed the extent of his network in the city.'

Coupland had in fact encountered the Dutchman's legacy prior to that, when it transpired he'd bankrolled the illegal transportation of Albanians into the UK for the purposes of sex trafficking. The public outcry hadn't been as loud then as it was later when youngsters from the city started going missing, and even then the responses had been 'tiered' in relation to which part of the social strata the victims had come from.

Once it was clear the threat was no longer confined to faceless migrants and belligerent runaways and had progressed to putting local children at risk, the Government had been impelled to take action. Coupland chose his next words carefully. 'Some of your officers from SENET stepped in to oversee our investigation once the extent of the Dutchman's involvement was clear.'

They'd tried to take over was closer to the truth. But when it became obvious the investigation was going pear-shape they'd stepped back at an alarming rate.

'From what I remember hearing, it was a joint enterprise with you in a pivotal position on the ground,' Commander Howorth acknowledged. It was as close to the truth as they were likely to get.

'It was a steep learning curve in a very short space of

time,' Coupland said with honesty.

'I can understand why you'd think this briefing is pointless then.'

'I wouldn't say that, sir…'

Ash fell from the end of Coupland's cigarette as he floundered with what to say next. Unsure whether the Commander's words had been intended as a reprimand or not, he played out the worst-case scenario in his head. Returning to Salford Precinct station in the morning with his tail between his legs, being the butt of everyone's jokes for the foreseeable. It had been too optimistic to think he could get through his first day on the job without putting someone's nose out of joint, he supposed. But to hack off the head honcho running the show? Nice one, knobhead, he muttered silently.

A look flashed across the Commander's face as though sensing his discomfort. 'There are many officers here who don't have the same direct experience as you. Certainly, they don't have first-hand experience of the Dutchman's legacy. Their involvement to date has been at arms' length.' He paused, as though considering his words. 'I want every person in my team to truly understand what these victims have suffered, not just have an abstract idea of it. So if it sounds like I'm going a bit painting by numbers on this it's because I want everyone from civilian staff to IT support to fully commit to it. Trust me, what you've heard this morning was just the warmup act. If they…' he jabbed his finger in the direction of the building behind them, 'don't go home today sick to their stomach at the evil this man and his cronies continue to peddle then I've failed.'

Coupland's mouth turned down at the edges as he

considered the Commander's words. He felt sorry for them. Officers who to this point had thought they'd seen it all. He nodded slowly, dropping his cigarette onto the tarmac before crushing it underfoot. 'Better be getting back, then, sir. I believe we've got sick bags to hand out.'

*

This time the buzz was louder in the conference room. Less cautious, now acquaintances had been made. The bonhomie of a common goal. Some of the officers had returned to their seats, others were seated but continued their conversations with colleagues several chairs away. A hush descended as the Commander entered the room, several pairs of eyes locked onto Coupland as he followed him in, eyeing him suspiciously as he returned to his seat.

'I think it's time,' Commander Howorth began once he reached the lectern and turned to observe the audience, 'that we spare a moment to reflect on the victims. I'd like to draw your attention to the back of the file…' he instructed, holding up the case file that had been issued at the start of the briefing. He opened the file and read out the page numbers he was referring to.

Each page contained a brief victimology of a sample of the young women and children confirmed as being victims of the network. 'These are just the tip of the iceberg,' he reminded them.

'It would be a logistical impossibility to include every case,' he added. 'You will become familiar soon enough with the numbers. For the purposes of this briefing we have only referenced a handful of victims across several cities in the UK. Make no mistake the numbers are replicated in every city across Europe and beyond.'

The Commander stepped away to give everyone time to digest the file's contents. He remained silent, moving to the side table occupied by his cronies to take a swig from a bottle of water. The only noise that could be heard was the turning of pages and shuffling backsides.

Coupland opened the file where instructed and began to read.

The Commander was right to step away. There were no words to describe what was contained in those pages. No polite way to give the horror of it justice. It never ceased to amaze him that someone could carry out acts with this level of depravity and still be considered *human*. Shouldn't their behaviour mean they forfeited that classification? Even wild animals, creatures whose survival depended upon them preying on animals further down the food chain, didn't do *this*.

Each new page in the case file was dedicated to a victim. A 'before' photo was displayed at the top. Beneath it the victim's age and where they were from, together with a few lines taken from their loved one's victim impact statement:

Natalie Davenport, 14, Newcastle. Abducted on the way home from school. Missing for six weeks before her body was discovered in a disused railway siding. The Public Protection Unit found over a dozen on-line videos charting her abuse.

'She was our sunshine. Nothing will ever be the same again.'

Gemma Tovey, 12, Bristol. Went missing after going to the local shopping centre with a friend. It was two years before her remains were discovered. By then the video of her rape and strangulation had been viewed 630 times.

'She loved going to gymnastics and listening to Katy Perry songs.'

Toby Roberts, 7, Salford. Abducted while playing a game of kickabout in front of his house. His broken body had been found in woodland. The public protection officer who found the online video of his injuries being inflicted was signed off work for six months.

'He loved football, had just joined his local junior team. How could this happen?'

Coupland's gaze lingered on Toby's name. This case had come close to breaking him. Toby Roberts had blindsided Coupland's investigation. Given the number of female victims that had fallen prey to the Passmen, his team hadn't expected a young boy to go missing. Yet it was Toby's love of football that helped identify the passman who killed him. Aiden Nichols, a property developer who in his spare time coached the little boy's junior football team.

Like all victims' loved ones Coupland had come into contact with in his career, Toby's parents took up residence in his head. Their squatters' rights earned by his part in the massacre of their life. For he'd been the one to break the worst possible news. The one who'd obliterated all hope, and without hope there was nothing. Nothing that mattered, anyway.

No murder was harder or less palatable than another, but Coupland felt responsible for not keeping pace with the network as it shifted its shape to keep one step ahead. He wrapped that guilt around him like a hair shirt.

Beneath the personal details of each victim were more photos. Stills taken from the digital clips and live streams found online which captured their abuse, passed off as entertainment: Hollowed out eyes. Faces contorted in pain. Resignation that no one was coming to rescue them.

Each victim had been pumped with enough drugs to be compliant. Not so out of it they couldn't put up a bit of a fight where it mattered, just so long as those pay-per-view sickos got value for their money.

The last picture on each page was the crime scene photo, capturing their final resting place. Not so much resting place, Coupland corrected himself. More a dumping ground where they'd been tossed aside like rubbish. Worse than that. Most folk put more thought into what they did with their rubbish than had been put into what should happen to those broken bodies.

Dehumanised. Stripped of their uniqueness. Left in hedgerows, shallow graves, beneath a pile of stones.

Around him officers shook their heads at the images, swiped hands over mouths too dumbfounded to speak.

Of course, nothing could replace the sheer horror of seeing the victims in the places they'd been discarded. A paper report couldn't evoke the sights, the smells. The post-mortem commentary. But Commander Howorth, aided by a carousel of grotesque images that flashed by on the projector screen, did the next best thing. Images of the victims as they appeared online. The search engine they'd been found in. Where the 'products' listed for purchase were classified by gender, age, ethnicity.

Shock and disgust replaced the academic curiosity he'd seen on the officers' faces earlier. Revulsion, not only at the monsters who carried out the abuse, but at the keyboard paedophiles all too ready to flash their plastic.

Satisfied that the case notes had been digested, the Commander returned to the lectern.

'It's only right that I give every one of you an opportunity at this point to step away from this task force. There will be no shame, no blame, if you choose to do so. This case will demand more than you may be prepared to give, more even, than you've got. Make no mistake. It will take its toll on you. So, before we step off completely into the unknown I shall say this just once. If anyone wishes to withdraw, please do so now.' His gaze swept the room as he said this.

No one moved.

He nodded, satisfied. 'Then this is as good a point as any to break for lunch.'

It was a whole minute before Coupland realised that the officers around him had vacated their seats. He looked up to see the Commander striding along the corridor in the direction of his next nicotine fix. He closed the case file on his lap, put it on the empty seat beside him. He slumped back in his chair and loosened his tie. His crisp clothes and new shoes felt wrong against his battle-worn body. Everything seemed tainted. He tried but failed to push away images from cases he'd worked over the years. Murders that had the Dutchman's hallmark all over them. Images that wouldn't leave him. Skid marks of blood and semen against broken skin. He remained sitting for another ten minutes, until his breathing returned to normal and the rage coursing through him abated.

*

The after-lunch graveyard shift was traditionally the most dreaded time to brief any group – stomachs were full and minds were drifting as the blood flow was still diverted to digestion. This was the time when all participants wanted to do was rest their eyes, check messages, emails and social media.

The Commander had thoughtfully assigned this slot to Noah and Jared from the Digital Forensics Unit to explain to the uninitiated how the dark web worked. Using a series of flow charts projected on screen they described how, with a fake IP address, the perpetrators could make their location untraceable.

Coupland knew that IP referred to Internet Protocol. He'd had Krispy, the junior DC at Salford explain it to him more than once, in words that a dim witted five-year-old could understand. Internet Protocol was like a computer's postal address. It had a string of numbers that told another user your location. 'We've made significant inroads identifying members of these sites…' said Noah, looking at Jared to pick up the thread.

'Because credit card companies have at long last started playing ball with us…' Jared explained, looking at Noah to pick up the thread once more.

'Our digital forensic labs can even trace suspects who pay using bitcoin.' As their nervousness waned, they moved around each other picking up and finishing off each other's sentences, enjoying the attention.

'As you know, the Dutchman's site goes by the name of Utopia. It specialises in live streaming, where viewers can pay to watch victims being abused in real time. We know there are high level subscribers to this network. Wealthy men with pockets deep enough to buy whatever they want, including starring in their very own snuff movie.'

The pair described how, prior to joining the taskforce, their days had been spent tracing the identities of those who subscribed to Utopia. 'The evidence we gathered is pretty solid,' said Jared. 'These men will go down for a long time. Our main priority now is to find the identity of

59

the people providing the *Lights, Camera, Action* side of the production, even if all that entails is a camera on a tripod in a dingy bedsit.'

Coupland was reminded of the scene that had greeted him when searching for Kayleigh Lomax and Bethany Davies, also abducted by Aiden Nichols. The stinking bedroom with sweaty sheets. The camera with its blinking red eye… Two girls hiding in the bathroom. Only one brought out alive. He wondered if Kayleigh received the therapy her parents had been promised. Coupland was a murder detective, he could only be on their journey so far. He had to believe that social work and mental health services picked up the baton and ran with it, even if only for a while. These agencies weren't in the business of providing happy endings, but they were supposed to offer better outcomes.

Maybe it was better he didn't know. Maybe that's why this taskforce mattered so much. Wasn't prevention better than cure?

Something Jared said brought Coupland back to the present. 'If we can track down where the victims are being held – and where the films are being made – we can cause a major disruption to their operation which should flush the Dutchman out of his hiding place.'

Coupland raised his hand. 'What form will this disruption take?' he asked, in a voice louder than was necessary going by the number of suits several rows in front of him who turned to look in his direction.

Noah and Jared looked to the Commander for an answer.

'We'll carry out a series of simultaneous raids once we are apprised of the locations. We will liaise with local hospitals to ensure emergency care is available on standby. Given what we've seen online in terms of how these victims are treated, some may need urgent medical care upon their rescue.' The Commander thanked Noah and Jared before beckoning to someone sitting on the front row to approach the lectern.

Coupland sank into his chair as the next speaker came into view. Despite the Commander's ringing endorsement, no introduction was needed as far as Coupland was concerned. There was no way the man now standing beside Commander Howorth had been present for the earlier briefing, Coupland would have spotted him. He must have turned up just before the end of the lunch break, when Coupland had slipped out to search for a fire exit door he could wedge open for an uninterrupted smoke.

He huffed out a sigh. Amjid Bloody Akram. DCI with the National Crime Agency last time he'd had the pleasure of his company. He hadn't changed much by the look of it. Medium height with short-cropped hair. The glasses he used to wear had been replaced with contact lenses, either that or he'd had laser eye surgery. Even so he looked older than Coupland remembered, but then several years had passed since they'd worked together.

They'd last crossed paths when they'd worked on the investigation into people trafficking bankrolled by the Dutchman. Their collaboration hadn't been an entirely happy one. During their previous encounters Amjid had come across as an all-round decent guy before flicking a lever that turned him into a right royal pain in the backside. He'd accused Coupland several times during the trafficking investigation of getting ahead of himself, wading into territory he had no right being in. He'd been right, of course, but then it had been Coupland's team who'd caught the case first and as far as he was concerned it was finders keepers.

To top it all, he'd faced the biggest allegation of his career as a result of a less than text-book arrest, when Austin 'Reedsy' Smith had made an allegation of police brutality against him. An allegation that resulted in his suspension and kissed goodbye to any chance of future promotion, not that he'd been arsed about *that*, though it narked him that his reputation in the division had been compromised. Time might have passed since both officers had seen each other; question was, would Amjid be willing to bury the hatchet, at least in anything other than Coupland's skull?

Coupland flicked through the case folder until he found Amjid's career history. It had been added as an appendix. Maybe he was only here in a speaking capacity, he hoped. Coupland skim-read down the page. Since their last rodeo Amjid had spent the intervening years productively. A transfer to the City of London police, no less. As well as responsibility for policing the city's business district, the 'square mile' in the historical centre of London, it held national responsibility for economic and cyber-crime. Coupland rolled his eyes. Amjid's career was a bit niche. There were far too many specialists in the force for his liking, not enough boots on the ground to do the actual job of policing.

He watched the senior officer take his position at the lectern, waiting for hush to descend before addressing those seated. He didn't have the gravitas of the Commander but the group listened attentively as though fearful the boss was going to ask them questions afterwards.

Amjid began by stating his role in the infiltration of EncroChat during 2020 while he was still at the NCA. EncroChat was a smartphone service provider that offered modified encrypted communications between subscribers. Dodgy mobile phones, in layman's terms, with a texting facility that couldn't be accessed by anyone other than the recipient. Used in the main by organised crime gangs to plan criminal activities, it enabled them to keep one step ahead of the police. As a result of Amjid's team deciphering these messages, over 1000 arrests had been made across Europe. The breakthrough and subsequent arrests had made national news headlines. Fair play to the guy, Coupland conceded.

Amjid spoiled it by peppering his presentation with management phrases like 'surge activity,' and 'dialled up muscularity,' which might have given those in the audience with Masters degrees a slight tingle in the nether regions, but left Coupland decidedly flaccid. This was what happened when folk became legends in their own lunchtime. They started to believe what was said about them. Started making what they did sound a damn sight more complicated than it actually was.

'I'm proud to be partnering this taskforce,' Amjid stated, putting the kybosh on Coupland's hope he was just passing through. 'It's essential we keep the mission statement baked into everything we do.'

'Did he just say baked?' Coupland asked the person beside him, perplexed. 'Perhaps they should have drafted Paul Hollywood in and be done with it.'

Amjid's cool gaze settled on him for longer than

necessary, making Coupland wonder if he'd forgotten to use his indoor voice again.

Amjid explained how the team he now managed had the power to recover money held in bank or building society accounts through civil litigation, rather than using confiscation orders made by the criminal courts following convictions. Known as civil account forfeiture, the process was similar to the confiscation process, but the individual did not have to be convicted of an offence for the assets to be recovered. Instead, it had to be proved 'on the balance of probability' that the property had been obtained through unlawful conduct.

What it meant to Operation Maple was that financiers who came under the scrutiny of the task force risked having a confiscation order made against them if they didn't play ball. Finally, a tool to hit the banks where it hurt, if their chief finance officers didn't comply. One of these confiscation orders had been made against Lyndon Bank, on an account with £32,000,000 in it.

'We have reason to believe that the funds going through this account have been diverted to a media company by the name of Peta Productions, which in turn has a subsidiary, which we believe, although we haven't yet been able to prove, is linked to Utopia. Whilst investigations continue to determine the connection between these organisations, I am confident that our actions send out a clear message that we will continue to pursue those involved in enabling crime.'

Coupland shifted in his seat. Amjid's statement was starting to sound a little too political.

As though able to read his thoughts, Amjid let his gaze linger on Coupland. 'If our suspicions are correct, not only will this disrupt the Dutchman's activities, it finally gives us leverage to get the people funding him to talk.

'This has been a game changer – individuals do not have to have been convicted for us to pursue, seize and take the proceeds of crime passing through the city of London.'

At the end of the briefing Commander Howorth stood up at the front of the room and announced refreshments would be provided, after which the real work would begin. Amjid thanked the group for their attention and made as if to leave. Commander Howorth spoke quietly in his ear before leading him over to where Coupland waited beside a table about to be laid out with cakes and biscuits.

Coupland swallowed down a sigh. He supposed he was about to find out whether Amjid bore grudges.

'I believe you've worked together on a couple of cases,' said the Commander.

The two men looked at each other and nodded. 'A long time ago,' Amjid clarified, already distancing himself.

Coupland rewarded him with a smile. 'They were challenging investigations,' he acknowledged.

Someone called the Commander away. Amjid caught Coupland's eye, his smile sardonic.

'Look,' began Coupland, thrusting his hands into his trouser pockets. 'I know things got a bit fraught last time we worked together…'

'Assaulting a chief suspect can do that,' Amjid threw back, 'We can't all work fists first and think afterwards.'

'If I recall it was a head butt,' Coupland corrected him, 'but I take your point.' His mouth formed a thin line as he recalled the flash of anger that nearly cost him his career.

Austin Smith, known as 'Reedsy', had been convicted

for his part in the trafficking of migrants from Albania into Salford and his role in the subsequent death of a young girl he'd transported across the city for the entertainment of a wealthy paedophile later linked to the Dutchman. Coupland had apprehended him during a raid on a property where the migrants were being held captive. His attempt to evade capture hadn't gone down well with Coupland one little bit, his complaint resulting in Coupland's suspension. He'd been murdered in his cell at HMP Manchester on the say-so of the Dutchman in order to protect his identity.

'You'd be a good cop if you didn't have so much rocket fuel for breakfast.'

Coupland's mouth stretched into a smile. 'Cheers,' he said. 'I think.'

Amjid studied him. 'Look, when you get involved in operations like this you have to constantly look at the bigger picture. I remember you accused me of forgetting what it was like to be at the sharp end.' Amjid barely paused to take a breath. It was as though he'd been saving these slights up to throw at him at an occasion such as this. He wasn't so much burying the hatchet as sharpening the blade before taking aim.

Coupland grimaced, readying himself for the blow. He certainly wasn't expecting what came next.

'What you said was right. In a fashion,' Amjid conceded. 'We can't all be running around on the tarmac, though. Someone needs to be in the control tower directing take-off and landing.'

Coupland said nothing. Decided it was unwise to suggest that if he was using aviation metaphors the rocket fuel Amjid accused him of having for breakfast was a wise choice, all things considered. He rearranged his features to look suitably chastened.

'Anyway, all water under the bridge now. We are on the same side, after all,' Amjid concluded.

'I'm with you on that,' Coupland said agreeably.

Despite the natural pause in conversation, Amjid seemed reluctant to leave. Coupland eyed the buffet table with something akin to regret. At this rate all that would be left would be gluten free.

He bared his teeth but Amjid was not to be shaken off. 'I know on the face of it, what my team is doing seems tedious,' the senior officer continued, 'not quite as dramatic as watching someone's movements before breaking down their front door. Yet we've all got a role to play.' Amjid looked about him to check what he was about to say couldn't be overheard. 'The Dutchman gets a lot of protection to help him stay below the radar. Do you hear what I'm saying?'

Coupland did, but he wanted him to say it anyway.

'We're operating in a situation where we can't be sure requests for warrants will be authorised, where cases brought before the courts could be thrown out, not to mention tip offs,' he said, grim faced.

Coupland's ears pricked up. 'Shouldn't we be spending time weeding out those folk as well, then?'

'If it was as simple as that, yes. Though the kind of money available to this network would mean that whatever link we closed down, another would open up again the next day and we'd have to start all over again trying to track down who'd replaced them.' It was the age-old problem. Money really did talk.

'Then we put the thumbscrews on key players and

keep twisting them,' Coupland reasoned.

'Easier said than done.'

'Isn't everything?'

'What we do is find other ways to crack the nut.'

Coupland's eyes narrowed. 'Meaning?'

'If we dig deep enough, we'll find financial irregularities that'll put some of the big players behind bars. Remember, Al Capone was put away for tax evasion. At the end of the day, jail is jail.'

Coupland was indignant. 'Bugger that! Don't tell me you're satisfied putting this scum away for white collar crime. They'll serve, what, three years then out again. No joining the sex offenders' register, their reputation and career intact. They need to be punished for the crimes they've committed, and by that I mean rape, sexual abuse, murder.'

Amjid was a master of keeping his emotions in check but Coupland could tell he was riled. He jerked his thumb towards his chest. 'Do you think it's what I want?' He shook his head as he answered as though making his view abundantly clear. 'I don't want to soft soap any of this, it just gives us a way in.'

He held the palm of his hand out to stop Coupland's objection. 'Hear me out. I'm not saying this is how it's going to be, Kevin. I was brought in to find a way to put the Dutchman and his ilk behind bars. My job is to put a stranglehold on the finances, so that those protecting him will start to speak out. We need someone to give us his real name for a start. What you lot here do with that is up to you. Of course I want him put away for as long as possible. The rest of his life, if we're lucky. But a win is a win and I'll take that.'

He sounded like a losing contestant telling the game show host he'd had a lovely time. In Coupland's mind there was no room for compromise. He desired only one outcome – watching a judge hand down multiple life sentences before the Dutchman was carted off in a prison van. That or a hearse. He wasn't fussed either way, truth be told. As Amjid said, a win was a win.

Coupland offered an olive branch in the form of a nod. He accepted that they had to start from somewhere. He just hoped as far as the Dutchman was concerned they could bloody well finish it.

'I believe we've got what it takes to bring him down,' said Amjid. 'It's the right time.'

Coupland wasn't sure there was ever a right time to catch a monster. For the countless victims they left in their wake it would always be too late.

Commander Howorth signalled for Amjid to join him at another group. Coupland barely had time to pick up a slice of carrot cake when a couple of suits standing nearby sidled over.

'How long have you been attached to the taskforce?' one of them asked. 'Only you seem to be in with the bigwigs already.' He appeared put out by this, but was unsure whether he should vent or suck up to him.

Coupland inclined his head in the direction of the Commander and Amjid who were busy holding court. 'Only so far as having my card marked,' he replied honestly. 'This is my first day. Same as you, I take it?'

Both men nodded. The one who'd spoken had a Birmingham accent, not quite Black Country but close enough. He had a hipster beard which Coupland reckoned put him at about thirty-five. Anyone older than that should know better. 'Are you both from the same unit?' he asked, wondering if it was considered rude to stuff his face while they answered. Cakes and treats had been banished from home by Lynn in her overzealous way to encourage them to eat healthy. 'I've restocked the fruit bowl,' she'd call out when he prowled round the kitchen rummaging through cupboards and drawers searching for a sugar hit. Healthy eating wasn't all doom and gloom. The weight he'd lost had stayed off. The slob he'd fast been turning into a couple of years back was long gone. He looked better for it, and if the truth be told – though getting him to admit it was like pulling teeth – he felt better too. He'd always been punchin' with Lynn, who spent so much time in the company of charismatic consultants he couldn't afford to become complacent. Even so. Free buffets didn't count, he told himself as he swallowed down the last bit of cake and eyed up a chocolate brownie.

'No, we met when we were on secondment to Europol at the same time,' the Hipster answered while helping himself to a vegan flapjack. 'I'd just completed my Masters and wasn't sure where I wanted to specialise.'

'Did it help you decide?' Coupland felt obliged to ask.

Hipster nodded. 'Absolutely! Sorry, I didn't introduce myself. I'm DCI Shane Swain, based at TITAN, the organised crime unit for the North West. We monitor top tier organised crime gangs who operate internationally.'

Coupland nodded like he gave a fuck, his attention turning to the DCI's companion who was positively salivating at the opportunity to brag about his career. In contrast with his bearded chum he was clean shaven. A long foppish fringe made him look more bookish than he probably was, black framed glasses giving his eyes an owl-like appearance.

'DI Benjamin Taylor. I'm a CHIS handler with the South East Regional Crime Unit,' he stated when Coupland's gaze fell on him. Covert Human Intelligence Sources, previously known as 'grasses', were considered key in the fight against organised crime, even if most of them were duplicitous bastards. 'Prior to this posting I was seconded to Europol to get a better understanding of the Dutchman's international operations. The intention being to develop intel sources within his network.'

They spoke as though they were attending a particularly competitive job interview. Coupland resisted the temptation to ask where they saw themselves in five years' time.

'And what about you?' asked DCI Swain. A crumb had lodged itself in his beard, making him look as though he suffered from a worrying infestation.

Coupland kept his professional face on. 'Nothing to write home about as far as I'm concerned. I'm just your typical common or garden murder squad DS. I operate more at the hoodie-wearing gangbanger end of the spectrum, but I've mopped up the aftermath of a few turf wars. Brought down the odd crime lord or two due to luck and a prevailing wind.' Coupland's mouth turned down at the edges. No point mentioning Kieran Tunny's release which would see him back in the bosom of his manor, boomerang style.

'So how do you know the Commander?'

'I don't. He knows me because of a case I'd worked on previously involving the Dutchman.' There, thought Coupland. Stick that in your career bragging pipe and smoke it.

'And what about the chap from City of London Police?'

'Oh, you mean DCI Akram,' said Coupland. Apart from the two DCs from the Digital Forensic Unit, Coupland was the lowest ranking officer in the room. He was buggered if he was going to spend his time kow-towing to all and sundry though. Maybe appearing well connected wouldn't be a bad thing. He made a point of catching Amjid's eye and wiggling his fingers at him like they were besties. Amjid regarded him, inclining his head a fraction, his face resembling someone trying to pass wind quietly.

Coupland turned his attention back to Swain. 'Me and Amjid go way back...' he said, concealing a smile.

Something DI Taylor had said sparked Coupland's interest. 'Have they brought you on board to recruit in-house snitches then?'

Taylor shrugged. 'I guess they're covering all their options. There's a UC in position but I'm not hearing great things about him.'

Undercover officers performed deep, long term infiltrations into top tier organised crime gangs. The deployments were dangerous and psychologically challenging. Some forces were reluctant to rely on them.

'In what way?' asked Coupland.

'Nothing specific. I heard he can be difficult to manage, that's all.'

'Is that so?' Coupland commented, already deciding that he was someone worth getting to know. 'So, your job is to make him redundant?' he probed, his gaze resting on DI Taylor.

'I wouldn't quite put it like that.' A look passed between Taylor and DCI Swain.

'Spit it out, we're all on the same side,' Coupland prompted, trying to make it sound good-natured.

Swain glanced over his shoulder, guiltily, like someone about to spill top secret beans. 'We heard talk earlier of him being pulled out,' he muttered. He spoke out of the corner of his mouth, like a crap ventriloquist.

'Rumour has it he's gone rogue,' said Taylor, not to be outdone. 'Problem with these guys is they enjoy the adrenaline rush too much. Start to thrive on it.'

'Must be hard though,' said Coupland, 'never really knowing when it's safe to switch off.' Even the good ones found it hard to re-settle. 'Sounds like you've already written him off.'

'Just repeating what somebody else said.'

Coupland made a point of stepping back to look at them wide-eyed. 'Without verifying what qualified them to make that claim? I don't think I'd be mouthing that off to all and sundry. I like to fact check my information before I pass it on, what with us living in the era of fake news and all that.' He paused to let that settle.

'Anyway,' he added once they looked suitably hacked off. 'I really must go and make up a doggy bag before those cream horns get carted away... I look forward to working with you,' he added as an afterthought, his face giving way to the lie.

*

'So, how was it for you?'

Coupland turned in the direction of Superintendent Lara Cole's voice. He rapidly chewed the remains of some sort of French fancy, swilling it down with water from a tumbler left on a side table. 'On the basis that I haven't been marched off the premises by security I'm presuming it's gone okay. I didn't knowingly step on anyone's size tens.'

'Early days yet,' she acknowledged.

'Mind you, I was only sitting and listening. I'm presuming now the briefing's over we'll get down to some actual work.'

Cole smiled. 'Would you mind popping next door for a moment?'

Coupland studied her face. Having only met her for the first time that morning he wasn't sure whether he should be worried by this request or not. He looked back at the cake table regretfully and followed her into her office. She closed the door behind him, though unlike their earlier meeting didn't invite him to sit down. He might not be getting carted off by security, but he might still be getting the boot. Perhaps his face, and size tens, didn't fit after all.

She removed her jacket and draped it over the back of her chair, before resting both hands on it like a mini altar. Her face was inscrutable, like a news reader when nothing major has happened.

'This morning wasn't just about setting the scene. There was a bit of a beauty parade going on. The Commander insisted on eyeballing every operative who'd been approved for the taskforce before any decisions were made regarding who was going to make up the core investigative team, or the inner circle, as he insists on bloody calling it.'

Coupland's ears pricked up. 'Is that why he followed me out to the smoking shelter then, to suss me out?'

Cole scowled at his interruption, confused. 'It's why he asked DCI Amjid Akram to join you both after his presentation. He was aware of past tensions and wanted to reassure himself that they wouldn't carry forward into this operation.'

So, the encounter hadn't been as innocuous as he'd thought. Just as well Amjid didn't bear grudges. No wonder DCI Swain and DI Taylor acted as though they were at a job interview. Turned out they were all being evaluated.

'I take it the Commander now has all the information he needs to make his selection?' Coupland hadn't realised how important this job was to him until his gut started clenching at the thought of losing it before he'd even started.

'I'll put you out of your misery,' said Cole, a smile pulling at the corner of her mouth as she regarded him. 'You've made it to the top table. You've been assigned to the team tasked with ID-ing the key members of this ring,' she told him, 'but be warned, as the lowest ranking officer you're going to be doing a lot of the heavy lifting.'

'Suits me fine,' said Coupland, his face breaking into a grin.

Cole held up her hands. 'I wouldn't get too excited. Our biggest problem is that on paper the Dutchman doesn't exist. No phone records, no car registrations, no HMRC records. We might know him as the Dutchman, but we're none the wiser as to who the hell he actually is.'

Coupland nodded his understanding. He'd wanted a role where he could make a real difference, and now the opportunity had landed right in his lap. *Don't fuck it up*, his inner voice warned.

'Who else will I be working with in this team, Ma'am?'

She made a wafting motion with her hands. 'If you get yourself over to the top floor, pronto, you'll find out.'

CHAPTER THREE

Coupland stepped out of the lift into a hive of activity. Room dividers split the open plan office space which spanned the top floor into smaller work areas. Baffle boards surrounded a cluster of desks creating workstations, each equipped with a computer and telephone. A line of filing cabinets flanked one wall. A super-sized TV screen had been mounted on another.

Civilian personnel seemed to be doing most of the fetching and carrying – wheeling incident boards into position, unpacking kitchen appliances and charging up iPads to be distributed to the team – although a couple of officers had rolled up their sleeves to give them a hand. Coupland looked around for someone he recognised.

'Go and look for your name on the notice board,' one of them called out to him. 'That'll tell you where you're to set up camp.'

Coupland headed in the direction they pointed. As he passed one workstation he glanced inside. Noah and Jared, otherwise known as Operation Maple's entire Digital Forensics Unit, were setting up a bank of computers across a row of desks, checking network compatibility, making sure it recognised all their devices. Coupland's chin dropped a fraction. If anyone expected *him* to do anything more than switch his computer on, he'd be buggered. No point hiding from the truth.

Jared caught Coupland's eye and raised a hand in greeting. Coupland nodded.

The notice board was located above the water cooler, or water station, as the sign plastered on the front of it claimed. Big mistake putting it there, in Coupland's view. Only the folk who drank water would see it.

The roles to be assigned had been made into four column headings on an A3 sheet of paper taped to the wall: Overseeing enquiries. Coordinating interviews. Managing intelligence. Exhibits. The names of the assigned officers were listed below each heading. Beside each name was the workstation they'd been allocated.

Delighted to find his name under a heading that contained the word intelligence, Coupland headed to his new workstation. His good humour started to wear thin when DCI Swain and DI Taylor greeted him from a workspace that looked worryingly like where he was headed. He eyed the four civilian computer operators set up at the back of the room with something akin to envy. The part of his job that Coupland liked the least was having to work with other people, especially folk that were new to him. Trust issues rearing their ugly head again, he supposed, albeit justified, going by what Amjid Akram had to say.

'Looks like we'll be working together,' said DCI Swain.

'Can't have everything,' Coupland muttered, turning the edges of his mouth up in a smile as he got closer.

'Are you happy with this desk?' Swain asked him. Coupland clocked the proximity of his desk and the gents' toilet, shrugged. 'It'll come in handy when my prostate starts playing up,' he said.

'I'll swap with you, if you like?' DI Taylor offered,

obviously the peacekeeper of the two.

'It's fine, it's only a desk, I don't intend to be using it that often.'

'That's the spirit,' said Commander Howorth, exiting the gents, still zipping up his fly.

Five officers had been selected to form the so-called 'inner circle' of the team. Alongside Coupland, DCI Swain and DI Taylor, who brought OCG monitoring and CHIS handling to the table, they were joined by a DI with ginger hair and several days' unshaved stubble which he had a penchant for scratching when he spoke. 'Joe Edwards,' he'd said by way of introduction. Twelve years ago he'd been one of the Met officers involved in the investigation into phone hacking by the press, he'd told them as he introduced himself. 'The investigation was controversial at the time, not least because we had unprecedented access to material that, under law, is privileged. In normal circumstances we'd have needed a court production order to access such material.'

The investigation revealed that the phones of murdered schoolgirl Milly Dowler and victims of the 7 July 2005 London bombings had also been hacked. The resulting public outcry led to several high-profile resignations in the newspaper industry. He'd been brought in to handle the press side of things. Not in the usual, issuing of police statements, type of action, he'd been keen to stress, but had yet to elaborate further.

There was something about the fifth member of the team that Coupland couldn't quite put his finger on. Impeccably dressed in a single-breasted suit and plain tie, he had the demeanour of someone who'd never raised their voice except on a rugby pitch. His wavy hair was short and combed back bouffant style. Coupland placed him in his mid-40s, so they were similar in age, yet he gave the impression of someone much older, or rather old in his ways. He'd looked a little taken aback when he first strolled over to where the rest of them were setting up their desks, as though the office layout wasn't what he'd been expecting. It was like watching a Hollywood A lister discover they were sharing a dressing room.

Coupland must have been the only officer there used to working in an open plan set up but at least the others were putting on a brave face. Mr Low Key had said very little while everyone introduced themselves. Spoke only when spoken to; even then his answers were clipped and to the point. Whereas the others were more than happy to fill a silence with their career highlights, he preferred to keep shtum. Coupland wasn't sure what to make of him, which of his own tried and tested workplace headings he'd file him under: *Good Guy* or *Wanker*. The IT boys along with Joe Edwards were the only ones so far to make it into the first category. Swain and Taylor, on the other hand, had been relegated on sight to the second.

Commander Howorth had been doing the rounds, checking everyone was able to log into the system and had been given their passwords, in the same way a dinner party host makes sure guests' drinks are kept topped up. When he clocked the lone figure looking slightly adrift from everyone else he made his way towards him. 'Sorry I wasn't here to make introductions, Tony. Let me put that right straight away,' he said before clapping his hands together and asking for everyone's attention. 'I'd like to introduce you all to Superintendent Tony Romain. He'll be responsible for assimilating intelligence and guiding actions. He will be heading up this operation on a day-to-day basis and you will all report to him.'

He paused to let that nugget sink in. Coupland wasn't fussed, though he did notice a couple of chins jut out in consternation.

Commander Howorth continued: 'For those of you unaware of Tony's career experience, he was previously a Protection Officer assigned to the Royalty Protection Squad, SO14. The last two years he's been attached to the Met's Art Crime Unit, specialising in high end art and antique theft.'

He turned to Tony, sweeping his arm wide, 'I'm sure you'd like to say a few words.'

Tony Romain's hand casually moved to button his suit jacket as he rose to his feet. 'Of course. Thank you, Peter,' he acknowledged, his home counties voice demanding attention. He threw an apologetic look at Coupland and the rest of the team as if to say *At least I saved you from having to listen to this twice.* 'We have a huge task ahead of us…' he began, sounding like a general addressing troops before they went into battle. Although he moved his hands around a lot they stayed parallel with each other, as though he was holding an invisible ruler between his palms. Every so often he'd straighten his tie despite it never being out of place. The way he carried himself suggested he was accustomed to better things. He'd have been right at home hobnobbing with diplomats and visiting dignitaries working for the Royal Protection Squad, and as for tracking down counterfeit art… a sly look at his biography in the case file on his desk told Coupland he'd graduated with a first-class honours degree in art history from Cambridge.

Coupland looked around at the assembled teams hanging on every word. He was certainly charismatic; the jutted-out chins weren't exactly doing a happy dance but they looked a lot less sullen than they had when he'd first started talking. A few more tugs of his tie before joking that he'd only been selected because he sounded like he'd stepped out of Downton Abbey. Everyone laughed even though it was obvious that's what they'd been thinking. It made sense. If they had any hope of bringing the Dutchman's high-level cohort down, they needed officers who wouldn't have the door shut in their faces the moment they came knocking. Or the drawbridges pulled up.

'Things have moved on significantly in the last 24 hours,' said Commander Howorth, taking the helm once more. He beckoned over the group of civilian computer operators to join what was about to turn into a briefing. It would be their job to assess new information as it came in and build up databases to prioritise the lines of inquiry. This was the most important function. Prioritise it wrongly and a vital piece of information could be shuffled back into the middle of the pack and not investigated for several days. Days which could prove crucial. It was essential they understood the significance of what they were all doing.

'Never has there been a better time to commence this operation. In the last two years, seven passmen have been tracked down and jailed for their part in the abduction and murders of young women and girls found on Utopia. The Dutchman is getting anxious. He is tidying up his act. I don't mean he has shut the site down,' he said, raising his hand, palm outwards. 'He's simply exterminating anyone on his supply chain capable of identifying him.

'A week ago Dutch police discovered a "torture chamber" following a raid in a warehouse near the city of Rotterdam. Inside were several cells made out of sound-proofed shipping containers. Torture tools were found including a dentist's chair, hedge trimmers, scalpels and pliers. The place was nicknamed the "treatment room", apparently.'

Nice.

Coupland considered the type of person who wielded this torture. Did they kiss their wife and children goodbye each morning and climb into their car contemplating the day ahead? The many ways they could slice, drill, yank? Did they stop for a sandwich at lunchtime? Wonder what was for dinner while cutting up body parts?

'Recovering DNA from a site like that is a painstaking business. Trace samples so far belong to two British gangsters reported as missing since 2020. Both were under investigation for human trafficking, though there wasn't enough evidence to haul them in.'

Now there never would be. Coupland huffed out a breath. He felt many things for those who robbed others of their freedom before selling them on. Pity wasn't among them.

'Can any of this be linked to the Dutchman though?' someone whose name Coupland couldn't remember asked. 'He got his name through serving time in a prison in the Netherlands, he doesn't live there.'

Commander Howorth nodded. 'He has several residences, all funded by other people, which is why he's been able to evade us for so long.' He paused to take a breath. 'Surveillance footage shows a man leaving a restaurant in Bergen op Zoom, seven kilometres away from the torture chamber, two days before the raid.'

The commander nodded at Noah, who began tapping onto a laptop on his knee. The wall-mounted screen behind the commander sprang into life. Noah tapped some more, pausing when he found the image he was looking for. Several more clicks and a photograph of two men walking towards a blacked-out car came on screen. The car was parked a few steps away from the restaurant's entrance. The men wore woollen coats over dark suits. One held a mobile phone to his ear. The commander looked around the room until his gaze settled on Coupland.

'You're the only one of us here who has seen him in the flesh. Can you confirm this is the Dutchman?'

Every head swivelled in Coupland's direction as he moved closer to the screen. 'Can you make the image bigger?' he asked Noah.

The young officer obliged. Coupland stared at the face of the man holding the mobile phone. He focussed on the image. This man's hair was thinning on top, making his forehead look larger than it was. Two deep lines etched across it as he furrowed his brow in concentration. A business call, Coupland supposed. All at once he understood the pressure placed on eyewitnesses. No wonder so many cracked under the fear of getting it wrong. Doubting themselves when previously they'd been certain. He hadn't been looking for the Dutchman when their paths had crossed. He hadn't known he was in the city. It was a fleeting moment, a glimpse of him while he'd been waiting at traffic lights, heading to a nearby derelict estate to search for a murdered girl's mobile phone. He'd glanced across the road as a man and woman stepped out of the entrance to Pennant Tower, a prestigious development in Salford's financial district. Owned by foreign investors, it was largely unoccupied. The people who stayed there were seriously minted. The couple had been dressed for an evening out. Their body language was relaxed, unhurried. At the time he hadn't realised that's who he'd been looking at. It was only later, when his whereabouts had been pieced together, that they'd worked out it was the Dutchman. All this time he'd held onto the notion that he'd had a really good look at him, yet all he'd really seen was a guy in expensive clothes heading out for the evening. He didn't recall the thinning hair and the deep lines. Yet something about the eyes…

Coupland shifted his attention to the other man in the photograph to see if he looked familiar. The man had sallow skin and heavy-set features. The flattened nose of a trained fighter. It made sense the Dutchman travelled with backup. No matter how ruthless his reputation, he was past the stage where he'd want to get his hands dirty.

'Yeah, that's him,' Coupland said, his voice gruff.

He looked at the Commander. 'Where is he now?'

'This man entered the UK six days ago, flying into Stansted on board a Ryanair flight from Stockholm. CCTV picked him up climbing into a car with false plates.'

'So we lost him?'

'Yes.'

'And the name on the passenger manifest?'

'Robert Lewis. One of his many aliases.'

Coupland swiped his hand over his face. He could feel adrenaline charge through him. 'So what do we do now?'

'We wait.'

'Are you serious?'

The Commander fixed him with a stare. Coupland

dropped his gaze, remembering he wasn't in Kansas anymore. When he returned the Commander's gaze he looked suitably contrite.

'Europol have had surveillance officers track a dozen men that fitted this profile. Now we have a confirmed sighting, we can focus our attention on him and start to build up a case.'

'We've already got a case, sir,' Coupland persisted reaching for the case file on his desk and raising it above his head. 'It's all in here, the guy's banged to bloody rights.'

The Commander waved his hand at Coupland to put the file down. 'Not a single piece of evidence in that file can be attributed directly to this monster. He's been too clever for that. Every step of the way there are layers of individuals prepared to take the rap for him – his passmen and the well-rewarded trafficking gangs who have kept his supply chain going, for a start. Those no longer prepared to take the blame, well, we can only imagine what those poor bastards went through, maybe once the Dutch police find those bodies it'll give us some idea.'

The Commander scrabbled around to find a positive. 'The only arrests we can make at the moment are the arrests we've been making so far. The passmen who've been abducting and killing the victims, the gofers who drive around the city at their beck and call, and the saddos who log into this stuff to watch it. None of this enterprise can be directly connected to the Dutchman. He's the maestro who conducts the orchestra, but he doesn't play a single note himself.'

Some nodded at everything the Commander said. Others took copious notes.

Superintendent Romain spoke next. 'We have to play

the long game. Strip away his social and financial infrastructure. Right now he's being put up in a hotel, apartment or luxury home, at someone else's expense. What we need to do is put the fear of God into his supporters. Rubbing shoulders with a gangster is all very exciting until you're looking at the prospect of 30 years for aiding and abetting a network of sexual abusers and killers.'

'I think it's time to explain where you fit in to the operation, don't you?' Commander Howorth said to DI Edwards.

Joe got to his feet, keen to oblige.

'Does anyone understand what is meant by the term *Lawfare*?'

Coupland sighed into his chest as though the answer to that was obvious. He shook his head anyway.

Edwards' smile was smug. 'It refers to the misuse of the law by the super-rich to destroy their critics and opponents. Pretty much David and Goliath in reverse,' he explained, looking around the room. 'In the same way some newspapers refuse to cover topics relating to Russian oligarchs, for fear of costly litigation, so too they avoid anything to do with the suggestion of certain members of the establishment being corrupt. The deep pockets these individuals have mean they can instruct top tier law firms to issue what's known in the trade as SLAPPS: strategic litigation against public participation. Basically, it's a lawsuit designed to silence criticism.'

'So there's no such thing as free speech anymore?' Noah asked.

Edwards shook his head. 'Not if it's damaging to one of the big boys. Look, when it comes to the law we're a nation of hypocrites. Britain is among the most respected countries from a legal perspective, yet those legal principles enable those with immoral intentions and questionable ethics to do exactly as they please. It's been that way for years, and deep pockets wield power. These people control journalists, officials and media organisations through intimidation. It limits the way we can reach them. Step one uninvited foot over their threshold and they'll have the journalists in their pocket scream police harassment and wrongful arrest in their headlines. That or dig deep to find a scandal they can unearth to provide a diversion.'

'So we're buggered before we start,' Coupland summed up.

Edwards nodded. 'I'd say yes, other than the fact I've got contacts in the media who are sick and tired of being oppressed. Although they considered me the enemy back in the day, the lines of our engagement were clear. What I need to do now is get enough of them onside so that when the mainstream press starts to denigrate what you guys are doing – and trust me, they will – there'll be some who'll refuse to run the story. We have reason to believe the Dutchman's cohort includes senior officers, several judges and government ministers. If they can't hide behind fake news they will start to feel exposed. When they discover they can't deflect the attention as this thing starts heating up then there's every chance they'll turn their back on him, or at least not grant him so many favours.'

'So essentially we're smoking him out,' the Commander concluded.

A hush settled on the room.

'These people will stop at nothing to throw us off

track,' he added. 'So I need each and every one of you to bring your A game to the table every day.'

He looked around the room and nodded, satisfied. 'OK, that's enough for today. Things from here on in are going to start getting busy, so bugger off home while you can. There won't be many opportunities to clock off at a decent hour.'

Coupland took his time. Waited as the officers around him got to their feet reluctantly. Everyone was pumped now they knew the Dutchman was on UK soil. No one wanted to leave. This was definitely going to be a long game they were playing. Coupland just wasn't sure he could sit around on his hands while Amjid Akram and Joe Edwards put the frighteners on the so-called pillars of the community.

He followed the other officers to the door, then doubled back as though he'd forgotten something.

Commander Howorth and Superintendent Romain were deep in conversation. They stopped when Coupland marched up to them. 'Do you need something, Kevin?' asked the Commander.

'Someone mentioned an undercover officer earlier, I'd like to meet with him, sir.'

'Thought you might,' the Commander smiled, glancing at Romain. He was Coupland's new boss, after all.

'Any specific reason?' Romain asked.

Coupland shoved his hands into his pockets and hunched his shoulders. 'I'd like to get a measure of each link in this chain, sir. To get a better understanding of what part he plays in all this, given that we know the Dutchman's getting closer.'

'Makes sense,' agreed the Commander.

'Yet you're the only officer who has asked about him,' observed Romain, making it sound like a failing. 'It isn't possible for you to be hands on regarding every aspect of this investigation, Detective Sergeant. There's absolutely no need for us to engage directly with operatives on the ground. You're here to interpret what they find. Follow up on the leads they give us without blowing their cover.'

Romain came across as dry and emotionless but as a royal protection officer he must have been willing to put his life on the line.

'I appreciate that, sir, but it sounded to me earlier like some have written this fella off,' persisted Coupland.

'He's young but he's experienced. He's put his neck on the block on several occasions, from what I hear,' the Commander informed him.

'I don't doubt it,' said Coupland. 'It would be good to get a better idea what happens to the intel that he passes on. Make sure the jaded views I heard downstairs won't influence what is given priority and what's flushed down the pan.'

Romain considered this. 'I'll need to get it cleared,' he said, climbing onto the global wooden fence and trying it for size.

'No need,' boomed the Commander. 'I'll talk to his handler but what I say, goes. When the meet's set up I'll text you the location.'

*

A rare meal out, just the two of them. A bistro Lynn liked that served good food without the pretence of requiring diners to dress up like a dog's dinner. 'So, come on then, what's the occasion?' she'd asked him, a bemused smile on her face, after they'd been shown to their table and left with the menu.

'Do I need an excuse to treat my beloved?' he'd countered, wondering why they didn't do this more often.

'Yeah, usually,' Lynn answered reproachfully. 'Birthdays, missed anniversaries and whenever you've been a twat.'

'Christ, we'd never be away from here if that's all it took.'

Lynn considered his answer. 'When you've been a twat with bells on, then,' she qualified. 'So are you going to tell me what's really going on? What it is you've done or haven't done that you need the sanctity of a roomful of diners to stop me going postal?'

'Charming,' Coupland muttered. He knew in the life partner department he was often found lacking. That a proper husband would empty the dishwasher without being asked and never put plastic in the cardboard recycling box, despite being called out on it a gazillion times. His shortcomings were plentiful, yet she navigated round them like a bomb disposal officer crossing a field riddled with enemy land mines.

Her suspicion irked him more than it should, though as usual, she had a point. When he was in the bad books a change of scenery and a shared bottle of wine usually helped get them back on track, but that hadn't been his intention this time. For a start he wasn't aware he'd done anything wrong. Or rather, fucked anything up more than usual. He'd wanted to make a gesture, that was all, a show of appreciation that for all his fuckwittery she still chose to come home to him every night, for which he was baffled and grateful in equal measure.

It mystified him that she couldn't see his devotion. That she needed it spelling out in impossible ways like words and actions. They communicated through a vocabulary of sarcastic affection. He moaned and grumbled whenever she asked him to do anything despite being happy to do it. It kept her on her toes, he'd say. Like him getting on her wick, she'd say back. Lynn was the life raft he clung to. Though he'd be buggered if he'd ever admit it.

Despite his initial thrill at being selected for the taskforce, he was shrouded in an anxiety he couldn't shake off. Maybe today's briefing had heightened his fears, or he'd spent too long in the job. Seeing folk reduced to nothing in the blink of an eye could do that to a person.

He hated when this darkness oozed out of him, warping his sense of perspective. When Lynn was late home and not picking up her phone it wasn't because she couldn't hear the ringtone over the noise of the traffic, it was because she was being mugged at knifepoint at the cash machine, or being dragged down an alley. The bump in the middle of the night wasn't Tonto getting out of bed, but an intruder, not prepared to leave empty handed.

This wasn't catastrophizing. This was how Coupland's world looked on a daily basis. He was forever waiting for the wind to change. For his luck to run out. It was exhausting, living on the outside looking in, but it was all he knew.

Lynn's smile across the table made him resolve to do better. To *be* better.

'How about you order anything you want and I promise

I won't bitch about the prices?' he offered, deciding he had to start from somewhere.

CHAPTER FOUR

It hadn't been as plain sailing as the Commander had predicted. It had taken two days for Coupland's request to be rubber stamped. For the appropriate channels to be consulted. The territorial umming and ahhing and beating of chests that took place when party lines were at risk of being crossed. On two separate occasions he'd been asked by e-mail to explain why he wanted to meet with UCO 592, the undercover operative's code number, to which he'd replied, 'This has already been approved by Commander Howorth,' which was polite speak for go fuck yourself.

All Coupland knew about UCO 592 was that he went by the name of Jason O'Neill. His file was classified. The scant information he'd gleaned about him were the snippets of conversation from others on the first day in this job.

'Ignore them,' the Commander had advised when he'd told him about some of the comments made. 'People are quick to condemn what they don't understand.'

'But aren't we supposed to be on the same side?' Coupland had asked.

The Commander's response had been an enigmatic smile, like Coupland had much to learn.

Jason's handler hadn't been best pleased that Coupland wanted to meet him, but in the end seniority won out and the meeting had been arranged. This was the reason Coupland stood chain-smoking in the parking bay of an industrial estate that counted Strangeways, or rather HMP Manchester to use its Sunday name, as its notable neighbour. He'd been instructed to stay in view, and if it was safe to do so, Jason would make himself known to him.

Coupland had arrived early. The road into the industrial estate led into a turning circle, so he parked his car facing the only exit, a habit that had held him in good stead over the years. He took the opportunity to study his surroundings while he enjoyed his smoke. It was more a small development of workshop units than an industrial estate. The concrete buildings were single storey with metal up-and-over loading doors, suited to small businesses requiring warehousing space rather than somewhere to place personnel.

Despite the reputations of the residents in the big house looming in the distance and the trade in knock-off gear in neighbouring streets, known as 'Counterfeit Alley,' there was nothing to mark this particular location out as a problem hotspot. Still, Coupland's inbuilt antenna scanned for trouble wherever he found himself. An in-your-face Mercedes four-wheel drive turned into the road, its headlights flashing twice before pulling up outside one of the lock ups.

Coupland dropped his cigarette onto the floor, ground it out with his foot. He shoved his hands into his pockets as he strolled towards the car, nodding as the driver got out.

'I see you didn't get the memo about not dressing like the job,' said Jason, looking him up and down. Aged somewhere in his early thirties he was long and lean. He wore a Nike tracksuit zipped up to the neck, a heavy gold chain hanging over the top of it. Never one for brand names, even Coupland knew the trainers he wore were the best part of five hundred pounds and that the Rolex on his wrist, despite looking like it came out of a Christmas cracker, was the real deal. Coupland had heard about the amounts spent on these guys to make them fit in with the company they had to keep. It was one of the constant causes of friction when overtime was treated like a precious commodity. He looked down at his own ensemble: A pair of old Levis and a zip-up hoodie replaced his regular suit. His GMP lanyard and badge tucked under a greying t-shirt below it.

'Pardon me for not looking street enough,' he growled. 'I can't even claim for the smokes I've gone through waiting for you to show up, never mind getting sign off on a rent-a-villain costume.'

Jason raised his hands in apology, his sunbed-tanned face splitting into a wide grin. 'Yeah, sorry I'm late. Had a bit of unexpected business to attend to.' He unlocked the metal shutter and pulled it up, stepping inside. Coupland followed him in, waited while the shutter clanked shut behind him. 'Everyone calls me Jay,' he said, lifting his fist in readiness for Coupland to bump it with his own.

Coupland's hands remained by his side. 'I've been called a bit of a C before now but let's stick to Coupland, that way we both know where we stand,' he said, taking in his surroundings. He wasn't sure exactly what he'd been expecting the interior to look like, but he hadn't expected to see a full-sized pool table and mini bar. 'Jesus wept, I always suspected I was in the wrong job,' he muttered.

'Now I'm bloody sure of it. Have you any idea how hard it was to get HR to cough up for a new kettle for my team last year?'

Jay laughed. 'What were you expecting, a crack lab?'

Coupland's grunt in response suggested that was nearer to the truth.

'I'm part of the supply chain, remember, not manufacturing.'

'Thanks for clearing that up,' Coupland drawled.

'Fancy a game?' Jay asked, picking up a cue and offering it to him.

'Are you off your head?' Coupland demanded, giving him a look that suggested his cue might be used for a very different purpose if he didn't buck his ideas up. 'I don't have time to fanny about, son. I'm here to find out more about your operation and then be on my way.'

'Your choice,' shrugged Jay. He pointed to two faux leather foam-backed chairs in what could loosely be called a mini kitchen. A sink and low-level units had been fitted against one wall. A kettle and microwave sat on top of a melamine work surface.

Coupland lowered himself into one of the chairs, while Jay pulled two cans of Red Bull from a fridge, setting one down in front of Coupland before sitting in the neighbouring seat.

'I'll pass, thanks,' said Coupland. 'Don't think my blood pressure could take it.'

'Saw you smoking outside,' Jay shot back.

'A cigarette I would never have had if you'd been on time,' Coupland lied. He eyed the blue and silver can with contempt. 'My ticker gets quite enough exercise as it is without artificial stimulants, thanks very much.'

"'Fraid we're all out of cocoa, Grandad,' Jay quipped, his head tipping to one side as he flashed Coupland with another grin.

Coupland wasn't quite sure when he'd started to sound like a grouchy old timer, but he was aware that at right this minute he was putting on a damn good impression. He wouldn't mind but he could give Billy Big Balls here a run for his money if he chose to. He sat forward in his chair and flexed his biceps. He might not know how to rock the Love Island look but he knew how to be menacing. He sent Jay a look that said don't bugger me about.

Jay's grin fell away. 'So, my handler tells me you wanted to see me,' he said. 'How come?'

'Didn't they tell you?'

'She gives me information on a need-to-know basis. Knowledge is power and all that. You know how it goes. She obviously thought you'd join up the dots.'

'That's what I'm hoping you can do for me. I'm part of Operation Maple, which is in its infancy. It makes sense to meet everyone involved in intelligence gathering. Especially those who have been on the ground for a while,' Coupland answered.

'I am honoured,' chimed Jay. 'Most people are happy to tip the housekeeper even though it's the chambermaid who empties the pot.'

'I suppose I'm a chamber pot kind of guy,' Coupland responded.

Jay threw his arms wide. 'In that case welcome to my world,' he said. 'I like to think of myself as the Lab Rat of the operation.'

'Agile and hard to exterminate?' asked Coupland.

'Low grade and expendable.'

Coupland wondered whether this meeting had been a good idea after all. The guy liked to showboat, and it was clear there were tensions between him and those he reported in to. He didn't want to make the situation worse. Even so, many of the decisions the taskforce would make over the coming months could be a result of the information Jay gleaned. Coupland needed to know that he was solid.

'How about we start with you telling me what you do around here?'

A look flitted across Jay's face, followed by a shrug. 'I gather intelligence on the big players in the area. I pass on information about any jobs about to go down. Larger than normal drugs shipments coming into the city, or new players stepping into the arena. I haven't been given specific terms of reference, if that's what you're after. My remit is pretty wide.'

'And how's it working out for you?'

'You should know better than to ask about intel I've already sent in. Need to know basis, remember?' he said, tapping the side of his nose with his index finger. There was a swagger about him that would irritate the hell out of most people. Or at least those trying to manage him. In terms of those he was trying to emulate, Coupland had come up against lifelong grifters a lot less convincing, he conceded.

'Suppose there's no harm in telling you about stuff that's already gone down,' Jay conceded when after staring at each other for what seemed like an age he was the first to blink.

That's more like it, thought Coupland. Jay was young. Stood to reason he'd want to show off a bit. Couldn't blame him. There was a time when Coupland went about thinking he was immortal. Now when he left for work he worried he was pushing his luck.

'Remember the brothers in Cheetham Hill who got sent down for shooting that bouncer? It turned into a tit-for-tat turf war?'

Coupland remembered something vaguely. Three more fatalities if he remembered it right. It hadn't been his patch, he had enough on his plate keeping Salford from turning into bandit country. The gangs in Cheetham Hill were as prolific as the Salford gangs and when one stepped into the other's territory GMP braced itself. He nodded.

Jay looked pleased. 'It was my intel that stopped a shipment of weapons coming into Liverpool. It was on its way to where the brothers were staying. They'd lined up a weekend of executions that would have turned into the Apocalypse.'

Coupland remembered *that* success story. Remembered the photo of the Detective Super in charge of the operation holding up one of the confiscated sub machine guns for the camera.

'It meant that instead of absconding, the brothers were made to stand trial. They got 35 years each and the rest of the gang were given a total of 80 years.'

'Good shout,' Coupland acknowledged.

Jay tipped his head. 'All part of the service.'

'How come you weren't moved onto another patch afterwards?'

'No need. My cover wasn't blown. I'm part of the criminal fraternity here. Why waste that?'

Coupland didn't look convinced.

'Guys like me aren't put in place to infiltrate a particular gang. We're infiltrating a community. It's taken real graft to work my way up to become a known face. Over time I've been accepted into the fold of some of the largest gangs in operation here. I'm not affiliated to any one in particular, but their acceptance works as an endorsement as far as all the other big players are concerned.'

Coupland was aware that if you wanted an informant that was well connected in the criminal world then you'd need to engage with a player. The downside with using a snitch, or CHIS as they were called, was that by their very nature they couldn't be trusted. It made sense that infiltrators were the better option. He could see why DI Taylor, as a CHIS handler, would take a different view. Still, he shouldn't let it blur his opinion of the man.

'How long have you been in position?' he asked.

'Eighteen months,' Jay answered, coughing out a laugh when he saw the look on Coupland's face. 'Add on another six months to get the backstopping right.'

Backstopping was when an undercover officer was given their new identity. They were issued with a new passport, and driving licence, bank cards and credit cards. Even their birth certificate was destroyed and replaced with another. Their DNA and fingerprints were removed from the national database until all traces of the person they were before was erased.

'Did you get sent away anywhere?' It wasn't unusual to spend time in a completely new location to build up a back story. Working behind a bar in Ireland, or for a family firm in Amsterdam.

'You could say that...' Jay smiled. He had one of those Jack the Lad demeanours that gave the impression he was unfazed by anything. Everything about him was convincing. Even his outlook.

'…I was sent to Winson Green.'

There was an established practice of sending undercover officers into jail to befriend a suspect in an effort to get evidence to prosecute him or try and get a confession. To do it in order to get himself known in the criminal fraternity seemed a little extreme.

'Did you have a specific target?' Coupland asked in an attempt to see if that's what he meant.

Jay shook his head.

Coupland worked hard at keeping his eyebrows in check. The category B prison in Birmingham had hit the headlines after the Justice Secretary launched an enquiry following the Chief Inspector of Prisons berating it following incidents of high violence, widespread bullying, squalid living conditions and poor control by staff scared out of their wits.

'No, I wanted to create a memorable legend which would set me up for when I got out.' A legend was a cover story, to explain the UC officer's presence. 'We can't just rock up out of nowhere and start giving orders like some big fucking banana. Think of me as a method actor. The Robert De Niro of undercover policing.'

Coupland tried not to roll his eyes. 'So, what's your story then?' he asked.

'I told anyone who'd listen that I used to work for my uncle. I made out he'd been a money lender who'd taken me on as extra muscle when he started getting on a bit. He's no longer with us, God rest his soul,' he added, making the sign of the cross. 'I made a point of putting myself in front of enough lags so any claim I made later down the line to have been inside could be easily verified.'

'I presume when you say memorable you mean keeping on the right side of the main players?'

Jay gave him a look. 'Where's the fun in that? That wasn't going to bring me to anyone's attention. The whole point of my time in there was to become a known face, but I also wanted to secure some allies for after I came out. That wasn't going to happen if I didn't speak out every once in a while, take sides occasionally, and throw a couple of punches to show I couldn't be pushed around.'

'Christ, have you got a death wish or something?' The repercussions of anyone discovering he'd been working undercover didn't bear thinking about. A cop in jail was a dead man walking. The only way he'd have left if the truth had come out would have been feet first.

'It's not the first time someone's accused me of that,' Jay acknowledged. 'It paid off though,' he laughed. 'As you can see I'm here, all in one piece.'

Coupland wondered what his handler had been thinking when she'd signed off on that deployment. If she'd been thinking at all. He could see why Jay likened himself to a lab rat. 'What were you supposed to be in there for?' Coupland asked him.

'Assault. It provided me with an instant hard man reputation without having to prove it. I was released after six months for "pleading guilty",' he added, making quote marks with his fingers.

Coupland frowned. That was six months of his life he wasn't going to get back, yet he didn't seem to care.

Jay clocked the look Coupland gave him. 'I don't have a home life, if that's what you're wondering.' No surprise there, thought Coupland. 'I split with my ex before I took on this job, so there's no one to mourn me if things go tits up.

'So, here I am, a walking talking encyclopaedia of the gangster A-Z. I'm on first name terms with some of the toughest dealers in Manchester. As well as all the local families I've got Yardies, Somalians, Albanians and Romanians on speed dial. All battling for a share of Manchester's drug scene. These cartels won't stop until we've become a nation of crack addicts.'

'What a time to be alive,' Coupland muttered.

As he listened, he got a sense that Jay was completely immersed in the life he was living. He wondered whether he ever clocked off, how that was possible. When he went to the pub, it would be as Jay O'Neill, the connected gangster with a history of violence. He wondered what the appeal was, because from where he was sitting there was nothing remotely rosy about his set-up.

The stress a UC officer faced – the investigation's lack of direction, not knowing when it would end and mounting expenditure not to mention risk to life – was considerable. Far removed to that faced by regular officers, whose main source of stress was admin and red tape.

Coupland inclined his head towards the pool table and mini bar. 'So what's all this in aid of?'

Jay shrugged. 'There's a lot of waiting around in this job. Thought I might as well put it to good use.'

'And what is the job exactly? The one folk round here think that you do?'

'I'm known locally as an enforcer. Most people understand that if I turn up on their doorstop something has gone badly wrong for them.'

'Who do you work for?'

'Myself. Anyone can hire me, for the right price. But I'm like Switzerland in all other respects. Completely fucking neutral.'

'How far do you go…?'

'Do you mean do I actually break anyone's legs?'

Coupland said nothing.

Jay shook his head. 'What do you take me for? I went through all the proper training, you know. I can't do anything to entice an offence but if not doing something would expose me then I'm left with little option. If I'm supposed to put the frighteners on someone I will. I'll intimidate and threaten, otherwise my cover would be blown instantly if I bottled it. I ask questions and order take, that's all. These guys trust me enough to ride along as extra security when they need it. Occasionally I carry bag loads of cash or drugs from A to B. Mainly airport runs but that's it.'

Coupland felt sure he wasn't being given the complete picture but there were choices he'd made in his own line of work he'd prefer not to share.

'Did they tell you that a couple of years ago a UK operative doing my job in Liverpool was found dead in the back of a burned-out Audi?' Coupland shook his head. 'No? Funny that… His death wasn't allowed to be reported by the press, allegedly to preserve the fact that other UCs were still in the field.'

Coupland sensed his scepticism. 'What do you think was the reason?'

'The murder was sanctioned at a high level. There's been no investigation into how the UC officer's identity was leaked and no one's allowed to ask why. The blanket of silence is a tad too convenient for my liking.'

'What does your handler say?'

'Nothing, other than telling me to drop it. It was like speaking into a vacuum whenever I brought it up. I could hear tumbleweed blowing down the phone line.'

'What about your colleagues, other UCs, what do they think?'

'We're not in contact anymore. Can't risk it.'

'What about the specialist officers relying on your information? You speak to them much?'

A shrug. 'No, why would I?' said Jay, puzzled.

Coupland thought back to the comments made about Jay during his induction. He'd thought they'd come from direct experience, not hearsay.

Jay's face cleared as he made the leap. 'Ah, I see my reputation goes before me. You heard someone slagging me off and wanted to see for yourself if any of it was true.'

'There was a bit of that,' Coupland agreed. 'Though I prefer to make up my own mind about folk.'

'Bad mouthing UCs seems to be a default setting, mate. Part of the unwritten exit strategy if you ask me. Keep whispering he's bent enough times so it becomes fact. It makes it so much easier for the higher ups to get rid of us once our deployment is over.'

It was notoriously difficult for UCs to return to normal duties. Working their own hours, without supervision, imitating the people they've been infiltrating until it becomes their normal way of life. Returning to their former police role requires the shedding of old habits, language and dress. After working such free lifestyles, discipline can be a problem. It was hard for regular officers not to be cynical, suspicious or have a paranoid world view; Coupland could only imagine what the world felt like to Jay.

'Water off a duck's back,' Jay shrugged as though he'd read Coupland's thoughts. 'They had me marked out as difficult from my training days. I remember the old guard looking at me twice because of the way I dressed and the fact I sounded just like the players I was going to be mixing with. Even though that meant it would be so much easier for me to fit in they held it against me. I mean, I get it. I'm as far removed from the establishment as you can get. My mam was a spoon burner. I was the sixth of seven children, and the sixth of seven children taken into care at birth. A revolving door of children's homes and foster care, I haven't seen my siblings since I was five. Every so often my mam would show up with her latest crack-head boyfriend and claim she was a reformed character, begging for me to go and live with her only for her to dump me back into local authority care once the novelty had worn off.'

'You did well to survive it.'

'What choice do you have?'

'Even with limited choices some folk manage to make the wrong one,' Coupland commented. 'So, given all you've gone through, why go into this?'

'I wanted to give something back.' A glint in his eye said he could read Coupland's mind. That with an upbringing like his surely he had nothing to give. That he was owed much more by a system that had failed in their duty of care to keep him from harm.

'Nah… I'd love to say that I was on some sort of moral crusade but that would be bollocks,' he shrugged. 'I was a roadman. I grew up in the city. Played on the same streets as many of the guys I'm now chasing down. I didn't need to be trained in how to survive undercover. It was ingrained. A way of life. I understood the lack of trust in the police. That in some areas it's second nature to sort out your own disputes. Whether you've been battered or burgled you don't ring the dibble, end of. Besides, what else am I fit for? I was destined for a life dictated by the criminal justice system, I just had to work out which side I wanted that to be. I look like a wise-guy. I think and talk like a wise-guy. I either revert to type and fall into a life of crime or put my skills to use for good.'

Those had been Coupland's sentiments twenty-odd years back, when it was a toss-up between whether he'd become a criminal or a constable. The company he kept. The anger bottled inside him. In the end reality won out. As much as they tried to make grifting look like La Dolce Vita, gangsters were more likely to end up in the ground than end their days in a shiny white villa in Spain. There was more to it than that, of course. A morality his peers couldn't seem to grasp. Though some would say, like his muscle mass, that had diminished over the years. Wasn't as finely honed as it used to be.

Jay's face split into his trademark grin. 'Turns out those stints with me mam weren't wasted. In this game you need to know that a tenner will get you a shot of W, a rock, or one wrap of B,' he said, referring to the street names for Cocaine, Crack and Heroin.

'Every cloud, eh?'

'As for that lot,' he added, referring to Coupland's new colleagues, 'they might not like me but they need me and that's what they can't stand.'

He jerked his thumb towards his chest. 'I can't win. If I'm not killed in the line of duty they assume I must be bent. Isn't that how witches were treated back in the day?'

Coupland had no answer to that. 'So where do you fit into Operation Maple?'

'What you really mean is how can a jumped-up muscleman-come-drug dealer contribute to bringing down the Dutchman?'

'In a manner of speaking, yes.'

'I don't spend my days sending kids on bikes to feed the local bagheads, if that's what you're wondering. I work a bit further up the narco ladder than that.'

'Go on, then. Impress me.'

'Where there's wealth there's an appetite for drugs. And supplying wealthy folk with drugs is lucrative. For a start you end up supplying their friends, then their business contacts, before you know it you end up finding out when anyone important is visiting the city by the quantity of coke your customers order, or the purity.'

It made sense. 'What happens when you send the information in?'

'You tell me, mate. I pass the information up the line with barely an acknowledgement these days. I'm none the wiser whether the junkie I'm dealing coke to is a paedo or just a posho who likes getting off his face.'

'They'd come back to you if they wanted you to delve deeper.'

Jay laughed as though Coupland were suggesting something ridiculous. 'What's started happening is they pass any useful information onto other UCs. Guys who haven't been living here and working here, who aren't known faces. They stomp all over my patch, making me look weak. I mean, in what universe would I let someone come and eat from my trough? Means I have to go and throw my weight around in another direction to show I haven't gone soft. When all's said and done, beating up a fellow officer is gross misconduct. This game is all about not letting someone take advantage. Not losing face. Meanwhile, the guys they send in get no intel because all anyone sees are nosey strangers and they clam up.'

'So why do they do that?'

'I'm guessing you already know the answer to that,' said Jay smiling. 'But let's just see if my answer matches up. You've heard the rumours saying I've gone rogue. Yet if you think about it, if the powers-that-be really thought it was true they'd pull me out. But I'm still here. So what does that tell you?'

'That they know you're doing a good job, they just don't want to come right out and say it.'

'Exactly. So, Einstein, have you worked out why these other UC officers keep being sent in?'

Coupland thought about this. 'Because someone wants to undermine what you've been doing.'

'Give the man a gold star.'

'Any idea who it is?'

'Haven't a Scooby's, which is why I haven't flagged it up the totem pole yet. Can't be sure who I'm talking to, can I?'

'Surely it's whoever is sending out these officers?'

'I'm not privy to information like that. We only have dealings with our own handlers. When they tell us to do something it's because they've been given instructions from on high. The less we know the better.' In case their cover gets blown, was left unsaid but it hung between them.

Coupland got to his feet, thanking Jay for his time. 'Is there a way I can reach you direct?' he asked. 'Without going through your handler?'

Jay was already shaking his head. 'No can do, mate,' he said. He pressed the mechanism to open the metal shutters. 'Don't you go stressing though,' he grinned, 'I'm like an unstable erection. You never know when I might pop up.'

'I'll have to take your word for that,' said Coupland stepping onto the pavement outside.

Jay's face grew serious. 'Before I joined the dibble I spent five years in the army,' he told Coupland as he accompanied him outside. 'Want to know the difference between the police and the military?' he asked, meeting and holding Coupland's stare. 'On the battlefield you know where the bullets are coming from.'

CHAPTER FIVE

Incident Room, Nexus House

Coupland felt the buzz in the incident room the moment he stepped out of the lift. The electricity in the air. DCI Swain, DI Edwards, and DI Taylor were huddled round Noah and Jared's computer screens.

'What's going on?' he asked.

It was Joe Edwards who answered: 'The Commander's taken a call from his equal number in the North East. The man that you identified in that photograph as the Dutchman has been caught on CCTV in Newcastle, boarding a train with three men. Destination Manchester Piccadilly.'

Coupland felt his pulse quicken.

There'd been a false alarm two days earlier. CCTV cameras at London City airport had showed a man seen with the Dutchman on several occasions check onto a flight to Newcastle. Police met it upon landing, arrested him and transferred him to Nexus House for questioning. Well versed in interview technique, he 'no commented' it throughout the ninety minutes Superintendent Romain and DCI Swain had spent with him. Coupland's request to interview him fell on deaf ears. The Super and Swain had more experience they told him, although a *No comment* was a *No comment* no matter how many years you'd racked up on the clock. He'd been held in custody until PACE guidelines had meant they'd had to let him go.

Now the Dutchman was about to arrive on their turf. 'What time does the train get in?' Coupland demanded, already heading back the way he came.

Someone coughed.

All eyes fell on the Super, who throughout this exchange had remained tight lipped. He half turned in his seat, ready to fill Coupland in on the information the others were all too aware of. 'There seems to have been a problem with communication,' he said.

'What kind of problem?' Coupland's shoulders had ridden up to his ears, his back curving as though weighing in for a fight.

'The train got in an hour ago.'

The noise that came out of Coupland's mouth was an attempt at a laugh, but came nowhere near. 'Is this a joke?' he asked, checking the expressions on the faces around him.

Some regarded him with a mix of curiosity and alarm.

'Do I look as though I'm laughing, DS Coupland?' Romain said through gritted teeth. His reference to rank was a form of control. A reminder of the pecking order in case the bolshy detective overstepped the mark.

Coupland carried on regardless. 'Come on, this is the first sighting of him on our doorstep in what, years?'

Romain nodded, though it was cautious, like someone who'd disturbed a hornet's nest.

'And it's gone up in smoke before we can do anything about it.' What he wanted to say was more primitive than that. There was no situation that a string of four-letter words couldn't make better, but he reined it in, reckoned the others would have pretty much covered it before he arrived. No point raking it over.

'I hope the cock up was theirs and not ours,' he added, not quite ready to let it drop.

'A mix up getting through to the Commander's direct line, apparently,' said DCI Swain, the curl of his lip showing what he felt about that piece of nonsense.

'Jesus wept...' Coupland muttered in response. There were thirteen regional crime units across the UK, ten based in England. Operation Maple spanned the North West, North East and combined Midlands regions, although intelligence from across the UK could be accessed on an as and when basis. 'How difficult was it to send out an email with a list of everyone's contact numbers?' Coupland asked, throwing his arms wide.

His question was met with silence, reminding him he was on new territory. They all were, which was why no one else spoke up in agreement. The Super's gaze raked over him, but there was no anger because he'd spoken out. More a curiosity as to what made him tick.

'I take it that's the station CCTV you're going through?' Coupland asked. Noah and Jared were studying multiple images of the station concourse, surrounded by half eaten protein bars and empty cans of energy drinks. What is it with this generation that didn't appreciate getting its caffeine from bitter as fuck vending machine coffee like everyone else. As for the protein bars, Coupland sighed, made a mental note to take them out for a slap-up burger when the investigation was over.

Noah nodded. 'NERCU sent us the image of the Dutchman and three companions walking along the platform ready to board the train at Newcastle,' he advised, referring to the North East Regional Crime

Unit. He indicated the monitor to the left of his desk. 'On this screen we've got the footage at Manchester Piccadilly and have rewound it to the train's arrival at platform eight.'

'That's assuming they got off there,' said Coupland, 'and not the however many stops there are between Newcastle and here.'

'Agreed,' Romain interrupted irritably, 'but we've got to start from somewhere.'

'We haven't seen anyone matching the men on the other screen get off the train, so DS Coupland might be right,' said Jared.

Coupland considered this. 'Or they decided to split up and get off separately,' he said, animated. 'Look for men helping folk off the train with bags, or a pushchair, or speaking into a phone. These guys know how to blend into the background.'

Noah's shoulders dipped. Frustration that neither he nor Jared had considered that possibility flashed across his face.

Coupland knew he had to dial it down a notch, nobody liked a know-all. 'I'm not all rugged good looks, you know. I have learned a few things over the years, and one of them is that villains run rings round us, it's what they do. Send me a copy of the file and I'll take a look. Many hands and all that.' He felt the weight of the Super's gaze. Didn't want to ruffle more feathers than he needed to. 'If that's alright with you, sir,' he added, happy to toe the line that little bit longer.

Superintendent Romain nodded.

*

An hour later and they'd had no luck spotting the Dutchman and his cohort get off the train at any of the stations on route to Manchester Piccadilly, where the train terminated. This made Coupland's suggestion that they'd disembarked separately, seem the most likely.

Noah found Coupland making himself a coffee and munching on a packet of chocolate digestives.

'Want one?' Coupland asked, offering him the packet.

'I didn't put into the kitty,' said Noah.

'Oh, there's a kitty?' asked Coupland, taking the packet back and helping himself to another couple.

'Yeah,' nodded Noah. 'I could find out who you need to speak to…'

'You're alright, kid. I'm sure they'll make themselves known. Anything I can help you with?'

'You were right about them getting off the train separately. They left from different carriages and didn't regroup on the platform, but I've picked up the trail again, Sarge. Can I show you?'

Coupland dropped the biscuit packet onto the countertop, nodding as he followed Noah to the bank of computers on his desk.

The Dutchman's image was frozen on one of the screens. Noah hit 'Play'. Coupland watched as he walked along the station concourse towards another man. Both men shook hands before heading towards the exit.

'Can you get me a blown-up image of this fella's face?' Coupland asked without taking his eyes away from the screen.

'Already done it, Sarge,' Noah replied.

'Good lad.'

Coupland continued to watch as both men were met

by the Dutchman's three travelling companions before leaving the station. He hadn't been that far off the mark after all. They'd taken their time to leave the train individually before meeting back up. He looked at the time stamp on the CCTV and sighed. Two hours ago. He looked on, watching as the men climbed into a black Range Rover waiting for them in the drop off zone of the station car park.

'I take it you've checked the registration…'

'Vehicle was stolen last night, Sarge,' Jared informed him, determined not to be slow off the mark a second time.

'Hang on a minute,' said Coupland. 'Back up a little.'

Noah did as he was told and rewound the footage on a slow speed so Coupland could tell him where to stop.

'There!' said Coupland, pointing, his excitement making Romain look over.

'Found something?' he asked.

'Not sure yet, sir,' Coupland answered, wanting to see it with his own eyes before he said anything else. Didn't want to commit to something that could have been a trick of the light or a figment of his overactive imagination.

He leaned in closer to the screen, instructing Noah to press play. Now he knew the Dutchman was heading to meet the man waiting on the concourse, he turned his attention to him, or rather the cup of coffee he was clutching. 'Can you blow up the image to see the logo on that cup?'

Noah did as he was asked. It was a branch of an artisan retailer that had a unit inside the station's entrance.

'If this fella paid for his coffee using a contactless card, we'll be able to get a trace on his ID.'

'Want me to give them a call?' asked Noah.

Coupland was already shaking his head. 'Nah, some requests are better made in person.'

The owner of the coffee stand at Manchester Piccadilly Station was very obliging, all things considered. It took him half an hour to track down the transaction data Coupland wanted. A lot less time than it would have taken for him to be processed through the custody suite for obstruction, so a win for both of them at the end of the day. Better still, a CCTV camera positioned above the coffee stand would provide a bird's eye view of the customers who bought their coffee there.

By the time Coupland left the station he had a copy of that particular camera's CCTV feed from that morning along with the transaction record from the coffee stand. His step quickened as he headed to his car. What if this was the breakthrough they'd been waiting for? A misguided tap on a flunky's debit card that helped them crack wide open one of the worst paedophile networks of their time.

Coupland checked himself with a sobering thought. Yes, the Dutchman and his cohort were in Manchester.

But if they were here, they were here for a reason.

CHAPTER SIX

Helen Harper stood at the bottom of the stairs and took a breath. *It's just a phase*, she told herself, exhaling slowly. *One of the many joys of having a teenager.* 'Ellie!' she called out, injecting as much lightness into her voice as was possible given her daughter's bus would be at the bottom of the road in less than 5 minutes. As it was she'd now have to negotiate the back end of rush hour and spend first break marking to make up for leaving the house late again this morning. She'd been leaving later and later these last few months, in line with Ellie's refusal, or inability – she still hadn't made up her mind as to which of those it was – to get up on time.

I'm old enough to get up and out of the house on my own, Mum, Ellie moaned every morning, shooting Helen a withering look for yet another parental faux pas she was committing.

I've yet to see that theory put into action, Helen replied more often than not, giving examples of countless occasions she'd gone to sit in the car, waiting to see when Ellie would finally emerge. There had yet to be a morning where she hadn't needed to go back in and rouse her daughter one final time.

That's only because I knew you hadn't gone, Ellie would snarl back, and so it continued. Helen wasn't quite sure when she'd become Public Enemy Number One in her daughter's life. It was long after the divorce, she reasoned. Though not so long after her ex's remarriage and gleeful announcement he was to be a father again, as though impregnating a woman half his age required great skill.

A tousled head glared down from the landing. 'You still here?' Two brown eyes identical to her own sent her a filthy look.

'Where do you expect me to be?' Helen shot back, irritation mounting at the sight of Ellie's pyjama top rather than blouse and tie.

'Hurry up and get dressed and I'll run you in,' Helen offered, trying to keep the reprimand from her voice.

'No way! You promised!' Ellie's voice had gone up a notch.

Helen sighed. She could do without histrionics at this time of the day. 'I said you could make your own way in so long as you didn't leave it to the last minute and miss your bus. Which is what has just happened,' she added, making a point of checking the bus app on her phone.

'It's bad enough that you're a teacher at my school, without me being seen travelling in with you every day!' Ellie retorted.

Helen forced herself to remain calm. 'Ellie, honey, I understand that. But you making your own way in clearly isn't working. Why don't I run you in today and you agree to try harder in the morning?'

Helen congratulated herself on how reasonable she sounded. As the head of guidance at Northdown High School, she could hardly offer parents and pupils advice on how to communicate better with each other if she'd spent the morning yelling at her own child. That's not to say it never happened. That a wrong word said here or there hadn't reduced one or both of them to tears at one point or another. Not for the first time Helen reminisced for the days when Ellie enjoyed being in her mother's company. When her chatterbox daughter confided in her about everything. Now she was unwilling to even pass the time of day.

'How about a truce?' Helen called up in the best sing-song voice she could muster. 'You let me give you a lift in this morning, and I let you choose which radio station we listen to.'

'No talking?' Ellie added in a tone suggested this condition was a deal breaker.

Helen swallowed back the hurt and pulled her lips into a smile. 'Agreed,' she said, once more reminding herself this phase would pass.

*

Incident Room, Nexus House
Coupland scanned the coffee transaction receipt he'd collected from the retail unit at Manchester Piccadilly to DCI Amjid Akram, using his contact details in the case file. He explained the relevance of the debit card holder and asked that this request be fast-tracked.

The swipe card reader had been issued by SumUp, and a quick Google search told Coupland the system was operated by Starling Bank. Not quite the top tier information request Amjid's team were used to, but Coupland hoped by contacting Amjid direct the card owner's details could be turned around quickly, without the need for all the usual red tape hoops to be jumped through.

Amjid's response was almost immediate. He'd make an

application to court for a production order once Superintendent Romain had signed off the request.

Coupland muttered a string of expletives before heading over to the Super's desk. Their workstations were adjacent to each other and he could have easily called over to him but he was reluctant to now he was on the back foot. It was one thing short-cutting the system when you got the outcome you wanted, now Coupland would have to own up to approaching Amjid first and it had backfired. He didn't need the others bearing witness to his cock up.

Romain was pretty decent about it, all things considered. No harsh reprimand, which would have been Chief Superintendent Curtis's style, or the sigh of resignation that was Mallender's. 'You know we have to do everything by the book with this investigation,' he'd said with the air of a disappointed head teacher. 'Any conviction sought on the back of a less than watertight audit trail will be kicked out by the CPS.'

Suitably chastened, Coupland made all the right noises, promising that from now on he'd be a compliance officer's wet dream.

Romain, nose wrinkling at Coupland's assurance, told him he'd call Amjid and get the action rubber stamped straight away. 'Make sure you pass the CCTV footage to Noah. He can cross check it against the time stamp of the coffee receipt. See if we can get a clear enough image of this guy to work with.'

'I was going to do that, sir. If that's OK?'

Romain was already shaking his head. 'Digital material must go through Jared and Noah so it can be logged and downloaded on their secure server—'

'—For audit purposes,' Coupland finished for him.

Coupland did as he was told, standing over Noah's shoulder as the junior officer hit 'Play' before fast forwarding through the footage until the date and time stamp on the footage matched that of the coffee receipt. 'There you go,' he said, leaning back in his seat, satisfied. 'There's your man.'

The image was a beauty. A clear full face shot as he asked the coffee barista for – Coupland glanced back at the transaction slip – a Fairtrade Soy Latte. 'Jesus wept,' he muttered, 'how can someone who's in the business of filming kids getting raped care so much about the coffee they drink?' Some folk operated from a skewed moral compass.

The man on the CCTV had dark hair, long enough to part at the side. A fringe which fell onto his forehead when he reached to tap his card onto the contactless reader. While he waited for his coffee he raked his fingers through his fringe as though guiding it back into place. His face was unremarkable, bland features you'd pass every day on the street without a second look. Still, it was *something*.

'Get that head shot circulated to all local divisions in Manchester,' Coupland instructed. He locked eyes with Romain. Sighed. 'Scratch that,' he said, nodding at his boss. 'We need to get him ID'd first.'

The Super looked pleased with himself, as though he'd made inroads with someone he'd expected to be difficult. Like it was that easy. Coupland kept his frustration in check. While they were playing the approval in triplicate game precious time was being lost. This coffee connoisseur could realise his mistake and go to ground.

Harder to do if he wasn't a career criminal, granted. He could hardly change his appearance and move address overnight without raising some eyebrows if he was a regular 'upstanding' citizen, whatever the hell that meant these days. Coupland hoped to Christ Amjid's team could pressure the bank to release their customer's ID pronto.

In the meantime, they had no choice but to sit tight and wait.

*

Canteen, Nexus House
'I hear he's on our doorstep.'

Coupland turned to see Superintendent Lara Cole standing in the canteen queue behind him. The only item on the tray she was holding was a lacklustre coffee that he doubted was worth shlepping across the building for when there was a state-of-the-art coffee machine in her office.

She saw him study her tray and pulled a wry smile. 'Busted. I suppose this is my way of seeing how the troops are doing without it seeming official.'

'Ma'am,' Coupland nodded. He was unsure whether he should offer to let her queue jump, given she'd only got one item, whereas he'd gone for the works: Today's special – fish, chips and mushy peas as well as an aubergine tray bake and two builders' teas. He couldn't keep up with the ever-changing etiquette. It was impossible to wave a high-ranking officer to go ahead of him in a queue without seeming like a brown nose. Harder still if they were female – no one wanted to be accused of being patronising or lecherous. He wasn't sure he was even allowed to acknowledge she was female. Coupland gave his head a wobble as he pondered this, grateful when the cashier started ringing his items up on the till.

'I'm meeting a friend,' he explained when Cole glanced at the plates balanced on his tray.

'I'd better make this brief then,' she said, waiting while he tapped his card on the card reader before doing the same.

Coupland chose a table close by and plonked his tray down, swallowed down a sigh when she pulled out the chair opposite him.

'So, the Dutchman's on our doorstep,' she repeated, taking a sip of coffee that must have been the temperature of gnat's piss by then.

'That's pretty much all we do know,' Coupland answered, his tone regretful.

'Let's hope the coffee shop fella you're tracking down is more co-operative than the last one brought in. I heard we had to release him without charge.'

'We had nothing on him, Ma'am, other than he bore a passing resemblance to someone on our wanted list. No wonder he was as cool as a cucumber.' Coupland hadn't been involved in interviewing him but it was easy to think you could do a better job watching from the side-lines. He wasn't about to start criticising his new colleagues. 'We're trying to build a better picture of where everyone fits in the network. It doesn't pay to rush in.' Coupland felt like he was having an out of body experience. Was he really explaining the benefits of exercising caution to a senior officer? Thank Christ none of his colleagues from Salford Precinct been there to witness *that*.

Cole didn't look too impressed either. 'Not quite the

response I was expecting from you of all people, Detective Sergeant,' she said, getting to her feet, coffee forgotten. 'I hope rubbing shoulders with the senior ranks hasn't made you lose the spark I'd heard so much about.'

Coupland kept his face in neutral. He'd never been accused of playing it safe before. The unfairness of it. Still, it was early days. Nothing worth getting bent out of shape for. 'Ma'am,' he said, inclining his head as she turned to go.

He raised his hand in greeting when Alex Moreton entered the canteen. They'd arranged to meet so that he could let her know how he was settling in. She had a vested interest, given she'd been the one to recommended him for this secondment. When he'd called her extension earlier she'd told him that she couldn't stay long but lunch would work if he grabbed something for her.

'Fan-bloody-tastic,' she said, eyeing the plates as she reached the table, 'I'm in desperate need of a carb fix.' She lifted the fish and chips he'd selected for himself from the tray and placed it in front of her. 'Nice one, Kev,' she added, saluting him with her builder's tea, leaving him to pick half-heartedly at a congealed aubergine, his mouth opening and closing like a fish out of water.

'What's twisting your boxers?' she asked between mouthfuls of extra salty chips, the glint in her eye confirming she knew damn well and was enjoying every minute. 'I'm saving you from all those trans fats, you should be grateful.'

'I don't need saving, thank you very much. It was a one-off treat, that's all, nothing wrong with a bit of comfort eating.' He watched as she tucked into his chippy meal with gusto. 'Carry on like that and you'll need to be hoisted into your inspector's tunic.'

'Whatever…' she said, breaking off a bit of her fish and putting it on his plate.

Coupland used his fork to spear some of her chips. 'Just protecting your waistline,' he said when she glared at him.

'You can't say stuff like that, it's not PC.'

'Just as well I'm not a PC, then,' he countered.

Alex put her fork down and sat back, a clear signal for him to hoover up what was left on her plate. 'How's it going?' she asked. 'You've been here long enough to get a measure of everyone. Is it what you expected?'

Coupland swallowed the chip he'd been chewing. 'I'm still finding my feet,' he answered truthfully. 'It's a pain in the backside having to work with different teams across several forces. The SIO's a bit of a jobsworth, too.'

'They have to be, Kevin. We're only just clawing our way out of special measures. The chief constable wants everything signed in triplicate in blood before he approves anything. That approach is bound to trickle down.'

Coupland didn't look convinced. 'Rank seems to matter so much more, the higher you go,' he observed. 'It's been made clear to me on more than one occasion I'm nothing more than the tea boy.'

Alex laughed. 'I wondered whether being involved in something as big as Operation Maple would change you but you're the same grumpy old bear you've always been.'

'Now who's not being PC,' Coupland shot back. 'Maybe you should have a word with Superintendent Cole. I get the impression she thinks I'm treading water. I wouldn't mind but she barely attends briefings. Since my induction she's been arms' length at best.'

Alex nodded. 'That's not surprising. From what I understand, her role in this is one of oversight. Commander Howorth has ultimate responsibility for the taskforce but her role is to monitor internal compliance. She might not attend briefings, but she has full access to what's going on. She's all over it, Kevin. Though if she involved herself too much in operational matters it might put Superintendent Romain's nose out of joint. Inflated egos and all that.'

'Not sure he's my greatest fan either.'

'Sounds to me like you've made yourself right at home,' she laughed.

As he looked at the remnants of his lunch he noticed large chunks of batter on the side of his plate that he must have cut away from the fish before eating it. He hadn't even been aware he was doing it. Even when Lynn was nowhere near, she managed to brainwash him into doing her bidding. Coupland shrugged. As control freaks went, he'd known worse.

'I'd best get on,' said Alex, getting to her feet. She could see Coupland wasn't exactly taken with the pearls of wisdom she'd offered. 'Perhaps the Super was giving you a pep talk,' she soothed, before heading back the way she came.

'Felt like she was goading me…' Coupland responded, though more to himself. He tried to fathom why Superintendent Lara Cole's words irked him as much as they did.

Wondered, on some level, if she had a point.

*

Northdown High School

Helen Harper wasn't sure what had made her go into teaching. When she reflected on it, there'd been a certain naivety about her choice. A hope, at the time, that she'd be able to transform children's lives. Make a real difference where it mattered, yada yada. A yen for travel and a misplaced belief she could go backpacking every summer was closer to the truth.

Though apart from her first summer after graduating, she'd never had the opportunity. A whirlwind romance with Ellie's father put paid to that. Or more accurately, the second blue line on the pregnancy test she'd carried out three months after they'd met in Greece had put paid to it. Those first few years had passed by in a blur. Ellie's arrival. Pete's lacklustre proposal and her reluctant acceptance. A move from the flat they rented together to their first mortgage made them seem so grown up. It was after the move to a bigger house in a better part of the city that the cracks first started to appear. Cracks that a baby, marriage, and several house moves had managed to keep hidden. The blame for their breakup didn't lie all one way. He accused her of always putting her job first, which she brushed off with a laugh, right up until the moment he stepped into the living room with his suitcase packed.

Mary Jackson, Northdown's headteacher, calling her name in the corridor as she beckoned her over brought her back to the present. 'I'm so glad I've seen you, Helen. I've been meaning to bring something to your attention, but I just haven't had the opportunity.'

Helen's smile was hesitant. The head had a way of catching you on the backfoot purely with the intention of getting you to agree to something because you couldn't come up with an excuse quick enough. Helen held her breath and waited.

'As you know Janet Clements is retiring next term.' She paused while Helen nodded. 'Such a stalwart of the school, they really don't make them like that anymore.' Little wonder, thought Helen. All those extra-curricular activities that she never turned down. The school trips and careers days she'd been guilt tripped into organising. Helen reckoned there wasn't an evening Mrs Clements didn't devote to the school, no wonder she was taking early retirement on the grounds of ill health. Whatever the head was building up to ask Helen to do she would point blank refuse. No way would she fall for any of her flannel.

'I know how busy you are,' Mrs Jackson observed, 'not just with school duties but running around after Ellie. It must be so hard on your own.'

'Ellie's no bother,' Helen stated, too stubborn to admit she found balancing work and home challenging. 'She's even making her own way into school these days so I'm able to come in earlier.' *Shit*. Why did she say that?

Mrs Jackson beamed at her. 'Really? That's excellent. In which case I don't feel nearly so bad about asking if you could oversee the breakfast club a couple of days a week. I can ask one of the other members of staff if you think it'd be too much?'

Crafty cow. She'd backed her into a corner and there was no way out without admitting she was finding it hard to cope. 'No, it's fine,' she said, mentally kicking herself. 'I'm sure I'll be able to fit it around my other responsibilities.'

'That's the ticket,' Mrs Jackson beamed. 'Maybe you could have a think about refreshing some of the activities. They do seem to be getting a bit stale.'

Give someone an inch… Helen reminded herself. 'OK,' she agreed through gritted teeth. 'Now I really must be getting on.'

'Morning Helen.' Dylan Breakwell, Head of the English department, slowed as they approached each other in the corridor.

Dear God, that's all I need, Helen sighed. 'Dylan,' she said crisply without breaking her stride. Her tone making it clear she had no time to stop and chat. She caught the bewildered look he threw in her direction. *Tosser.*

Breakwell was popular at the school. A tad too popular as far as some of the old guard were concerned, the ones who believed pupils didn't have to like their teachers in order to learn. That in fact liking them was a disadvantage. He'd settled in well after arriving the previous year. He'd come into teaching late, a series of jobs which he preferred not to elaborate on, other than to say none had given him any satisfaction or a reason to get up every morning.

He'd been at his last school five years. Was well regarded by all accounts. If the head of department job had come up there he'd have been happy to stay, he'd told them all in the staffroom on his first day, but he was ambitious and keen to make up for lost time. So when the vacancy came up at Northwood he felt compelled to apply for it. Best decision he'd ever made, he was fond of saying whenever the head was in earshot, and the annoying thing was the old bat lapped it up. There was an easy way about him that rubbed Helen up the wrong way. His confident assumption that he could make your day better just by speaking to you.

Helen had her hands full for the first two periods. Two of the more disruptive pupils in year ten had been sent to her following an altercation that had got out of hand. She spent the remainder of the morning trying to get to the bottom of their disagreement, before resorting to threatening to call their parents if they didn't speak up. She'd worked through first break, sipping a bottle of water while catching up on a report she'd agreed to write for the school board once her marking was completed. When she'd popped out in the corridor to refill it, her attention was caught by a group of girls loitering in the hallway because it was raining outside. 'Hello sir,' one of them called out as Dylan Breakwell walked by.

'He is well fit,' the girl who'd called out to him said to her pals.

'For an old guy, definitely,' said another.

Helen smiled at the fact that at thirty-eight, she was older than Dylan by a couple of years, which must make her seem positively geriatric to this lot.

Her smile quickly turned into a frown when she caught him perform a mini salute to them out of the corner of her eye. It wasn't unusual for young girls to form an attachment to a male teacher, especially one new to the school and keen to be liked. He was happy to chat to those who stayed behind after class but he really needed to draw up some boundaries. Helen refilled her water bottle and returned to class, trying not to let her dislike of him cloud her professional judgement.

Instead of checking on the progress of a couple of new pupils during her lunch break she had to drive Ellie home to pick up her hockey kit for a tournament after school. Funny how her daughter didn't seem to mind sitting with her in the car when she needed something in a hurry, Helen thought sourly, but knew better than to say it aloud.

She stayed in the car while Ellie rushed into the house for her kit, appearing at the front door after a couple of minutes shouting, 'Where are my socks?'

'Where they always are,' Helen informed her. 'Rolled up on the hall table so you'd remember to pack them on your way out this morning.'

'*Fucksake,*' moaned Ellie.

'I beg your pardon?' Helen yelled, knowing if Ellie had been out of earshot she'd be muttering the same thing but that wasn't the point. She wondered what those two year tens would think if they saw the unflappable Mrs Harper's irate face this moment, hands tightly gripping the steering wheel so she didn't storm into the house and throttle her daughter.

The journey back to school was in silence. Ellie's phone, which was permanently glued to her right hand, had pinged to say a message had come in. They were waiting at traffic lights that were taking forever to turn green. Long enough for Helen to peek at the notification banner as it appeared at the top of Ellie's screen. *Dylan Breakwell.*

Helen frowned. What the hell was he doing messaging Ellie? 'Does Mr Breakwell normally send you texts?' she asked, trying to keep the condemnation from her voice.

Ellie scowled. Her eagle-eyed mother had been snooping again. 'Yeah. He texts everyone. Why?'

'What sort of things does he text?'

'Reminding us when our homework has to be in. Or sometimes mentioning something he's forgotten in class.'

'Nothing of any interest to you then,' Helen sniped, instantly regretting it.

'Why not? Some of us care about our education, you know.'

'If that's the case how come you can't be bothered to get out of bed in the morning?'

And so it went on. Sometimes Helen wondered why she bothered. Showing her concern seemed to earn her nothing but scorn. Even so, this particular revelation couldn't be ignored. She'd have to speak to him. Warn him not to leave himself exposed to misinterpretation. She was head of pupil guidance, after all. It was her job to make sure safeguarding rules were followed. She'd have a word with him later.

The period after lunch didn't go quite as she'd planned. A year twelve boy turned up to his registration class as high as a kite. Another boy had been selling ecstasy tablets behind the sports pavilion. After extracting the other boy's name and finding cover for her own class she referred the matter to the head. Both boys were immediately suspended with exclusion being the most likely outcome for the boy dealing drugs, as this wasn't his first time.

Ellie was mortified. 'This is why it's humiliating having YOU as my mum,' she hissed as their paths crossed at the start of afternoon break.

A quick coffee in the staff room with Jenny. They'd worked there ten years between them and still managed to see off three headteachers. Jenny Doyle taught geography, had been married to an estate agent before going through a messy divorce. At least they'd got a good price for their house when they sold it.

Her friend eyed Helen with concern. 'What's up? You're looking a bit glum.'

'Oh, nothing.' In truth she'd love to put the world to rights with Jenny; problem was, once she started she wouldn't know where to stop. Should she bad-mouth a colleague for showing poor judgment? Or berate a system that punished bad behaviour by withdrawing education when it was needed most?

'Fancy a drink on Friday? About time we started dipping our toes back in the water,' Jenny said with a wink. 'We could ask some of the others.'

Helen smiled. 'Count me in,' she said, rinsing her cup under the tap before putting it away.

*

Dylan Breakwell stood by the window in his classroom, looking out onto the playing fields. Helen knocked on the door even though it was open, a courtesy as she was stepping into his domain. She fixed a smile on her face as she approached him.

'To what do I owe this pleasure?' he asked, turning towards her. His demeanour was friendly though she couldn't help feeling that he was mocking her. Perhaps he was getting her back for being brusque with him that morning.

'Can I have a word?' she asked as she joined him at the window. She hadn't realised his classroom looked directly onto the hockey pitches. Ellie and the rest of the team were warming up before their match. 'I hope you don't mind me mentioning this,' she began, trying to keep it upbeat.

She floundered for a moment, wondering how often

he stood by that window watching the hockey team train. On the pitch below, Ellie's team-mates stood in a huddle as they listened to their PE teacher.

'I don't want this to sound like a reprimand,' she said, knowing that's exactly how it sounded. 'But it's come to my attention you've been texting individual pupils.' She threw in a comment about it being against the school's rules and hoped he hadn't worked out that Ellie had been the one to drop him in it, albeit not by choice. 'I happened to see a message on someone's phone and asked them about it,' she added as though she needed to explain herself.

Instead of coming back with an excuse, Dylan thanked her, told her he'd take her comments 'on board'. 'Anything else?' he asked, though they both knew he was telling her to go forth and multiply.

'No, everything else is fine,' Helen replied, a feeling in her stomach telling her it was anything but.

*

Not for the first time, Helen cursed at the amount of paperwork teachers had to plough through each day. She only had time to watch the first half of Ellie's match before returning to her desk. Yet another night she'd have to work late. She texted Ellie to ask if she could get a lift home from one of the other girls' mums, and that there'd be something in the freezer she could reheat if she rummaged round enough. She remembered to add **'congratulations'**, the decibel level at full time making it clear who the victors were.

Not had a takeaway in like, ages, read Ellie's reply. The emoji beside it was two hands pressed together as if in prayer. Helen smiled, despite herself. **Fine, you choose**, she texted back, clicking onto a smiley face emoji before pressing send.

Remembering Ellie's over-reaction when that boy had been suspended earlier, Helen wondered if it was drugs, and not hormones going into overdrive, that were the cause of her daughter's unpredictable mood. Her heart sank at the thought she'd missed all the vital signs she warned other parents to look out for. Was Ellie just flexing her independence muscles, or was the distance between them widening? It was important to keep the dialogue between them going. Even if that meant having conversations neither of them wanted to have.

She decided to broach the subject this evening, after they'd eaten, once she had a glass of full-bodied red inside her.

*

Incident Room, Nexus House
Coupland had called Lynn to let her know they were waiting on a lead. That there was no guarantee it would come in that evening but if it did they'd be making a move.

'I'll see you when I see you then,' she said, adding 'Mind your cholesterol levels if you're getting a takeout.'

Coupland loved the fact that of all the harm his job exposed him to she still fretted over his fat intake. Even so, her words had struck a nerve. He waved over at Noah who was standing by the lift, his hand clutching a torn sheet of paper. 'Better make it just one battered sausage,' he called out to him, glancing guiltily at his phone to make sure Lynn wasn't still on the line.

At 8.00pm DCI Amjid Akram put a call through to Superintendent Romain. Starling Bank had expedited their request, providing the name and contact details of the customer who had purchased the Fairtrade Vegan Latte from the retail unit at Manchester Piccadilly Station.

Graham Prentice. A lawyer residing in one of the more affluent suburbs of Greater Manchester.

A strategy had been put in place in anticipation of the information coming in. It wasn't, as Coupland had hoped, a convoy of units to bring him in, followed by through-the-night interrogation.

'We tread carefully,' Superintendent Romain had reminded him.

'We saw him shake hands with the Dutchman!' Coupland had countered.

'The person who you have ID'd as the Dutchman. Until any of this is corroborated with hard evidence we have nothing.'

What he said was true, Coupland accepted grudgingly. They were in the intelligence gathering phase of this operation, a stage which could not be leapfrogged over just because the adrenaline had kicked in.

Amjid Akram's team were to run background financial checks on Prentice, while Noah and Jared were tasked with researching his digital presence. News reports, social media, and any online footprints that could provide a background picture of his character. Romain had put a request through to the Regional Organised Crime Unit's surveillance team to place a tracker on Prentice's vehicle so that his movements could be monitored, but until that happened someone would need to keep an eye on him. Coupland had been the first to raise his hand.

'Very well,' Romain had agreed, recording the actions in his logbook. He looked over at DI Edwards. 'You go with him.'

*

Graham Prentice lived in a modern new-build in an area of Altrincham favoured by Manchester's football stars. A tree-lined grass verge and extensive driveways obscured the properties from passers-by. Coupland and Joe Edwards, having located Prentice's house and made sure it couldn't be accessed by any unadopted roads or paths, had parked on the main road outside it. A PNC check on the car parked in front of the house confirmed it belonged to their man. All they needed to do was make sure the bastard didn't leave.

It was 11pm. The majority of the residents would be tucked up in their beds. They'd need to keep a look out for sharp-eyed dog walkers. If someone clocked them more than once they'd drive round the block a couple of times, return when the nosey-parker had gone to bed.

Coupland burped into his hand then sniffed it. 'Lucky for you I only had battered sausage,' he said, lowering the passenger window a smidgeon. Edwards threw him a look. 'You might want to lower it a tad more,' he informed him, shifting slightly as he raised his left buttock off the driver's seat. 'I think my Spicy Meat Feast is coming back to say hello.'

Coupland lowered the window while making a wafting motion with his hand. He had a feeling this was going to be a long night.

CHAPTER SEVEN

'I thought I'd missed you!' His relief tumbled down the line at her.

She smiled despite herself. At least she made a difference to someone's world. 'I heard it ringing as I put my key in the lock. One of these days I'm going to trip over that bloody cat in my race to answer.' They laughed. She threw off her jacket one handed while keeping the phone's receiver in the crook of her neck. 'How've you been?'

'Same old. You?'

She hesitated. 'You know me, busy, busy, busy…'

'You work too hard. What do I keep telling you? You should be taking it easy.'

'What, at my age?' she laughed, looking up at the ceiling. Chance would be a fine thing.

'You know I didn't mean it like that.'

'It's how it sounded.' Her tone was sharper than she intended. Time to steer the conversation onto safer ground. 'I'm making that meatball dish you like for dinner,' she told him, eyeing the M&S bag containing a microwaveable tikka masala for one and a bottle of red.

'Lucky you. Today's special was Mac 'n cheese, only the cheese always tastes like boiled plastic.'

'Could be worse,' she said, struggling to think of

something. 'Remember that boil-in-the-bag fish I gave you when you were little? Had a big piece of bone in it, you nearly choked.'

'No wonder I wouldn't go near fishfingers after that.'

'You were such a good eater, too.' She took a breath, indulging in the memory. 'Rememb—'

'—Look, I'd better go. Same time next week?'

'Oh…' she replied, swallowing back disappointment. 'Yes, that's fine. All being well.'

CHAPTER EIGHT

Helen Harper's body was discovered in woodland bordering Northdown High School at 6.30am by Alfie, a Black and Tan Dachshund and his owner, Gail Morgan. A keen fan of television crime dramas, Gail had dialled 999 making sure neither she nor Alfie contaminated the scene further by standing some way back from the body and warning every dog walker and jogger who passed by what they'd found.

By the time police arrived a modest crowd had assembled, phones held aloft like festival goers at some macabre concert. 'Show's over,' the officers putting the cordon in place stated, standing their ground until the ghouls quickly dispersed.

The victim had been dumped, rather than buried. There'd been little attempt to conceal her body, although it was hard to be certain how much of the foliage around her Alfie had disturbed. Bruising around her neck suggested strangulation, though it would be several more hours before pathologist Harry Benson would get round to performing the post-mortem and commit to it in writing.

Helen Harper's daughter, Ellie, had reported her mother missing at 10:00pm the previous evening when she'd failed to return home and didn't answer her phone. Ellie ran to the door at the sound of the doorbell, only to find two detectives standing on her doorstep.

Detective Sergeant Chris Ashcroft studied Ellie as he introduced himself and DC Timmins. Her face was pale and mascara was smudged around her eyes.

'I keep trying her phone, but all I get is her voicemail.'

Poor kid thought they were there to take a description, had no reason to suspect what they were about to tell her, apart from their sombre faces.

'Have you found her?' she asked, looking from one officer to the other. Her gaze settled on DC Timmins, as though, as the younger officer of the two, he was more likely to tell it to her in words she'd understand.

DC Timmins, known affectionately as Krispy by the rest of the murder squad team because of his love of a certain chain's iced donuts, felt as though the words would choke him. He let out a breath when Ashcroft took charge, asking Ellie if they could come in, if she could take a seat, if there was someone she could call to sit with her as they had bad news, and it was probably better if she wasn't on her own when she heard it.

*

Ellie's father arrived mid-morning to take his daughter back to his place. 'Just for a few days, to give us all a chance to get our heads round it,' he reassured her. He waited in the living room while she went upstairs to pack a few things. Ashcroft, along with Krispy, had stayed in the vicinity questioning neighbours either side of the property so they could return quickly once Ellie's father arrived.

It had been the woman living across the road who Ellie had asked to come sit with her. Val Corcoran. She used to keep an eye on Ellie when Helen needed to work late when she was younger. 'I'd fix her a bit of tea. Let her watch a bit of telly as long as she did her homework before her mum got back,' Val informed Krispy between sobs while she hurried upstairs to fetch a cardigan which she draped over her shoulders as she crossed the road to Helen and Ellie's home.

Her response to Helen's ex-husband had been cursory. A clipped 'Hello,' when he joined them in the living room, making her excuses to leave once Ellie had gone upstairs. Definitely no love lost there.

Ellie's father plonked himself down on the sofa his daughter had sat on beside Mrs Corcoran two hours earlier when they'd broken the news. He shifted under Ashcroft's scrutiny, pushed his hands between his thighs as though trying to warm them up. 'I still can't believe it,' he said, attempting a smile. 'God knows how Ellie's going to cope with this.'

'Early days yet,' said Ashcroft, moving to a nearby armchair, motioning for Krispy to take the other one. 'I'd like to ask you a couple of questions, while you're waiting for Ellie to come back down. Is that alright with you?' He pulled out his notebook and pen before sharing a look with Krispy, asking him if he'd mind doing the honours. 'Ellie mentioned that you were divorced from her mother. Did you share joint parental responsibility for your daughter?'

Mr Harper looked confused. 'What? Yes, of course. Things were difficult for a while – certainly around the time I left, but Helen didn't let that get in the way of me seeing Ellie.'

Ashcroft nodded. 'Can you think of anyone who

might have wanted to cause her harm?'

'No way,' said Harper, shaking his head. 'She wasn't a confrontational person. I can't imagine her killer is someone she's hacked off on parents' night.'

The head teacher at Helen's school had mentioned a pupil who'd been excluded on the back of an incident that Helen had reported the day before. DCs Turnbull and Robinson had been dispatched to the pupil's home to check the whereabouts of Noel Spencer during the previous evening. Rosie Pearson, the newest DC to join Salford Precinct's murder investigation team, had gone to the school along with DS Andy Lewis, known as Cueball, to interview staff and pupils.

'Was it normal for your wife to work late?' Ashcroft asked Harper.

'Ex-wife.'

'Apologies. Did your ex-wife usually work late?'

'Helen was dedicated. Ambitious. It wasn't unusual for her to work a 12-hour day.'

'Was she seeing anyone?'

'I'm the wrong person to ask.'

'How would you describe your relationship with her more recently?'

'Polite,' Harper said, his face darkening. 'Now look, if this is going where I think it is...'

'And where's that?'

'Barking up the wrong bloody tree, that's where. Helen and I, we co-parent Ellie, that's all there is to it.'

The sound of footsteps on the stairs was Ashcroft's cue to wrap things up. 'We'll leave it there for now,' he said, getting to his feet as Ellie entered the room. 'I'll be in touch when I have more information for you.' He slipped his hand into his jacket pocket and pulled out two business cards, handing one to each of them. 'In case you need to contact me. Any time at all.'

*

At 7.30am a leaflet distributor entering Graham Prentice's driveway glanced at a steamed-up car parked on the main road. Two minutes later she came back into view, eyeballed the inhabitants before sending a discreet nod in Coupland's direction. At that moment DI Edward's phone made a noise that sounded like an incoming text. 'It's the boss,' he said, reading the message before holding the phone so Coupland could see.

GPS tracker in place. Stand down.

The GPS tracker was capable of recording every stop Prentice's vehicle made, the addresses he went to, as well as the time taken en route. The places he frequented would be logged and visited by surveillance officers, background checks would be taken on the people he associated with. The intelligence gathering would grow exponentially over the next few weeks, as each associate was traced and eliminated from the investigation or became a suspect in their own right and a new surveillance thread was created. Coupland hoped to Christ they were able to wait that long.

They made a detour via both their homes on the way back from their surveillance detail. Coupland had a quick shower while Amy made them a pot of coffee. A suddenly shy Tonto stared glumly at his breakfast. Lynn was working day shift, had left a smiley face post-it note on the bathroom mirror. Coupland took a photo of it, sent it to her via WhatsApp with the message:

Not sure whether this was meant for me or your

fancy man.

He dried himself quickly and put on fresh clothes. His phone beeped, a red circle against his WhatsApp icon told him he had an incoming message. A reply from Lynn:

Better leave it where it is then 😊

Downstairs, Tonto was giving Joe the beady eye. Despite Amy's coaxing, his cereal sat untouched, his attention moving to Coupland as he stepped into the kitchen. The boy was sharp as a tack, needed constant stimulation that he relied on others to provide.

There was a telepathy between Coupland and his grandson that didn't include other members of the family. A meeting of minds. Whether that meant Tonto was old for his age or Coupland was immature was anyone's guess. Tonto's face lit up when Coupland picked up his spoon and started swooping it over his breakfast making aeroplane noises. 'I'm too old for that, Grumpy!' he laughed, grabbing the spoon out of his hand and proving his point by consuming several mouthfuls. He grinned at Coupland in triumph, lifting an empty bowl for inspection.

'Well, that showed me!' Coupland retorted, ruffling the boy's hair. He slurped a mouthful of the coffee Amy had poured, motioned to Edwards that they'd better get going. 'See ya!' he called out as they reached the front door.

'Wouldn't wanna be ya!' Tonto bellowed back.

'Nice family,' Joe observed as Coupland started the engine and pulled out into the traffic.

'They have their moments,' Coupland replied.

'Been a long time since I've enjoyed that kind of set up,' Joe said when it became obvious Coupland wasn't going to elaborate. Their next stop at the DI's flat made his statement abundantly clear. If architects designed living quarters for newly divorced men then Joe Edwards was living the dream. An open plan living room/diner with a kitchen just about big enough to heat microwave dinners and refrigerate beer. A massive TV had been mounted clumsily onto a wall bracket. A balcony with a small table and two chairs that had been moved to one side to make room for a clothes airer draped with towels and mis-matching socks. 'You get used to it after a while,' he said when Coupland commented on the music coming from next door. 'Not like I'm here much anyway.'

Coupland perched himself on the arm of an uncomfy looking sofa.

'You've got kids, then?' asked Coupland, eyeing a photograph on a side table. A funfair, going by the background. Edwards, flanked by a boy and girl not much older than Tonto. Rosy cheeks and wide grins.

'Don't be fooled by what you see there,' said Edwards, lifting the photo and examining it as though searching for clues. 'They're much older now. At the age where seeing me every other weekend gets in the way of going out with their friends.'

'Can you visit them mid-week?'

'Only if I can do a two-hundred-mile round trip that doesn't get in the way of my shifts. My ex's new fella got a promotion which meant them upping sticks and moving away. A chance to make a fresh start, she reckoned, knowing fine well it would call time on my relationship with my kids. You know the hours this job makes you keep.' He returned the photo to the table, his hand lingering on it as though fearful to let go.

'Must be tough,' said Coupland, grateful he'd never

had to deal with anything like that. The thought of Lynn not being there, of not seeing Amy or Tonto as much as he did. The idea of it broke him.

Joe's phone beeped, alerting him to an incoming text. He fished it out of his pocket and glanced at the screen. 'It's from DI Taylor,' he said, tapping onto his screen to open the message which he read out loud: 'Superintendent Romain has called for a briefing this afternoon. Wants everyone present.'

'Best get our skates on,' said Coupland, getting to his feet.

CHAPTER NINE

Noel Spencer, known as Spenny to his mates, lived with his parents half a mile from Northdown High School in an ex-council house in need of repair. The front garden was used to park a souped-up BMW Coupe in canary yellow. 'Not exactly keeping a low profile,' muttered Turnbull as he approached the front door and rang the bell. A PNC check on Spenny had revealed nothing out of the ordinary. A caution for dealing six months earlier but that was the extent of it. Yesterday's offence, dealing on school premises, would in all likelihood result in a stint in young offenders. The boy's father, Noel Spencer senior, on the other hand, was a different kettle of fish altogether.

The front door was yanked open by a man wearing jersey shorts that sagged round his crotch, and a t-shirt two sizes too small for him. 'What time do ya fuckin' call this?' he demanded, moving so that his bulk blocked the entrance to his property. He had the bashed in nose of someone used to going a few rounds and hands like a gorilla's.

'Is Spenny in?' Robinson asked ignoring his question.

'Who wants to know?'

The detectives held up their warrant cards.

'Fucksake, what is it now?' he demanded, as though he'd been having a perfectly lovely morning until they'd come along and ruined it.

'We'd prefer to speak to Spenny,' Robinson persisted.

'He's under fuckin' age.'

'With you present, of course,' Turnbull informed him, all teeth. 'Or we can do this down the station if you'd rather.'

'Shoulda wiped him on the fuckin' curtains while I had the chance,' he grunted, turning to shout down his boy.

Spenny's alibi was solid. He was getting a pasting from his father around the time of Helen Harper's murder, as evidenced by his trip to A and E when his mother got back. The drugs he'd been trying to sell belonged to his dad, who didn't take kindly to being told they'd been confiscated when the police had been called out to the school. The boy stared at the detectives from the relative safety of the hallway, ready to leg it if his dad laid into him again. Two black eyes and a swollen nose. When he spoke they could see broken teeth. Enough evidence to arrest the father for assault, though that wasn't always the answer. Turnbull's partner used to be a social worker, he knew from her that placing children into the care system wasn't always 'better.' He made a mental note to speak to the school, find out if there were any documented concerns regarding his welfare. See if they couldn't relax the suspension, given the tiptoeing required to stay out of his old man's way.

In terms of Helen Harper's murder, Noel Spencer could be crossed off the list of suspects.

*

Northdown High School

It looked more like a business centre than a comprehensive school. A curved roof arching over a glass fronted atrium, flanked either side by brick and steel panels painted in a garish maroon. It was modern. Fresh. The opposite of Ashcroft's old school which had looked tired long before he started there. By the time he left it was ready for demolition. Bought by a developer, it was now a luxury apartment block.

Two pupils wearing prefect badges held the door open for him as he approached the entrance. Flowers and candles had already been left either side of the main doors alongside messages of condolence which would eventually be passed onto the family.

'Are you here about Mrs Harper?' one of them asked.

Ashcroft nodded.

'I hope you get who did it,' said the other before they both shuffled towards the school office.

A wiry woman in a no-nonsense suit extended her hand to him in reception. 'Mrs Jackson?' Ashcroft asked, shaking her hand while introducing himself.

'None of us can believe it,' she said as she led the way to her office. 'Who on earth would want to hurt poor Helen? She was such a trooper. Always offering to take on more responsibility. She set a great example to the other staff.'

She moved behind her desk to sit down, motioned for Ashcroft to take one of the two empty chairs across from her. 'Your colleagues were very interested in Noel Spencer. I take it you've spoken to him now?'

Ashcroft nodded. 'He has a cast iron alibi. He's not the person who did this.'

Mrs Jackson breathed out a sigh. 'Thank God! I mean, I know these things happen. That every so often a pupil goes berserk and wreaks revenge on their teacher. But as headmistress you hope it never happens in your own school. I mean, how are your staff ever going to reprimand pupils again, after something like that?'

Ashcroft told her he didn't know. He paused. Made it look as though he was considering his next question even though it was the reason he was there. He reached into his pocket for his notebook and pen. 'Had Helen reported any problems with parents at all, or staff even?'

'Of course not, I'd have mentioned it!'

'Shock can do funny things to our memory. Maybe something she said in passing? Something that didn't seem like a big deal at the time?'

Mrs Jackson shook her head. 'No. She never raised anything like that with me. As her line manager she would have done, certainly if she wanted to take the matter further.'

'What if she didn't? Want to make it official, I mean.'

A nod. 'You mean if she wanted to confide in someone?'

'Yes.'

'She was very friendly with Jenny Doyle. She might have discussed that kind of thing with her, I suppose.'

Ashcroft opened his notebook and wrote down her name. 'Can I speak to her?'

Mrs Jackson rose from her chair. 'Yes. Yes of course. I'll need to get cover for her class.'

'How long will that take?'

'She's got the year elevens just now. I suppose I could do something with them. I'll send her in here. More private than the staff room.'

'It's appreciated,' Ashcroft said.

*

A statuesque woman with curly hair and large earrings stepped into the headteacher's office. She wore slim fit trousers over high heeled boots. A blouse that seemed to have every colour of the rainbow on it. 'DS Ashcroft?' she asked, moving round to the headteacher's side of the desk before lowering herself into her chair. Jenny Doyle's smile was cautious. Her eyes were bloodshot and watery. Her nose shiny from frequent blowing. Her hands fluttered to her face self-consciously. 'You'll have to forgive the state of me. Still can't get my head around it.'

'That's understandable,' said Ashcroft, when what he was really thinking was what the hell did she look like when she was pulling out all the stops.

'We held a special assembly this morning. To help the kids process the news. They're in bits. Every time I see one of them break down it sets me off all over again.' She pulled at a tissue tucked under her sleeve. Dabbed her nose with it. 'God knows what Ellie's going through.'

'I believe you and Helen were good friends?' he asked.

'Work colleagues first and foremost,' said Jenny, her mouth turning up at the corners. 'We socialised out of work and certainly helped each other through difficult times.'

'Sounds like a friendship to me,' observed Ashcroft, a smile tugging at the corner of his mouth. 'A good one.'

Jenny's smile grew wider. 'Me too. So, how can I help?'

'Had anything been troubling Helen recently? Anyone causing her concern perhaps?' Jenny frowned before moving her head from side to side.

'I need you to think back,' Ashcroft prompted. 'Was anything about her behaviour puzzling?'

'No way! She was straight down the middle! She never left you guessing about how she felt about something. Her ex got on her nerves but then newsflash, don't they all? She was having a few problems with Ellie but they were working through it.'

'Any idea what the problems were about?'

A shrug. 'Not really. Don't teenagers and problems go hand in hand? We'd arranged to go out on Friday to let off a bit of steam. Come to think of it, something *was* troubling her yesterday but she seemed reluctant to talk about it.'

'Going back to Ellie. Was there anything specific they didn't see eye to eye about?'

'Ellie accused her of being overprotective at times.'

'And was she?'

'You'd have to ask Ellie.'

Ashcroft put away his notebook and pen. He pushed himself out of his seat, thanking Jenny for her time.

*

Ted Harper lived in a modest new-build. Not long finished by the look of it. A wooden sign pointing customers to a sales office and a show home stood at the entrance to the development.

Ashcroft located the Harper's house easily enough, recognised the Volvo estate parked on the driveway, the 'Dad to be' sticker placed in the rear window. As he pulled up outside the front of the house he saw a face at an upstairs window that retreated when he stepped out of his pool car. He'd telephoned ahead to say he was coming. Harper's new family lived an hour's drive away from Northdown High School. Didn't want his trip to be wasted.

Ellie's father opened the door wide, stepping back to let Ashcroft through. The interior smelled of new carpets. Harper's feet were encased in moccasin slippers. A heavily pregnant woman came downstairs to join him, wearing fluffy blue socks. She looked pointedly at Ashcroft's feet as Harper introduced his wife, visibly relaxing when the detective pulled a pair of shoe protectors from his pocket.

'Good man,' Harper said quietly with a wink, before ushering him into the living room.

'How are you all bearing up?' Ashcroft asked as he followed Ted Harper into a room containing an L-shaped sofa and wall mounted TV but very little else by way of furniture. Ellie sat nursing a mug of hot chocolate, small marshmallows floated on the top of it. Harper sat beside his daughter, motioned for Ashcroft to join them.

Ashcroft sat on the 'L' end of the sofa so that Ellie was in his eyeline.

'It's been hard, hasn't it Ellie?' said her father, 'but we'll be fine.'

Ellie's head dropped as she studied the contents of her mug. 'I've not drunk this since I was like, six,' she said scornfully.

'Let me make you something else,' said Harper's wife stiffly, trying to make the best of an awful situation.

'Don't bother,' said Ellie.

Harper must live in cloud cuckoo land if he didn't pick up on the tension. So many changes had been thrust on them. A stepmother too close in age for Ellie not to be jealous of, and a grieving teen the new mum-to-be hadn't bargained for when she'd shacked up with Ellie's dad.

'Would it be possible for me to speak with Ellie on her own?' Ashcroft asked, his tone making it clear this was not a request.

'Of course,' said Harper reluctantly, getting to his feet. He gave Ellie's shoulder a squeeze. 'We'll just be in the kitchen if you need us,' he said.

'I won't,' Ellie shot back.

Ashcroft gave her a moment. The sarcasm was defensive, but must be exhausting. He pulled out his notebook and pen but didn't open them, instead placing them on the seat beside him. He leaned forward in his chair, resting his elbows on his knees. He waited for Ellie to look at him.

'I thought you wanted to ask me some questions.'

Ashcroft smiled. 'I know you want us to find the person responsible for all of this. Taking your mum away from you. Forcing you to live a different life from the one you expected.' 'He says I've got to leave Northdown and go to a school here,' Ellie told him, her tone defeated. Sometimes anger was all a person had.

'You feel powerless right now. I get it. We can't control what life throws at us. But we can control the way we react to it. You'll need time to adjust to everything that's happened. No-one's doubting that. Let's make sure the person who did this is put behind bars, yeah?'

Ellie nodded. 'I'd been such a cow to her,' she admitted. 'Mum's always—' she paused, took a breath, '*was* always on my case. I realise now she was only looking out for me.'

'In what way was she looking out for you?'

'The way she found fault with things. The friends I

hung around with. The way I dressed. The way I spoke. Especially to her. She hated that I was always late for school. Then the thing with Mr Breakwell. Saying he shouldn't be texting pupils. She really went off on one when she found out.'

Ashcroft kept his face relaxed. 'What kind of texts were they? Can I see?'

Ellie pulled out her phone and tapped on the home screen until she found them. She handed the phone over to him. 'See?' she said, as Ashcroft scrolled through. 'There was nothing wrong with them.'

She collapsed into herself, put her head in her hands. 'I wish I hadn't been so mean to her!' she sobbed. 'She was my mum. I loved her!'

'I'm sure she knew that,' said Ashcroft, making a mental note to find out more about this Mr Breakwell.

*

Northdown High School

At 2.00pm three police cars pulled into Northdown High School's car park. Dylan Breakwell, accompanied by DS Ashcroft, left in one, having accepted Ashcroft's invitation to answer questions at the station. DC Rosie Pearson along with Krispy and DS Andy Lewis emerged from the other two cars to take statements from pupils in Mr Breakwell's English classes in the presence of an appropriate adult.

An hour later Rosie telephoned Ashcroft to say that a pupil she'd just interviewed had boasted that she'd been to Breakwell's flat on several occasions. Krispy's text to Ashcroft half an hour after that confirmed two pupils claimed they were in a relationship with him. DS Lewis reported that a pupil told him she wasn't sure that what Breakwell made her do was normal, but she was too ashamed to ask anyone for advice.

Ashcroft's response had been the same to all three officers: *We need dates and times, locations, so these claims can't be written off as flights of fancy or wishful thinking on which there is no basis.*

Ashcroft briefed DCI Mallender immediately. Midway through the briefing Mallender telephoned Mary Jackson, the headteacher, informing her that he needed to speak to several of the pupils' parents urgently. He gave her the pupils' names, stated that he could be at the school by 5pm.

The situation needed to be handled with care. He'd have to explain to the parents what their children had claimed, and the procedure that now needed to be followed. That each of Breakwell's alleged victims would need to undergo a medical examination, after which trained counsellors would be made available to help them come to terms with what had happened. It would be a lot to take in, and there wasn't the manpower to break this news individually, given the speed with which the medical evidence needed to be collected to make the case against Breakwell stick.

'Look, there's something else we need to do...' said DCI Mallender, eyeing Ashcroft uneasily. 'Don't worry, I've already worked that out,' Ashcroft replied, reaching for his phone. 'Mind if I do the honours?'

Mallender nodded his approval.

Ashcroft scrolled down his contacts list. Found the number he was looking for. Hit 'dial'. Listened as the phone rang out.

*

Nexus House

Graham Prentice's name had been written at the top of a whiteboard in the incident room. A photograph of him had been pinned to the wall, a head and shoulders shot taken from a press release announcing his appointment as partner in a city law firm. Below it was a partially filled in association chart, showing his network of family and colleagues, gleaned from his social media profiles and company website. Noah and Jared had certainly pulled out all the stops.

Superintendent Romain looked up as Coupland entered the incident room behind DI Edwards. 'I take it there weren't any visitors at Prentice's place yesterday evening?'

'Nada, boss,' said Coupland. 'I'm guessing he fancied a quiet night in front of the telly with his missus.'

'Any movement since we left?' asked Edwards.

Jared held up an iPad with the Google Maps app open on it.

'I take it that's Prentice's car?' Coupland asked, pointing at a stationary blue icon.

Jared nodded. 'The three location markers you can see,' he said pointing out three red dots on the map, 'are his home, St Bartholomew's Grammar – he did the school run this morning – and his office, which he went on to after dropping his kids off.'

'Cosy,' observed Coupland. 'So what do we do now?'

'We wait until a pattern emerges,' said Romain, turning

to address the team. 'Any locations that can't easily be explained, we take a closer look at as possible places where the Dutchman is staying.'

Coupland chewed the inside of his cheek. 'We'll be checking all the obvious associations as well though?' he asked. 'Members of any sports clubs this guy belongs to, golf club buddies, that sort of thing?' He knew damn well questions like these irritated the hell out of competent officers who knew how to do their job, but he'd also seen how a failure to clarify things at the outset led to fuck ups. The detective's mantra: assume nothing.

'Once we've got names on that board the boys here will check every one of them out,' said Romain, making it sound like a punishment.

Coupland nodded.

'Amjid's team are running background financial checks on him,' added DCI Swain. 'We'll soon get a measure of the level of clout he brings to the network.'

'Any joy on the Dutchman's ID?' Coupland asked, already knowing the answer. That kind of breakthrough would have them dancing round their desks doing The Floss.

Swain shook his head. 'We've drawn a blank on the men who arrived in Manchester with him as well. Multiple identities are a stock in trade for these guys. We're just going to have to work through Prentice's contacts and hope we strike lucky.' Hope. It was what every detective thrived on to stay in the game. You give up on that and you might as well hand in your warrant card.

This was the part of the investigation that frustrated the hell out of Coupland. Waiting for results to come in which would inform what direction they would take next.

He'd never been any good at kicking his heels. Despite having no real desire to sit at a desk and push buttons he could see Noah and Jared were inundated with actions. 'Need a hand with your online searching?' he asked.

The young DCs failed to conceal their horror. 'We use specific algorithms to mine the data we're interested in. It would take us longer to show you what to do than do it ourselves.'

'Charmin',' grumbled Coupland.

Attention returning to the whiteboard he typed the name of the legal firm Prentice worked for into the internet search engine on his phone. Clicked onto his profile. 'He's head of Global Business,' he informed the others. 'Specialises in M&A, whatever the hell that is.'

'Mergers and Acquisitions,' said the Super, as though that explained it.

Coupland nodded anyway.

'According to his bio he's spent the previous two years based at the Netherlands office.'

'Handy,' Coupland observed.

'Took his family skiing last year with another partner from the firm and her children,' added Romain. 'Ruth Hunter Pepper. Between them they'd brokered a lucrative deal in the renewable energy market, the trip was their reward.'

'Nice work if you can get it.'

'She's a socialite apparently. Divorced. Daughter of an earl but wasn't given a title at birth. Likes living in the limelight. There are quite a few photos of them online attending the same glittering events. Award ceremonies and charity bashes. There's every chance she's a key introducer of wealthy subscribers to the Dutchman's network.'

Coupland keyed her name into his phone. Dozens of press association images came up. Sitting in the royal box at Wimbledon. A VIP guest at a society wedding. Everything about her spoke money and privilege. Did no harm that she was photogenic either. The paparazzi loved her. She was like the Audrey Hepburn of the corporate world.

'You really think she could be mixed up in something like this?' asked Coupland, before checking himself. Why would *anyone* become part of a sex abuse network? Thinking like a regular person didn't help.

'We don't know anything at this stage,' said Romain. 'They work together and socialise together. If I was constructing a profile of what the Dutchman's inner circle looked like, she'd tick a lot of the boxes. On top of that, she works with someone who has had direct contact with him in the last 24 hours. I know where I'd be putting my money.'

'So what now?'

'She's based in London. I'll get onto my equal number at the Met to put her under surveillance too. In the meantime, Jared and Noah will create a similar association chart for her, see who that throws up.'

Coupland's phone started to ring. He slipped his phone from his pocket and glanced at the screen. Frowned. Sending an apologetic look to Romain he hit 'Reply'. 'Now's really not a good time,' he barked into it.

'*Well hello to you too,*' Ashcroft responded.

Coupland felt a twinge of guilt for not keeping in touch. He moved away from his desk. Made a mental note to call him after his shift. Arrange to go for a beer or something. 'Sorry mate, can we do this later?'

Ashcroft swore in frustration. '*Hear me out, Kevin. I*

think you're going to want to know about this.'

Something in his voice had Coupland on alert. 'What is it?'

'We've picked up someone I think you'll be interested in.'

'You'd better keep talking then,' said Coupland.

He returned to the briefing, telling the assembled group he had a colleague from Salford Precinct station on the line. He hit the loudspeaker button on his phone, informing Ashcroft he was now speaking to Superintendent Romain, SIO of the intelligence unit he'd been seconded to. Ashcroft explained how he'd brought in a teacher by the name of Dylan Breakwell on suspicion of his involvement in the murder of a teacher at the same school. That while questioning some of his pupils the team had uncovered evidence of grooming and sexual abuse. Some pupils claiming he had filmed them 'for a bit of fun'.

Romain exchanged a look with DCI Swain before nodding at Coupland.

'Cheers Chris,' Coupland spoke into his phone. 'We'll arrange for Breakwell to be transferred to Nexus House. He's not to be questioned until he gets here.'

'I don't suppose I can sit in on his interview?' Ashcroft asked.

Coupland didn't need to look at the Super for the answer to that. 'No can do, buddy.'

An awkward silence fell between them. *'Understood,'* said Ashcroft, before ending the call.

Two hours later Dylan Breakwell was in the custody suite at Nexus House, seeking counsel from his duty solicitor who'd driven behind the police van transporting him in a battered Nissan Juke.

Ashcroft, who'd escorted Breakwell to the Custody

desk, was in no hurry to leave. He leaned against the countertop while Breakwell was taken away. Waiting. Ashcroft wasn't the explosive kind, but it was obvious something was troubling him. He clenched and unclenched his jaw like he was chewing on something really difficult.

Coupland sidled up to him. Showed him his teeth in what he hoped was a friendly gesture. 'I appreciate this,' he said.

'I could tell. One minute you were saying you didn't have time to spare, next minute you're saying I have to tell it to your boss and I could tell by your heavy breathing you'd run all the way to him.'

'It was hardly heavy breathing.'

'Trust me, it was. You need to come down that running track with me when you've finished your stint with MI5.'

'It isn't MI-'

'Yeah, you're OK, I worked that out too.'

Coupland dipped his head, embarrassed. 'I was under strict instructions not to tell anyone,' he said, hearing how much of a Jobsworth he sounded.

'And you've always done as you're told, haven't you?'

Coupland winced. 'Are you pissed at me?'

'No, mate.' Ashcroft sighed. 'Well, maybe just a little bit.'

'Look, let me explain what I'm doing here.'

'No, save it.' There was no heat in Ashcroft's voice, just acceptance. 'You weren't sure I could be trusted. When DCI Mallender started acting all edgy when I brought Breakwell in I guessed it had something to do with the Dutchman – and your sudden career move.'

Coupland gave him a look.

'You used to bitch about him every chance you got,

then for the last couple of months we didn't get a peep out of you. Call it a fluke but your vow of silence seemed to coincide with your announcement that you were joining Organised Crime.' He held his hand up, palm outwards, 'Don't tell me anything you could end up regretting. Besides,' he added, making a shooing motion with his hands, 'you've got an interview to conduct.'

Coupland's nod was slow. 'What about the others? Do they know what I'm doing now?'

Ashcroft shook his head. 'All they know is that the investigation has been bounced over here on the say so of DCI Mallender. No questions asked.'

They'd headed out to the car park while they'd been talking. The driver of the van that Ashcroft had travelled in with Breakwell sat scrolling through his phone.

'Better head back,' said Ashcroft. 'If you need anything from us…'

'Yeah, yeah,' said Coupland. 'Look, now the cat's out of the bag regarding the real reason why I'm here there's nothing to stop us going for a pint some time? Or one of those bloody awful smoothies you're always knocking back when you're on a health kick.'

Ashcroft nodded. 'As long as you're paying. All that overtime you must be raking in…'

CHAPTER TEN

Interview Room, Nexus House

There was nothing remarkable about Dylan Breakwell, other than the amount of confidence it was possible for someone as ordinary as him to exude. Medium height, he was a tad on the heavy side, with blonde hair that curled around his face making him look cherubic. He sat back in his seat, his gaze sweeping the interview room as though searching for clues as to why he was there. He looked intrigued. Like someone finding themselves in a situation they'd only previously heard about but never experienced, comparing it to the reality.

This was Dylan Breakwell's second interview. The first interview, the evening before, had been a basic fact-finding session that ran out of steam once he started 'No commenting' to anything relevant to the allegations made by the pupils. Superintendent Romain had called a halt to it. Stated they'd reconvene the following morning.

Now, sitting at his desk, Coupland watched the live screening of Breakwell's interview with Superintendent Romain and DCI Swain, on his computer. Although Breakwell's body language was guarded, his arms resting on the table-top touched only at the fingertips. A lot less closed off than if he'd folded them in front of his chest. His shoulders were relaxed too, and there was a slight slouch to his posture that suggested he was comfortable with the environment he found himself in. That or he was already resigned to his fate.

Coupland studied his face for tells: a blink, scratching his nose, a twitch or yawn; there were none. His confidence made him over-answer their questions. Provide more detail than was asked for, information that with any luck would trip him up later. Coupland's request to interview him had been turned down flat. According to the Super, DCI Swain had more experience preparing interview strategies for this type of crime. Coupland wondered when questioning nonces had become a bloody science, but he sucked it up, reminding himself it was all about the result. He didn't quibble about Romain's place in the room. He was SIO after all.

Coupland looked up to see Noah trying to attract his attention. He removed his headphones, asked the DC what was up.

'I've done some social media searches on local forums close to Hadfield Grammar, Breakwell's previous school. You know the sort of thing: *Lost Dogs* and *Items for Sale*. People taking chunks out of each other over parking violations. According to Hadfield Residents' Forum, Dylan Breakwell left his previous post under a cloud. An unsubstantiated claim by a "problem" pupil. Locals reckoned the headteacher let him go for a quiet life…'

'Did they now?' asked Coupland, reading the report Noah brought over to his desk.

Breakwell's DNA had been sent to the lab to be compared to DNA found on Helen Harper but it was a technical exercise as he'd already confessed to her murder.

According to him they'd had an altercation in the school corridor as they were leaving. She'd seemed distracted when he'd tried making conversation. He asked her if she had a problem and she asked him if he thought it was appropriate ogling the hockey team from his classroom window. She seemed to have a real bee in her bonnet about it. Told him he needed to clean up his act or she'd have no option but to report it to the head. He couldn't let that happen. He'd followed her out of the car park then rammed his car into hers on a quiet road. She hadn't realised it was him when she got out to inspect the damage. There'd been a struggle. The only way he could stop her shouting for help was by putting his hands around her throat and squeezing hard. His level of detail had been full on up to that point. Graphic certainly, in his description of how her eyes almost popped out of their sockets. The sound she made when she slumped to the ground. The fact she'd wet herself. What he was less forthcoming about was how he moved her body to the woodland path by the school without being seen and how he'd disposed of her car. The vehicle, or rather its burnt out carcass, was found five miles away on farmland. It had been set alight by someone who knew what they were doing. Very little would be gleaned from it that would help with the investigation.

He'd had help. Of that there was no doubt. By someone proficient in moving bodies and tampering with evidence. Someone who tidied up after men who groomed young girls.

A Passman.

Coupland glanced back at his computer screen. He didn't need to put his headphones back on to work out Breakwell was 'No commenting' through the remainder of the interview. Tutting, he got to his feet.

*

Coupland knocked sharply on the interview room door. Snatched a glance at Dylan Breakwell as Superintendent Romain stepped outside before closing the door firmly behind him.

'This had better be good,' Romain grunted.

'He wasn't exactly spilling his guts last time I looked,' Coupland said, adding 'sir,' after a couple of beats. He handed him Noah's report. 'Thought you'd want to see this.'

He summarised as Romain skim read. 'Several posts on social media claim Breakwell was being over-familiar with pupils but there was no evidence to substantiate it from what I can see. The only pupil who spoke out about him was a known troublemaker facing exclusion for assaulting a classmate. Some reckoned the kid made the allegations up to deflect from her actions.' Coupland paused. Waited while the Super had finished reading. 'Want me to contact the headteacher, see what truth there is to these rumours? Ask him if he didn't take action because he didn't want a scandal?'

Romain considered this, before nodding. 'See if you can get hold of the excluded pupil as well, get their version of events.'

'Agreed,' said Coupland. He'd intended doing that anyway but if it helped the boss feel he was easy to manage then it was a win-win. Coupland felt as though he was on a roll.

He nodded towards the interview room door. 'I could go in there now and put the feelers out. See how he reacts when I mention the allegations made by his old pupil.'

Romain was already shaking his head. 'We've got a

strategy worked out. He coughs up the names of whoever helped him get rid of Helen Harper's body and we'll cut him a deal to get a couple of years off his sentence.'

Coupland looked less than impressed. 'Hardly a jackpot. Besides, last time I looked he was No Commenting to anything to do with grooming his pupils.'

'Our priority is to track down the network. We've got an opportunity here to identify a passman who in turn may lead us to others further up the chain.'

'We've also got a duty to make him accountable to the youngsters he abused. Secure justice and help them gain closure,' Coupland reminded him.

The Super's nod was non-committal. 'Go and speak to his old school. See where that gets you. Anything relevant feedback to me ASAP.'

CHAPTER ELEVEN

Hadfield Grammar School

Richard Centre, the headteacher at Hadfield Grammar School, welcomed Coupland with as much warmth as a mortuary fridge. 'I really can't see how I can help,' he insisted when Coupland turned up unannounced at the school's reception an hour after getting the green light from Superintendent Romain.

He led Coupland along a corridor adorned with students' artwork and posters about sexual health into a dismal office that looked as though it hadn't been decorated since the 1980s. The school's catchment area was two sprawling council estates and a mill town decimated by factory closures. There was a feeling of exhaustion about the school. As though its fighting days were over and it was coasting its way to closure.

Coupland got straight to the point. 'Dylan Breakwell tendered a letter of resignation three weeks before the end of term and you accepted. I want to know why.'

Richard Centre glanced at the paperwork on his desk, as though he'd find an answer there, if he looked hard enough. 'No specific reason really,' he said, his gaze eventually meeting Coupland's. 'His work had started to slip and he felt he was letting the pupils down.'

'And you didn't make him wait three more weeks so you didn't have the expense and inconvenience of bringing in a supply teacher?'

'His mind was made up.'

'So it had nothing to do with the allegation of rape made against him by a pupil around the same time?'

'That was completely unfounded! She was a troubled young girl who had formed an unhealthy attachment to Dylan. She was attention seeking, that was all. Nothing worth involving the police over. Or ruining a man's career.'

'Dylan Breakwell's career, or yours if the local authority became aware of the complaint? It wouldn't be the first time a scandal has hit the school, would it?' Coupland regarded him. 'A crack den in the boiler room, one online article claimed.'

'A gross exaggeration!'

'Maybe the affair you had with the French teacher distracted you from what was going on under your nose.'

'That was ages ago! My wife and I have moved past that unfortunate episode.'

'More like an unfortunate season, than an episode, from what I understand.'

Centre flinched, but Coupland wasn't done. 'I've seen the league tables. Exam results have been falling year on year. It can only be a matter of time before the school is put into special measures. The allegation made against Breakwell may have been the last straw as far as the school – and your position as headteacher – was involved.'

Centre slumped back in his chair, threw his hands up as though in surrender. 'I had no evidence to go on,' he said, shaking his head. 'Other than the word of a young girl.'

'I understand other members of staff came to you with concerns about him.'

Centre jerked forward in his seat. 'Let's put that into

perspective right now,' he demanded, jabbing his index finger down onto his desk. 'Half-arsed comments in the staff room don't count. No one put their concerns to me in writing.'

'Maybe they knew you wouldn't take them seriously. Or you'd made it clear to them you didn't want anyone rocking the boat. I mean, what are you, six, maybe five years off retirement? Soon be home and dry if everyone keeps their head down.'

'I've had enough of this!' Centre got to his feet and swept his arm towards the door. 'I'm afraid I'm going to have to ask you to leave.'

'And I'm afraid it doesn't work like that. A teacher you provided a glowing reference for has confessed to murdering one of his colleagues.'

Centre's face grew pale.

'Several pupils have come forward to say he was abusing them.' Coupland tilted his head, drummed his fingers on his chin. 'Hmm, what are the chances, I suppose, of him doing something like that before? Wonder what the local authority will make of that, eh? There'll be an internal enquiry at least, I'd have thought. Oh, and yes. Before you ask, we will be informing them. Got to be thorough about these things. Might make you look a little less incompetent, mind, if you started to help, not hinder.'

Centre's head dipped, defeated. 'What do you want?'

'I want to speak to the pupil who made the original complaint.'

'She never came back here. She attended a pupil referral unit after her exclusion.'

'Her address then,' said Coupland. His expression clear that he wouldn't leave until he had it.

*

Coupland was climbing into his car in the school car park when he heard someone calling his name. He recognised the woman hurrying towards him as the secretary from the school office. She'd been the one to buzz through to the headteacher when Coupland had turned up out of the blue. 'Have you got a minute?' she asked him as she drew level. The name badge on her jacket lapel said Kate Whiting.

'What is it?' Coupland asked, stepping away from his car. She was slightly out of breath, her cheeks were flushed and she glanced back at the school as though fearful someone might see. 'Do you want to go somewhere else to talk?' he asked, sensing her unease. The headteacher's office looked onto the playing fields rather than the car park but that didn't stop another member of staff seeing her talk to the detective on her own. Coupland suspected that gossip in the staff room was as rife as any station he'd worked in. That news of his visit would spread like wildfire.

She shook her head in reply. 'No time. If the phones don't get answered he'll know I'm not there. I can't be long.' She opened her jacket to reveal a file she'd concealed. 'He's just asked me to shred the contents of this file.'

'What is it?'

She placed it into Coupland's hands. 'It's Dylan Breakwell's personnel file. You said that's who you came to speak to him about?'

Coupland nodded.

'Breakwell was good at his job,' she told him, 'in so far as I could tell. If I ever had reason to go into his classroom the kids were always fully engaged. No real issues with unruly behaviour like some of the staff. But he *was* sleazy. He had this way of looking at you just a little bit too long. I wasn't the only person who thought that. Some of the female teaching staff said the same. It got so they'd shudder when they referred to him. We used to wonder what he was like around the female pupils. We had no evidence, you see. Nothing really to go on that could be considered a cause for concern. Then when Gayle Woodall spoke up about him, well, it came as no surprise to any of us. It didn't help her case any that she'd got a reputation in the school for getting into bother.'

'What case? From what I've been told nobody ever made anything official.'

'Yes, well that's where you've been told wrong, isn't it? Because Maureen Webster in the art department helped Gayle draw up her complaint and Eliza Evans, a newly qualified teacher who shadowed Dylan for a while, compiled a log of concerns she had about him being over-friendly. It's all in there,' she said, patting the file he was holding like it was precious cargo.

'I'll need to speak with them now,' Coupland told her, putting the file in his car before turning to follow her back inside.

'I'm afraid that won't be possible with Maureen. She took early retirement and not long after was diagnosed with terminal cancer. She passed away six months back.'

'And the other? You mentioned there'd been two teachers who'd helped Gayle make her complaint.'

Kate nodded. 'Eliza left just before Mr Breakwell. She's in Thailand now, teaching English to orphans. She sent me a text not long after going out there to let me know how she was settling in.'

'You've not heard from her since?'

Kate shook her head, unconcerned. 'We weren't friends as such. I suppose I took her under my wing a little. She didn't have any family to speak of. She was an only child and her parents died when she was small. It must have been tough. It made sense that she'd want to help other disadvantaged children.'

'Did she discuss her plans with you?'

Kate shook her head. 'No. She spoke to Dylan Breakwell about them. Made sense I suppose, given the amount of time she spent shadowing his class. They were bound to become friends, which made it all the more odd when she supported Gayle's complaint and started compiling a report on Dylan's behaviour.'

'How do you know she discussed her plans with Breakwell?'

'Her letter of resignation arrived out of the blue the second day she failed to turn up for work. In it she'd stated she was going to volunteer at some orphanage or other. We were all shocked but that's when Dylan told us she'd been planning it for a while.'

'Did he now?' mused Coupland. He thanked Kate for coming forward, asked if she could text him Eliza Evans's mobile number. He gave her a card with his contact details on it.

'Yes, of course. I thought you'd probably want to speak to her.'

Coupland assured her that he would. Though the timing of her departure, and the fact she hadn't been in touch since she left so abruptly, didn't bode well at all.

Coupland returned to his car, picked up Breakwell's personnel file and started reading. His phone beeped, alerting him to an incoming message. Kate Whiting, the school secretary, texting him with Eliza Evans's number as promised. Coupland replied immediately, thanking her and asking for Eliza's last known address before she left for Thailand.

He called Eliza's number. As he suspected, the line was dead. He constructed a 'test' text anyway and hit send. Within seconds the text was returned marked undelivered. Not enough to start a full-blown murder enquiry, granted, but enough to be concerned about the young teacher's welfare.

The next call he made was to Nexus House. Despite selecting DCI Swain's extension he was surprised when he picked up.

'How's the interview going?' Coupland asked.

A half-arsed laugh rumbled down the phone. 'Breakwell stopped "No Commenting" long enough to demand a break. The boss has gone to update the Commander with the fact there's no news. You can imagine the mood he's in. I've been told to put together some fresh questions. I was going to give you a call. I heard you're at his previous school?'

'Just leaving now,' Coupland told him. 'You might want to hold off questioning him again until you've seen his personnel file. Oh, and I suspect we've got a missing teacher on our hands.'

'How so?'

'One of Breakwell's ex-colleagues is potentially unaccounted for. I suspect she's suffered a similar fate.'

'Shit.'

'Couldn't have articulated it better myself.'

'How long before you get back?'

'I need to speak to the girl who made the original complaint about him. A Gayle Woodall. None of her claims were verified at the time and the more I'm hearing the more I reckon she was pressured into keeping quiet. I'm going to be an hour tops, then I was going to check out our missing teacher's last known address.'

'DI Taylor can do that. Besides, forensics need to be in there pronto, especially since we don't know what we're going to find. I'll update Superintendent Romain. He'll want everything coordinated from here, remember, audit trail and all that.'

'Understood,' Coupland said reluctantly.

'That frees you up to speak to this Woodall girl then come back here with a file that with any luck will turn out to be Breakwell's undoing.'

'Never say the L word out loud,' Coupland warned, 'Christ knows there's precious little of it as it is, without you jinxing it.'

'Ah, that's where you're wrong, see. If you're willing to help me put together a fresh interview strategy, I'll speak to the Super, see if he'll let you sit in when I question Breakwell again.'

'Deal,' said Coupland, stifling a smile.

A text had come in while he'd been on the phone. Kate Whiting, the school secretary:

Here's Eliza's address. She lived with her aunt until she passed away so the place is hers now. I suppose she must be renting it out.

The address she'd given was 45 minutes' drive away. He could check it out first. See if there really was any reason to be concerned. He could speak to her lodgers, ask when they'd last heard from her.

And if no one answered? Then he'd kick down the door, see what condition the place had been left in. Only he'd be doing it without the Super's consent, a sure-fire way to have the team lose confidence in him, and for the CPS to throw out anything he found as inadmissible.

Swallowing down his impatience, he forwarded the content of the school secretary's text to DCI Swain as agreed.

*

Gayle Woodall wasn't at home when Coupland called round to her house. His warrant card was needed for the safety chain to be removed, a woman he took to be Gayle's mother checking it closely before telling him where she was.

'She'll be on her way back from the job centre. Likely as not be on the bus now and the signal's crap so I can't call her to tell her to come straight home. She sometimes goes to a mate's house. You know what they're like at that age. Prefer to be anywhere but home.'

Coupland shuddered. When Amy was Gayle's age she'd shacked up with a serial killer. Not that any of them had known it at the time. Coupland tipped his head, said he'd wait by the car. The thought of Tonto's father making him crave nicotine.

Breakwell had confessed to Helen Harper's murder far too easily for Coupland's liking. As it was he was facing a life sentence. In the grand scheme of things, no matter how many jail terms were tacked on for grooming and sexually abusing his pupils it wouldn't alter his existence as he'd soon come to know it. It was done for anyway. A life as a respected professional traded for a lifetime of being told when to eat and sleep. Of living in virtual isolation due to the nature of his crimes. He'd likely die in jail, though that probably had nothing to do with the length of the sentence handed down to him.

DS Ashcroft had sent him the statements taken from the pupils who claimed to be in some sort of relationship with Breakwell. Coupland had read them several times over. Could almost recite them line by line.

'He told me I was special…'

'He said he'd never felt like this before…'

'He promised it wouldn't hurt…'

Ashcroft had included photographs of the interior of Breakwell's flat. He'd circled specific items that matched the descriptions given in those statements. A fridge filled with cans of coke and chocolate milk. A bottle of vodka and ready-rolled joints on the coffee table. A video camera and tripod beside the bed.

A thorough search of his home and the contents of his personal belongings at school had resulted in a video camera, two laptops, and an iPad, together with two mobile phones landing on Noah and Jared's desk marked urgent.

The medical evidence from the victims was starting to come in. Bite marks. Grazes. STDs. It was possible Breakwell had been abusing these pupils for his own sick fun. Or that he was involved with an entirely different network of sickos. Ashcroft's sixth sense was right. Something in Coupland's gut told him this level of organisation was beyond your average group of Nonces 'R' Us. Breakwell was part of the Dutchman's network alright. They just needed proof of the connection. As for Breakwell doing the honourable thing by giving up the names of the people he reported in to, Coupland wouldn't hold his breath.

A girl aged about 17 hurried up the hill clutching her bag. Coupland knew instinctively this was Gayle by the way she contained herself. Making herself smaller so as not to attract unwanted attention. He'd seen it before in abuse victims. The need to be invisible.

She looked at Coupland as she drew level with his car but she didn't really see him. Right now he was a threat. An obstacle she must pass before she entered the sanctity of her home.

He decided not to move from the car. Instead he waited until the front door opened, her mother ushering her in before pointing him out. She must have been watching from an upstairs window, waiting until she saw her walk up the road. A nod over her daughter's shoulder and Coupland stepped forward, his mind formulating the questions he dared ask versus the ones he wanted to. He stepped into the hallway. Waited while Gayle turned to look at him before introducing himself, explaining the reason he was there. He ascertained her mother's name was Carol, and if she hadn't been present, there was no doubt he'd have been given short shrift.

A quick glance at her mother reassured Gayle everything was OK. 'I'll be back down in a minute,' she said, hurrying up the stairs.

'You'd better come through.' Carol beckoned Coupland into a modest kitchen, pointing to one of the two chairs either side of a small square table. Went about the process of making him a drink even though she hadn't asked if he wanted one.

'Might as well, she's away having a shower,' she told

him when she plonked it down in front of him.

Coupland nodded his thanks.

'Don't get carried away, it's only instant,' she warned. 'I'm sure you're used to better.'

'All goes down the same way.' He picked up his mug, blew across the top of it while he waited for her to say whatever it was she was building up to.

'Go easy on her,' she said eventually, her finger worrying at a silver cross around her neck. 'She's had a hell of a time of it. Leaving school under a cloud didn't help, not to mention the fact everyone thought she was a liar.'

'Because of what happened with Dylan Breakwell?'

'I can't stand hearing that bastard's name. Not after the damage he's done.'

Coupland took a sip of his coffee. 'Why was she excluded?'

'Didn't they tell you? I mean, I'm guessing you went up to the school first before you turned up here?'

Coupland nodded once more. 'Yes, but only because I wanted to find out how I could reach Gayle. I prefer to make up my own mind about people. I want to hear what *she* has to say. But there are more important questions I want to ask her as well – relevant to an investigation I'm involved in, and given what I've seen I don't think she'll be up to them all. So, perhaps you can tell me?'

Carol's features softened. She placed a hand on her chest. Looked away momentarily. A woman unused to kindness in any form.

'I can see she's troubled,' said Coupland.

'Scared out of her wits more like.'

'What of?'

'The future,' she answered simply, turning to look at him. 'She was wild when she was younger. Some would say that was my doing, that I wasn't a proper mum to her, and they'd be right.' She took a breath. 'Me and her dad split up when she was small. I reacted badly. Started drinking while she was at school, didn't stop till she went to bed. Poor sod brought herself up, learned she couldn't rely on me for anything.'

The sound of footsteps overhead. A door closing. A shower running.

'I met a fella. He moved in after a while. Didn't seem to mind the benders I went on. Turns out while I was sleeping it off he was creeping into her room. It happened a few times before she plucked up the courage to tell me.'

'What happened?'

'What do you think? I told him to sling his hook. Made him pack up his things and go that same night. It's what any decent mother would do.'

Some wouldn't. Preferring to blame the child for the trouble they caused. Resenting them for the attention they were getting. Some family dynamics were fucked up. 'Did you report him?' Coupland asked.

Carol shook her head. 'That's when it all started to change for her, I think. When she realised he wouldn't be punished for what he'd done. She didn't see why she should have to follow the rules when others didn't. She started playing truant. Giving cheek in class. They were quick to give her detention, but no one bothered to question why she was acting up. I think she was desperate to tell someone, but no one stopped to ask.'

'Then along came Breakwell,' said Coupland.

Carol nodded. 'He talked to her. Listened to what she

had to say. Made her feel special. She told him what my ex did to her. Didn't realise that what she was confiding in him made her an easy target. He showered her with attention, small gifts and such like. I was oblivious to what was going on.' She studied Coupland's face. 'Not in that way. I gave up the drink five years ago. Haven't touched a drop since.'

'Pleased to hear it.'

'Her attendance improved and so did her grades. For a short while anyway. She was a young girl who thought she was in love, willing to do anything to make him happy. He started taking things further. Making her do things she didn't want to. She'd go round to his flat and there'd be other men... When she said no, Breakwell taunted her, told her he was getting bored. He told her there was another girl in her year he was interested in. If she didn't buck her ideas up he'd finish with her and move onto this other girl. She went into school the next day and beat her up. The awful thing is the girl had no idea about any of it. I'm convinced he came up with a random name just to wind her up. The point is, to everyone else it looked like Gayle had attacked her for the hell of it. When she tried to explain Mr Breakwell's involvement the head wouldn't listen.'

No surprise there. Once Gayle was excluded, the problem, as far as the school was concerned, would go away.

The sound of running water stopped, followed by footsteps across the landing. Carol lowered her voice: 'Whenever she goes out, the first thing she does the moment she gets home is shower. She scrubs herself raw day in day out. Says he's left her dirty.'

'Have you tried getting her some counselling?'

'She refuses to go. Says she doesn't want to keep reliving it over and over.'

'You mentioned earlier that she sometimes goes to see a friend. At least she's got someone to talk to if she wants.'

Carol's mouth formed a grim smile. 'She doesn't really have any friends. Sometimes it's easier to lie, pretend everything is normal when it isn't. Make believe we're living a different life.'

'Nothing wrong with wishful thinking.'

'Why are you here?' Gayle was standing in the doorway studying him. She wore a long-sleeved baggy sweatshirt over leggings. She'd towel dried her hair, which hung round her face like rats' tails.

'I'm investigating the grooming and sexual abuse of pupils at another school. I understand you may also have been a victim of this person. Dylan Breakwell.'

Gayle moved to the empty chair and dropped into it. 'There's no may about it. Even though that tosser of a headteacher didn't believe me at the time.' Gayle's forehead creased in confusion. 'How did you get to hear about it though? I was persuaded not to go to the police.'

'I work in a team dedicated to bringing people like Dylan Breakwell to justice. Unlike me, certain members of the team are damn good at trawling the internet. They found comments posted on social media from people who thought you'd been poorly treated.'

'Didn't make any difference at the time, Mr Breakwell accused me of egging folk on to make those comments.'

'And did you?'

'I didn't talk to anyone about it.'

'It was me,' admitted Carol. 'I wanted people to know how badly she'd been treated. I told friends, neighbours, people I worked with. I wasn't to know it would backfire and make her look like an attention seeker.'

'It wasn't your fault, Mum,' Gayle said, turning to her mother.

Carol moved to the kettle to make Gayle a coffee. 'Here,' she said, handing her a mug.

Gayle took it gratefully, circling her hands around it. 'So what do you want from me?'

'To ask you a few questions, if I may?'

'I'm not sure how I can help. I'm done with it all,' she said off-hand.

Coupland tried a different tack. 'You ever hear from that teacher who helped you write your complaint, the one who went to Thailand?'

Gayle shook her head. 'Why would I? She was just another person who didn't really give a toss. Did what she had to then moved on. A bit like you will, in the end.'

Coupland didn't rise to it. 'Bit odd though, don't you think, not keeping in touch, given the effort she must have put in at the time?'

'Not from where I'm sitting.'

Coupland changed direction once more. 'What was the inside of Mr Breakwell's flat like?'

Gayle regarded her mother in alarm. 'Do I have to do this?'

Carol looked at Coupland, the expression in her eyes asking the same thing. 'If it helps his investigation…' she said eventually.

Gayle nodded, took a breath.

'Dylan's flat was modern. All glossy furniture and a

big TV. When I went round there he used to get me a Coke and tip a bit of voddy in it. Said I needed loosening up. We'd play on his Xbox, but it was obvious he wanted more. I did too, I suppose. He'd use his phone to take selfies of us, then after a while he just wanted to take photos of me. He said the videos he took were a bit of fun, that everybody did it. That was when he started hurting me.'

'He hit you?'

'No. He used things that were painful,' she said, not meeting his eye.

'Why isn't any of this in the letter you sent to the head?'

'Because I couldn't tell Miss Evans about things like that, I was too ashamed.'

Jesus wept.

'What about the men who used to come to Mr Breakwell's flat? You ever seen any of them before? Or since?'

Gayle turned to her mother.

'All I want to know is whether these men could have been local,' Coupland explained.

'No, I'd never seen them before,' Gayle said quickly. 'They didn't look local, you know what I mean?'

Coupland needed more than that. 'Can you describe any of these men? Did they have any distinguishing features?'

'Apart from their hard-ons?'

'The detective's only trying to help, love.'

'Is he though? Sounds to me like all he's doing is asking dumb fucking questions!' Gayle rubbed at her arms. The sleeve of her sweatshirt rose up exposing angry scars.

'She's right,' Coupland said before her mother could say anything more. 'I'm sorry. I really don't want to rake up awful memories for you, but I do want to catch the men who went into that flat with the intention of having sex with an underage girl. Of course you weren't looking at what they were wearing or whether they had a tattoo or spoke with a lisp. I hate asking these questions but it's funny the things we can remember at times. Things we don't expect to be important.'

Gayle considered his words. 'Mum, can you leave us a minute?'

Carol regarded her daughter, surprised. 'Why? There's nothing you can't say in front of me.'

'Please…'

'Fine!' Carol threw her hands in the air. 'I'll go and watch TV in the front room. Let me know when you're done.'

Gayle watched as Coupland got up to close the kitchen door. Waited until he sat down again. 'There's not one single person who knows everything about what happened. I told my story in bite-size pieces. The full version is too much for any one person to bear,' she said, looking down at her hands.

'You had to bear it,' said Coupland.

She threw back her head to eyeball him. 'God only gives us what we can stand. Do you believe that?'

'I'd have to believe in God first.'

A smile. 'Giving up the booze turned her into a bit of a God botherer,' Gayle said, inclining her head towards the door and the living room beyond. 'Seems a bit hypocritical, but if it helps her then so what. I never told her all of it but in turn she didn't really want to know. Knowing might have set her back and neither of us wants that.'

Coupland waited.

'You asked me about what they looked like. The men that came to the flat. To me they all looked the same. Sleazy, desperate. I never thought that one day someone would ask me to describe them. I never thought that day would come.' She paused, as though gathering her thoughts or steeling herself, Coupland couldn't be sure. 'There was this one bloke. A right posh git. He spoke like one of them actors on those shows set in the old days with stately homes and servants. Wore a poncey scarf.'

Coupland nodded his encouragement. Willed himself to say nothing.

'He had a ring on his little finger. It was gold. Had something engraved on it but I couldn't tell you what.'

'How often was he at the flat?'

'Couple of times a month.'

'How long did he stay?'

Gayle looked away. 'Long enough. I put up with it all for much longer than Mum thinks. That's how much I loved Dylan.'

Piece of fucking work, thought Coupland, struggling to keep his professional face on.

She turned to face him. 'Can I ask you something?'

Coupland nodded.

'Do you think some people are born to be victims? That they give off a scent or something, that lets others know they're easy prey?' She scratched the back of her hand over and over, forming deep red welts.

Coupland let out a sigh. 'From what I've seen some people are skilled in manipulating the trust of others. Dylan Breakwell is one of them. Everything that took place in that flat, everything that took place between you, is down to him, not you.'

It was clear she wasn't listening. Her gaze had settled on something over his shoulder. Not a physical thing. A memory. The lost look in her eye, the way she moved her hand up and down her scarred arm and started to rock, told him it wasn't a good one.

Carol returned to the kitchen, her way of signalling he'd outstayed his welcome. Coupland got to his feet.

'Look, I've taken up enough of your time but I just want to say this. Breakwell is in custody, and the evidence against him will put him away for the rest of his life. But you mustn't live out his sentence too. We have specially trained counsellors who are working with his other victims. Can I ask one of them to contact you?'

A quick glance at her mother.

'It can't do any harm, love,' Carol urged. 'Though God's love is all we really need.'

Gayle shared a look with Coupland. Nodded.

*

Coupland didn't remember the journey back to Nexus House. His mind was still in Carol Woodall's kitchen, speaking to a young woman who blamed herself for the abuse she'd suffered.

How many Breakwells were out there, infiltrating schools, sports clubs, positions of trust? If Coupland were to draw an organisation chart to illustrate the extent of the network, Breakwell and those like him operated at the shop floor level, where the victims were groomed and put through their paces.

If they could crack Breakwell, get him to give up the name of the person he reported in to, it'd be a start. Coupland knew it wasn't as simple as that. These human skid marks never divulged their real names. They wouldn't be listed on Breakwell's smartphone contact list as 'Passman' or 'Sick Fuck Team Leader', but they'd have a way of reaching each other. Burner phone most likely. The curse of every force up and down the country.

His phone rang. He hit the hands-free button, barked his name. It was DCI Swain.

'A welfare check has been carried out on the address you gave us for Eliza Evans.'

'And?' Coupland grunted.

'No sign that it's been occupied recently, which fits in with her working away. Officers saw no signs of a struggle, or of her belongings being disturbed, although several things did cause alarm. Uneaten breakfast items haven't been cleared away from the kitchen table and have now gone mouldy. The washing machine is full of clothes and the fridge hasn't been emptied. Not normally how you'd leave things before going on holiday or leaving the property for a while.'

'What about her passport?'

'No sign of it as yet. Interestingly, the neighbours weren't aware of her plans to go to Thailand, never mind plans to stay there.'

Coupland huffed out a sigh. 'It doesn't look good.' Breakwell knew how to pick them, he'd give him that. An orphaned young woman whose closest relative had passed away. Persuading her colleagues that she had gone to work abroad was guaranteed to buy him time before anyone started asking questions. All so that he could move to another school to do it all over again?

Groom. Abuse. Film. Kill anyone who gets in the way. Repeat.

'Listen, I've spoken to Superintendent Romain. He's given the green light for you to sit in when I next interview Breakwell.'

'Top man,' said Coupland, putting his foot down on the accelerator.

CHAPTER TWELVE

Nexus House

The pace in the incident room had stepped up several gears. Eliza Evans, as yet unaccounted for, was getting the full belt and braces approach for someone suspected of going missing in suspicious circumstances. Her social media would be scrutinised. Her mobile phone company would be approached to determine when her phone had last been used, and to triangulate the location. Her bank would be contacted to see if any transactions had been made in the intervening time. Passenger names on flight manifests to Thailand would be checked and a request would be made to Interpol to check the names of British citizens recently employed or volunteering at state orphanages there.

A photo of Eliza, lifted from her Facebook profile, had been placed on a new incident board beside Helen Harper's. A third board listed the names of pupils from Northdown High School abused by Dylan Breakwell. Gayle Woodall's name had been added to that list.

Having waited for Coupland to return, Superintendent Romain gathered the team together for a briefing, although Commander Howorth was running this one. There was nothing like the whiff of success to bring the shiny brass buttons out.

The Commander nodded as Coupland took a seat.

'DS Coupland's visit to Hadfield Grammar School has resulted in an unexpected discovery which may well prove to be significant to this investigation. Eliza Evans, previously a newly qualified teacher and thought to be working in Thailand for over a year now, is missing.' He nodded at Coupland to summarise for the team.

'Apart from a note addressed to the headteacher resigning from her post, the only person Eliza supposedly told about her plans to work abroad was Dylan Breakwell. This seems unlikely, given the concerns she'd raised about him to the headteacher following claims made against him by a pupil. I suspect she's gone the same way of Helen Harper, her remains just haven't been discovered yet.'

Commander Howorth nodded at Jared to report on his progress: 'We're waiting on Eliza's mobile provider to get back to us regarding her phone activity, but she hasn't posted anything on Facebook or Instagram since her last day at school. Prior to that she would upload photos or memes two or three times a week.'

'What the hell's a meme?' asked Coupland.

Jared smiled, was about to oblige him with an explanation when Coupland held up his hand: 'Scratch that – will me understanding make any difference to this investigation?'

Both Jared and Noah shook their heads.

'Then move on. I'm OK with being an old fossil.'

DI Taylor spoke next. 'We're waiting on Amjid getting back to us regarding Eliza's bank account activity. I've also asked officers at Heathrow, Gatwick, and Manchester to include stopovers in their search through flight manifests, not just direct flights. What's worrying is the way she left her flat – like she expected to return later that day, and the fact her neighbours knew nothing about her supposed trip. In the past she's asked them to pop in and water her plants, move her mail, that sort of thing.'

'What about the headteacher at Hadfield Grammar?' asked the Commander. 'Could he be implicated in any of this? I understand he played down the complaint he received when it was clearly a serious allegation, corroborated by two teachers.'

Coupland blew out his cheeks. 'He's more useless than dangerous, sir. Coasting to retirement.'

'What about the retired teacher, Maureen Webster? Have we checked out her death wasn't suspicious?'

'A rapid decline witnessed by her husband and monitored by her GP. Nothing sinister.'

'And the girl...' began Romain.

'Gayle Woodall?' clarified Coupland.

Romain's nod was impatient. 'Is she willing to undergo a medical examination for evidential purposes?'

'Not a chance,' Coupland told him. 'I'd go so far as to say putting her through that would be detrimental to her mental health right now.'

'It'll mean we can't include her statement as evidence to the CPS of Breakwell's abuse.'

'Trust me, that's the least of her concerns. She's in desperate need of support right now. I said I'd get the counselling team to contact her.'

'That's not possible,' said Romain. 'The counselling service is only available for victims who have undergone a forensic examination. We simply don't have the resources for anyone else.'

'I know how it works, but she shouldn't be held to ransom like that. Enough pupils have come forward for us to bring an abuse case against Breakwell. We can't withhold access to support on the basis she won't co-operate with the investigation.'

'Actually we can,' Romain countered. 'In most cases that's all the leverage we have.'

'I think she's self-harming,' Coupland continued. 'At the very least the rituals she performs show she's riddled with anxiety. I'm no expert, but she needs serious help and she needs it now.'

Romain pursed his lips. 'Fine,' he said in a resigned voice.

Just as well, thought Coupland, keeping his face in check. He'd already contacted the counselling centre on his way back to Nexus House. A member of the emergency duty team would be contacting Gayle this evening. A little bit of persuasion had been needed to put her at the top of an already burgeoning pile, but he couldn't sit back while she waited her turn. The state of her. The fact that despite what she'd gone through she got out of bed every morning. That she got on a bus and signed on for work. Some folk got plaudits for kayaking down the Amazon, yet no one was braver than a survivor who managed to put one foot in front of the other despite what life had thrown at them.

'You happy for us to crack on with Breakwell's interview then?' Coupland asked, rubbing his hands together. 'PACE clock going tick tock and all that.'

Commander Howorth fixed Coupland with a stare. 'We need information from a man who's got no reason to play ball with us. Think you can appeal to his better side?'

'I'm prepared to give it a shot,' Coupland said, showing what he hoped was a reassuring smile.

Interview room, Nexus House.

Inside the interview room Dylan Breakwell and his solicitor sat on one side of the table, Coupland and DCI Swain on the other.

'This interview is being recorded onto a secure digital network,' said Swain, stating the time and date as well as listing those present. He summarised the previous interview, asked if Breakwell wanted to add anything.

'No thank you,' said Breakwell, all genial.

Coupland saw this as an opportunity to strike first. 'Ever had sex with underage girls?' he asked without bothering to refer to his interview plan.

DCI Swain shot a look at him. His look suggesting they'd barely sat down and he was already going off piste with the questions.

'Of course not!' Breakwell bristled.

'Ever invite your pupils to your flat after school?' Coupland asked, locking his gaze onto him.

'This is preposterous!'

'Why is it preposterous? You've already confessed to being a killer. I'm not sure where your moral boundary's set but I'd say it was pretty low, wouldn't you?'

Breakwell bowed his head. 'What I did to Helen Harper was unforgiveable. For that I am truly sorry.'

'Can you tell us how you disposed of her body?' Swain interrupted.

'No comment.'

'Can you describe where you left her body?'

'No comment.'

Swain opened his iPad, tapped on several keys until

he located a photograph of an area of woodland close to the school. He turned the iPad around so that Breakwell could see it. 'Are you familiar with this location?'

'No comment.'

'This is where Helen Harper's body was found. Can you tell us how it got there?'

'No comment.'

'I think that someone helped you dispose of her body. Who are you trying to protect?'

'No comment.'

Coupland swallowed down his frustration. Leaned forward in his seat to get Breakwell's attention. 'Can you confirm that you worked at Hadfield Grammar School since qualifying to become a teacher in 2016 until you left in 2021?' he asked.

'Yes,' answered Breakwell, nodding.

Coupland thanked him as though his answer had been really helpful. 'Do you remember working with a newly qualified teacher by the name of Eliza Evans during the latter part of your time in that post?'

Breakwell tilted his head as though giving the matter some serious thought. 'Vaguely. It's hard to remember everyone I've met during my career.'

'Wish I could say the same,' said Coupland. He tapped his temple with his index finger. 'Once you're lodged in here you're going nowhere,' he said, baring his teeth. 'So, back to Eliza. She resigned her post just before you resigned yours. Does that help jog your memory a little?'

'Ah, yes. She left to work in Thailand.'

'So I understand,' said Coupland. 'Yet none of the members of staff at the school – or her neighbours for that matter – were aware of her plans. Only you, which is a bit odd.' He held Breakwell's gaze and waited.

'What's odd?'

'That she'd choose you of all people to confide in.' Coupland made a point of opening the file in front of him, skimming through a couple of pages. He looked up to see Breakwell straining to read the contents. He rearranged his features into a frown. 'Hadn't things got a little awkward between you? You know, given she was one of the teachers who supported Gayle Woodall when she accused you of sexual assault.'

Breakwell clicked his tongue. 'It wasn't sexual assault, it was rape!' he snapped.

Coupland's eyebrows shot theatrically into his hair line. 'Glad we've cleared that up so quickly,' he said, looking at Breakwell's lawyer.

'I mean she *accused* me of rape, not sexual assault!' Breakwell sounded rattled. Looked as though he was about to burst a blood vessel.

'I must insist on having a word with my client,' said Breakwell's solicitor, staring at Coupland stony-faced. Linda East was a seasoned brief, known for her no-nonsense attitude and straight talking. Breakwell would be hard pushed to get anyone better.

'I'm sure you would,' agreed Coupland. 'Just when I was starting to enjoy myself, too.'

Coupland could feel DCI Swain's glare all the while the senior officer summarised the reason for the break for the purposes of the tape, asking Breakwell to confirm this had been at his request. Swain gathered up his interview book and iPad before stepping out into the corridor, Coupland in his wake.

'What the hell was that?' he demanded, rounding on

Coupland once they were out of earshot of the interview room.

'I was winding him up a little,' Coupland explained. 'And it worked. Till you reverted to your "How did you move the body?" line of enquiry when he went all no comment again. I listened to the previous interviews you've conducted with him, where you kept banging on and on with the same questions as though he was going to reward you with different answers at some point. Personally, I don't see that happening!'

'How can you be so sure?' Swain persisted, all sullen.

'Christ, man, are you blind?'

'Watch it Coupland, I'm two ranks above you.'

'Christ, sir, are you blind?' Coupland corrected himself, meeting Swain's gaze head on. 'He's scared out of his wits. He isn't going to cooperate in a month of Sundays, so if I were you I'd bin that interview strategy and start again.'

'The boss will kick you out of the interview room if you carry on like that,' Swain warned.

Coupland shrugged. 'Won't be the first time that's happened to me.'

'I can see why you haven't progressed beyond sergeant,' Swain observed.

'And I can see why your shoes are spotless,' Coupland shot back. He jerked his thumb towards the interview room door. 'Now we can stand here pulling each other's hair or we can go back in there and get that piece of shit to give us a name.'

'There's a protocol to follow...'

'I know there's a protocol. And I'll do everything I can to stay within it,' Coupland assured him, breaking eye contact.

Swain looked at his watch. 'We reconvene in fifteen minutes. Just enough time to draw up a new strategy.'

Coupland tried not to roll his eyes. 'I'll catch you up,' he said, 'I need to do something first.'

To the casual observer looking down from any window at the rear of Nexus House, Coupland looked as though he was chain smoking in the car park while scrolling through his phone. They'd have been right, of course. His fingers swiping the phone's screen until he found what he was looking for. 'Thank Christ for that,' he muttered, clicking on the image to save it for later. One last lungful of nicotine and he was ready to go back inside.

*

Interview room, Nexus House
Seated across the table from Dylan Breakwell, DCI Swain kicked off the formalities by asking him to confirm, for the purposes of the tape, that no questions or other discussions relating to the offence had been conducted by any officer during the break. He really was dotting the 'I's and crossing the 'T's on this one, thought Coupland. More was the pity.

Once the preliminaries had been taken care of, Swain began:

'Digital recordings found in a box in your wardrobe at your home address are currently being examined by our Digital Forensic Unit. The material examined so far is of a sexual nature, filmed at a location that appears identical to the interior of your flat. I can also tell you at this early stage, Dylan, our officers have already identified two of your pupils in those recordings.'

DCI Swain paused, flashed a look at Coupland before continuing. 'This proves that you've been lying to us. That at least two pupils have been in your flat, and that you have had sex with them. Is there anything you want to say in response to this?'

Coupland bit back his frustration. As damning as the digital evidence was, there was still nothing to link Breakwell to the Dutchman's network. His admission to abusing and filming the girls would incriminate him, but prove useless in terms of bringing others to account.

Breakwell whispered into his solicitor's ear. His solicitor whispered back. Breakwell looked at her and nodded.

Breakwell's solicitor spoke next. 'My client admits that he has had intimate relations with the pupils concerned, but would like to stress that the recordings he took were for his own personal use.'

You don't say, thought Coupland.

'You know we can cross check them against digital clips uploaded on the dark web,' he said. 'We're particularly interested in a site that goes by the name of Utopia. It's the equivalent of Netflix for sad sacks,' he added for Linda East's benefit. Utopia was the Dutchman's sleazy pay-per-view website. Breakwell's videos appearing there would prove there was a link between them.

Despite this threat, Breakwell's face remained impassive.

'Who are you trying to protect?' asked Swain.

'No comment.'

'Have you heard of anyone referred to as the Dutchman?'

'No comment.'

Jesus wept, they were back to square one again. Did the man not bloody listen? Coupland drummed his fingers on the tabletop to get his attention but Swain ignored him.

'If your accomplices were in here instead of you they wouldn't think twice about giving you up,' Swain added, sounding like a headmaster trying to track down who'd graffiti'd the bike sheds.

Breakwell stared at the wall behind him.

'I get it,' said Coupland, sitting forward in his seat. He regarded Breakwell. 'You're already facing life for murder, never mind what you'll get for filming yourself raping children.'

He paused. Waited until Breakwell stopped looking at the wall and focussed on him instead. He summoned a smile he didn't feel, made his voice sound sympathetic. 'The predicament you're in must be tough. The people you work for will have warned you what'll happen if you grass them up. That they'll be able to reach you in prison, make your life a living hell.' He leaned forward in his chair until his chest was touching the table's edge. Jabbed his finger on the table top as though pointing out a stain; all the while his eyes bore into Breakwell's. 'I've got a newsflash for you. Your life's going to be a living hell anyway. Everyone knows there's a pecking order in the criminal world. That bank robbers look down on burglars and burglars look down on rapists and rapists are thrilled to high heaven when a nonce comes along. Now, that's a way of life you're going to have to learn to navigate, and I'm a great believer in if you can't do the time, don't do the crime. But what about your family? They didn't ask for any of it.'

He slipped his phone from his pocket. Refreshed the

screen to show Breakwell's Facebook profile. He held it up, scrolling through recent posts until he found what he was looking for. A photograph taken in a restaurant. Along with Breakwell, people of various ages sat either side of a long table. 'Family celebration?' asked Coupland.

Breakwell nodded.

'Happy days, eh? Shame to think this is the last time they'll ever look like this.'

Breakwell sent him a questioning look.

Coupland pointed out a white-haired couple with suntanned faces. Back from a winter break in the Canaries by the look of it, enjoying their pension while they still had all their faculties. 'Your parents?' Coupland asked.

Breakwell inclined his head the tiniest fraction.

'It's them I feel sorry for. The rest of your family will soon wash their hands of you. *Uncle Dylan.* Airbrushed out of every photo with your nieces in. Your nephews will get the shit kicked out of them, but they'll learn to live with it. Your brother and sister will make a pact never to speak of you again. But your mam and dad? For them that's not an option. They'll have to live with the shame of knowing they created a monster. They'll blame themselves, of course. Pick over every moment of your childhood wondering what they did that sent you down this path. They'll try to remember happier times, but even those memories have been snatched from them. They'll still go on their holidays,' Coupland nodded, 'but it won't be the same. When other holidaymakers ask if they have a family they'll leave you out, then feel guilty.'

Coupland let the words sink in. 'You've resigned them to prison visits they won't want to make. To have strangers frisk them and search inside their mouths before sitting

205

in a hall full of volatile men. Each visit they'll try not to notice your cuts and bruises, your limp. Your Mam'll cry when she gets in the car. Your old fella will hate what you've done to her. When they pictured how they'd spend their retirement, Dylan, that's not what they saw.'

'What's your point?' Breakwell choked out the question, his eyes fixated on the photo of his family as though consigning it to memory.

'You've resigned them to living every day of your sentence with you. Knowing that from now on in every move you make, every shit you take, someone'll be biding their time. They'll learn to fear calls coming from a withheld number. Calls that inform them you're in the medical wing with a nail in your eye or you've been scarred with boiling water and sugar. It won't matter if it's the Dutchman's gang or a chancer trying their luck, you'll be ripe for the picking.'

DCI Swain said nothing. They both knew Coupland had crossed a line, but it was his backside that would be strung up, no one else's. If this got them the result they needed, Coupland was more than willing to take one for the team.

A tic had developed in Breakwell's left eye.

'Help us, Dylan,' Coupland soothed, 'and we'll arrange for you to serve your time at Wakefield.'

Breakwell started rubbing at the imaginary stain on the table that Coupland had pointed out earlier.

'The locals call it Monster Mansion but don't let that put you off. Imagine, 600 nonces living under one roof. It's like a convention centre for the dregs of humanity. Now be warned, even in a shit hole like Wakefield there's a pecking order. Sex offenders and child killers compete for the title of the lowest of the low and the thing is with nonces, they are so much more imaginative than the rest of the criminal fraternity when it comes to teaching someone a lesson. What they can't do with a chair leg and a bottle of Reggae Reggae sauce…'

Breakwell paled.

'Play ball with us and we'll take care of you. Get you one of those Perspex isolation cells in the basement, complete with cardboard furniture.' He sounded like a timeshare tout flogging the benefits of a Benidorm duplex. He flashed his teeth by way of encouragement.

'All we need is a name that leads to a conviction.'

Breakwell had stopped rubbing the table. His hands hung limp by his side.

'It's the best chance you've got,' he added, before gesturing to the photo, to Breakwell's parents. 'Don't they deserve having one less thing to worry about?'

Breakwell dropped his head onto his chest, started whimpering.

'Is there something you'd now like to tell us?' asked Swain.

Breakwell nodded.

Told them everything he knew.

*

Coupland was halfway through a cigarette in the designated smoking shelter when he became aware of a presence behind him. 'Never a wise move to creep up on a fella having a much-needed smoke,' he grumbled, turning to lock eyes with the Commander. 'Didn't realise it was you, sir. Obviously,' he muttered.

'Enjoy your cigarette, Kevin,' the senior officer said,

lighting one up for himself, 'after this afternoon's performance what I have to say can wait.'

Coupland nod was slow, as he tried to process the level of threat in the senior officer's statement. A final cigarette before the firing squad appeared? he wondered.

Dylan Breakwell had been an easy enough nut to crack. Despite his heinous acts he wasn't immersed in the Dutchman's world. Most days the path he trod was a normal one. He'd have been easy for the network to control. To scare. But at the end of the day how his parents felt won out.

Coupland finished his cigarette. He was tempted to light another but didn't want to push his luck. Instead, he shoved his hands in his trouser pockets, kicked at a bit of gravel with the toe of his shoe. He tried to work out how his bollocking would go. Officers weren't supposed to offer unapproved inducements to suspects during the course of an interview. Then again a Perspex box in the basement of Wakefield Prison was hardly a week in the Bahamas.

Even so, referencing Breakwell's family like that. Piling the pressure on. He'd merely been telling it like it was, though that wouldn't stop the stuffed shirts at the CPS determining that any answers given following their little tête-a-tête were inadmissible in court.

Breakwell had already admitted to killing Helen Harper. As a result he'd been charged with one count of murder. Following a brief appearance at the magistrates court in the morning he'd be remanded into custody, with any luck Wakefield Prison, if Superintendent Romain's call to the prison service went the way it had to. What was in jeopardy was how they could use the fresh information he had given them. The name he'd put forward. A direct arrest of this person was no longer on the table due to the manner in which they'd come by it, but that had never been part of the game plan. This was a strategic operation and the name Breakwell had offered up was another link in the chain.

Coupland watched Commander Howorth toss his cigarette butt onto the pavement, winced as he ground it into a thousand little pieces.

'Good work in there,' Howorth commented, inclining his head in the direction of the building.

'I know I didn't exactly toe the line,' admitted Coupland, 'but given the Dutchman is on our doorstep we've got a real chance to flush him out. The problem is we don't know how long he's here for, so I felt applying a bit of pressure was necessary.'

Commander Howorth studied him. 'You're not listening, Detective Sergeant. I said good work. End of.'

'Oh.' Coupland swallowed. 'Thanks.'

The Commander eyeballed him. 'This isn't the first time I've gone after the Dutchman. Five years ago I was assigned to a unit whose remit was the same as ours – to bring the bastard down. We got nowhere near him because we underestimated his reach and I don't intend doing that a second time. I need people who are good at adapting to situations as they come up. There's a time and a place for strategists, but it's rarely on the front line.'

Coupland looked at him nonplussed. 'So, what are you saying?'

'Jesus, man, keep up.' He pointed his finger at Coupland in an accusing manner. 'I'm saying that anyone watching from an upstairs window will think I'm ripping you a new hole, when what I really mean is you played a blinder in there. Good work detective sergeant. Got it?'

'Loud and clear,' said Coupland, making sure he looked suitably chastened.

In reality, those further up the network's chain were going to be the real challenge. They were career criminals. Hard men with fearsome reputations who only mixed with other hard men. They had one job. To put a ring of steel around the Dutchman. To exterminate anyone who got in his way. They did it mercilessly, and they did it well. The strategy to bring them down needed to be as brutal as they were. Coupland hoped to Christ that when it came down to it, he wasn't the only one prepared to do whatever it took.

*

Coupland attempted to chill out when he got home that night but he couldn't pull it off. He sipped a beer he didn't want, looked on as Lynn and Amy shared a joke. He tried tapping into their light-heartedness, found he was going through the motions. His mouth stretching into a grin he couldn't feel.

Later, he waved away Lynn's offer of the TV remote control. Wasn't sure anything on the box that evening could take his mind off the horror of child rape. He looked on oblivious while she channel-hopped TV dramas and reality shows, looking for something that would pique his interest. Eventually she clicked off the TV, laid the TV switcher on the sofa between them.

'You know you don't have to put on an act for us, right?' she asked. 'You're home. This is your safe place.'

He was grateful that she didn't tempt fate by saying

nothing could harm them. Twenty years of nursing, she was all too aware of the damage that could befall someone without stepping through their front door.

'You're working longer hours. You spent the other night cooped up in a car. It's bound to be taking its toll.'

'Thanks for the vote of confidence,' he huffed.

'You know what I mean,' she soothed. She had one of those voices that made everything seem better but Coupland didn't want his mood lifting. He felt narky and wanted to dwell in it, look for conflict where there was none.

'You think I'm past it,' he accused her, hating himself. 'Perhaps I should put in for a desk job. Is that what you want?'

'You can be a right knobhead at times,' she said, getting to her feet. She picked her Kindle up from the coffee table. 'Think I'll have an early night,' she told him, her tone making it clear it wasn't an invitation for him to join her.

CHAPTER THIRTEEN

'I called yesterday but there was no answer.'
'I had to work late. Is everything OK?'
'Same old. So, what's for dinner tonight then?'
'I'm making lasagne,' she lied. Though she was looking forward to the bottle of Primitivo on the kitchen counter. It'd go down nicely with some cheese on toast.
'Sounds lovely. Curry pie today. How can something made up of my two favourite meals be so disgusting when combined?'
'I have no idea. Look, is there any chance you could start calling me later? It's such a rush to get back in time.'
'No can do I'm afraid. They start locking us up after association time. I'm pushing it as it is.'
Someone barked his name. He answered in a muffled tone. The clang of heavy doors shutting, the echo of shouted conversations bouncing around the landing. Chairs scraping as the occupants got to their feet, the grating noise of metal against metal.
'If I don't go now he's putting me on report. I love you.'
'I love you too,' she answered, but the line had already gone dead.

CHAPTER FOURTEEN

Morning briefing, Nexus House

The incident room was Bedlam. Mark Novak, the name Dylan Breakwell had given them in the interview room the previous day, was written on a new incident board with a question mark beside it. Breakwell had described him as mid to late 30s with dark hair and a stocky frame. He drove a 70 plate Toyota Hilux. The fact he was proving difficult to trace didn't dampen the buzz in the room.

'There are no Mark Novak's on the electoral register,' Jared stated. 'Not with that spelling anyway. There's a Mark Novac and a Marek Nowak, and several other derivations of the name but not an exact match.'

'Breakwell heard his name spoken only once, likely in error, when he overheard him answer his phone. He's never seen it in print, can't be certain of the spelling. We're going to have to be creative.'

Noah and Jared had run different versions of the name through social media sites to see if they could find a profile to match. Jared explained: 'It's not unusual for people who don't want to be found easily on social media to change part of their profile name. Teachers or police officers for example might spell their name backwards or might throw in extra letters to their surname to limit who can find them.'

'Or do like me and don't bother setting up a profile in the first place,' said Coupland.

'There's always that.' Jared smiled, like he was talking to an old soldier on Remembrance Sunday. 'The point is, we can't find this guy on social media and there are several versions of his name.'

'He has to live reasonably close to Breakwell as he'd turn up at his flat within half an hour of his phoning him,' said DCI Swain.

'Could be coming from work,' reasoned DI Taylor.

'Most of their activity was at night. He'd bring clients to be "entertained" by the pupils Breakwell had enticed to his flat. Then there's the removal of Helen Harper's body…' he reminded him.

'Fair point.'

'Did this fella move her body on his own then?' asked Taylor.

Coupland shook his head. 'Breakwell says he turned up with another bloke after Helen's murder. Both of them wore gloves.'

DI Taylor opened an electronic map on his computer, located Breakwell's current flat and the flat he used to rent while working at Hadfield Grammar. He pinpointed an area of equal distance between the two. 'Gorton is half an hour's drive from both locations,' he said.

'Hang on,' said Jared, tapping onto his computer keyboard and studying the results on his screen. 'According to the electoral register that's where Marek Nowak lives.'

DI Taylor nodded, satisfied. He studied the map once more. 'The closest Toyota garage is here, on Ashton Old Road,' he said, indicating another point on the map. 'I'll get them to send over a list of customers who purchased a 70 plate Hilux from that area. We can then cross check the names and addresses and see if we can get a match.'

'Agreed,' said Romain. 'Put a rocket up the garage if you need to. I want to know everything about him ASAP.'

Romain recorded the actions in his daybook. He'd sat tight lipped when Coupland and DCI Swain had returned from interviewing Breakwell the previous day and had avoided looking at him when he'd spoken during the briefing. Coupland was aware he'd watched the interview live in the observation room with the Commander. He couldn't decide what was hacking him off more – that Coupland had gone off-piste during the interview – or that apart from the Commander waving his finger at him, he hadn't been disciplined.

'OK, this is all well and good but what I don't understand,' said Superintendent Lara Cole who'd joined them for the briefing but had so far been sitting quietly, writing notes, 'is how their paths ever crossed in the first place? If they're not in the same social circle, how were they introduced?'

'Oh, you'll love this—' said Coupland, delighted to do the honours. Here was his chance to show Lara Cole that he hadn't been coasting since he'd joined the team. That when it came to getting suspects to talk he was nothing if not effective. He tried to catch Romain's eye, his thick skin undaunted by the senior officer's chilly demeanour.

'Noah,' said Romain, ignoring him, 'play the segment of Breakwell's interview where he explains this, on the big screen.'

'Yes sir,' said Noah, clicking onto the interview link saved in the shared drive. He donned a pair of headphones, fast forwarding through Breakwell's 'No comment' answers to Swain's questions and Coupland's death stare while he listed what options were left to him. Breakwell's meltdown when he realised they amounted to sod all.

As he watched the playback, Coupland congratulated himself on not making a fist or banging his hand down on the table once. His nonverbal signals were improving.

Noah paused the tape at the point where Breakwell was explaining when he met Nowak or Novac, or whatever he liked to call himself, for the first time. He glanced at Superintendent Romain, waited for him to nod before pressing 'Play.'

Breakwell had calmed down at this point in the interview. Had become biddable. Hopeful even. As though the information he was going to give them could make up for killing at least one teacher and raping more pupils than would ever truly come to light.

DCI Swain: 'Dylan, are you familiar with the term *Passman*?'

Breakwell nodded.

Swain: 'For the purposes of the tape please answer yes or no.'

Breakwell: 'Yes.'

Swain: 'Can you explain what passmen do?'

Breakwell: 'They check the girls I provide. If they like the look of them they'll introduce them to paying guests.'

Swain: 'What's a paying guest?'

Breakwell: 'Someone who…' he'd paused then, floundering for the right words.

Coupland: 'Someone who wants to immerse themselves in the full child rape experience?'

Breakwell shuffled in his seat. 'I suppose that's one

way of putting it.'

Coupland and Swain had shared a look.

Swain: 'Where did your first meeting with your passman take place?'

Breakwell: 'He turned up at my door one day and gave me a mobile phone. Told me I was to contact him if I had any problems.'

Coupland could be seen scratching his head, a perplexed look on his face.

Coupland: 'Someone must have put you in touch with each other. How were you recruited?'

Breakwell: 'I got a call out of the blue one day from my bank. It was odd right from the beginning. I mean, I hadn't been in touch with them for anything and as far as I was aware my account was in order. I answered the phone and said "Hello". This man, who claimed to be from my bank, says "Someone's been a naughty boy." I didn't know what the hell he was talking about. At first I thought it was a scam. Then he started reading out a list of transactions, several purchases I'd made online from a company called Utopian Enterprises.'

Coupland: 'Purchases?'

Breakwell: 'Films I'd been watching online.'

Coupland: 'That's more like it. No need to be coy.'

Breakwell: 'I thought there must be some mistake. I mean, I've been watching this kind of stuff online for years and nothing's ever come of it. These transactions are normally secure.'

Coupland: 'You mean hidden?'

Breakwell sighed. 'They're not supposed to show on your account, no.'

Swain: 'So what happened then?'

Breakwell: 'He said the bank was duty bound to report me to the police, however, there was another option, if I was willing to consider it. He asked if I'd ever considered making my own films and uploading them.'

Coupland: 'Not like he had to convince you there was a market for it.'

Breakwell: 'I suppose not.'

Coupland: 'OK... I've got to check here. I mean, I'm not the sharpest knife in the block but I'm guessing you realised at this point that he didn't really work for the bank? Or at least this wasn't an official call?'

On the large screen Breakwell could be seen squirming.

Coupland: 'But enough of your interest had been piqued for you to ignore that minor detail.'

Breakwell: 'I suppose so. He asked if I'd be willing to make the kind of films I'd been downloading. He said there was good money to be made, plus the obvious perks.'

It had taken all Coupland's strength not to punch him. Right then. In the neck. Instead he'd rammed his hands under his thighs, reminded himself this was all being recorded.

Even as Coupland watched it back he was aware he was grinding his teeth.

Breakwell: 'I asked for his name. He said I didn't need it. Someone would be in touch shortly. When the call ended I checked my phone and saw that it had originated from a withheld number. I tried calling him back by using the phone number on the back of my debit card but the recorded greeting stated all calls are recorded for training purposes. Even if he did work for the bank there was no way he'd risk speaking to me on an inbound call.'

A nod from Superintendent Romain and Noah pressed 'Stop.'

The financial investigation unit would check it over but it didn't take a wild leap of imagination to figure that Utopian Enterprises was the trading arm of Utopia, the Dutchman's sadistic site that traded on the dark web.

'The information has to have originated from a bank though,' Lara Cole stated after some thought.

Coupland nodded. 'Think of all the sensitive information bank staff have access to, day in, day out. Who's paying rent on extra-marital love nests, who spends their wages downloading grubby videos. Nothing illegal in those, although I'm guessing they're the kind of transactions people would rather not be made public. If a bent bank employee knows what kind of material Utopia has on its site, then there's every chance they'd see customers with transactions from Utopian Enterprises as fair game.'

Superintendent Romain spoke next: 'Whether the person who cold-called Breakwell to recruit him into the network actually works for the bank is irrelevant. What matters is that a member of staff is collecting this information and passing it on. Whether it's a staff member acting solo or there's a team of them, Breakwell's bank is now implicated.'

It took a few moments for Coupland to digest this. 'Which Amjid's business unit can use as leverage to get it to comply with the investigation,' he said eventually. 'I'll call Amjid.'

'Requests like this need to be put through by someone with a rank of inspector or above. I'll do it,' stated Romain.

Coupland tipped his head in deference.

Romain referred to his logbook. 'The Public Protection Unit have confirmed that several of Breakwell's videos appear on Utopia. Older ones, filmed a couple of years back, have amassed tens of thousands of views. Some of the most recent material has been uploaded this month.'

Coupland huffed out a breath. What a thing for the parents to have to be told.

'Have we got an update on the missing teacher?' Lara Cole looked directly at Romain as she asked this.

'Her name hasn't shown up on any passenger manifests to Thailand, although Interpol's enquiries with the Thai authorities are ongoing. No one by that name or description is working for any of the state registered orphanages.'

'Has a postal redirect been set up for her address?' Lara Cole asked.

Romain jerked his head at Taylor as though saying *you take it from here*.

Taylor shook his head. 'No Ma'am, and a search of her unopened mail revealed dental fines for appointments she didn't show up for, confirmation of renewal of her gym membership, things you'd expect to be cancelled when someone's planning to leave the country for some time.'

Taylor floundered as though unsure whether to say more. An impatient nod from Romain told him to continue. 'Regarding the resignation letter that she sent to the headteacher. The paper it was printed on doesn't match the printer paper that Scenes of Crime officers found at her home, nor does it match the paper used at the school.'

Superintendent Cole underlined something in her notes before speaking. 'Get it checked against any paper found in Dylan Breakwell's flat. If it's a match then we have reason to presume she's come to serious harm, and that he's our chief suspect. I'll liaise with the Commander to put out an urgent missing person appeal and get search teams on standby.'

Romain looked as though he was chewing a wasp as he wrote the action in his daybook.

Coupland sensed a little tension. Two alphas flexing their muscles was all they needed.

'Have we got a confirmed last sighting?' asked Romain.

'Two days before her letter of resignation arrived at school,' said Coupland.

'How did she get to work?'

'She travelled by bus,' said Noah. 'We've been working through on-board CCTV footage the bus company sent us. We found footage of her travelling on the number 26 at 7am that morning, though we've been unable to find her making the return journey at the end of the school day.'

'Maybe she decided to walk,' said Swain.

'Or she got a lift,' said Coupland.

'Or she still hasn't actually left the school premises,' Romain said darkly.

'We need to narrow this down. We don't have the manpower to run multiple searches,' stated Cole. She let out a slow breath before turning to her equal number. 'At the moment Breakwell is charged with one count of murder, with multiple charges of child sexual offences pending. We need to inform the CPS that we are going to question him in relation to a missing person, presumed dead.'

Romain nodded his agreement, his gaze settling on

Coupland. 'Under the circumstances, and the rapport you've built with Breakwell, I'd like you to conduct a post-charge interview with him in relation to Eliza Evans' disappearance.' He couldn't have looked more grudging if he'd tried.

Coupland didn't need asking twice.

CHAPTER FIFTEEN

Wakefield Prison

Coupland didn't relish entering the prison that counted Levi Bellfield, Ian Huntley, Mark Bridger and Robert Black as inmates at one time or another.

It was a means to an end, he reminded himself as he waited in line to be searched and prodded before stepping through a series of heavy airlocked doors.

Dylan Breakwell was barely recognisable as the popular but perverted teacher who'd given them a run for their money in the interview room several days before. He already blended in with his surroundings. His skin was a little greyer than it had been the first time they'd met. His face more guarded. A damn site less cherubic. His eyes blinked several times as he came into the room as though they'd acclimatised to the dimness of the prison's basement and needed to adjust to the upper level.

'Told you we'd come good on our promise,' Coupland said when the prison officer escorting him brought him into the legal visits room where Coupland waited at a table bolted to the floor. He watched Breakwell lower himself gingerly into the chair opposite. 'Those strip searches can be a shock to the system, granted,' he acknowledged, enjoying the look Breakwell sent in his direction. 'Had your induction yet?'

Breakwell nodded.

'Good stuff, the sooner you get used to the routine the better. Get a few things sent in from home and you'll soon have the place looking cosy.'

Breakwell looked confused. 'Do the police normally pay visits to people they've locked up?'

Coupland's smile was tight. 'I'd love to say it was all part of the service but I'd be telling porkies. Don't get me wrong, most cops would gladly pay to see the skid mark they've scraped off the street in his new habitat, but sadly we don't have the time.'

'So why are you here?'

'I'll get round to that, Dylan, don't you worry.' Something occurred to him. 'You know, you're going to have to work on that patience deficit. Remember on the outside, how everyone runs around like blue-arsed flies wondering where the time goes?'

Dylan nodded.

'Well, think on. No one ever wonders that inside.'

Pleasantries over, Coupland ran his hands over the file on the desk in front of him, flattening the corners. 'Now I'm going to have to caution you…'

*

Nexus House

Coupland updated the team on his return to Nexus House. 'Breakwell's adamant he hasn't killed Eliza, and as much as it pains me to admit it, I believe him.'

'Some killers get a kick out of the police running round after them for information once they're behind bars. Especially in solitary. Maybe he's holding back his confession to eke out a few more visits. I suppose even your company's better than nothing,' said DCI Swain.

'I wouldn't be so sure,' said Joe Edwards. 'Remember I'm the only one whose actually spent the night with this reprobate.'

'And I'm the one who had to explain why spooning on the back seat was wholly inappropriate,' Coupland deadpanned.

It was only when the officers around him started laughing that Coupland realised what had been missing from the unit up to that point. They'd all been so intent on getting everything right they hadn't settled into being a team. Banter, piss-taking, whatever you wanted to call it, was a way of cutting through all that, but only worked if the person doling it out was also capable of receiving it. The grin on Joe's face proof, that like Coupland, he had no problem when the joke was on him.

Superintendent Romain, preferring to maintain his distance, didn't join in with the laughter. He appeared more relaxed though, which Coupland put down to Lara Cole's absence. He guessed there really was such a thing as too many cooks, especially one that kept questioning the ingredients. 'Did you speak to the SOCO regarding the printer paper found in Breakwell's flat?' he asked DI Taylor.

'Yes. It's a match, sir.'

All eyes settled on Coupland. 'Breakwell admits he typed up the letter to make it look like it was from Eliza – and dropped it off at school – but claims he was ordered to do it by Mark Novak,' he told them.

'Did he not wonder why?' asked Edwards.

'He said it crossed his mind that Novak or his mate were going to kill her but decided there was nothing he could do.'

'Nice,' said Swain. 'And without evidence to the contrary the existence of that fabricated letter puts him in the frame for her murder.'

'I rather think that was the intention,' observed Romain. 'There've been no withdrawals from her bank or transactions made since she went missing, the only activity are direct debits that she'd set up for her gym, Netflix and house insurance.'

'What next?' asked Swain.

'The Commander is fronting a televised appeal to go out in the lunchtime and evening news. We're sharing the clip of her taking the bus to work in the hope of jogging people's memories. Social media appeals will start doing the rounds on Twitter, Facebook and Instagram. Meanwhile DI Edwards is going to lobby his contacts in the press to get them to keep the story on the front pages for the next few days.'

A tall order, only possible if it's a slow news day, Coupland reckoned, unwilling to burst anyone's bubble.

'And then?'

'If the televised appeal doesn't bring any new sightings of her, we start searching for her body.'

*

Press briefing, Hadfield Grammar School
Commander Howorth turned his sombre face to the journalists assembled for the briefing of missing newly qualified teacher Eliza Evans, unaccounted for since she unexpectedly resigned from the grammar school she'd secured a position with after qualifying. A flattering photo

of Eliza had been blown up into a poster and placed onto a board beside the Commander. The press officer had advised him to hold the press briefing in front of the school with her old colleagues in the background, due to the fact there were no grieving relatives to plead for the public's help in finding her. It was better not to emphasise the fact that nobody was missing her.

'Eliza finished what was to be her last day at school before setting off for home. We have reason to believe she didn't make it home, nor has she left the country for a job abroad, as her resignation letter stated. We are increasingly worried about her. If she is watching this, or someone is watching this who knows where she is, then I urge you to get in touch with us. We are also asking members of the public to contact us if you remember seeing Eliza on her journey to work that morning. Footage of her getting onto her regular bus and alighting at the stop closest to school will be shown directly after this message, along with ways that you can contact us.'

Representatives from a good cross-section of the press had turned up. Eliza was young, female and attractive. The perfect ingredients in a missing person piece to stir up just the right amount of moral panic. How long each journalist continued to show interest depended upon how the investigation developed, which basically meant how long it took before she turned up dead.

*

Incident Room, Nexus House
DI Taylor wasted the best part of an hour on the phone choosing options from an automated menu, before being left on hold listening to a cover version of Mamma Mia. Finally, in a fit of frustration he slammed down the

phone, jumped in his car and drove the few miles to the Toyota garage near Gorton.

He returned to the incident room two hours later holding an A4 sheet of paper with the Toyota logo on it, up in the air. 'Seven customers matched the criteria I gave them, with one partially matching the name Breakwell gave us. A Marek Nowak, which if I'm correct matches an entry in the electoral register?'

He regarded Jared, who nodded. 'I ran a PNC check on him and it's come back clean.'

'And since passmen are so-called because they have no prior convictions…' said Edwards.

'Then this is our man,' said Taylor. He read from the printout he was holding. 'Marek Nowak paid for his Hilux using the finance option. The application form he had to complete has him down as running a ground maintenance company. You know, the kind of firm that's contracted to work on new build housing developments, mowing common areas of grass and trimming the hedges?'

Coupland and Edwards nodded.

'The direct debit leaves his account on time every month. Here's his address.' Taylor handed the printout to Superintendent Romain.

'Want us to pick him up, boss?' asked Coupland.

Romain was lost in thought for a moment. He tapped the edge of the paper on his desk like a newsreader at the end of their broadcast. 'No. We watch and wait,' he said eventually. 'Search ANPR to get a picture of his movements. I'll apply for a tracker to be placed on his vehicle.'

To the rest of the team, 'If we can establish a link between him and Graham Prentice then it gives us the evidence we need to step up the surveillance on him to the next level.'

He turned to Noah. 'I want a full association chart by the end of the day. We know that Dylan Breakwell and Marek Nowak are connected, and we know that Graham Prentice and the Dutchman are connected. We now need to get the connections in the middle of this chain right.'

And if they get it wrong, thought Coupland, and these men continue to be at large. What then?

TWO MONTHS EARLIER

OCTOBER

CHAPTER SIXTEEN

BSHC Bank, Canary Wharf

DCI Amjid Akram arrived at the glass and chrome head office of BSHC Bank in Canary Wharf at 8.30am, flanked by four financial investigators. He showed his warrant card to the receptionist, stating that he needed to speak to CEO Jonathon Exmouth as a matter of urgency.

Flustered, the receptionist ran through her range of usual questions anyway, 'Is he expecting you?' followed by 'Can I ask what it's regarding?' to which Amjid didn't reply.

'I'll see if he's available,' she said eventually, before picking up her phone. She spoke into it quietly, stealing a glance at the detective to make sure he wasn't listening in.

'His executive assistant will escort you,' she said after replacing the phone in its handset. She indicated behind them towards a descending glass lift.

'Is there anything else I can help you with?' she asked as the lift doors opened.

Amjid told her there wasn't.

'Enjoy the rest of your day,' she told him.

I'm sure I will, Amjid thought, when the executive assistant, without a word of greeting, ushered them inside before pushing the express button to the executive floor.

'Mr Exmouth is a very busy man,' she attempted whilst

they were her captive audience. 'If you can give me some idea as to what this is regarding I may be able to locate the information you require without the need to disturb him.'

Amjid wasn't great with heights, had positioned himself in the centre of the lift so the officers around him obscured his view. 'Mr Exmouth will want to speak to me, regardless of his schedule,' he responded, eyes fixed on the shoulders of the officer in front of him.

'Of course, no problem at all,' Exmouth's assistant replied in a tone that suggested the opposite was closer to the truth.

When the lift doors opened she stepped out briskly, making a sharp left towards a corner office without bothering to see if the visitors had kept up with her. There was an unoccupied desk by the door, which Amjid took to be the vantage point from which she normally protected her boss. Knocking on a door marked *Jonathon Exmouth, Chief Executive Officer*, she stepped inside, appearing moments later motioning for the detectives to approach. 'Mr Exmouth will see you now,' she said, before returning to her desk, the offer of refreshments gone the same way as her smile.

This wasn't the first time Amjid was an uninvited visitor in a senior banking executive's office. He stepped forward into the room until he was standing before Exmouth's large desk, his fellow investigators keeping in step with him like some synchronised dance troupe. Amjid held out his warrant card for inspection before introducing his team. He fished a business card out of his pocket which he laid on top of the desk. *DCI Amjid Akram, Economic Crime Unit.*

Exmouth glanced at the card in the way a driver looking

for a parking place might glance at a traffic warden.

'To what do I owe this pleasure?' he asked, managing a smile, though not bothering to get out of his chair.

No matter where Amjid went they were all on the defensive. Not one bank chief confident enough in their organisation's due diligence to offer him a warmer welcome. To co-operate with his requests without threatening to get lawyered up. There'd been a trend in recent years, blind eyes turned to tax evasion while welcoming new investors and their unexplained wealth with open arms. Legislation was yet to go through parliament that would make these executives responsible, though Amjid had enough tools in his bag to get them to do his bidding without having to wait for unpassed laws.

'I'm glad you consider our presence to be pleasurable,' he said agreeably. From the safety of the centre of the room he studied the view through the floor-to-ceiling windows, his gaze settling on the building opposite. 'Your neighbours across the way there, on the other hand, gave me quite the chilly reception.'

The head of the Swiss bank that he was referring to had used his company credit card to pay for strip clubs, Tinder dates, holidays and dinners to the tune of £165,000. He was now serving four years in a Category C prison. His exit through the bank's pillared front doors handcuffed to Amjid had made front-page news.

'Rest assured, we're not here to scrutinise your expense accounts,' Amjid informed Exmouth. 'Not today, anyway,' he added, causing the officers by his side to smirk. 'What I do want is carte blanche access to your branch network, starting specifically in the northwest. We suspect a member of staff is playing fast and loose with customer accounts, though if it's happening in one area you can be assured it's happening in another,' Amjid stated. 'My investigators need immediate access to the bank's mainframe and security cameras. Our infiltration needs to be swift and confidential.'

A look of alarm flashed across the banker's face. 'Am I allowed to ask what exactly you suspect is going on?'

Amjid inclined his head a fraction. 'We've reason to believe certain members of your workforce have been passing on customer account details to a third party, and that this third party uses this information to blackmail customers into engaging in illegal activity. Given the nature of certain transactions appearing on their account they do not feel in a position to report this blackmail.'

Exmouth looked troubled. 'What is the nature of these transactions?'

'Subscriptions to a paedophile network. Fees for viewing young girls being abused online. Snuff films.'

'No one I should feel sorry for, then.'

'Maybe not. But these men have been blackmailed into performing despicable acts, including murder.'

'What's the extent of this network?'

'Europewide, possibly global.'

Exmouth considered this.

'If your bank gets tarred with this kind of crime, it could be catastrophic,' Amjid added. 'Joe Public might not understand white collar crime such as insider trading and the LIBOR scandal, but if they get wind your bank is helping recruit key players in a sex abuse ring you might as well pack up and go home now.'

'We'll do whatever you need,' Exmouth said, bowing his head.

CHAPTER SEVENTEEN

The search for Eliza Evans stepped up pace. Response to the press appeal had been disappointing. Too many months had elapsed for the public to recall with any certainty the last sighting of her. A large number of the volunteers who turned up to help with the search had their own attention-seeking agenda. Influencers posting selfies on social media or live streaming their efforts on Tik Tok.

Cell site analysis showed that Eliza's phone was last operational the afternoon Kate Whiting, the school secretary at Hadfield Grammar School, received a text from her saying she'd arrived in Thailand safe and well. Except the cell site it pinged from was located in the North West of England rather than the Far East. Less than five miles from the school. The most recent activity prior to that was Eliza's last day at work. She'd scrolled through social media sites during her lunch break then at 16.27 that afternoon her phone was switched off.

Thirty officers had been deployed to carry out a finger-tip search of the woodland surrounding her home and the fields bordering onto the school. Located in a rural area, there was no CCTV surrounding the school beyond the property itself. If she'd climbed into a car that had pulled up beyond the school gates there was no way of knowing.

Forensic scenes of crime officers attended Eliza's home, looking for bloodstains or evidence of cleaned-up blood. The contents of her rubbish bin were bagged and searched. The clothes in her laundry basket sent for forensic analysis. They removed her toothbrush, hairbrush and bedside paperback to determine her fingerprints and DNA. A check of the garden failed to find any freshly dug or recently planted areas. It wasn't unusual for killers to dispose of bodies close to home for fear of their vehicle being stopped and searched or being involved in a crash. As the search progressed a drone was brought in, enabling the search team to do a wider sweep of the area.

If Eliza was dead by the time Breakwell passed off his forged resignation letter as hers, then her body would have already significantly decomposed, making the task of forensic examination increasingly difficult. Given her home bordered on woodland, the possibility of her being buried there was high, giving risk to animals carrying off body parts to forage on. If she had been buried in a shallow grave then there was every chance her body would be gone. Cadaver dogs were brought in to facilitate the search.

Assuming there was anything left of Eliza to find.

CHAPTER EIGHTEEN

City of London Police HQ, London

DCI Amjid Akram skim-read through the report that had been handed to him by a member of his forensic examination team.

Via camera security checks and electronic footsteps on BSHC Bank's mainframe, a bank employee by the name of Jennifer Shimmin was identified as the person whose password had been used to carry out transaction searches on customer accounts for purchases made on the dark web. Based at the bank's city centre offices in Manchester, she was Credit Card Fraud Team Leader. It was her job to review and authorise suspicious-looking transactions referred to her by her team. All the while she was compiling her own list of customers with dubious spending patterns for her own nefarious purposes. Amjid couldn't think of a job role better placed to accumulate this information.

On one occasion a security camera caught her entering a branch interview room and inserting a KVM switch – a hardware device that enabled a user to control multiple computers from one keyboard – into a laptop, gaining access to the bank's internal systems. Once in she was able to run a number of searches for customers with transactions that originated from the dark web. She was seen copying this information onto a memory stick before leaving the branch to go on her lunch break. Covert surveillance officers positioned across the road from the bank photographed her handing the memory stick to an unidentified man outside Pret a Manger on King Street.

Selling on this information was clearly lucrative. Each day Shimmin was under surveillance she wore high end clothing teamed with designer bags and shoes. Her tan suggested she splashed out on a lot of foreign holidays.

Two weeks after receiving Superintendent Romain's initial request to find the leak in BSHC Bank, Amjid contacted him to provide an update.

*

Incident Room, Nexus House
Coupland's mood after Superintendent Romain's phone conversation with DCI Amjid Akram was a damn sight better than it had been before it. The forensic search of Eliza Evans's property found no sign of blood or unexplained DNA. All that meant with any degree of certainty was that she hadn't been attacked at home. The Super had announced the search for her body was being scaled down, but Coupland knew what it really meant. 'Yeah, like when your ex tells you they want a break but there's a strange car parked outside your front door and some Boyzone member lookalike is loading her suitcase into the boot.'

'You've just described my last break up, only she swore it was only temporary,' said DI Taylor.

Coupland regarded him. 'And how long ago was that, dare I ask?'

'Two years and nine months, not that I'm counting,' he

answered, looking glum.

'The investigation will continue as a "no body" murder,' Romain reiterated, before answering his desk phone. 'Amjid…' he said, reaching for his desk pad and pen.

'But there's no closure without a body,' said Noah, reminding them how for someone who rumour had it had hacked into GCHQ as a student, he was inexperienced in the ways of the world.

'The fact there are no relatives to want closure makes it an easy decision,' Coupland explained in the voice a parent might use to tell their child Santa wasn't real.

He wondered how this generation got rid of the horrors of the day. Several cans before logging onto Call of Duty, perhaps. An evening spent obliterating evil, even if it was only in the virtual world.

When Romain's call ended he logged into his emails, peering closely at something on-screen before raising his voice to share the news.

'Amjid's team have found the bank employee responsible for passing on customer account details to the Dutchman's network. Going by what he's sent through they've gathered enough evidence for us to arrest her immediately. I want you to bring her in…' he said to DCI Swain, forwarding the bank employee's details to Swain's inbox. 'Then I want you to persuade her to arrange a meeting with the person she's been passing the information onto,' he said to DI Taylor.

'Joe, Kevin, hang fire for now. If she's willing to cooperate and set up a meeting with this chap then I want you two to swoop in and pick him up.'

'Now you're talking,' said Coupland, his frustration

that Eliza Evans's body hadn't been recovered yet temporarily forgotten.

*

BSHC Bank staff car park, Manchester City Centre branch
Jennifer Shimmin smiled distractedly at the man who climbed out of his car at the same time as she'd stopped beside her own vehicle, a BMW 3 series, her hand feeling around in the bottom of her bag for her keys. She was about to say something inane like can't see for looking when he moved towards her, something resembling an ID badge in his hand.

She waited politely while the officer cautioned her. She'd seen folk get arrested on TV, on those fly-on-the-wall programmes where camera crews follow a police van round, filming officers as they pull bags of weed out of teenagers' pockets after chasing them through ginnels. She had no intention of putting on a show for anyone by resisting arrest. Not as though she could, even if she wanted to, in these heels. His colleague stepped out of the passenger side of the car, moved to the rear door closest to where she was standing. Held it open. She nodded quickly to show they'd get no trouble from her.

*

Briefing, Nexus House
'Her ex-boyfriend was the one who got her involved. Someone had damaged her car and driven off while it was parked at the supermarket. Left her with repair costs of fifteen hundred pounds and a job that required her

to have a vehicle to drive between different offices. The boyfriend – as he was then – said he knew someone who'd pay good money for customer account lists. Sold them onto rival firms.' DCI Swain talked the team through Jennifer Shimmin's statement.

'She worked for a bloody bank. Couldn't she get a loan, an overdraft even, for Christ's sake?' asked Coupland.

'She'd already exhausted her credit options. Was no stranger to living beyond her means,' said Swain.

'So, she met with this guy…' prompted Coupland, keen to learn the extent of her involvement.

'Who told her he was only interested in certain types of transactions, the kind nobody wanted to be visible on their accounts. She told him she knew what he was after. That she and her colleagues would snigger every time they saw transactions from a porn site or sex shop. He explained that wasn't what he was meaning. That he was looking for transactions from sites a lot darker than that. The kind that the police, if they ever saw what these people were buying, would be very interested in.'

'So what exactly did she think she was getting mixed up in?' asked Edwards.

Coupland was wondering the same thing.

'Blackmail, pure and simple. As far as she knew, the data she was passing on was used to extort money from terrified paedophiles.'

'That's OK then,' said Coupland, only half joking.

'A search of her home has uncovered several memory sticks full of data…' stated DI Taylor, who'd conducted the interview alongside the DCI.

'You mean lists of nonces and their buying habits,' Coupland stated.

Taylor nodded in agreement, '…along with twenty grand in cash.'

'She's prepared to cooperate fully. Hoping for a conviction for extorting money rather than anything that ends up with her going on the sex offenders register,' added DCI Swain. 'She's already provided the names of two other bank clerks she'd roped into the scam, one based in the North East branch and one who works for a competitor.'

Superintendent Romain nodded. 'Be sure to pass on this information to Amjid. His team's surveillance at the bank is ongoing and may well result in other employees being referred to the relevant regional organised crime gang units around the country.' It did no harm to throw a bone to other divisions. You never knew when you'd need the favour reciprocating.

'Sir,' Taylor replied.

'And the piece of work she passes this "data" onto,' said Coupland, for want of a better word, 'did she give you a name?'

Taylor shook his head. 'She only knows him as "Chadders", that was the name her ex used when he put her in touch with him. He was just an acquaintance, he knew him in passing, that was all. Having said that, she has a direct dial number for him which she has called under my supervision, and has arranged to meet with him tomorrow.'

At last, they were moving up the chain.

CHAPTER NINETEEN

St. Ann's Square, Manchester City Centre

St. Ann's Square was a pedestrianised public square in the heart of Manchester's city centre, flanked by churches and high-end shops. It was here that many of the flowers, balloons and candles had been laid in memory of those killed after the Manchester Arena bombing.

Coupland took a sip of his takeaway coffee and glanced at his watch. The bastard was late. Either that or he'd got wind of Jennifer Shimmin's arrest and had no intention of turning up. DI Taylor had listened in while Jennifer had made the call. Had given her the thumbs up when 'Chadders' suggested the Starbucks on the corner. She'd told Taylor she'd met him there a few times. It was close enough to her work she could slip out whenever she wanted, and not far from the designer stores she was so fond of frequenting in her lunch hour. Chadders wasn't to know that instead of coming from work she'd been released temporarily from police custody. They'd instructed her to sit at a table outside. To keep her hands on her lap, only moving them onto the table when she was handing over the memory stick. She mustn't leave it on the table, they'd stressed, she had to hand it to him, and more important, he needed to be seen holding it.

Two tables along, a female surveillance officer pretended to take Instagram-worthy photos of her latte

247

with her phone. A quick nod at Coupland told him she had the angle she needed to capture the handover.

Coupland glanced at his watch once more and sighed. His own takeaway coffee was tepid and he'd spent the best part of twenty minutes staring at designer watches in the jeweller's window opposite the coffee chain. Joe Edwards, standing by the war memorial in the centre of the square, pretended to talk into his phone.

For the second time while Coupland had been there the jeweller's door opened and a fat-necked security guard stepped out to give him the once-over before moving a few feet away to light up. Seeing others smoke had the same effect on Coupland as watching someone yawn. Placing his coffee cup on a nearby bin he located his cigarettes and lighter, using this opportunity to survey his surroundings. The morning rush hour was over. The people out now were in no hurry to go about their day. Two women strolled through the square pushing grizzling toddlers in buggies. A glum-faced couple sat on a bench. A man around retirement age dressed in lycra leaned against the perimeter wall of the church doing stretches. Coupland had no idea what he'd do if he had time on his hands. Tonto had put paid to that, but even so, it wasn't like there was anything he hankered after. He'd never been one for hobbies. Or exercise. Or mixing with other folk if he didn't have to. An image of his old man getting shit-faced in his sheltered housing flat loomed before him. *Make an effort, knobhead*, he muttered. The security guard threw him a look before stubbing out his cigarette and returning to his post.

Keen to rid his head of mawkish thoughts, Coupland slipped out his phone and dialled Joe Edwards' number.

'Reckon he's a no show?' he asked.

Edwards stole a glance in his direction before turning back to face Starbucks. 'Give him time,' he said.

Coupland's shoulders dipped. 'I'm going to have to find somewhere else to stand. The fella on security keeps giving me the beady eye.'

'P'raps he knows there's not a snowball in Hell's chance of you buying anything from there.'

'How very dare he, then!' Coupland shot back. 'For all he knows I might have won the lottery.'

'If you had, surely the first thing you'd do is go clothes shopping,' Edwards quipped, turning to give him the once-over. In anticipation of today's arrest Coupland had ditched his usual cop-in-a-suit attire in favour of his hooded sweatshirt and jeans. He wore a padded jacket over the top of it, which granted, he'd had his doubts about, but Lynn and Amy could be persuasive. Coupland was about to say something derogatory to Edwards when the other officer's face grew serious. Something beyond Coupland's shoulder had caught his eye. 'The eagle has landed and is about to fly right by you,' he said, stepping back.

Coupland willed himself not to turn around. Keeping his phone clamped to his ear he studied Chadder's reflection in the shop window as he walked past. Shimmin had described him as medium build and wiry, said he'd acted a bit cocksure for her liking, but business was business. Coupland could see what she meant, clocking the swagger as he headed towards their rendezvous. Bandy legs, arms bent like a cowboy reaching for his holster. He didn't look as though he was concealing a weapon, there were no tell-tale bulges around his hips or waist. Some fellas just liked taking up as much room as possible, reckoned it made them look bigger.

Coupland stayed in position, watching as Chadders glanced up and down the square before dropping into the seat opposite Jennifer. He took a sip of the iced tea she'd ordered for him, neither of them bothering with small talk. Without waiting to be asked Jennifer reached into her bag, pulling out the memory stick before placing it on the table between them.

'Shit!' Coupland spoke low into his phone. She wasn't supposed to leave it there, she was supposed to put it in his hand.

The female officer at the table adjacent to them looked as though she was checking for messages on her phone. She didn't bother tapping on the camera icon. There was no point taking photographs yet, Chadders hadn't done anything incriminating.

As though realising her mistake Jennifer covered the memory stick with her hand, gesturing with her free hand that she wanted something in return. Chadders frowned. Shrugging, he reached inside his zip-up top and pulled out an envelope which he dropped onto the table. Jennifer removed her hand from the memory stick and picked up the envelope, peeking inside before nodding and placing it in her bag. 'Come on…' Coupland muttered. The WPC angled her phone, ready to take pretend photos of her tepid coffee.

Using the back of his legs to push back his chair, Chadders got to his feet. He picked up his drink and swigged back the contents.

'Come on…' Coupland repeated.

In his peripheral vision the doorway of the jewellers

opened. The security guard marched out, angling his head in Coupland's direction. He opened his mouth.

'Do one,' Coupland hissed before he had a chance to say anything, turning in his direction to bare his teeth.

The security guard slunk back inside the store.

Coupland's attention returned to the coffee shop opposite. To the table that still had a memory stick on it. To the shyster who was about to leave empty handed.

'Nice doing business with you,' Chadders said, placing his empty cup beside Jennifer's latte mug. Another sideways glance in both directions then he picked the memory stick up.

A nod from the female officer that the action had been caught on camera and both detectives walked briskly towards the table. Chadders had just pocketed the stick when a twenty-a-day voice growled his name. Turning, he saw two men stride purposefully towards him. The one that grabbed his arm was a mean-looking fucker and he'd worked for some mean fuckers in his time. His ginger haired companion showed Chadders his warrant card before reading his rights. The mean looking one twisted his arms behind his back. Kept on twisting.

*

Nexus House

The atmosphere in the interview room was electric. 'Chadders', aka Andrew Chadderton according to the ID in his possession when he was checked into the custody suite, lived in Sale, on the outskirts of Greater Manchester. Interrogation of his bank accounts and online presence revealed that he was married with two kids, a mortgage, car finance, and a Facebook page from where he ran an executive travel business. His website boasted a fleet of black Mercedes. A publicity photo had been taken of them, parked in front of what looked like a stately home.

'Where's his wife now?' asked Superintendent Romain.

'Took the kids to stay at her sister's when we turned up to search the family home. From the size of the bag she took with her I think she'll be gone for some time,' DI Taylor informed him.

'He's got previous, sir,' said Jared. 'Served three years for blackmail and extortion.'

'Ideal qualities if your job's recruiting paedophiles into an illicit network,' said DCI Swain. 'Check out the cons he associated with inside. Might give us a fast track to others in his line of work.'

'Will do, sir,' Jared answered, making a note into the jotter on his desk.

'What did the search on his property throw up?'

'We found just shy of forty grand in cash, sir. Multiple electronic devices and burner phones. We also found a stash of memory sticks going back over several years, the sheer volume suggests he has dozens of bank staff providing him with data,' reported DI Taylor.

'We carried out a search and found Dylan Breakwell's details on one of the memory sticks,' added Noah. So, Andrew Chadderton had recruited Breakwell.

'Nice one!' said Coupland. 'Am I the only one who feels like Christmas has come early?'

'He's certainly our golden goose,' agreed Romain. 'We just need to work out where we want him to lead us before we go in that interview room.'

'What's wrong with going in there and winging it

a little?'

'There's every chance he'll throw us the low hanging fruit in order to protect those further up the food chain.'

'I thought he was a goose, boss, what's he doing throwing fruit?'

'I think, DS Coupland, that if we question him without sufficient knowledge of his position in the network, the eggs he'll be laying for us will be more your battery farmed variety rather than solid eighteen carat.' The Super had a point.

DI Taylor provided an update on Marek Nowak. 'Apart from his home, the tracker on his car shows him moving between the same three sites in Stockport. I've checked them out and they're all legit housing developments, with his firm contracted to maintain the grounds.'

'Any newly dug borders or recently installed kiddie playgrounds?' asked Coupland, his thoughts returning to the whereabouts of Eliza Evans. They already knew Nowak disposed of Helen Harper's body – Breakwell had told them as much. His hands were definitely dirty.

'I went to each site myself. There was nothing obvious,' Taylor replied.

'Did you refer to the site plan on each development?' asked Romain, his mind moving along the same line as Coupland's. 'Made sure nothing has been added that wasn't in the original specification?'

Taylor's hesitation gave them the answer. 'Damn,' he muttered, his face clouding over. 'Sorry everyone. I'll get onto it straight away.'

Coupland knew what it was like to be on the receiving end of Romain's pursed lips. 'No harm done,' he said, 'we're looking at body retrieval, not rescue.'

The death stare Romain sent in his direction told him he was overstepping the mark. Perhaps in his book only those with the rank of inspector or above were permitted to show empathy, Coupland thought sourly.

He regarded the association chart Noah had constructed for Marek Nowak. His gaze running along the list of friends he saw regularly. Colleagues. People he socialised with on an occasional basis. None of their names appeared on anyone else's association chart.

'Are you checking for sports clubs or medical centres they have in common?' Coupland asked aloud. 'Do their kids go to the same school?'

'They're all in different towns, Sarge,' said Jared.

'Maybe we're looking at this the wrong way. Association charts matter more when we're dealing with the movers and shakers in this network. If we start thinking of the Dutchman as the Chief Executive of Utopian Enterprises then the people he associates with in the network are his board of directors – the door openers and palm greasers of this set-up – whereas Breakwell and Nowak are foot soldiers. They don't mix with each other outside of work because their roles require little in the way of socialising. They are sent to do a job and they do it. Dylan Breakwell works on the production line and Marek Nowak is responsible for quality control. Between them they make sure the goods – the videos, the "live entertainment" nights – meet the network's grubby standards, removing anything that might cause a problem.'

'Like Helen Harper?' asked Jared.

'Yes, exactly like Helen Harper, or anyone else who asks questions or starts being difficult,' agreed Coupland.

Taylor nodded. 'We know that Andrew Chadderton

recruited Dylan Breakwell and paired him with Marek Nowak. It's clear that he's been a significant part of the supply chain. Remember, he's the one who contacts the customers on those bank transaction lists. The one who works out who is capable of grooming and committing abuse, and who is capable of killing, or disposing of bodies.'

'He's like a one-man Job Centre Plus for nonces,' Coupland summarised.

'It's one thing exploiting someone's perversion by incentivising them with more of the same if they agree to make films and host parties, but how do you get them to kill?' asked Edwards.

'Motivate them with money?' suggested Taylor.

DCI Swain didn't look convinced. 'That'd have to be one hell of a financial reward to make murder appealing.'

Coupland wasn't so sure. 'It's all relative. I've known fellas who'd kill for the price of a pair of trainers,' he said eventually.

'Yeah, but these passmen are so called because they have no criminal record. Of "good character" in any cop's book. To go from unblemished to killing on demand…' stated Edwards.

Coupland was inclined to agree. Try as he might, he couldn't fathom out what they stood to gain. The Super was right, the only person who could help them work this out was cooling his heels in the custody suite. Meanwhile the PACE clock was ticking. They had to use the next few hours wisely.

'How do you suggest we handle Nowak then, Boss?' asked Coupland.

Romain considered this. 'We stay at arm's length. If

we track his movements long enough he may lead us to others like Breakwell. We don't know for certain the size of this network, but let's reel as many of these bastards in as we can.'

It was reassuring to hear the Super swear. It made him appear human. That getting a result mattered because of the lives that would be saved rather than the career opportunity it offered.

Romain got to his feet. 'I need to update Superintendent Cole and the Commander on our interview strategy,' he said, his face suggesting this was a task he didn't relish.

'I didn't know we'd actually agreed on one,' said Swain.

'We haven't,' Romain admitted. 'Though no one outside this room needs to know that. I've taken the decision that in the absence of an alternative I'll take a leaf out of DS Coupland's book for once and wing it.'

Noah glanced up from behind his computer screen. 'Sir, can I show you this before you go?' He waited for Romain's nod. 'Andrew Chadderton's Facebook posts are mainly photos of him and his drivers ferrying rich tourists around the city, but I think you'll be interested in a photo he posted a couple of months ago.'

Romain peered over Noah's shoulder to get a better look, his face brightening. 'Damn right I'm interested,' he concurred, a grin splitting his face from ear to ear. 'The others need to see this. Put it on the big screen!'

Noah did as instructed, his fingers flying quickly across his keyboard. A final click and the image appeared on the wall-mounted screen for everyone to see.

The photograph was a selfie. Chadderton kitted out in a chauffeur's uniform, standing in front of one of his gleaming Mercedes. In the background stood the

Drummond Hotel, resplendent after a recent makeover. It wasn't the selfie as such that had caught Noah's attention, nor was that the cause of Romain's obvious delight. It was the couple caught in the background, walking down the hotel steps towards the waiting vehicle, that set the room buzzing. Graham Prentice, dressed in black tie. His work colleague, socialite Ruth Hunter Pepper in a shimmering dress beside him.

'Get in!' growled Coupland, punching the air.

'Are we looking at a crazy coincidence here?' asked Edwards.

'I'm not a gambling man,' said Coupland, 'but if I was, I'd bet my house, my pension and the clothes on my back that this isn't the first job he's done for Prentice. That now we've found this connection we'll unearth a shedload more.'

Coupland turned to Superintendent Romain. 'I think you've just got your interview strategy, sir,' he said, hoping to Christ he'd get the opportunity to sit across from Andrew Chadderton and look him in the eye.

'I think you might be right,' said Romain, his smile making him look ten years younger.

*

When the Super returned, the photograph of Andrew Chadderton, Graham Prentice and Ruth Hunter Pepper had been placed on the top of another new whiteboard with arrows and lines now going in several directions.

'The Commander has approved my request to increase the surveillance on both Graham Prentice, and Ruth Hunter Pepper. We are going to red flag all of their contacts.'

This meant that covert intelligence would be gathered on every person they associated with. A significant and expensive undertaking, but the fact it had been approved meant that top brass – in this case Commander Howorth's level and above – agreed that Prentice and Hunter Pepper were the most likely route to the Dutchman.

Even so. Coupland massaged the back of his neck with his hand, his fingers kneading the top of his spine. Why did he get the feeling Romain was holding something back? 'Did the Commander say anything else, Boss?' he asked.

Romain frowned. The grin he'd sported less than an hour ago already a distant memory.

'The Commander has taken a call from his equal number in the Netherlands regarding the forensics gathered from the torture chamber they discovered at Rotterdam.'

'The one that came with its own dentist chair and pliers?' asked Coupland.

'Yes,' Romain replied. 'At the time of discovery we understood the remains found at the site belonged to human traffickers suspected of double crossing the Dutchman.' His voice took on a sombre tone. 'However, the DNA of several missing girls has also been identified.' He paused to let that settle in. 'Specifically, DNA belonging to two schoolgirls reported missing from their home in Antwerp in 2015. Dutch police have since found images and film clips recording their abuse, uploaded onto Utopia.'

Coupland felt as though he'd been slammed in the chest. His brain went into go slow mode as he tried to compute what the Super was saying. Hoped to Christ he'd got it wrong. 'Hang on a minute, sir. Are you saying a monster belonging to this network abducted these girls and tortured them online in 2015? That the link to those images has been available for other sickos to watch all this time?'

Superintendent Romain shook his head.

'Then what are you saying, sir?' asked Noah. The room went quiet.

'The first videos of the girls were posted online in 2015. More followed at regular intervals. In each one they look older. Emaciated, but older nevertheless. Their murders were filmed and posted online this year – six weeks before police raided the site.'

The room fell silent as the detectives gathered round digested this.

'So they've been alive all this time, held captive by the network?' Coupland clarified, not yet able to believe it.

Romain's nod was slow.

'This changes everything,' stated DCI Swain.

'How?' asked Coupland.

'It means that despite keeping several steps ahead of us the Dutchman is feeling the pressure.'

Coupland addressed his next question to the Super: 'He was seen close to that site prior to the raid, wasn't he? We saw the photo taken of him – the one where I ID'd him – coming out of that restaurant.'

Superintendent Romain nodded.

'We know he's scaling down his operations to stay below the radar,' said DCI Swain. 'Killing off the girls he's holding captive is another way of obliterating any link that leads us to him.'

Coupland picked up Swain's line of thought. 'What if

he's got similar set ups over here? His presence in Greater Manchester, right now, may be more significant than we realise. He could be overseeing victims as they are literally sent to the slaughter.'

Romain's nod confirmed they weren't alone in that view.

'Gold Command has upgraded his presence here as posing an imminent threat to life. He must be stopped by any means necessary.'

Coupland was aware of Superintendent Cole's absence. He wondered what her response had been when informed of Gold Command's decision. Lara Cole, responsible for oversight, who required clarification for everything, would have wanted to know what was meant by those three words. *Any means necessary*.

Coupland understood the potential risk. A reprimand. A disciplinary. A jettison off the force if it went belly up. But if they got it right. If they risked everything and got it right…

'I've prepared an interview strategy for Andrew Chadderton. The Commander wants you in with me,' Romain said, eyeballing Coupland.

Coupland got to his feet.

*

Interview room, Nexus House

Andrew Chadderton, AKA Chadders to his mates, sat stony faced while Coupland went through formal introductions and digital recording formalities. Chadderton had asked for the solicitor sitting beside him by name, rather than accept the duty solicitor, and they'd spent their first five minutes together discussing each other's children. Some lags preferred to stick with the same lawyer throughout their criminal career, made the paper trail simpler for a start.

Coupland sat on his hands while Superintendent Romain asked a series of 'safe' questions, aimed to determine Chadders' capacity for lying and whether he was any good at it. All well and good under normal circumstances, but then the current circumstances could hardly be described as that.

As though reading Coupland's mind, Romain quickly got down to the reason they'd brought him in. 'I have officers going through the items removed from your home with a fine-toothed comb. Your laptop, notebook, memory sticks, you name it. We have already found files containing the personal details of BSHC bank customers – among others – who made purchases from illegal sites on the dark web, including Utopian Enterprises. Purchases that identified them as potential candidates for the paedophile pyramid scheme you were recruiting for.'

Chadders' face cleared. 'Oh, I get it. Well, it explains why that double-crossing tart was so keen to meet me today. I take it she's hung me out to dry?'

'You can hardly blame her,' said Romain, 'once she understood the gravity of the situation...'

'She decided to point her finger in the opposite direction,' Chadders finished for him.

'It's our understanding that Ms Shimmin was unaware of the intended purpose of those files.'

'No shit?'

'You, on the other hand,' said Coupland, 'knew damn well who and what you were looking for. Like my boss here says, there are officers working through the data found on your property as we speak.'

There was a knock on the interview room door. Coupland got to his feet, opened it wide enough for Noah to hand him a sheet of paper. He glanced at the content, reading it a second time when he got to the end, his pulse quickening. He winked at Noah before closing the door and returning to his seat, laying the paper on top of the case file he'd brought in earlier. He leaned forward, placed his hands on the tabletop to indicate to Romain that he wanted to ask the next question.

'You know, Andrew – you don't mind if I call you Andrew, do you?' he asked.

He was rewarded with a shrug. 'Call me what you like, makes no difference to me.'

Coupland smiled as he silently ran through all the names he'd much rather be using. Names which, if they hit their target, would get a lively response. Now wasn't the time for that kind of needling though. He'd save that pleasure for later. 'I've been looking at your file, Andrew. I see you spent three years inside. Must have been tough.'

'Had its moments.'

'Care to share any of them with us?'

'Not really.'

'I hear you had a hard time of it when you first went in. Bit of a gobshite by all accounts. According to the hall manager on your wing the prison officers had to lock you up during association time for your own safety. Reckoned you never knew when to keep it buttoned.'

Coupland made a point of looking at the report in front of him. Waited while Chadders followed his gaze. 'Six months in and everything changed. The other inmates stopped taking a pop at you. Your cell could be left open during recreation, and you even got a job on the landing. Now, either you saw the error of your ways and stopped rubbing folk up the wrong way, or someone started protecting you. I've got to say my money's on the latter. Call me old fashioned, it's just a feeling I have. You know, how leopards don't change their spots as often as they make out. Once a gobshite always a gobshite in my book. So, what I want to know is, who was it started watching your back?'

Chadders cocked his head. 'Why does it matter?'

Coupland sat back in his chair. Not quite enjoying himself, but close enough. 'Because everything in prison has a currency. Someone does you a good turn, you have to do something for them in return. It's one of those unwritten rules that you ignore at your peril. By all accounts you spent the remaining two and a half years throwing your bantam weight around without a single incident. Whoever had your back had something special in mind for you. Did they tell you at the outset what your debt was going to be?'

Chadders was already shaking his head. 'It wasn't like that.'

'It never is. At first. Then before you know it they turn up at your cell door with a bag of drugs they want you to hide. Except they had something special in mind for you, didn't they? Must have done a bit of homework into your past. Then again, you'd made it easy for them, bragging to everyone who'd listen about the bank manager you'd blackmailed into crediting large sums of money into your account. You'd been seeing her, what, for a couple of weeks when you started asking her to push through a loan you'd applied for. When she refused you threatened to tell her husband about the two of you in the back of her car if she didn't play ball. In the end she relented but it didn't stop there. Every few weeks you'd give her a call, next thing a couple of grand would arrive in your account as if by magic.'

Chadders smirked at the memory.

'Happy days, eh? In the end she had enough. Confessed to her husband and her line manager, went home that night and topped herself. I'm guessing your lack of remorse makes you an ideal candidate for someone looking to hire a blackmailer. Someone skilled at making people do things against their will, at least long enough until they realise they're enjoying it, and that person was you.'

'I'd have brought my waders if I'd known you were taking my client on a fishing trip, DS Coupland,' said Chadderton's solicitor.

'Better hold on tight then,' said Coupland, 'I've a feeling we're about to get into some choppy water.'

He regarded Chadders once more. 'This fella. The one who had your back. Did he come right out and tell you he worked for a paedo ring or did he leave you to work it out?'

Chadders sighed. 'It wasn't like that, alright? We didn't discuss work in the beginning. We just got talking one day, after this bastard had beat the crap out of me for giving 'im a bit of banter. He claimed I was out of order but I'm not into all that "respect your elders" shit. Seems to me there's a lot of fellas in jail who can't take a joke.'

'A life sentence can do that to a man,' observed Coupland.

'He asked me what line of work I was in. I told him. He said he could sort me out with something a lot more lucrative if I went to work for him when I got out. In return he'd look out for me, make sure I didn't end up in the infirmary. Seemed like a no-brainer.'

'And the name of this charmer?'

Chadders smiled, triumphant. 'Aw, shame, is he not on that sheet your hoppo brought in?'

Coupland turned his attention to the report in front of him. Made a show of running his finger down the names the prison hall manager had provided. Nodded as though conceding Chadders' point.

'I understand these are the people you hung around with inside,' Coupland said. 'If I need to, I'll contact every last one of them. Let them know that as an associate of yours they are now under investigation for their part in a global nonce ring.'

Chadders stared at Coupland. 'You can't do that!'

'Oh, I can, and I'll be doing that the moment this interview ends.' Coupland made a point of counting the names aloud. 'One, two, three, four, five…' He regarded Chadders' solicitor. 'Once I caught a fish alive.' He grinned. 'That was just for you…'

Then back at Chadders: 'That's five lags I'll be speaking to. Five old-school cons who'll be mightily pissed to see the police at their door. Or the tactical unit if I really want to mix things up a little.'

The solicitor tutted before addressing Superintendent Romain, a pained look on her face. 'Are you really going to let him sabotage the interview by making false claims?'

Romain threw her a look. 'We've reason to believe the network your client works for poses an imminent threat to life. I can assure you there's nothing false about the so-called claims my detective sergeant is making.'

Chadders' face fell. 'Hang on a minute. What's this about a threat to life? I can't be held responsible for the actions of others.'

'You mean the monsters you recruited? The ones you persuaded to groom underage girls, with the added incentive of employee "perks".' Coupland shuddered. 'Remind me what that included again… Trying out the goods? Taking a starring role in their dodgy home movies?'

Chadders said nothing.

'Remember Dylan Breakwell? A schoolteacher now on remand for a string of offences including murder. He was one of your recruits. We have reason to believe you introduced him to his passman, Marek Nowak, who may well be looking at perverting the course of justice and unlawful disposal of a body, at the very least.'

'I don't know what you're talking about.'

'Oh, and we're looking at conspiracy to murder for you, in case you're interested.'

Chadders opened and closed his mouth but no sound came out.

'I'm sure your lawyer would like to say the case against you isn't as bad as it looks but at the fees she's charging that would be just wrong.'

'I didn't conspire with anyone to commit murder!' Chadders spluttered. 'Fucksake, you've got to believe me!'

'I'm sure you'll keep telling yourself that,' said Coupland, 'but in your heart of hearts, this whole business must have smelt very fishy.' He glanced back at the solicitor, as if saying *see what I did there*.

'Look, I knew there was bad stuff going on, and since

it involved nonces it wasn't difficult to work out what the bad stuff was likely to be. But anything more than that?' Chadders shook his head vehemently. 'There's no way I'd get involved!'

'What were you told the passmen did?'

'They moved girls and punters around. End of.'

'Like a taxi service?'

A shrug.

Coupland scratched his chin. 'That doesn't make sense. You run a transport business. If all that was needed were lifts here and there surely you could have provided that?'

'Mine's more for high-end clients, executive travel and all that,' he said.

'Rather than terrified girls and bodies that need getting rid of,' added Coupland.

Chadders looked down at the table. There weren't many places to look in an interview room where you couldn't be sure you weren't being scrutinised. Whether by the person doing the interrogating or their colleagues watching remotely.

Coupland shared a look with Romain. A brief nod told him it was time to throw Chadderton a lifeline. 'No matter what you're convicted with it's safe to say you'll serve time. But what you choose to do over the course of the next few hours could make a significant difference to the sentence you're given.'

Chadders' head lifted. 'How much difference?'

'Hard to be specific,' said Romain.

Coupland painted a much clearer picture. 'Could be the difference between that wife of yours coming to see you regular as clockwork or sending you a Dear John letter in time for your next anniversary.'

Chadders stared at him.

'And those kids of yours calling another man Daddy.'

The con's face grew pale.

Coupland made a sympathetic clucking noise. 'Children, eh? The reason we age so quickly and the reason we cherish every day.' He leaned forward, as though they were the only people in the room. It took some effort to look like he gave a crap about Chadders' future but no one could accuse him of not going the extra mile. 'Now if we could show the CPS that you were willing to help us, and that all you were really involved in was the recruitment side of the operation, then that future of yours could start to look a lot rosier than it does right now. A CPS deal and a sympathetic jury, well, you could be back home in the bosom of your family long before they realised they weren't missing much.'

Chadders opened his mouth to object to Coupland's insult; a glance at his lawyer made him close it again.

Nearly there, thought Coupland. One more twist and we're home and dry.

'We're all guilty of assuming things, Andrew. That's how mistakes happen.'

Chadders' eyes narrowed. 'What do you mean?'

'Don't assume I'm as daft as I look, and I won't assume you feel indebted to the fella who roped you into all this.'

Coupland placed the first of two photographs on the table. A screen shot of the selfie Chadders took in his chauffer's uniform outside the Drummond Hotel. 'Remember taking this?' he asked. An innocuous question, met with a confident nod.

Coupland smiled appreciatively. There weren't many perks to his job but waiting for some lowlife to put their foot in it and carry on digging was right up there on his leader board of magic moments.

With the dexterity of a croupier on a blackjack table he placed a blown-up shot of the same selfie on the table beside it. His smile grew. In this photo Graham Prentice and Ruth Hunter Pepper could be seen heading towards Chadders' chauffer-driven Mercedes.

Chadders' face fell.

'What about this couple?' Coupland asked. He made the question sound like an afterthought. The 'silver bullet' to catch him unawares. 'They high-end enough for you?'

Chadders folded his arms across his body as though his hands needed to do the work of his ribs. He looked as though he was going to collapse in on himself, nowhere near as confident as he had been ten minutes earlier. It never ceased to amaze Coupland how some criminals failed to grasp the basic principle of cops and robbers. That when caught with their hand in the till or holding the smoking gun they had the audacity to think they'd been hard done to. That their life of criminality was going oh so well until the nasty copper came along and ruined everything.

Coupland waited.

'It was a fare, that's all. A corporate booking to take a couple of lah-de-dahs to some posh knees up.'

'You see, that's what I thought, wasn't it?' Coupland said, turning to the Super to corroborate his claim.

'Understandable, given the context of the picture,' agreed Romain.

'Yeah, only it got me to thinking. There's been a tracker on this fella's car for quite some time, yet we've got nothing on him. Not in terms of the places he visits,

269

anyway. Nothing *incriminating.*

He turned to the superintendent, 'Is that the right word, boss?' he asked, waiting for Romain to nod.

'Sounds accurate to me.'

Coupland smiled appreciatively. 'So it got me wondering. The fella in this picture. This Graham Prentice. What if he uses *your* cars to go about his business? I mean, we haven't been tracking your vehicles so we're none the wiser where you've been taking him.'

Romain spoke next. 'However, we do have a trace on his finances. So we'll be able to get a list of all the bookings he's made with you over recent months.'

'And just to be on the safe side, in case your booking system leaves a lot to be desired, we'll also check with the ANPR camera network. That way we'll get to see exactly where your shiny fleet of vehicles go to every day.'

'A tad clunky but it gets results,' said Romain.

'A bit like me,' added Coupland. 'Only problem is, there's a chance that information might show you're more involved than you can afford to admit.' He rubbed his hand over his chin, made a show of looking thoughtful. 'If only there was a way out of all this sticky stuff, eh?'

The Super placed his elbows on the table. Made a steeple out of his hands. 'There is a way you can help us,' he said, 'and if it results in lives being saved it may help reduce your sentence.'

Chadders flinched. 'I can't go back inside! Jail was hard enough the first time round. I don't think I could hack it again.'

This was probably the first truthful thing he'd said since his arrival at the station, Coupland acknowledged.

'What my client means, is that although he may be

willing to help the crown in any way he can, certain assurances will need to be made, in terms of guaranteeing the protection of him and his family in the lead up to any trial and beyond.'

'Nice to see you're finally earning your retainer,' said Coupland.

Romain slipped a sheet of paper out of the file in front of him and slid it across the table.

Chadders' solicitor picked it up and began to read.

'We anticipated our conversation might take this turn, so I took the liberty of drawing up this agreement. I'm sure you'll find its contents satisfactory.'

The solicitor slid the agreement across the table to her client for his approval.

'Let me know if you need help with any of the long words,' offered Coupland.

Chadders' lips moved as he read through it. Finally, he lifted his head and nodded at his solicitor.

'Very well,' said Romain, 'shall we begin?'

Chadders huffed out a breath. 'What exactly do you want to know?'

'We want to know everything. Which means you start talking and don't stop until I bring your slippers and a cup of Horlicks,' Coupland told him. 'Think you can do that?'

CHAPTER TWENTY

Incident room, Nexus House

The incident room was standing room only. If there'd been any doubt about the significance of Andrew Chadderton's co-operation with the investigation, the presence of Superintendent Lara Cole and Commander Howorth spoke volumes, especially as they'd been fully briefed the previous evening.

DCI Amjid Akram, along with four members of his team, had flown up specifically for the briefing and occupied chairs that Coupland and a civilian worker carried over from a stack piled against the back wall.

Turning Andrew Chadderton into a prosecution witness was a significant breakthrough.

A nod from the Commander and Superintendent Romain began.

'Following Andrew Chadderton's arrest, and the tireless work of Noah and Jared who have worked through the night searching the data files on his computer, we have amassed a list of eighteen operatives working at ground level throughout the Northwest of England. Men holding down day jobs in positions of trust: teachers, sports coaches, taxi drivers. One of these men was Dylan Breakwell, currently on remand for Helen Harper's murder and the grooming and sexual abuse of pupils in his care. In addition, we now have the identities of four "Passmen", though the boys here tell me there are many more names for them to check out.' He regarded the junior officers who were scrolling through lines of data on their screens while listening to the briefing. 'It is likely these numbers will increase,' he concluded, nodding at Coupland to continue.

'Andrew Chadderton paid cash to branch staff working in several high street banks to provide him with contact details of customers who had transactions on their accounts originating from the dark web. He approached these customers with the sole purpose of recruiting them into the network as either groomers or passmen. He'd been given orders from on high to select the passmen based on their social standing in the community. It wasn't enough that they passed all the criminal record checks. He'd been told to look for professionals who were married with kids. Engaged in community activities. Recipients of business awards or other accolades that put them on a social pedestal. At his bosses' behest he invited potential candidates to "sample" the girls being groomed, then made sure everything they did was caught on camera. It was the threat of those images being made public that turned them into the Dutchman's puppets. From then on in they would do anything – even commit murder – to preserve their reputations.'

'Who recruited Chadderton?' asked Amjid.

'A con by the name of Lino Pavel. They met in jail and were released within three months of each other. Pavel had been serving time for GBH.'

'What's his background?'

'A mid-tier gangster with a reputation as an enforcer. According to Chadderton he works for a gang trafficking

Albanian girls to the UK to be set up as sex workers. DCI Akram and I put away a similar gang a few years back.' Amjid shared a look with Coupland. 'There's always that fear as you shut down one operation it's replaced by another, and here we are.'

'What do we know about this gang?' asked Lara Cole.

'They've been running for five years, Ma'am. Your typical mix of low-lives who alternate criminality with stints behind bars. It's the guy they report into who is the most significant in all this.'

'And who is that?'

Romain took over once more. 'Graham Prentice. A corporate lawyer we suspect has been bankrolling – or at least co-ordinating the bankrolling – of the bulk of this particular operation. He's been on our radar for some time now,' Romain added. Coupland sensed more tension, as though Romain felt the need to justify what they'd been doing for the last two months. He was relieved to know he wasn't the only one Cole made feel that way.

'DI Edwards and I had the pleasure of camping outside his house a while back,' Coupland stated in a show of solidarity. It was easy for observers to find fault.

'Seriously, trafficking's his side hustle?' asked Edwards.

'Seems so,' said Coupland.

'But there's been a tail on him since he met the Dutchman at Piccadilly Station. Apart from those few moments caught on CCTV of them greeting each other before heading off in what turned out to be stolen cars we've been unable to find any evidence of them meeting up again, or of the location they went to after leaving the station.'

'We can thank Chadderton's executive travel company

for that. It was set up as a front to transport members of Prentice's circle around the various locations he uses to host "special" parties. He uses fake number plates to avoid detection.'

'What happens at these "special parties"?' asked Lara Cole.

Coupland blew out a breath. 'Chadderton stresses he's never stepped foot in one. From what he's overheard from the guests that he's ferried to and from them, they're upmarket knocking shops. He picks up guests from their hotels then hangs around with the other drivers until he's sent for several hours later.'

'He's never seen the girls? Doesn't know how they're brought in, or where they're being kept?' questioned the Commander. 'I don't believe him.'

'Neither do we,' said Romain, 'but you can hardly blame him for not wanting to implicate himself.'

'We can keep working on him, boss, see if he can cough anything else up before he goes into protective custody.' Coupland addressed this to Superintendent Romain though they both knew it was the Commander's decision. The room fell silent as the gathered officers waited for him to speak.

Commander Howorth shook his head. 'Let's get him shifted. I'll feel happier knowing he's off the premises.'

Romain looked less than happy about this but said nothing.

'I'll get his transfer kickstarted,' said Lara Cole. 'Where's his family?'

'Staying with relatives at the moment, Ma'am,' said Coupland. 'We've spoken to his wife. She's agreed to stay there for the time being. She didn't seem too enamoured with the idea of swapping their four bedroomed semi for a flat in Whalley Range.'

'Them's the breaks when you consort with a villain,' Cole muttered.

'What about this Lino Pavel?' asked Joe Edwards. 'Do we pass his details on to the surveillance team?'

'We're already stretching their resources,' stated Lara Cole. 'Besides, Chadderton will be coughing the goods up on him soon enough.'

'Agreed,' stated the Commander, keen to push on. His gaze shifted to the back of the room. 'Amjid, now we know the significance of Graham Prentice, can you execute a full audit on his finances: Who he pays money to and vice versa. Whether he syphons his money away in shell companies and offshore accounts. There's a hell of a lot of data to be verified, and the presence of you and your team will make disseminating the information that bit easier.'

Amjid nodded. 'Yes, of course. We can already see a link between one of Prentice's personal accounts and a shell company by the name of Peta Productions that we've been tracking. Turns out all the income generated is channelled directly into Utopia.'

Romain shook his head. 'Layer upon layer of deceit,' he observed.

'Pretty much,' agreed Amjid.

'What about the operatives Noah and Jared have identified?' DCI Swain asked Commander Howorth.

'We leave them alone for now. If we round up twenty-two men in a dawn raid tomorrow, all we'll achieve is removing the middle tiers of this network. When we do swoop, we need to inflict maximum damage, and to do that we need the scalps of several top tier members so the message we send out is loud and clear.'

Superintendent Romain turned to DI Edwards. 'Joe, can you keep on at your press contacts to keep Eliza Evans in the news? In light of recent developments I feel we should classify her as a MISPER once more, rather than a "no-body" murder, given we've no evidence of her demise. Are you in agreement, Peter?' he asked, looking at the Commander for approval.

DI Taylor had obtained copies of the original site plans for each development Mark Nowak's maintenance company was contracted to work on. A second inspection of each site confirmed the ground hadn't been tampered with since the original landscaping had been completed. Eliza Evans wasn't buried there. That didn't mean Nowak wasn't responsible for abducting her, they just didn't have any evidence. Some investigations never provided the answers you were looking for. How a young woman could leave work one day and simply disappear. Nowak would stay on their watch list. The network he belonged to was so devious, so slick, there was every chance that Eliza would never be found, though no one wanted to give up on her. Not yet.

'Without doubt,' said the Commander, nodding. 'We also need to start baring our teeth. I accept we don't want to go after the small fry, but there's nothing to stop us leaning on Prentice's professional contacts. Amjid's done a sterling job of putting the fear of God into some of those stuffed shirts. It's about time we made our presence known too.'

'I was thinking of something along those lines,' stated Romain.

'Any reason you were looking at me when you said that, sir?' asked Coupland. Romain's smile telling him it wouldn't be long before he found out.

ONE MONTH EARLIER

NOVEMBER

CHAPTER TWENTY-ONE

'It's been over a week, is everything alright?'
'I had a run in with someone.'
'What happened?'
'Do you really want to know?'
'I suppose not. Were you hurt?'
'Yeah, but that didn't stop them putting me in the slammer for seven days. The screws can't be seen to lose face when something kicks off and the other guy has connections.'

Prisons, like any other establishment, had a pecking order. Though some inmates had an easier time of it than others, no one's time was easy. The tabloids loved to print headlines about TVs and PlayStations, but if someone's locked up for 23 hours a day, what else were they supposed to do? She'd always been a 'Prison's too soft for them' kind of person till that god awful day the judge uttered her loved one's name followed by the words custodial sentence.

It wasn't just about being kept away from the life they should be living. It was the claustrophobia of living cheek by jowl with someone they didn't choose. Sharing an unscreened toilet, their cell mate complaining about the smell of their shit. How bad must their life be like on the outside, that this was the better option?

'Listen, the guy I had the run-in with. He wants another word.'
'What? With me?' Dear God, what the hell was he

getting mixed up in?

'You still there?'

'Yes, of course. I was just thinking about dinner tonight. Thought I'd do that lamb tagine…'

CHAPTER TWENTY-TWO

The front of the restaurant was understated. Warm lighting and green foliage provided a welcoming entrance. Gastronomic accolades including two Michelin stars were on display in the softly lit reception area. There was an air of expectation about the place. People didn't just come here for great food, they came for the experience and to be seen.

'Good evening, Lord Dray, Lady Dray, lovely to see you again,' the woman behind the reservation desk greeted the couple in front of Coupland with gusto, not bothering to check her computer. As if by magic a young man appeared from behind a curtain, helping the woman slip off her coat before hanging it on a rail behind him, repeating the process for her husband.

'This way please,' said the maître d' sweeping his arm towards the dining room.

'Did he just bow then?' Coupland asked Superintendent Romain, voice low. Romain pretended not to hear.

The receptionist was deferential to Romain as she checked his booking. He had a natural air of entitlement, and it was hard not to be intimidated by his cut glass accent. He'd told Coupland on the way over that although they were on duty, he should call him by his first name for the duration of the evening. He'd sounded pleased with himself, like an MP getting down with the kids on a sink estate.

Coupland told the boy who sprang out for his coat that he was alright thanks, he'd prefer to hang it over the back of his chair.

'Let the man do his job,' Romain urged him, under his breath, waiting as Coupland handed the coat over reluctantly.

'What about my cloakroom ticket?' he asked when the maître d' appeared to take them to their table.

'What about it?' said Romain, placing a hand on Coupland's shoulder in order to propel him away. 'Not as though anyone's going to mistake it for theirs.'

The main restaurant was a collection of booth-style seating and large circular tables. There were hardly any tables for two. Folk who dined here liked to eat in packs by the look of it, showing off to friends how much they could spend. Several tables were occupied by corporate diners. Loud men and women in business suits, faces shiny with drink as they compared bonuses. Diners at another table wore grungy leather jackets and sweaters over jeans. A footballer who'd been given a red card the previous weekend wore a Gucci tracksuit and trainers. Dress codes didn't seem to apply to the seriously wealthy. Coupland had stuck to his good work suit. His shirt was clean on and he wore the spare tie the Super brought from home, 'in case you didn't have anything appropriate.' Romain wore green corduroys with brown loafers, a tweed jacket over a checked shirt. 'That's some dressing up box you must have, Tony,' Coupland had quipped before it occurred to him the boss probably dressed like that when he wasn't working.

'Remind me again why we're doing this,' he said once

they were seated.

'You heard the Commander. We need to start being visible, make the Dutchman's contacts feel uncomfortable being around him.' In the two days since Andrew Chadderton's arrest he'd been moved into protective custody, with witness protection officers assigned to him around the clock, keeping him in one piece while surveillance on the Dutchman's inner circle was completed. Amjid Akram's economic crime team had come up trumps. A dubious looking credit on one of Graham Prentice's business accounts gave the DCI the power to freeze the account and threaten the bank with special measures if they didn't cooperate fully with his investigation. Within twenty-four hours Heritage Bank's vice president of operations had boarded a BA flight to Manchester, arranging to meet Romain and Coupland at the restaurant he used regularly when he was in town. Romain had agreed to his choice of restaurant but declined his offer for them to dine as his guests.

'These expenses'll take some explaining, if you don't mind me saying, Tony,' Coupland said, enjoying himself. 'I promise I'll stick to the set menu.'

Romain shrugged. 'The Commander was happy to sign off on the choice of venue. Reckons we'll kill two birds with one stone.'

'How so?'

'Gives us an opportunity to get our faces in front of people we may well be seeking out in the not-too-distant future.'

'By seeking out, you do mean arrest and detain?'

'I very much hope so, Kevin. Don't think because I'm not as gung-ho as you I don't feel as strongly about putting these vile offenders away.'

Coupland's nod was slow. He'd been described as gung-ho for so much of his career, he had no idea if it was meant as criticism or praise.

Their table had four place settings on it rather than three. Coupland had been about to ask who else would be joining them when the maître d' returned with two men who looked as though they'd stepped out of a tailor's window.

'Ninian Carmichael,' said the taller of the two, shaking hands with Romain as though meeting organised crime officers in his own time was what he lived for. He grasped Coupland's hand and nodded, before introducing his colleague. Coupland missed the name but picked up 'Head of our legal division.' Obviously Ninian wasn't as happy on meeting with them as he made out.

Introductions over, they took their seats. Romain enquired about their journey and asked how often they came to Manchester. Ninian admitted it was his first time this year. Coupland didn't blame him, the number of underlings he must have to do all the grim jobs. They ordered the tasting menu for the table, both detectives declining the wine flight, opting for soft drinks.

'Surely you can bend the rules a little this evening?' Ninian cajoled.

'Isn't that attitude the reason you're sat here tonight?' Coupland asked, showing them his teeth.

They sat quietly as the sommelier lectured them on the provenance of the wine being served, Coupland running his finger around the top of his water glass, gagging for a beer. He felt Romain's gaze bore into the top of his head. He didn't need to catch the senior officer's eye to know he was being warned to cool his heels.

Romain waited for the wine to be poured and the sommelier to scurry off before speaking. 'We mustn't forget the reason we're here,' he began. 'Financial irregularities came to light during an investigation conducted by my colleagues from City of London Police. Anti-money-laundering procedures weren't followed in relation to payments made into an account belonging to Graham Prentice, who is a person of interest in an ongoing investigation.'

'I feel the need to interject at this point—' said the lawyer.

'Interject away,' said Coupland, enjoying the moment.

'—that although we accept there may have been a lack of due diligence in relation to this particular client account, it was an isolated incident. We would like to make it absolutely clear that whatever the investigation into Graham Prentice relates to, our bank has no part in it.'

'Thank you for clearing that up,' Romain said. 'My colleague from the Economic Crime Unit, DCI Amjid Akram, informs me that I can count on you to, shall we say, to fill in some blanks we have relating to your client.' Blanks that quoting the Data Protection Act would have stopped in its tracks, if their backs weren't up against the wall.

'This is the part where I go for a leak,' said the lawyer, getting to his feet. Made sense. He could hardly defend his client against breaching the Data Protection Act if he witnessed him do it.

'DCI Akram discovered that similar payments were made on a regular basis. Two of these payments came from individuals who are also customers of your bank. Charles Falconer, and Sir Edward Jamieson.'

Ninian's nod was cautious. 'The majority of their investments with us are managed by our private bank, yes.'

'It isn't clear what these payments are for. Would you be able to shed any light on that?'

Ninian's face went blank. 'Services rendered?' he offered.

'It's the *type* of service we're interested in,' Romain persisted. 'Given Mr Prentice is a partner in a law firm, we can't imagine why six figure sums arrive in his personal account so regularly.'

'Isn't this something you could ask Mr Prentice directly?'

'When the time is right,' Romain informed him.

'But right now you're more interested in building a case against him,' Ninian stated.

'Got it in one.'

'I take it you think he's money laundering?'

'Actually no. It's a lot more serious than that. But he isn't operating alone. We know he's mixed up with some seriously wealthy, albeit morally corrupt, business partners, as well as some seriously *dangerous* ones too.'

Nicely done, thought Coupland, watching as Ninian considered this.

'What I tell you isn't going to come back to bite me?' he asked, mind made up.

Romain shook his head. 'My colleagues are already running background searches on these people. I want you to paint a picture of what they're like, so we can work out our best way to approach them.'

'I'd prefer to do that without an audience,' Ninian said, glancing at Coupland. Romain jerked his head towards the bar where Ninian's sidekick sipped a cocktail through a straw.

Coupland shrugged as he got to his feet. 'I need a blast of fresh air anyway,' he said, patting his jacket pocket.

*

Susan Dray eyed her husband across the restaurant table as though seeing him for the first time. It was a long time since she'd really looked at him. Properly. At home, they tended to talk to the side of each other's heads, and when they were out there were so many others vying for his attention she never really got a look in. She grabbed her moment, while he was off-guard. Let her gaze settle on him. His impeccable silk scarf looped around his neck like a resting thespian actor. He looked so at home in situations such as these, only those who knew him well would sense he was distracted. Work probably – he never seemed able to switch off. His gold signet ring clinked against his water glass as he lifted it. He pulled a pair of reading glasses from his breast pocket, perching them on the end of his nose in order to read the menu. Wine was ordered without glancing at the wine list. The woman beside her announced she'd started working for a charity, then proceeded to tell them about a fundraising dinner she'd been asked to arrange. Simeon promised to buy tickets for the table and pledged prizes for an auction. No one asked about the charity or who it supported, though the men raised a glass to Simeon's generosity. How much they spent on good causes was a serious sport, second only to being seen doing it. He'd need a new dinner jacket.

A new bow tie. Insist she splashed out on a new dress.

Simeon Dray loved being the centre of attention. He seemed to thrive on dressing up. Didn't seem anywhere near at ease when wearing casual clothes. It was as though he thrived on pomp and ceremony. As though the ordinary minutiae of day-to-day living held no interest to him. My husband the judge. She smiled as she thought this. That after all these years, despite her staunch liberalism, she still got a thrill from saying it.

*

Outside, Coupland smoked his way through two cigarettes. Time enough for Ninian Carmichael to spill the beans on his high-net-worth clients. His stomach rumbled, reminding him it had been several hours since he'd last eaten, if a packet of crisps and a cup-a-soup he'd found in the office kitchen counted. He went back into the restaurant, headed towards his table.

'Well I never. Mr Coupland as I live and breathe.'

Coupland swore under his breath at the sound of the familiar voice behind him. His face took on a pained look as he turned round. 'Fancy seeing you here, Kieran. Lost your way?' Salford gangsters rarely operated outside of their own peer group, never mind territory. Yet here he was, an hour away from the heart of his city and no sign of altitude sickness.

Kieran Tunny chuckled. 'Thought I'd start living a little. Push the boat out so to speak, after all I've got a lot to celebrate.'

Coupland said nothing. Chewed the inside of his cheek. Behind Tunny at one of the few tables for two sat Tunny's on-off partner, Bella, pushing round the remnants of her dessert with a fork.

Despite being incarcerated for the last few years Tunny looked remarkably well. He'd none of the fresh-out-of-jail pallor associated with newly released cons. He'd managed to stay in shape too. Although a big man, he wasn't physically imposing – he had henchmen for that. Henchmen who this evening were conspicuous by their absence. Coupland looked back the way he had come, to the restaurant's entrance, and the street beyond. 'Given your lads the night off?' he enquired. 'I'm guessing you couldn't persuade G4S to reset their tags?'

Kieran's smile was wide. 'That's what I like about you, Mr Coupland. You never miss an opportunity to take a swing. Keeps me on my toes.'

'Glad to be of service, Kieran.'

'So, what's your excuse for being dressed up like a dog's dinner? I don't expect a policeman's salary to cut much sway here.' A glint came into Tunny's eye. 'Unless you're here in a professional capacity, of course.'

'Maybe I'm keeping an eye on you, Tunny. Waiting for you to slip up so I can send you back where you belong.'

Tunny considered this. 'Why would you meet anyone here though? Hardly your normal stomping ground.'

'Don't let me keep you,' said Coupland, already moving away.

'Hang on,' said Tunny, moving after him to catch him up. 'You can't bugger off now, just when it was getting interesting.'

As a rule he always showed Coupland deference. Despite his formidable reputation for serious violence when needled, he valued respect and loyalty above all else. He was literally, if previous gangland assassinations were anything to go by, part of a dying breed. He was the sort of likeable rogue portrayed on TV. Not so appealing if you lived on the same estate and had to put up with turf war feuds and police raids in the early hours.

'I can do what I like, Tunny.'

'Indeed you can, Mr Coupland.' Tunny threw his hands wide. 'I don't mean any harm. Especially when I owe you for saving my life.' Coupland had stopped Tunny's would-be assassin in his tracks when he'd put a blade to Tunny's throat. A close shave in every sense of the word, given he was sitting in his local barber's chair at the time.

'You repaid that debt a long time since, if I recall,' Coupland told him. 'We don't owe each other anything.'

Tunny smiled. 'Remember when we were young, Mr Coupland?'

'Depends how far back you are going.' Most of Coupland's childhood was packed firmly away in a box marked 'Do not open.' Memory Lane was a no go zone as far as he was concerned.

'Come on, don't be coy. All us kids used to play out on the streets. Cops and robbers. Now we're all grown up and playing it for real.'

Coupland shrugged.

'Only problem is, working out who is who,' Tunny added unperturbed.

'What's that supposed to mean?' Coupland narrowed his eyes. He knew Tunny was playing him, yet he'd gone ahead and bitten the bait anyway.

'You come across as a right little Pollyanna, sometimes, Mr Coupland. Hard to believe we grew up in the same city.'

'Think you're mistaking me for someone who gives

a toss.'

Tunny's eyes scanned the crowded restaurant, his gaze settling on a group of diners seated around a large table. A familiar looking man wearing reading glasses and a silk scarf. The gold signet ring on his little finger sporting a family crest. 'I think you care far more than you like to let on. It's one of the many things we have in common.'

'And your point is?'

Tunny turned his attention back to his old adversary. 'I'm saying I'm not the only one who is out of his comfort zone tonight.'

Coupland said nothing, though on this Tunny was right. They didn't belong here. They'd crawled through too much shit to pass themselves off as civilised and everyone around them could see that. They were imposters, but then Coupland had felt like an imposter most of his life.

Tunny grinned. 'I read somewhere once—'

Coupland raised his hand, palm outwards. 'I'm going to have to stop you there, Kieran. We both know you don't read.'

Another grin. 'Fine! I hold my hands up to that. Someone posted a saying on Facebook. Can't remember who it was by. That we're the sum total of the five people we spend the most time with.' He let that sink in. 'Interesting, don't you think?'

Coupland blew out a sigh. 'There's no hope for me, then, given I spend all day chasing bell-ends.'

Tunny's face grew serious. 'Be careful, that's all I'm saying. The people in this room are not like us, Mr Coupland. Try as we might we'll never be accepted by them.'

'I'm not looking for acceptance.'

'So it's definitely business that brings you here, then.' Tunny smiled. 'But what kind of business would that be?' He paused, waiting for a reply that didn't come. 'You're a decent man, Mr Coupland, I would hate to see you get involved in something over your head, that's all.'

Coupland gave a small bow. 'Thanks for the career advice, Kieran. I'll be sure to forget it the moment I… sorry, what were we talking about?'

Tunny made a rumbling noise that turned into a throaty laugh. 'If you say so. Remember this though. The folk in these sorts of places might act all high and mighty, you know, give you the impression they should be treated differently to everyone else. With deference even. Trust me, some of these fellas are not so fragrant. Get on the wrong side of them and they'll cunt up quicker than a rat in a fight.'

'Your pearl of wisdom is duly noted, Kieran. Now if you don't mind…'

Tunny nodded, his smile lingering as he watched Coupland make his way back to his table.

'He looks a rum sort,' observed Ninian, his head inclining in the direction Coupland had come from. 'Someone really needs to have a word with the management. Stop all these folk coming in clutching gift vouchers they've been given to celebrate their anniversary or retirement or whatever else their work mates have clubbed together for.'

'Funny you should say that. He is celebrating something as a matter of fact,' drawled Coupland, deciding not to add 'evading a life sentence for conspiracy to murder' in case it put him off his appetiser.

CHAPTER TWENTY-THREE

Commander Howorth's office, Nexus House

Coupland wasn't sure what he'd been expecting when he accompanied Superintendent Romain to a private briefing in the Commander's office, but he knew as soon as he walked in this wasn't it.

The Commander's desk sat in front of the only window in the room. A desktop computer, laptop and electronic notebook occupied one side of his desk. A printer occupied another. The remaining surface was cluttered with handmade gifts made by primary school aged children, young ones at that: Unrecognisable animals made out of glued together pebbles, a mug with a wonky handle. Several ball point pens stood in a painted plant pot beside a notepad. A notice board on the adjacent wall showed two graduation photos, a young man and woman with the same bullet shaped heads smiling at the camera. Coupland looked back at the desk, frowning.

'The joy of second marriages...' the Commander explained, following his gaze, '...is that you get the chance to do it all again, minus the fuck-ups.'

Coupland had made the mistake before of thinking of work colleagues one dimensionally, as though they operated in a vacuum with no life of their own beyond the job.

'I've a youngster in the house, as well,' he blurted.

'I didn't know that,' said Lara Cole, who had stepped into the room behind them.

Coupland was about to say *pot calling kettle* but there was no requirement to share personal details. He'd heard through the grapevine she was divorced. A career jockey by the sound of it. Kids stayed with their father so she could focus on climbing the greasy pole. It was hard for women, Coupland accepted, or at least harder for women married to the wrong man. With Lynn working shifts, childcare had been a juggle. They'd got it wrong more often than they'd got it right, but they were through the other side of it, more or less intact. It couldn't have been all bad.

He wondered if Cole saw much of her kids. What her relationship with them was like. If, when she finally left her desk and let herself into an empty home, she felt the sacrifices had been worth it.

'The little fella's not mine,' Coupland added, feeling the need to explain, 'he's my daughter's.'

'So you're a grandad then.' The Commander laughed, enjoying himself, even though they both knew he had a good ten years on Coupland. Cheeky bastard, thought Coupland, laughing back.

They were seated at a table that wouldn't look out of place in the Cabinet Office in Downing Street. The Commander and Lara Cole on one side, Coupland and Romain on the other.

They'd been summoned first thing. A lot had been riding on last night's meeting and Romain was keen to show they had delivered. In truth the discussion regarding Graham Prentice and his associates had finished by the time Coupland and Ninian Carmichael's legal advisor returned to the dinner table yesterday evening. Coupland had taken his boss's willingness to move onto other topics as a sign the banker had come up trumps.

Once Ninian's taxi arrived to take them back to their hotel, Romain had shared what he'd learned and as a result even Coupland was feeling upbeat.

'As soon as Carmichael understood the severity of the crime being investigated he practically rolled over in order to distance himself and the bank from Graham Prentice's activities,' stated Romain.

'Do you trust him?' asked Commander Howorth.

Romain considered this. 'Yes, I do. He went completely into survival mode, his eye contact was strong and he's agreed to provide us with dates of the events he referred to should we need them.'

A nod from the Commander told him to continue.

'As you already know, two people who made signification donations to a business account set up by Graham Prentice in the last six months are also customers of the same bank – Heritage Bank.'

'Private bank clients,' Coupland chipped in.

'Indeed,' said Romain, keen to crack on. 'Charles Falconer is a senior partner in a city investment brokers. We're talking serious wealth. The company manages assets worth more than a billion pounds and that's the money Ninian knows about. His home in Kensington is owned by a company registered in the Cayman Islands. He owns an apartment in New York and holiday homes in Antigua and Florida. He also owns Pennant Tower.'

Coupland couldn't resist butting in. 'Which is where I saw the Dutchman when he came to Salford.'

The Commander looked visibly impressed. 'This means

their relationship isn't just financial. The Dutchman has been on the receiving end of his hospitality, which makes me wonder what this Charles Falconer gets in return.'

'I think we know the answer to that,' said Cole.

'As vice president of Heritage Bank, Ninian has also enjoyed Charles Falconer's hospitality on a number of occasions. He wanted to stress this was purely in relation to his services as a representative of the bank, nothing else. He did name several celebrities and politicians he's seen socialising at these events, even the odd royal has been spotted on Falconer's yacht in Monaco.'

If it was the same odd royal Coupland was thinking of, Falconer kept some seriously dodgy company.

'And this other person? You stated there were two,' prompted Cole.

'Sir Edward Jamieson. An inventor and serial entrepreneur. Better known these days for being a philanthropist. He donated 10 million to his old university then flew to Africa in his private jet to oversee an orphanage he was having built in his wife's name.'

Coupland shook his head. 'He builds an orphanage one minute then transfers money to a sex trafficker the next. Does he not realise one act doesn't cancel out the other?' The sheer hypocrisy of it.

'I'll get onto Interpol,' said the Commander, 'get them to speak to the relevant authorities in Africa.' He looked at Romain. 'A career in Public Protection has made me cynical, but when you said orphanage all I could hear was stock in trade.'

'Jesus H. Christ,' muttered Coupland. He hadn't considered that. Whatever their social standing or walk of life, the members of this network were connected by the moral void at their centre.

If we really are the sum total of the people we mix with, thought Coupland, in order to put these bastards behind bars he needed to seriously lower his game, not up it.

'Thanks to the surveillance on Graham Prentice we have identified three key players in the network: Ruth Hunter Pepper, Charles Falconer and Sir Edward Jamieson.'

'It's like one of those naff jokes. A socialite, a billionaire and a philanthropist walk into a bar...' said Coupland, 'all connected by a lawyer who doubles as a sex trafficker in his spare time.'

'I say we bring Graham Prentice in. The Dutchman is in Manchester and Prentice knows damn well where he is,' said Romain.

'He hasn't led us to him so far,' Cole reminded him.

'That's because he's smart. He's been using Chadderton's executive travel service to ferry him around but that option isn't available anymore.'

'There are plenty of other firms out there who'll drive him around. Plus, they'll be harder to keep track of.'

'So we bring him in and broker a deal. It's our best chance...'

Both superintendents fell silent, though Coupland suspected that was because he was in the room and they didn't want to spit their dummies out in front of junior.

'You bring Prentice in and the network will drop him like a ton of bricks,' stated the Commander, not caring whose ego he was stamping on. 'He might meet and greet the Dutchman when he comes into the UK but it's the Jamiesons of this world who break bread with him. Tony, get your team to work out who cuts more sway with the Dutchman. Whether it's Jamieson, Falconer, or Hunter Pepper, then go after *them*.'

'Thanks Peter,' said Romain, getting to his feet.

Coupland took this as his cue to leave, taking care not to look at Lara Cole as he walked to the door.

*

Incident Room, Nexus House

The incident room fell silent as Coupland and Superintendent Romain returned to their work station, making Coupland wonder if they'd heard the bickering next door.

'You might want to see this, sir,' Noah called out before The Super sat down, indicating something on his computer screen. The junior detective stepped back from his desk so that Romain could take his seat. 'You too, Sarge,' he said to Coupland, clearing his throat.

Interest piqued, Coupland made his way over to Noah's desk.

The press photograph was innocuous by itself. Four men dining in a top-notch restaurant was hardly breaking news. It was the caption above it that was attention grabbing: *Cash strapped Greater Manchester Police pick up the bill for Banker's Michelin meal.*

The article beneath it was flim flam dressed up as fact. Coupland and Romain were both mentioned by name although it was Coupland's face that was clearest, staring at a camera he hadn't known was there. The restaurant manager declined to comment when approached by the Evening News, stating 'The restaurant respects the privacy of its customers,' though it would have been helpful if he'd mentioned the bill had been split, debunking the claim made by the paper.

'The dinner was arranged last minute, how the hell did it get leaked to the press?' barked Romain.

Coupland's jaw clenched. 'I've got a damn good idea, sir,' he said. 'Mind if I go and check out my theory?'

'Be my guest.'

Coupland narrowed his eyes as he felt in his pocket for his car keys.

Kieran fucking Tunny.

*

A couple of North Face ninjas leaned against the wall outside the café on Bolton Road, smoking roll ups. Dressed head to foot in black, with hoods pulled over baseball caps and scarves draped round their necks, ready to be yanked into position when it suited.

No face, no case, bruv.

It was reassuring to learn that despite his time enjoying the hospitality of His Majesty Kieran Tunny had settled back into his normal regime. He was painstaking about his daily routine, frequenting the same café in the morning for his breakfast, the same pub for his lunch and then home for tea.

'Boss man's inside then,' Coupland said to the posse standing guard as he approached the café door.

'What's it to you?' asked the ninja nearest to him.

Coupland swung his arm wide enough for the young gun to flinch, bringing his hand down hard on his shoulder in a mock friendly gesture. 'You're as frightening as undercooked bacon, son. Now, jog on,' he said, releasing his grip, before stepping inside.

The café was a greasy spoon in every sense of the word, serving full English or bacon rolls with tea in chipped mugs. The only thing that marked it out from other similar establishments along the road was the plastic bag on the counter containing everyone's mobile phones. A security measure Tunny insisted on to make sure his conversations weren't recorded.

The tables were occupied by men of all ages discussing football and fighting, though not necessarily in that order. All eyes fell onto the interloper, bringing their conversation to an abrupt halt. Tunny, spearing a pork sausage with the tip of his fork, sent Coupland a look that would have stopped most men in their tracks.

'I'll have what he's having,' Coupland called over to the café owner.

A quick look in Tunny's direction told him it was OK to do as the interloper asked.

'A more paranoid person would think you were following me.' Kieran laughed.

'Oh, I'm following you alright, Kieran. Following you all the way to the jail door if I get my way.'

Tunny jerked his head at two head-the-balls sat across from him. Juggling plates and mugs of tea they moved to another table. Coupland sat down without waiting to be asked.

'Something twisting your melons?' asked Tunny. 'Oh, great photo by the way. That photographer really captured your best side,' he stated.

'Was it you?' Coupland growled, causing several shaved heads to turn in his direction.

'What?' Tunny sounded bewildered. 'Hang on a

minute,' he said, face clearing, 'are you being serious?'

'Not like you haven't got form,' grunted Coupland.

Tunny had made the mistake a few years back of getting one of his lackeys to take a photo of Lynn and Amy and send it to Coupland to rattle his cage. Coupland's response had made both men realise what he was capable of.

'That was a long time ago,' Tunny placated him. 'A case of crossed wires, if you remember.'

'I remember warning you not to overstep boundaries and yet here we are. You can't help yourself, can you?'

Tunny raised his hands placatingly, prompting one of his henchmen to step forward.

'It's OK, Fido,' growled Coupland, 'get back in your kennel.'

The henchman looked at Tunny, waited for him to nod before stepping back.

'It's all very well you coming round here with your accusations, Mr Coupland. Are they actually based on anything, other than the fact that I'm a free man has stuck in your craw?'

'I don't know Kieran, let me think. Maybe you wanted to take a pop at my reputation? Have a go at the Force in general? It doesn't really matter…'

'If I wanted to discredit you, or embarrass the Force, or cause whatever the hell else you want to pin on me, I'd have had one of my lackeys take a photo of you and me chewing the fat last night. Think that would have made a much better headline, don't you?'

Coupland huffed out a sigh. There was no denying he had a point.

The café owner placed a fry up and mug of tea in

front of Coupland along with fresh cutlery. 'If you need anything else I'll be out front having a smoke,' he announced before retreating.

Coupland tucked in. He'd had better, but it did the trick.

'You know, Mr Coupland, you keep insisting on treating me like the enemy when that couldn't be further from the truth.'

Coupland took a swig of his tea. 'That's reassuring to hear, Kieran.'

'We've even collaborated on a couple of occasions, if I remember it right.'

Coupland preferred not to comment. Instead he made a show of clearing his plate. He was there because he thought Tunny was responsible for the press leak. Knowing that he wasn't meant that someone else was to blame, leaving few suspects. Commander Howorth and Amjid Akram had hinted there were moles working on the inside. Chief Superintendent Curtis had stated it outright. This changed things. Now, Coupland was less bothered about the press leak and more bothered about the leaks they didn't know about.

Tunny waited for him to set down his knife and fork. 'I heard you got a promotion.'

'You heard wrong then.'

'You're based over at Nexus House. Sounds like a promotion to me.' Tunny paid kids to hang around police station car parks taking down the number plates of officers' private cars. Made it easier to follow them home. To threaten, bribe. Knowledge was power and all that. Looked like Coupland's new location had been rumbled.

'I've heard there's a special unit been set up. Tracking

down that arch enemy of yours.'

'You, you mean?'

Tunny laughed, but there was steel in it. 'Word gets around, Mr Coupland. No need to take it personally.'

'If you know as much as you do, Kieran, you'll know it's not up for discussion.'

'I know I saw someone in that restaurant last night that I haven't seen in a long time. Since the day I was sentenced, as a matter of fact.'

'Oh yeah?'

'The beak who sent me down. Simeon Dray. He was there last night, large as life.'

Coupland shrugged. 'That's Lord Dray to you and me, Kieran. He's entitled to dine where he likes, last time I checked.'

'That's a matter of opinion,' said Tunny. It must be hard to be sent down by someone and not bear a grudge, Coupland supposed, and Tunny had appeared in the dock opposite him a good number of times, he didn't wonder.

'The fella's a danger to society,' said Tunny.

'How can he be? He put you away good and proper.'

'Let's just say, as far as he's concerned, justice isn't blind.'

'Say what you've got to say, Kieran, and be done with it.'

'He's known on the con circuit for being lenient towards nonces.'

'What?' Coupland's eyes narrowed. 'If you're trying to take a pop at him for sending you down—'

'Which I'm not – even though my conviction was overturned.'

'A technicality, Kieran, you know it as much as I do.'

'I'm not having a pop at him. Honest, Mr Coupland. Cross my heart and hope to die. Check him out if you don't believe me.' Tunny paused. 'It just seemed odd, that's all. You being there the same time old sticky beak is dining with his missus and a group of hangers-on. I reckoned you lot were onto him at long last.'

Coupland's brow creased. He made a mental note to fact-check what Tunny was saying. It was likely bollocks at best, but all the same...

'Your enemy is my enemy, Mr Coupland. Remember that. You know my view on nonces. In fact nonce is too good a word for them. If I can be of any assistance—'

'—Save it. The answer to that is no. Don't ask me again. In fact I'd better get going, given there's a phantom photographer about,' he said, pushing himself to his feet and placing a crisp ten pound note on the café counter. 'Last time I was seen speaking to you I was hauled up on a disciplinary.'

'I suspect that wasn't the main reason,' Tunny shot back.

Coupland said nothing.

'I have friends in every city, Mr Coupland. There's always someone I can call on should you need—'

'What? Muscle? A weapon? I'll stick to my side of the fence if it's all the same to you.'

'From your lips to God's ears,' said Tunny, smiling. 'Times like this, there's no you and us. Just us. And we want the same thing. Go safely, Mr Coupland.'

*

Nexus House

There was now a fourth whiteboard in the incident room. Two photographs taken through long lenses, captured by the surveillance team in London, were stuck to it. Ruth Hunter Pepper attending a charity ball in her role as ambassador for a children's charity. In the other photo she was in the passenger seat of a Range Rover, driven by a man wearing sunglasses.

Superintendent Romain was studying the association chart below it, which showed her known network of family and other contacts.

'Do we know who this man is?' Romain demanded, jabbing his finger at the driver wearing Ray Bans.

'They'd have listed his name below if they'd known it,' said DCI Swain.

Coupland placed his jacket over the back of his chair and went to join them.

'Any luck with the press leak?' Romain asked.

Coupland shook his head. 'Wasted trip.'

'I've been onto my contact at the Evening News,' Joe Edwards told him. 'They said it had been copied onto a memory stick posted though their letterbox first thing. The envelope it came in had "from a concerned member of the public" written across the front of it.'

'Don't suppose they've got CCTV?'

'Not a chance,' Edwards replied. 'This is small scale stuff but there'll be more on its way. We're putting powerful noses out of joint so they need to discredit us. Expect more news stories denigrating what we're doing, just don't expect them to be as tame.'

'The guy in the Ray Bans is Lino Pavel,' said DI Taylor, getting up from his seat to take a closer look. He'd been on the phone, had followed their conversation while waiting to be put through to the DI in the regional crime unit in London. He moved to the board containing photos of Graham Prentice's contacts, jabbed his finger at a nasty looking piece of work. 'If it isn't him, it's his double,' he said confidently. 'He's the con who recruited Andrew Chadderton in jail. The one bankrolled by Prentice to smuggle in Albanian women and put them to work as sex slaves.'

'Why would Hunter Pepper be dirtying her hands letting him ferry her around?'

'It makes sense if her role is matchmaking girls to clients in the network. It's in her interest to suss out the latest intake from the person who supplies them.'

It also meant she was more pivotal to the network than originally thought.

'What do we know about Lino Pavel?' asked Romain.

'He was serving a sentence for GBH when he recruited Chadderton in jail. Despite his trafficking history he's evaded any significant jail time,' said Noah. 'Must have a good lawyer.'

'Is that right?' Coupland said, his brain switching up a gear. 'Maybe my trip this morning wasn't wasted after all.'

He recounted his conversation with Kieran Tunny. The claim the gangster had made that Judge Simeon Dray – who happened to be in the same restaurant as them yesterday – had a reputation among the criminal fraternity for being lenient on paedophiles. He provided enough of Tunny's criminal career history to make his observation credible. 'It's possible he has an axe to grind,' warned Coupland. 'I wouldn't have thought any more of it if you hadn't just made that comment about Pavel evading justice.'

Romain nodded, satisfied it was worth looking into. 'Leave the boys to run their searches. If there's anything to find on him they'll track it down.'

Coupland didn't doubt it.

Romain considered their options for a moment while he decided what action they should take next. 'From what I've learned this morning I'm convinced Ruth Hunter Pepper is the one to bring in. Shame she's in bloody London. Would've liked us to be in on that arrest.'

'I'll ring my equal number back,' said Taylor. 'Give them the green light to pick her up.'

Five minutes later he was off the phone. 'She's booked onto a flight from Heathrow to Manchester this evening, sir. Due to arrive at 8.40pm. Under the circumstances they're happy to keep surveillance on her until she lands in our neck of the woods.'

Romain smiled. 'Looks like the pleasure will be ours after all.'

CHAPTER TWENTY-FOUR

Emergency briefing, Muster room, Manchester Airport

British Transport Police, GMP uniformed and plain clothed officers, along with specialist firearms officers, gathered in the muster room twenty minutes before flight BA1398 was due to arrive from London Heathrow. Flanked at the front of the room by DCI Swain and DI Melvin Jones from BTP, Superintendent Romain outlined the arrest warrant that had been issued and the protocol officers were to follow.

'Flight Captain John Estler has been alerted that officers are on standby to detain Ms Hunter Pepper and will await our instructions before releasing the cabin doors,' DI Jones informed the group.

Romain spoke next. 'Do not board the plane. Uniformed officers are to keep their distance. Remember, wait for her to open her mobile phone before making a move on her and seizing it.' This would allow them to go through her search history and contacts.

'Are we all clear?' Romain asked.

A chorus of grunts was his answer.

'Let's get to it, then,' he said, dismissing them.

*

Ten minutes had elapsed since the pilot had announced *'Welcome to Manchester, we look forward to you flying with us again soon.'* Passengers who had clamoured for their overhead bags now stood in the central aisle, restlessly staring at their phones while waiting for the cabin doors to open.

'Doesn't normally take this long,' a plump woman in a crumpled business suit said to the passenger seated beside her.

Ruth Hunter Pepper smiled back stiffly. She'd managed to avoid getting into a conversation for the duration of the flight, she was damned if she was going to get embroiled in one now. A brief glance at her Omega watch confirmed they were being cooped up longer than normal, but that in itself was nothing out of the ordinary. She curled her lip. They were in Manchester, for God's sake, what more could they expect? A few minutes here or there made no real difference to her day. Her driver would wait. The work she was on her way to oversee would carry on regardless; she was a figurehead, after all. She viewed her fellow passengers' agitation with something akin to pity. She'd never had need to apologise or explain herself. How tedious it must be, to start a conversation saying 'Sorry I'm late.'

The silly woman beside her was now on her feet, yet there was no indication from the flight crew they'd be going anywhere soon. Ruth sighed. Travelling cattle class was no fun. She reached into her bag and slipped out her phone, returning the 'Flight mode' icon on her home screen to *off*. She tapped onto the *Outlook* symbol, ready to scroll through her emails.

'Finally,' the woman beside her muttered. Ruth looked up in time to see the cabin doors open and the inevitable surge forward at the prospect of freedom. She slipped her bag over her shoulder as she got to her feet, barely acknowledging the flight attendants wishing everyone a pleasant stay.

Once clear of the airbridge she picked up pace, for no reason other than the insufferable woman she'd ignored during the flight was still in her wake. She looked away quickly, glancing at her phone as she tapped several icons to check for messages. The idiot woman seemed to lose interest, her attention shifting to two men waiting beside the baggage reclaim belt. Perhaps she's lonely, or a drug mule, Ruth thought, the idea making her laugh.

Her laughter froze on her lips when both men walked towards her. 'Not so fast,' said one of them, reaching for her phone while the other one began reading her rights.

'Best not to cause a fuss,' said the idiot woman as she sidled up beside her, propelling her through a door marked 'Authorised personnel only' before slapping her in handcuffs.

*

The idiot woman was DS Catherine Arnott, attached to the Met's Organised Crime Unit. She'd been following Ruth Hunter Pepper for the best part of a week. It was to her credit – and experience – that Ruth had been oblivious to her existence until today.

DS Arnott escorted Hunter Pepper to an unmarked BMW saloon, where Superintendent Romain waited in the passenger seat. After placing her into the rear of the car, the arresting officer, DCI Swain, thanked Arnott and wished her a safe flight back to the Smoke. She'd expected no more than that; after all, it was hard not to be precious about the turf you worked on. She'd studied Operation Maple's case file long into the night when she'd been given the brief to watch Hunter Pepper. She hoped they threw the book at her.

*

Nexus House
Coupland watched the convoy of police vehicles enter the compound to the rear of the custody suite. An unmarked BMW pulled up closest to the door. DCI Swain and the Super stepped out of it, flanking Ruth Hunter Pepper as they led her inside. She lived up to her publicity photos, he conceded. There was a shine about her that was impossible for ordinary folk to maintain. She wore clothing that only women who were chauffeured around could wear. Silk, by the look of it. Skyscraper heels and a jacket that suggested she didn't come to Manchester often. She seemed to glide, even in handcuffs. She was bound to use this celebrity of hers to her advantage. Have them run round after her, if they were daft enough. He hoped the Super's royal protection detail meant he'd see through the facade, or at least not be intimidated by it. He finished the cigarette he'd been smoking then headed back indoors. Might as well find out.

*

Noah and Jared had been part of the convoy returning from Manchester airport. Noah cradling Ruth Hunter Pepper's mobile phone like a new-born baby. Back at their desks Jared scrolled through her contact list which he'd downloaded onto his computer. Noah searched through her WhatsApp messages and calendar.

Graham Prentice had been saved in her contact list

as a work colleague but they were already aware of that connection. There were several high-ranking business entrepreneurs, including Sir Edward Jamieson.

'They all piss in the same pot,' stated Coupland, hovering around their desk.

Each name was painstakingly logged and cross checked against the increasing number of network members they'd been able to identify.

Coupland was only bothered about the Dutchman. 'I bet my eye teeth he's in that phone, just not where you'd expect him to be.'

'Let's hope so,' said Noah, as he slipped on his headphones, though whether to get on with the job or block out the gobshite leaning over him was anyone's guess.

Commander Howorth had already stated he wanted Tony Romain and Lara Cole to interview Hunter Pepper, who was insisting on representing herself. 'I'm the best God-damn lawyer I know,' she'd informed the custody sergeant when he'd pressed her for a decision and there'd been no turning her.

'Probably better to have another woman in there,' the Commander had added, 'don't want her claiming later that we were heavy handed.'

'So I'm seen as a soft touch?' Cole had bristled, however there was no changing the Commander's mind either.

'They'll have their work cut out for them,' DCI Swain muttered out of earshot, his undergarments chafing him because he'd been benched.

DI Ben Taylor had been checking airport CCTV. 'A silver Mercedes waiting in the arrivals pick-up zone stayed for an hour before driving off without a passenger. Registered to an executive travel firm – legit,' he added, reading the question on the DCI's face. 'I checked the booking with their office – it was to take Ruth Hunter Pepper to the Midland Hotel.'

'Shit,' muttered Swain. He wasn't the only one hoping its next stop had been to pick up the Dutchman, Coupland guessed. As though it would have been that easy. 'The good news is that means he isn't wondering where she is,' he said in a rare moment of optimism, 'buys us a bit of time, if nothing else.'

DCI Swain's desk phone rang. He said his name into the receiver and waited. 'We're on our way,' he said, before ending the call. He got to his feet, indicating that Edwards, Coupland and Taylor do the same. 'Interview's about to start. Commander Howorth wants us in the observation room, pronto.'

Coupland, already on his feet, was at the door in a flash. 'Game on,' he said, wringing his hands.

*

Observation room, Interview Suite, Nexus House.
Watching a suspect's interview from the observation room was like studying wildlife in their enclosure at the zoo. Lots of time spent waiting around as the animals sniffed each other and checked out their surroundings. Some withdrawing into a corner to contemplate, others only too keen to show you their backside.

Superintendent Lara Cole carried out the formalities before starting with non-contentious questions. Ruth Hunter Pepper played along nicely. She was far too polite for Coupland's liking. Too helpful. Too obliging. Some people used a charm offensive to mask their contempt for others. Adopting a 'cleaning lady voice', a way of talking to people they regarded as underlings or inferior. *'You are a darling, Mrs H, oh, and can you give the guest bedroom the once over, we've got visitors…'*

Considering Lara Cole had taken him to task for not being more gung-ho, he was surprised she was letting Hunter Pepper get away with being so condescending. Maybe Commander Howorth had had another word. Or they'd agreed Tony Romain would be playing bad cop to her good cop.

Coupland was about to find out.

Romain sat forward in his chair, his expression mirroring Ruth Hunter Pepper's disdain. 'When you first came onto our radar, I have to admit some of my colleagues were confounded as to how someone like you could become embroiled in a sex abuse network. After all, socialite, high ranking professional, either way it didn't make sense.' He sat back in his chair to let that settle. The view through the observation window was one way, but Coupland nodded anyway, satisfied.

'However, your financial history tells us another story. Your father might have been an earl, but when he died he left crippling debts and a crumbling country estate. A corporate lawyer's salary – even as partner – wasn't going to put a dent in the mounting repair bill any time soon, not to mention school fees. Winchester, if I'm correct?'

Ruth's nod was slow.

'For the tape, please.'

'Yes,' Ruth replied.

Romain acknowledged her response with a nod. 'So, that's the hard part out of the way. We've established *why* you're not just mixed up in this network, but instrumental to it. That for all your grand ways, like everyone else you're in it for the money.'

Ruth's eyes narrowed. 'I take it you intend to ask me a question, Superintendent Romain, or are you simply demonstrating your powers of speculation?'

'Indeed I am,' Romain stated. 'To the former, that is.' Coupland was getting to like Romain's style more and more. He might be a stuffed shirt with his team but he could rattle posh suspects without raising an eyebrow.

'I have several questions, in fact. But first I must warn you that our Digital Forensic Unit are interrogating the data on your mobile phone. I'm confident they will find the information we need, but I'm giving you the opportunity to co-operate with this investigation. I want *you* to give me the identity of the lynch pin in this network. The man known as the Dutchman, by those not in his inner circle. I believe that you have travelled to Manchester to meet with him.' His face took on a serious look. 'We also intend to question you in relation to a missing schoolteacher by the name of Eliza Evans, and the remains of two schoolgirls found in The Netherlands earlier this month.'

Ruth's demeanour changed in an instant.

She glanced at the clock on the interview room wall. 'I would like to request a break,' she informed Romain.

'No surprise there,' muttered Coupland as Tony Romain and Lara Cole got to their feet.

*

Incident Room, Nexus House

'How's it going, Sarge?' asked Noah when Coupland returned to the incident room alongside Joe Edwards and Ben Taylor. DCI Swain was huddled in the Commander's office with Lara Cole and Tony Romain, going over their interview strategy.

'She hasn't coughed up the Dutchman's ID yet if that's what you're asking,' said Coupland, 'we're relying on you guys for that.'

'She might,' said Taylor, 'once she knows we're on to her about the trafficking.'

'There's no evidence to directly link her,' stated Edwards. 'Not yet, anyway.'

'She doesn't need to know that,' reasoned Taylor. 'Seems to be the approach that Romain's taking…'

Coupland was standing by Jared's desk. He could never work out how he and Noah divided their tasks between them; both seemed fully conversant with each other's work.

'Listen, I know you're up to your gonads at the moment but did either of you get anywhere with the intel on Judge Simeon Dray?'

Jared nodded. He retrieved a printout from a pile on his desk and handed it to Coupland. 'Sorry Sarge, meant to give you this earlier.'

Coupland skim read through the A4 sheet of paper. Swore and scratched his head. Read it through again, taking his time, muttering 'Jesus wept,' every so often.

'Any use?' Jared asked, attention already returned to his original task.

'You could say that,' said Coupland, signalling for a bit of quiet.

He waited while Taylor and Edwards gave him their attention.

'Judge Dray handed out ten sentences last year that were considered to be unduly lenient. All of them increased by the appeal court. Last July he declined to jail a man who tried to rape a girl of three, saying the defendant was "experimenting" and had "got carried away". The appeal court jailed the man for three years.'

'Christ,' said Edwards.

'Only that's not the worst of it. He jailed a sex trafficker for ten years, even though the standard tariff for that crime is more than double that.'

Taylor considered this. 'There's nothing illegal there,' he commented. 'Incompetent, yes. Narrow-minded and arrogant, certainly, but he isn't breaking the law.'

'He is if we can prove the defendants being given the light touch are part of the Dutchman's network and he stood to gain by being lenient.'

'How do you propose we do that? The surveillance teams are already stretched to the limit.'

'We could pay him a visit.'

'And say what? *We're on to you, Your Honour*, and then pray he never presides over any future case you take to court?'

Coupland sighed. It was bad enough that the only reason Simeon Dray had come to their attention was because Kieran Tunny had given him a heads-up. To not be in a position to do anything about it was rubbing salt into the wound. He thought of schoolteacher Dylan Breakwell, and how his victims would feel if a judge like Dray handed down a ludicrous sentence. What kind of message would it send?

He was aware that Edwards and Taylor were watching him, as though worried he was going to do something rash. He was saved from proving them right when DCI Swain returned to the office, with a thunderous-looking Romain. 'It seems Ms Hunter Pepper is tired. She's insisting we wait until morning to continue the interview.'

Everyone's gaze fell on the wall clock. It was 10.30pm. Hard to argue, but it rankled.

'What happens in the meantime?' asked Jared who was pulling far too many all-nighters for Coupland's liking.

'We go home to our families,' said Coupland.

'Those who've still got them,' Joe Edwards reminded him.

CHAPTER TWENTY-FIVE

The ringtone blaring its familiar tune shattered the comforting silence.

'Is everything OK?'

'S'all good,' he said after a moment's pause.

'You don't normally ring at this time.'

'Normal left the station a long time ago.' His tone was sharp, aggressive even, but then nothing about their set-up was desirable. *'That fella I mentioned to you before. The one who keeps giving me a bit of bother.'*

'What about him?'

'He needs a favour.'

'Another? Isn't it enough that I did what he asked last time? What the hell is going on there?'

He explained, leaving nothing out. Just as he'd been instructed.

'What sort of favour?'

CHAPTER TWENTY-SIX

'COME AND GET IT!'

Andrew Chadderton, AKA Chadders, threw down the controls of his PlayStation and stifled a smile. This safe house malarkey wasn't nearly as bad as he'd feared. He got to play Gran Turismo as much as he liked without getting an earful from his missus, and no kids demanding lifts here and there. He was enjoying the peace and quiet, truth be told.

Sure, he got bored. He hadn't stepped outside the four walls of the budget hotel they'd moved him to since agreeing to turn King's Evidence. He missed the banter with the other drivers and flirting with the hotel receptionists when picking up guests.

The protection officers assigned to him were decent enough, for feds. Their shifts overlapped so he was never alone. Meant one of them could pop out for a takeaway while he shared a beer with the other. The place was a bit of a dump by most folks' standards, but it was alright for a fella reliving the single life.

He wasn't sure what the permanent set-up was going to be like. It was too soon for Janeece and the kids to visit him so they hadn't had a chance to talk things through yet. To see whether they still had a future. Then again, a fresh start might be just what they needed.

'You know, if this police lark doesn't work out you

could always go and work for Deliveroo,' he called out, pushing himself up from the sofa, shoving a hand down the front of his jogging bottoms to adjust himself as he made his way into the kitchen. Felt himself shrivel at the sight of the gun pointing directly at his head.

'Fucking Hell!' was all he managed, before his executioner pulled the trigger.

*

The call came through as Coupland helped himself to his second beer of the night. Admittedly it was hot on the heels of the one he'd just finished but then he was making up for lost time. Tonto was in bed by the time he got home most nights, it had been the same with Amy. He'd had to make do with standing outside the boy's bedroom door, measuring his breaths. Imagining the steady rise and fall of his chest.

Lynn was in the front room. Despite being on earlies she'd stayed up when he'd called to say he was coming home, had clinked her cup of camomile tea against his beer can before they'd settled down in front of the TV. No chat. Just a shared appreciation of the quiet. Everyone he loved most was under this roof, yet they were the people he spent the least time with. Life was messed up.

He answered the phone on its second ring, didn't want Tonto waking to find Grumpy on his way out again. He stated his name, looking regretfully at the unopened beer can on the kitchen counter.

'Fuck,' he muttered as he listened to what the caller had to say. He looked up to see Lynn standing in the doorway. She pointed upstairs to let him know she was calling it a night. Blew a kiss in his direction. He rewarded her with a tired smile, continued to listen as he picked up his car keys and made his way to the door.

*

Coupland pulled into the budget hotel car park, located a space between two police vans. He made his way over to the scene of crime manager who issued him with a bodysuit and shoe protectors. He gave his name to the officer manning the inner cordon, before making his way to the third-floor apartment where the fatal shooting had taken place.

DCI Swain and Joe Edwards were talking to a SOCO in the hallway that separated the living room from the kitchenette and bathroom. Coupland waited for the officer to step away before joining them. It had been Edwards who'd made the call. DCI Swain had specifically asked for Coupland to attend the locus. He wasn't sure what he could bring to the table that the others couldn't but he was flattered all the same.

Edwards raised his hand in greeting. 'His protection officer was taking a dump when he heard the gunshot. Ran through to the kitchen to find Chadderton's brains all over his pizza.'

'Did he get a look at the killer?' asked Coupland.

Edwards shook his head. 'Saw a guy dressed in black climb onto a motorbike. Tried taking a photo on his phone but the image is a waste of time.'

'Hardly matters. Not like we can't guess who's behind it,' stated Swain.

There was nothing out of place in the living room. A brief look in the bedrooms didn't flag up anything untoward. Executions tended to be carried out with the minimum of fuss. In. Out. Job done.

Coupland's nose wrinkled as he moved towards the kitchen. The air was pungent with the tang of blood and sulphur. Chadderton's body lay where it fell, one side of his head missing. He must have been lured by the pizza which had been placed on the kitchen table, unaware he was heading into a trap. Edwards had been right. There was brain matter everywhere, including on top of the pizza. He'd seen enough.

'What happened to the officer who went out for the pizza?' Coupland asked when he returned to the living room.

'He was found unconscious in the alleyway behind the hotel. Came to as he was lifted into the ambulance. He doesn't remember anything,' Edwards informed him.

DCI Swain scratched his beard and swore. 'There's no chance Ruth Hunter Pepper will open up to us after this.' There was no point contradicting him. What he said was true.

'I could speak to my press contacts, organise a news blackout?' Edwards offered.

Swain nodded. It would do no harm to contain news of the killing for a couple of days.

'Where's the officer who found him?' asked Coupland.

'Sat in a van downstairs, awaiting his fate. He'll have his backside handed to him for this.'

'For what?' asked Coupland. 'Taking a dump on duty? The blame lies far higher up the tree than that.'

Swain's eyes narrowed. 'What are you suggesting?'

'I'm not suggesting anything. I'm stating a fact. Only a handful of personnel knew where Chadderton was staying. Looks like one of them has blabbed.'

*

Nexus House 2am

Andrew Chadderton's incident board was placed against the others in the incident room. The selfie he'd taken while waiting to pick up Graham Prentice and Ruth Hunter Pepper was placed at the top of the board. His crime scene photo beneath it. Coupland was busy drawing a line of dashes across several of the boards, tracing the link from the Dutchman to Graham Prentice, then onto Chadderton, adding a question mark midway between the two, representing his killer.

The office floor was deserted. Coupland, Edwards and DCI Swain the only ones present. The bulk of the room was in darkness, except for the fluorescent lights above their section which gave off an eerie glow. Swain had telephoned Superintendent Romain from the scene, assuring him he had everything under control and there was no need for him to come out. Romain would relay news of the incident to the Commander, but precious little could be done after that until morning.

Edwards was putting together a list of staff who'd known the location of Andrew Chadderton's safe house. After writing down the names of the protection officers who'd provided round the clock security and their DCI, he'd drawn a blank. Access to this information was restricted. Details stored on the part of the police computer that required several levels of clearance.

'That counts me out,' said Coupland.

'And me,' stated Edwards.

'It's not a bad theory, but it doesn't prove anything,' said Swain. 'If an officer's bent they'll circumnavigate the system by stealing someone else's password and log in as them.'

Coupland considered this. 'OK, so we do this the other way round. Find out who accessed information on the safe house and ask them to confirm they'd made the request.'

'You're not Professional Standards, Kevin, no one is answerable to you. Besides, that doesn't tell you who the culprit is, just whose password has been hacked,' said Swain.

'Bollocks,' said Coupland. 'I was never any good at problem solving at school.'

'I'm guessing you didn't put that down on your police application form.'

'They didn't have forms in those days. As long as you could add up using your fingers and toes you were in.'

'Look, this is getting us nowhere,' said Edwards reasonably. 'How about we get some shut eye and pick this up first thing with clear heads?'

'Agreed,' said Swain, moving to his desk where he'd left his jacket and car keys an hour earlier. Coupland wasn't about to argue.

The sound of the lift doors opening made them turn in unison to see Superintendent Romain striding toward them. Clean shaven and sporting fresh clothes, he glanced at Andrew Chadderton's incident board before turning to face them. 'In approximately five hours I'll be hauled in front of the Commander to reassure him we're all over this. So that's what I want from you now. Reassurance. Buckets of it. Start talking.'

3.15am

It was daft o'clock before Superintendent Romain sat back in his chair, satisfied that, wherever the cock up lay that led to Chadderton's murder, it wouldn't be found at their door. Coupland climbed into his car, swiped a hand over his face. He drove on autopilot. No music, his thoughts clattering round his head like marbles in a jar. He was halfway home when he noticed the same car had driven behind him for the last ten minutes. He hadn't paid much attention at first. His head was full of brain-spattered pizza, when the car behind's lights flashed several times before pulling out as if to overtake him. He wondered whether Chadderton's execution and the person driving erratically behind him were connected. Deciding it wasn't safe to lead the lunatic to his home he floored the accelerator to put some distance between them, swinging left into a Travelodge car park.

The road was quiet, but when a vehicle drove past the breath caught in his throat. He was in a state of hyper vigilance. When the car doubled back on itself and entered the car park he knew it was a threat. He floored the accelerator once more, heading straight at the vehicle before swerving at the last minute. He jumped out of his car then ran towards the other vehicle, yanking open the driver's door.

'What the hell!' he shouted, the adrenaline surging through him as he slammed his hand down hard on the car's roof. 'I saw a car in my rear-view mirror, didn't know who it was…' He was aware he was paranoid and jabbering. Everywhere he looked he saw Andrew Chadderton with half his head blown off.

He clocked the look of alarm on the undercover officer's face. He stepped back to give him space as he got out of his car. Slowly, as his breath returned to normal, so did his state of mind. He locked his hands together, placed them behind his head as he huffed out a sigh. 'Ignore me. Our key witness was murdered in his safe house this evening. For a minute there I thought someone was trying to take me out, too.'

'You'd have been right then,' said Jay O'Neill, moving towards him.

CHAPTER TWENTY-EIGHT

'I don't understand,' said Coupland, back on alert. 'How come you knew where I was?'

'I've been following you since you left the crime scene,' Jay told him. 'I needed to speak to you but didn't want anyone to see me.'

'Couldn't you use the phone like everyone else?'

'The amount of surveillance you guys engage in and you're still happy to pick up a phone?'

'When you put it like that…' said Coupland. With the adrenaline drained out of him he was exhausted. 'Look mate, it's been a bastard of a night. Can you cut to the chase so I can go home?'

'Your key witness was Andrew Chadderton, right?'

Coupland nodded.

Jay eyed him steadily. 'He was murdered by Lino Pavel.'

Coupland screwed up his face in concentration as he tried to recall where he knew that name. 'The con who recruited him in jail?'

'I'll have to take your word for that.'

'How do you know it was him?'

'Told me himself. Acting on orders from above,' Jay added.

'How do you know him?'

'He's an enforcer like me. I've been trying to get in with him for a while and he rocked up the other day offering me a job.'

'He's more than an enforcer,' stated Coupland. 'He traffics girls to the UK, then sets them up as sex workers for a man named Graham Prentice, a known business associate of the Dutchman.'

Jay considered this. 'He's asked me to provide muscle at some posh event that's coming up soon. His words not mine. Asked me if I'd be his wingman.'

'Where's the event?'

'Said he'd text me the details nearer the time.'

Coupland's interest was piqued. 'Will you send them on to me when you get them?'

Jay nodded. 'That's not what I wanted to tell you though.'

Coupland waited.

'Lino told me he's been given another job.'

'Yeah?'

'The person who contracted him to take out Chadderton has asked him to take out a cop. He showed me the photo they sent him.' Jay gave Coupland a look. 'The guy in the photo was you. Filling your face alongside a couple of suits in some restaurant.'

Coupland swallowed. 'Did he happen to say why I'd been singled out?'

'We don't get a back story. Just a photo and a part payment. Balance settled when the deed is done.'

Jay read the expression on Coupland's face. 'Was it you that got Chadderton to turn?'

Coupland's nod was slow. 'Then they'll see you as a threat. Simple.'

Andrew Chadderton had been on Graham Prentice's payroll, like Pavel. It made sense that Prentice would get

Chadderton taken care of, in-house. He was as ruthless as the Dutchman when it came to tidying up loose ends. Or in Chadderton's case, loose lips.

'Have you met the fella pulling Pavel's strings?' asked Coupland.

'If I did, don't you think I'd tell you?'

'You realise you're dealing with people directly involved with the network we're trying to shut down? You're putting yourself at enormous risk.'

'Take a look in the mirror mate and repeat what you just said.'

'I knew what I was signing up for.'

'So did I,' shrugged Jay. 'A bullet's a bullet, whether it's fired by a drug baron or a sex trafficker. Dead is dead.'

'We've got a mole,' Coupland admitted.

'Welcome to my world.' Jay's face was grim.

'I'm not sure if I'm more at risk reporting this or keeping shtum.' Coupland was struggling to take it all in. 'I have to go. I need to think about what you've told me.'

Jay nodded, headed back to his car. 'Don't think too long,' he called out before climbing inside.

Coupland climbed into his own car, gave him the thumbs up before starting the engine.

*

Home

Coupland put his key in the lock, let himself in. He trudged up the stairs, pausing by Tonto's bedroom door. Waited for his rhythmic breathing. He moved on. Lynn was asleep. Not wanting to disturb her he crawled on top of the bed and slept in his clothes. At 5.00am he cried out, waking her. Eyelids heavy, she peered at him in the half light, wondering whether to wake him or not. Deciding to leave him be, she closed her eyes. She didn't sleep for the rest of the night.

*

Incident room, Nexus House

Despite Joe Edwards' best efforts with his contacts in the press it was a tabloid that broke the news. A front-page photo of CSIs standing outside Andrew Chadderton's hotel beneath a caption that read: SUPERGRASS EXECUTED IN COLD BLOOD. The first the team had known about it was when Commander Howorth stomped into the incident room wielding a rolled-up copy above his head like he was about to swat a really annoying fly. Several, in fact, given the way his eyes darted around the room, finally settling on Edwards. 'What in God's name is this?' he bellowed, tossing the paper onto his desk. 'I'd been given categoric assurance that this wouldn't happen,' he said, throwing a sidelong glance at Superintendent Romain. He ranted for a full five minutes, Edwards having the grace to sit and take it. Coupland had been about to come to his defence when Edwards caught his eye, a brief shake of his head warning him to keep quiet.

'Why didn't you want me to say anything?' Coupland asked once the Commander had stomped back to his office with Romain in tow. Obviously the Super's new arsehole was to be ripped in private.

The room was relatively quiet. DCI Swain was attending Andrew Chadderton's post mortem, not that any surprises were expected there. Ben Taylor had been dispatched to take statements from Chadderton's protection officers. Noah and Jared, ensconced in headphones, continued to interrogate the data on Ruth Hunter Pepper's smartphone. Coupland had wanted them to try and hack into the restricted witness protection database to find who'd accessed Chadderton's file. The Super had nearly blown a gasket when they'd run the idea by him.

'I had a feeling you were going to mention our mole,' Edwards told him.

'You'd have been right then.'

Edwards pulled a face as though he'd tasted something sour. 'Be careful where you start pointing your finger when you talk about the leak,' he warned. 'Without any proof it's better that you play dumb. Start ruffling feathers and you'll get kicked off the investigation.'

That was the least of his problems, if what Jay told him was anything to go by. He hadn't told anyone what the undercover officer had disclosed to him in the early hours of this morning. He wasn't sure what he wanted to happen. Not the bit about getting his head blown off – he was quite certain he didn't want that. But if declaring the threat meant he'd be taken off the taskforce – he didn't want that either.

'There's a risk the information we're gathering will be compromised if we do nothing. Are we supposed to sit and let that happen?'

'I don't think it will be,' said Edwards. 'Once news of Chadderton's arrest – and subsequent disappearance into police protection – came to the attention of the Dutchman, it will have been obvious what Chadderton was up to. As far as Ruth Hunter Pepper is concerned, he doesn't know she's here.'

Coupland shook his head. 'She won't help us now. Not when she finds out that Chadderton's dead.'

'She isn't going to find out though, is she? What with being in the cells overnight.'

Coupland considered this. 'What if we try a little reverse psychology. We tell her what's happened to Chadderton, see if the fear of her being thought of as a grass makes her roll over.'

'It didn't turn out so well for Chadderton.'

'So, we make sure round the clock protection means exactly that. No popping out for protein shakes or sushi or whatever socialites eat when they're not attending galas.'

Edwards threw him a look. 'I can't see how it can possibly work, to tell you the truth, and I certainly can't see the Commander buying it.'

'Why don't we put it to him and find out?'

He looked at his watch. 7.45am. When his alarm had sounded first thing he'd reached out to Lynn's side of the bed, the cold space telling him she'd long gone. He'd thrown himself under the shower, gave his razor a swerve. Put on a clean shirt. Stepped into yesterday's suit. He'd dry swallowed a blood pressure tablet while tiptoeing past his grandson's room. Two piss poor coffees later and the day showed all the promise of one about to turn to shit. Ruth Hunter Pepper's second interview was scheduled for 8am. If he was going to persuade the Commander to change the interview strategy, he'd need to do it right now.

*

Observation room, Nexus House, 8am.

Superintendent Tony Romain rested his forearms on the tabletop while Superintendent Lara Cole went through the digital recording formalities. A comfortable stance from which to pose his first question to Ruth Hunter Pepper. A quick glance at his notes – handwritten for speed given the last-minute redirection from Commander Howorth – and he began.

'I must inform you that Andrew Chadderton, who has worked as a driver for you on several occasions, was murdered last night in what we believe to be a cold-blooded execution.'

Ruth Hunter Pepper looked at him with something akin to relief. 'No comment,' she answered through the remainder of the interview.

*

What Noah Rainey and Jared Ozin loved most about their work was that no one had a scooby what the Digital Forensic Unit actually did. Left alone with their headphones on they'd mostly be ignored until their heads popped up behind their screens to signify they had something to share. Senior officers nodded and went along with everything they said because they didn't want to look stupid. In these days of austerity nobody could afford to come across as past their best. Noah had tried on more than one occasion to explain to his folks what his work entailed. 'I'm an investigator. But instead of knocking on doors I search the digital network, looking for missing data in the same way my heavy-footed colleagues would look for a weapon.' His parents had been able to grasp that part in the main, but had struggled with how data could help him find a suspect.

He smiled as he stared at Ruth Hunter Pepper's phone. *This* would be the example he could use to finally explain it. He'd have to wait until the trial was over, of course. He couldn't share information that might jeopardise a case. But one day soon he'd show them a photo of this phone and tell them *this was how we discovered the Dutchman's identity*.

Ruth Hunter Pepper's phone contained several instant messaging services including ordinary SMS texts, Facebook messenger and WhatsApp. She used these primarily to communicate with the people on her contact list, rather than use emails, unless it was related to her legal work. There were 768 contacts stored on her phone. Noah had worked through the entire list, cross referencing it with the list of the socialite's known associates they had already compiled. Jared then checked each social media profile to establish their identities. Those whose details checked out and gave no other cause for concern were eliminated from their 'Network' list.

At the point the Commander had stomped into the office to lambast Joe Edwards about the press leak, just under three hundred names remained on that list. Progress, definitely, although the Commander's demeanour had made it clear he was in no mood to hear that they *thought* they were on the right track. He dealt in absolutes. They were either on the Dutchman's scent or they weren't.

Dampening down their excitement they'd kept their headphones on even though they'd switched them off earlier. People didn't include them in the conversation if they thought they couldn't hear. Just how they liked it, as it enabled them to listen in when it suited. Despite

DS Coupland's confidence, DI Edwards had sounded doubtful that Ruth Hunter Pepper would cooperate once she learned about Andrew Chadderton's murder. If he was right then all eyes would be on the DFU to bail them out. He shared a look with Jared and grinned. They lived for this buzz. Scrutinizing data in ways no one else thought was possible. To think their careers teachers used to shake their heads at them. Talk about the gaming generation like it was something to be pitied. 'And Lo, the geeks shall inherit the earth,' said Noah, his attention returning to the screen in front of him.

The phone numbers they were most interested in were those that had been saved on Ruth Hunter Pepper's phone with only a first name. The message history for these contacts typically consisted of locations and dates. They'd so far been able to group these contacts into messages relating to four destinations: Rotterdam, Frankfurt, Manchester and London. There was no doubt that these contacts were 'punters' being advised of the locations of sex parties. Bank details were provided so they could deposit their 'fee' for each soiree, with frequent flyers earning privileges as they built up their loyalty points. Jared had cross checked the bank account details with those of the shell company DCI Amjid Akram had reported as being a front for Utopian Enterprises. A match.

Only one phone number engaged in chat relating to all four destinations. This same number had messaged Ruth commenting on specific girls: 'She needs to be fresh faced.' 'Too much makeup on the last one.' Evidence she had a hand in where they went and how they looked.

There'd been one missed call and three texts from this

number since Hunter Pepper's arrest.

Noah spoke over the desk to Jared, grateful they were on their own. 'It's him, isn't it?'

Jared had been double checking the data to make sure they hadn't overlooked anything. He regarded Noah and nodded.

*

Ruth Hunter Pepper was taken back to the cells while Tony Romain and Lara Cole gathered their files together, their faces giving nothing away.

When they stepped into the observation room five minutes later their expressions showed what they really thought.

'The PACE clock hasn't timed out yet, sir, we've got another 24 hours if we need it,' said DCI Swain.

Commander Howorth stood with his hands behind his back, tight lipped. His silence demonstrating his fury far more than his hissy fit earlier.

Coupland raised his hands. 'I'm sorry. I really thought she'd talk. The Dutchman rules by fear but she didn't bat an eyelid when she heard about Chadderton.'

'Yeah, I know, I was there,' snapped Romain. He turned to the Commander. 'I'll apply for an extension if I have to, sir. We need her to start talking.'

Coupland was sure he wasn't the only person in the room thinking *fat chance*, though some things were better left unsaid. He thought back to his conversation with Jay O'Neill the previous evening. He hadn't told anyone that Lino Pavel was responsible for Andrew Chadderton's murder. With a mole in the unit, the last thing he wanted was Pavel finding out he was onto him, especially since

341

the next bullet he intended to fire had Coupland's name all over it.

Commander Howorth strode purposefully from the room, clearly in no mood for a post-match analysis. Swain and the others circled round Romain, putting in their two pennies' worth.

'A word, DS Coupland,' said Superintendent Lara Cole when Coupland made a move to join them.

He followed her into the hallway, waited while she opened an interview room further down the corridor and beckoned him into it. He assumed she was going to give him a roasting. He deserved it. He'd called it wrong and made the team waste precious time. Whatever she wanted to dish out, he'd take.

She peered at him closely. 'You look a little strung out this morning. Everything OK?'

'No one likes being on the back foot.'

Cole wrinkled her nose. 'I'm sensing it's more than that,' she prompted.

'Too much caffeine makes me antsy,' he offered.

'You've got a couple of rest days coming up. How are you going to spend them?'

Coupland looked taken aback. 'I wasn't intending to take them, Ma'am. Things are only just starting to get going. We haven't got the capacity. I haven't got the time…'

'Your rest days are mandatory here.'

'We've only just got to grips with the extent of this network, we're making inroads, I can feel it. You can't expect me to…'

'I'm not. I'm telling you. It's an order.'

Coupland stared at her.

'I've seen too many officers reach burnout because they refuse to take their foot off the pedal. They think they're indispensable.' Her tone softened. 'Look, I should know,' she said, 'I'm one of them.' It was well known she never arrived at her desk later than 7.30am, never left before 9.00pm. 'If you look up job pissed in the dictionary you'll see a photo of me, and trust me, it isn't all it's cracked up to be. My husband soon got tired of it, the job always coming first. Said I was never really present, and he was right. Truth was, the banality of day-to-day living didn't interest me. I've always felt guilty about the children though.'

She gestured to the four walls around them. 'The irony is of course that I barely have any life beyond this place. I've become a creature of habit. Only this is my habit. Family is the big stuff,' she reminded him, 'not this.'

Coupland shifted under her gaze. 'Look, there's probably something you should know...' He told her about last night's warning, but not who'd given him the heads-up. The last thing he wanted to do was put Jay in danger.

Lara Cole regarded him. 'And you're only telling me this now? You must take this seriously, Kevin. Perhaps you should consider taking yourself off the investigation?'

Coupland looked at her aghast. 'If I packed it in every time someone threatened to take a pot shot at me I'd never leave the house.'

'What about your family, has any threat been made against them?'

'Absolutely not,' he answered, though he'd fretted about it ever since.

'Can you send them to stay with relatives, just to be sure?'

'My daughter and her son, yes. My missus is more likely to dig her heels in. She has a responsible job. She wouldn't take kindly to being told she'd have to stop doing it for a while.'

'What does she do?'

'She's a nurse at Salford Royal. In the neo-natal unit.'

'Maybe it won't come to that. You could talk to her about varying her route to work, alternating shift patterns, that sort of thing.'

Coupland nodded.

'If we are to take any solace from this, it's the fact that we've obviously got those high up the network worried.'

'Little comfort if you're six feet under,' said Coupland shivering as a cold draught brushed over him.

'Take those rest days, Kevin.'

Coupland shook his head. He was hardly going to rest while there was a bounty on his head. 'I can't leave the team short-handed. We lose traction when we're not operating at full pelt.'

'Exactly. Exhaustion, fear, anger, how will that impact your performance?'

'I've been running on empty for the best part of twenty years, what difference will it make now?' Coupland cocked his head. 'Can I ask a favour, Ma'am? Could we keep what I've told you between us? I don't want anyone else getting wind of it. Loose lips, and all that.'

Lara Cole sighed. 'You're not an easy man, are you?'

'I never pretended to be.'

'I think you did. At first. You were certainly more agreeable than now.'

'My old boss told me to wind my neck in. And my old Chief Super. And an ex-colleague, come to think of it. Warned me to dial it down a few notches. No one likes a gobshite.'

'And yet here you are.'

Coupland clicked his heels and swept his arms wide in a theatrical bow.

'Are we done, Ma'am?'

Lara Cole tutted, throwing her hands up in surrender. 'We're done.'

*

Incident room

Noah's face lit up when Coupland entered the room. 'Where is everyone, Sarge?' he asked, looking behind Coupland as though expecting to see the others marching in single file behind him.

'Working on a strategy to flog a dead horse. Why?'

'We've isolated a mobile number which we believe belongs to the Dutchman.'

Coupland's breath quickened. 'Are you serious?'

'We know better than to joke about something like that, Sarge.'

'Does this mean you know who he is? And more important, where he is?'

'No,' admitted, Jared, deflated. The downside of working in the realm beyond most folk's imagination was they always expected more.

'Now we have his mobile number getting that information will be relatively straightforward,' Noah added in their defence.

'But you need to be clear what it is you actually want,' added Jared.

The Dutchman in a body bag would be a start, thought Coupland. He retrieved his mobile from his pocket and called Superintendent Romain, reiterating what the boys had told him.

'Halle-bloody-lujah,' Romain replied. 'I'll gather the troops.' His tone suggested that if the news was good, Coupland's crap interview strategy would be forgiven. Time enough for Coupland to buy up all the protein bars from the first floor vending machine, placing them in front of the junior detectives like a pagan offering.

*

Briefing, Incident Room, Nexus House
'It's twelve hours since Ruth Hunter Pepper was taken into custody. During that time there's been a missed call and three texts from one mobile number. It's a number that she has had a communication thread with over several years. The conversations refer to known locations we know the Dutchman has been seen in. They reference parties that have been held for the purposes of sexual exploitation, and discuss some of the girls they have provided for the duration of those parties.' The young officers stood before the assembled group with confidence as they explained the significance of the mobile number they had identified. 'More recent texts refer to another event that they are arranging. They don't mention specifics—'

'—They never mention specifics,' added Jared, nodding for Noah to continue.

'But we think it is soon.'

'The fact they're both in the same city at the same time suggests that,' stated DCI Swain, unconvinced.

'Yes, but reading through the thread of their texts we've identified a pattern to their behaviour. The pattern tends to be that when an event is coming up, he arrives first, then she does, followed by their high-level associates, or dodgy guests, for want of a better description. We took the liberty of checking domestic flight manifests for over the next 24 hours to see if any names tallied with the names on our board...'

'And?' prompted the Commander.

'Sir Edward Jamieson flies into Manchester tomorrow morning and Charles Falconer arrives in the afternoon.'

'So whatever's taking place is imminent,' said DI Edwards.

That tied in with what Jay had told Coupland the previous evening, though he wasn't about to cough that nugget up. The UC officer had agreed to give him the details of the party he'd been asked to provide muscle for when he received them. Coupland hoped by then to come up with a convincing enough lie about where he'd got the intel from.

'...They've developed a pattern of communicating over the years, a form of shorthand, if you like, that we think we have mastered...'

Coupland's ears pricked up. 'What are you getting at?'

'We're confident we can reply to his texts, make him think it's Ruth.'

'What, and ping his location through cell site analysis?' Coupland asked, pleased with his use of technical jargon.

Jared paused as he formulated an answer. 'If he was

with one of the main service providers then that would have been a possibility… However, if he's using a specially adapted phone – and we believe that he is – then the signal won't be picked up by the main carriers and he'll stay hidden.'

'Just when I thought I was getting the hang of all this technical stuff,' Coupland shrugged.

'What's this number saved as on her phone?' asked Edwards.

'Just the letter "L",' stated Noah.

'Is there any other way we can track him down?' asked Taylor.

'There's no benefit to finding out where he is right now,' stated Romain. 'We need to hit him at this event, where all his sponsors and fellow paedophiles will be. Remember, maximum impact.' He eyeballed Noah and Jared. 'Do you think you'll be able to elicit information from him relating to this event?'

The young men nodded.

The Commander looked less than convinced. 'He must suspect something has happened to Hunter Pepper by now, given she's not responded to his texts. How many did you say he'd sent?'

'Three, sir,' answered Noah, 'but here's the thing… Since she's been in custody there's been a missed call from this number but no voicemail. An hour later the first text arrived, hoping she'd had a pleasant flight. At midnight he sent her a question mark.'

The Commander put out his hand to stop him. 'By which time he's worked out that the reason she can't get to the phone right now is because she's been picked up by us. It's an occupational hazard, after all. A call to the hotel would clear up her whereabouts.'

A blush crept up Noah's neck. It was tricky contradicting senior officers, so many took it personally. 'You'd think so, wouldn't you, sir? But then this morning, just after 8am, he sends another text. Just one word. "Sorry."'

'Jesus wept,' said Coupland. 'As someone who has sent more one-worded texts to my much better half over the years than you two have had hot dinners, I can safely say our man here is in the dog-house. He doesn't think she's banged up, he thinks he's in her bad books.'

'And that,' says Noah with all the confidence of a snake oil salesman, 'is our way in.'

*

It took an hour for them to put together a script of leading questions aimed at finding the location of the party and the girls that had been groomed for it. Coupland, excluded from taking part in that piece of work, bore no grudges. 'If the Dutchman gets suspicious, back off,' said Romain. 'We can't afford for him to pull the whole event because he smells a rat.'

'Remember you can't make him think she's at the hotel in case he checks it out. You'll have to make it look like she's still mad at him,' said Taylor.

It was agreed that Jared and Noah formulate the texts using phrases that matched the Dutchman and Hunter Pepper's speech patterns. There was only so much micromanaging that could be done.

Coupland wasn't sure why he was surprised Hunter Pepper and the Dutchman were in a relationship. For all he knew she could have been the woman with him in the car park at Pennant Tower, the first time Coupland had clapped eyes on him. Sex traffickers weren't precluded from having relationships with each other, he reminded himself. In fact it probably made it easier. Negated the need to lie, quite so often.

He hadn't realised he was loitering over Noah's shoulder until he caught a look that passed between both junior DCs.

'We've got this, Sarge,' said Jared, fiddling with a switch on his headphones before turning back to his screen. The others had already backed off, although Coupland noticed no one had actually left the room.

'I'm going to grab a bite to eat. Anyone want anything?' he asked.

'No, but I'll walk out with you, could do with a bit of fresh air,' said Edwards, slipping his jacket on.

Coupland shrugged. He'd be lighting up the moment he stepped out of the building but they'd worked together long enough for Edwards to know that.

'So what are you really after?' asked Coupland once they'd exited the building. He lit up immediately as though making his point.

'There's a mole in our midst and we're several dummy texts away from coaxing the Dutchman into showing himself. Aren't you worried?'

Coupland coughed out a laugh. His name was top billing on an executioner's hit list; he was bricking it. 'What's the point worrying about things you can't change?' he lied. He'd never quite got to grips with the Serenity Prayer. Accepting the status quo was a failure in his book. If something was wrong he fixed it. It's what he did. It's what drove him on.

'Yeah, but since when do moles become selective? If

they passed on the address of Chadderton's hotel why not pass on that Hunter Pepper is here, rather than let the Dutchman be hoodwinked into thinking she's at liberty?'

Coupland dragged the nicotine into his lungs and held it there. He'd been wondering the same thing. He bleeped his key fob to unlock his car then remembered his promise, bleeping the door shut once more.

'Is that some sort of OCD ritual?' asked Joe.

Coupland exhaled the smoke in a long sigh. 'Nah, I used to smoke in the car, now I don't.'

'Who says you can't teach an old dog new tricks, eh?'

'Less of the old,' said Coupland. 'Anyway, about your hypothesising, you got anyone in mind?'

'Not really. One of the civilians has been on leave the last couple of days. I didn't want to mention it because I thought you'd judge me.'

Coupland threw him a look. 'I am judging you, let it go.'

Edwards raised his hands in surrender.

Coupland finished his cigarette, dropping the butt in the cigarette bin positioned by the main door. 'The money this network has at its disposal, it can afford moles right at the top of the chain,' he said eventually.

'You mean the Commander?'

'Why not? He's on his second marriage, has two families to support.' Coupland remembered something. 'He didn't want Andrew Chadderton kept in the cells for a second night. He insisted he was moved to a safe house straight away.'

'Wasn't that a good thing?'

'Obviously not.'

'Superintendent Romain has a lot in common with the

people we're investigating. Wouldn't he be the easiest to turn?'

'That's the kind of rationale Professional Standards have been trying to apply to me for years. It's a tad narrow-minded.'

'I suppose,' Edwards conceded. He turned to go back into the building, having declined Coupland's offer of an all-day breakfast. 'Look, in the absence of any real evidence let's stay vigilant, and if anyone asks to meet you on the top floor of a multistorey car park, make sure you don't go alone.' He'd meant it as a joke, but the grin Coupland rewarded him with fell away as quick as it came.

*

Coupland was sitting in the cafeteria at Salford Royal Hospital, stuffing his face with egg and sausage smothered in beans, when Lynn slid into the seat opposite him. She lifted a pot of tea, milk, and a mug from her tray, along with a freshly made salmon and cucumber sandwich, which she placed on the table. 'This is nice,' she said, fixing him with a smile.

'Who says we don't know how to live, eh?' Coupland stated, pouring her tea while she slipped her phone out of her pocket to check the time.

'Should be fine for half an hour,' she said.

She eyed the remnants of his full English. 'I'm guessing the stress you're under is making you crave greasy food.'

'Reckon you might have a point there,' he said, grinning, his face stretching in a way it never did when he was at work.

'Might help if you started having breakfast in the morning,' she stated, taking a sip of her tea, content to leave the conversation there. Coffee and back-to-back cigarettes had been his breakfast staple since his last year at the secondary modern, they both knew it was never going to change.

'I was surprised when you texted. Thought you were up to your eyes in it just now.'

'We are. We're waiting on a piece of information coming in that might mean I can't come home for the next couple of nights.'

'Just so long as you keep away from firearms and sharp implements.'

'I'll try my best.'

She studied him over the rim of her mug. 'Should I be worried?'

'Will my answer make you stop?'

She laughed because the answer was obvious. She reached across the table, placed her hand on his arm. 'What's wrong?'

'Nothing. Not really. I'd just feel happier if you and Amy went away with Tonto for a couple of days. Out of harm's way.'

'Would you now?' she said, raising an eyebrow at him. 'So we've been safe as houses all these years, have we?' She caught the look on his face. 'I didn't think so. It's what goes with the turf.' She gave his arm a playful squeeze. 'If I'd wanted an easier life I'd have gone for a drink with the teacher who asked me out the night before you did. Came in with a nasty injury to his hand after a slip up with a staple gun. Imagine how quiet life would have been with him, over the years…'

'Oh yeah?' Coupland cocked his head at her.

'Shh… I'm still imagining…' she joked. 'Look, I know

Amy's view is the same as mine on this and I'm going nowhere. We're not chattels you can move about at whim.'

'That's me told,' he said, leaning over the table to kiss her, a gesture which surprised them both. If he'd known then how different everything would be the next time he was there, he'd have begged her to change her mind. He'd have held onto her tight. Kept her safe.

Instead, he returned to Nexus House, oblivious.

*

Incident Room, Nexus House
Noah and Jared sat back and read their work, satisfied:

Finally, an apology.

Not one of my better moments, I admit. I was getting worried though. Why aren't you at the hotel?

I needed space to think things through.

And now?

I'm still thinking.

You're still coming tomorrow night though?

Of course.

Thank you. How are preparations going?

Don't worry about a thing. It'll go like clockwork. It always does.

You're so clever… Any chance I can see you tonight?

Let's wait until tomorrow.

If I must. I'll be busy for the first hour or so, you know how it goes. The judge has asked me to give him a personal tour. Can hardly say no since I'm his house guest… Till tomorrow then.

Noah printed out the transcript a dozen times, ready for circulation at the next briefing.

*

Coupland's phone rang as he was turning out of the hospital car park. It was Joe Edwards. He hit the hands-free button. 'I take it the boys have had a result?'

'You could say that. They managed to exchange several messages without raising suspicion. It's all happening tomorrow, apparently. Some big do that Ruth Hunter Pepper's helped organise. Only

problem is we're none the wiser where. Their texts just stated that they'd meet each other there.'

Coupland's thoughts shifted around as he listened. 'I may be able to help with that,' he answered. It'd mean a detour to a certain lock-up at the back of Strangeways but given Jay hadn't contacted him, he'd been given no choice.

'The boys have excelled themselves. Once they realised Hunter Pepper and the Dutchman were an item they searched through photographs she'd posted on Facebook from her personal profile. Found one going back about three years ago. A selfie taken on a yacht in the Caribbean. The pair of them, arm in arm, sipping champagne.'

'Seriously?'

'Better than that, she's tagged him in it. Must have been a moment of madness but it's there all the same. Available for anyone to find, if they knew where to look.'

'So we finally have a name for him?'

'We do indeed. Leon Dachman. The boys are putting together a bio on him as we speak.'

If there was a moment that made Coupland take back all his bitching about digital forensics, this was it. He felt as though he'd been injected with a new lease of life. *This* was what they'd been waiting for. The moment they'd been working towards for so long. 'Leon Dachman.' He tried out the name for size. It was a moment before he realised Edwards was still on the line.

'Was anyone else mentioned during their texts?'

'Not exactly,' stated Edwards, *'But he did mention that he's staying with a judge…'*

'Did he now?' said Coupland. 'That's very interesting.' Pound to a penny it was Simeon fucking Dray.

'Apparently he's asked him for a guided tour of the building where the party's being held,' Edwards told him. *'Or at least, I think that's what he meant.'*

Coupland shuddered. 'One more day...' he said, 'are we really this close?'

'We need to get the courts to sign off search warrants, once we've found out where this shindig is taking place.'

'I'll get you that address,' said Coupland, with more confidence than he felt. 'But for Christ's sake Simeon Dray can't be approached to sign anything off...'

'Already ahead of you there,' said Edwards. *'The application will be taken to a magistrate in Preston once we've got an address to put on it.'*

'Which is a cue for me to pull my finger out,' said Coupland, ending the call and pressing his foot down on the accelerator.

*

One look at the figure slumped on the ground in front of Jay's lock-up and it was obvious why the undercover officer hadn't been in touch. Coupland stepped tentatively towards him, not daring to breathe out until he saw his eyes blink. The blood on his tracksuit top had dried in patches. The cuts in his scalp needed stitching.

'Come on let's get you to the hospital,' said Coupland pulling him to his feet.

Jay winced and doubled over. Coupland waited while he steadied himself before yanking up his tracksuit top to take a look. Angry red marks covered his torso.

'It's not as bad as it looks.'

'Only if you're happy pissing blood for a week.' Coupland glanced about him. If the people who'd done this were hanging about he'd be powerless to do anything if they wanted a second go. Not much he could do about that now.

'So, what happened?'

Jay rubbed the back of his neck as he straightened himself. 'I'm just parking up when two blokes open the car door and drag me out. They caught me unawares, start giving me a right kicking before I can get my shit together. I managed to fight 'em off but…'

'What?'

'They could have finished me off there and then if they'd wanted to.' Jay closed his eyes. 'This happens sometimes, before I start a new job. A way of testing my mettle, I guess.'

'There must be easier ways of earning a living.'

'I was thinking of joining the SAS next.'

'Good choice. Look, let me take you back to yours. If you insist on healing yourself at least do it in your own bed.'

Jay's 'home' was a top floor luxury apartment in Ancoats, the type that came fully furnished in order to maintain the lifestyle the occupants aspired to. There were no personal effects. The place could be vacated at a moment's notice.

Before Jay collapsed on his bed he wrote down the address Lino Pavel had given him onto a sheet of paper torn from his notebook and stuffed it in Coupland's pocket. 'Now get out of here before someone sees you.'

'You still reckon you'll be able to make it?'

Jay opened a swollen eyelid and fixed his gaze on Coupland. 'You don't ring in sick to people like Lino. I'll be there. Besides, you're the one on his death list.'

'If I can get through tomorrow I'll be fine. They'll all be locked up after that.' When he looked back on the bed Jay was spark out.

Back in the car Coupland pulled the scrap of paper from his pocket. Used his phone to take a photo of the address Jay had written down, sent it to Joe Edwards.

CHAPTER TWENTY-EIGHT

'*Hello?*'

'It really isn't a good time right now, can you call back?'

'For God's sake! Sometimes I think you forget where I am. We can't come and go as we please, you know.'

'All right, I get the message, no need to be so cranky.'

'Talking of messages, someone here wants to have a word. Hold on a minute…'

'Hello? Are you still there?'

The voice that answers is deeper. Older. He gets straight to the point. Why it's important to do as he says.

The consequences if that doesn't happen.

CHAPTER TWENTY-NINE

Next day. Conference Room, Nexus House

The briefing took place in the conference room, where Coupland had attended his induction three months earlier. Not everyone at this briefing had been present on induction day. Due to the size of today's operation, personnel from several regional crime units would be deployed. Representatives from each unit sat on tables at the back of the room, along with specialist firearms units, and officers from the National Crime Agency.

A blown-up photograph of Grafton Manor, the address Jay O'Neill had passed on to Coupland, was on the large screen at the front of the room. The property was in Hale, a village that boasted some of the priciest homes in Britain outside London. The chances of bumping into a celebrity, or a premiership footballer, climbing into or out of garish coloured sports cars in this neck of the woods was very high. Not as high as stumbling into richer-than-Midas paedophiles later this evening, thought Coupland, as he stared at the Edwardian building. A trawl through the internet found interior shots of the downstairs reception rooms, featuring parquet flooring, oak panelled walls, fireplaces with high ceilings.

'Owned by a family who live overseas, the property has been leased out to a shell company set up by none other than Graham Prentice,' stated Commander Howorth.

Joe Edwards turned to Coupland, seated beside him in the main body of the conference room. 'Recognise the building?'

Coupland's mouth turned down at the edges as he shook his head.

'Andrew Chadderton had a publicity photo of his executive car fleet taken in front of it.'

Coupland's face cleared when he recalled the image. 'That figures.' His face grew serious. 'A property that size, all those empty rooms. Trafficked girls. There's every chance this lot had set up camp there while we've been up the road running round like extras out of The Bill.'

'We always knew they were active,' Edwards reasoned.

Coupland's nod was impatient. 'Yeah, but this close?'

Commander Howorth sent a warning glare to Coupland to keep it down. Appeased by Coupland's apologetic nod, he continued. 'Thanks to the information gleaned from texts between Ruth Hunter Pepper and Leon Dachman, formerly known as the Dutchman, we have a better understanding of how the top tier of this network operates. Along with Graham Prentice, they organise the strict, invitation-only sex parties held in the UK. Attendees pay a hefty subscription fee, which includes their drug of choice and an underage "companion" that matches their profile. Those who like a little more hard-core action can – for an even heftier fee – star in their very own snuff film. They literally pay to get away with murder, relying on those further down the network – the passmen – to dispose of the bodies. Many of these killings, along with the abuse generally meted out by these men, are captured on film and available to watch via Utopia, the Dutchman's pay-per-view live streaming site available online. This operation is repeated in many cities across Europe, with upwards of fifty attendees at any one event. At a fee of a quarter of a million euros per person, per party, I can see why he has protected his territory so fiercely.'

Jay O'Neill's information had provided them with the location and the time the party was due to start. He and local enforcer Lino Pavel were to report to Graham Prentice at 7pm, when they'd be shown round the area they'd be expected to patrol. They'd be provided with a guest list at 7.30pm, and under no circumstances would anyone not on the list be allowed to enter – or leave.

Coupland had refused point blank to explain how he'd come by this information. He suspected, when the Commander agreed so readily to work with it, that he remembered the introduction he'd set up three months earlier between Coupland and the undercover officer, guessing it had paid off.

'The hired muscle will be there not just to keep the uninvited out, but to prevent the trafficked girls from escaping. We have been granted a PACE extension in relation to Ruth Hunter Pepper. Her release would have jeopardised the whole operation. However, we need to strike before Dachman becomes suspicious by her absence. They've agreed to meet there and he'll be expecting to see her after his business with Judge Simeon Dray has concluded.'

An officer at the back of the room raised his hand. 'Any idea what this "business" is?' he asked.

'In return for being lenient on members of the network who end up in his court, the judge expects an early-bird preview of the girls who'll be there, only it's a lot more hands-on than window shopping.'

The officer sighed and shook his head.

Commander Howorth surveyed the room. 'The raid will be carried out at 8.00pm this evening.'

Coupland looked at his watch. It was 6.00pm. In two hours he'd be coming face to face with his nemesis.

Bring it on.

NOW

CHAPTER THIRTY

Salford Royal Hospital

"*The Forgotten Missing Women. Enough is Enough*"

Lynn wasn't one for buying newspapers. She got all the misery she needed from the news app on her phone. For some reason this headline jarred her. Without thinking about it she stepped into the newsagents which she normally walked past every evening, picked up the latest edition, tapped her card against the payment machine. As usual the headline contained the bulk of the story. The piece was intended to take a swipe at the police, the journalist using recent cases like hand grenades to get their point across. A newly qualified teacher, missing, presumed dead. According to the article the police had all but given up. She thought of Kevin and his colleagues sitting around in cold cars, on shift up to 36 hours straight with no sign of let up. There was no mention of that. She was tired, wondered if that was making her fret more. She worried about this taskforce he'd joined. Hoped he remembered to mind his manners, take his meds, keep dodging the bullet that had been after him his entire career. She pulled up the collar of her jacket, set off across the road for the bus.

*

Grafton Manor

The convoy of Tactical Aid Units snaked their way along the approach to Grafton Manor under the cover of darkness. Simultaneous raids were being carried out at the homes and workplaces of Marek Nowak and the twenty-two groomers and passmen found on Andrew Chadderton's computer at the time of his arrest.

The homes of Judge Simeon Dray and corporate lawyer Graham Prentice, amongst others, would be searched. The Metropolitan Police were coordinating a search of socialite Ruth Hunter Pepper's home along with properties owned by Sir Edward Jamieson and Charles Falconer. Interpol would be conducting searches in two apartments registered in Leon Dachman's name, in Frankfurt and New York. All digital devices and computing equipment would be seized. This was just the start of it. If all went to plan the network would topple like a house built on sand when the tide came in.

If all went to plan.

The rear doors of six armoured units in front opened, spewing out a sea of black as firearms officers took up position. A voice warbled over the radio checking with Superintendent Romain that the transmission was clear. Coupland, in one of the rear vehicles, pulled his Kevlar vest over his hooded 'Police' sweatshirt, put on his police issue baseball cap. In the vehicle behind his van officers from Immigration Enforcement bided their time. It was their job to round up any non-UK victims found on the premises and take them to a safe place. Underage UK victims would be taken into the temporary care of social services. Armed police lined up at the entrance to the building in silence. Superintendent Romain's voice came over the radio confirming the targeted sites were in view.

Lino Pavel, deliberately distracted by Jay O'Neill who'd been showing him a local gangster rapping on TikTok, was caught unawares when a CS gas cannister fired into the entrance hall landed at his feet.

'POLICE RAID! STAY WHERE YOU ARE!'

An explosion of noise erupted as tactical officers surged inside. The sound of heavy boots on polished flooring, of furniture being upended. The front of the building was flooded in light as portable beams were trained on the entrance.

Lino Pavel, dazed and confused, was led outside by Jay who disappeared just as a handy-looking cop in a Kevlar vest and baseball cap barrelled towards him and told him he was under arrest. Moments later a man in a velvet dinner jacket and bow tie was brought out in handcuffs. Coupland, having cuffed Lino Pavel, led them both into a cage at the back of a van.

Satisfied they were secure, Coupland pushed his way into the building, through the tide of officers leading well-dressed men outside in cuffs. He recognised some of the faces from the ones that had stared down at him over the last three months: Sir Edward Jamieson. Charles Falconer. Graham Prentice. Many looked on, bewildered, as officers read them their rights.

A man in his fifties sporting a silk scarf remonstrated with DI Taylor. 'Who the hell do you think you are speaking to? What makes you think you can walk in here and speak to me in such a manner?'

Judge Simeon Dray. Coupland flared his nostrils. Three steps and the only thing separating them was the stench of Dray's cologne. 'Who do we think *we* are?' he snarled, spit flying from his mouth as he spoke. 'Says the man who lets nonces walk free with a slap on the wrist. Now we know why… you sick fuck!' Coupland's mouth twisted as he resisted the urge to smash the bastard's face to a pulp.

'I've got it from here,' said Ben Taylor.

'I don't think so,' stated Coupland, pulling the judge's arms back before signalling to two passing NCA officers. 'I've reason to believe this suspect is concealing drugs about his person,' he informed them, standing back, satisfied, as Dray was carried out before being placed spread-eagled on the gravel drive face down while the officers searched him. It wasn't a fraction of what Gayle Woodhall and others like her had suffered, but it was a start.

Coupland's satisfaction was short-lived. After all, there was no show without Punch.

'Has anyone eyeballed the Dutchman?' he demanded.

Several officers around him shook their heads.

He ran through to the rear of the property where officers were taking down the names and contact details of the kitchen and waiting staff who'd been hired for the evening. Those who'd been given permission to leave loitered outside, smoking, waiting for their colleagues. Rather than wait for the others, one man, after giving his details to an officer stationed by the exit, climbed into the driver's seat of a black BMW. This man's hair was thinning on top, making his forehead look larger than it was. Two deep lines etched across it.

'What name did he give you?' Coupland barked at the officer.

'Rob Lewis,' came the reply after he referred to his

notes. A false name the Dutchman had used before.

'Fucksake!' yelled Coupland. He ran at the car just as the engine started, yanking the passenger door open and hoisting himself inside. He wasn't ready for the first punch that came his way. The taste of blood running from his nostril confirmed the Dutchman had hit his target.

Whack! Coupland retaliated with a side-on punch that would have KO'd a lesser man.

The car moved forward with a jolt then stopped. Coupland looked through the windscreen. They were at the side of the house. Behind them was a dead end. The only way out was through the front gates, which had been blocked off by armoured vans. The guy was on a suicide mission if he thought he was going to get through them. Coupland ran his tongue around the inside of his mouth, thinking.

'So, Leon, now butt in if you think I'm being unfair. But you're fucked, aren't you?'

The Dutchman pulled a gun from his pocket, aimed it at Coupland's head. 'If I am, then so are you.'

Coupland had played this scene through countless times in his mind. The moment he and the Dutchman came face to face. It usually involved chasing him down an embankment or shoving him from a bridge. None of them included the monster aiming a gun at him.

'I want you to get onto that radio of yours. Tell your colleagues to move those vehicles,' Dachman ordered.

'I'm afraid I can't do that.'

'Tell them if they do not move those vehicles, I will kill you.'

Coupland coughed out a laugh.

'I think you've put far more importance on me than I

merit,' he said, shaking his head. 'Not like I matter much, in the grand scheme of things. Now if I'd have been a politician, or a celebrity, or even a minor royal for that matter, you'd have been in with a chance. They'd likely shift the vans and send you a helicopter. As it is you've saddled yourself with the booby prize. A middle-aged detective from the arse end of nowhere. Some days are a bastard, aren't they?'

'I SAID GET THE FUCKING VANS MOVED!' yelled the Dutchman.

'AND I SAID NO!' Coupland yelled back, collapsing his body so that his head dropped between his knees. The hit was instant. The spray of warm blood on the back of his neck and the metallic tang in the air confirmed the marksman's accuracy. When Coupland looked to his right Dachman was leaning back against the headrest, eyes wide open, as though the bullet in his head had caught him by surprise.

Coupland pushed himself upright. He knew better than to reach for the gun Dachman was still holding. An involuntary spasm could have cocked the trigger. One wrong move and it could still go off. Better left to ballistics to sort out.

A firearms officer in dark blue overalls and a ceramic helmet opened the passenger door. Coupland climbed out.

'What took you so long?' Coupland grumbled. He'd pressed his 10 zero button, the emergency call sign button, on his radio the moment he'd jumped into the car. 'Not like you had roadworks to deal with.'

'You're welcome,' said the officer, slapping him on the back.

Superintendent Tony Romain hurried towards him. 'You OK?'

'Slightly deaf in one ear, sir, other than that I'm fine.'

'Get yourself checked out,' Romain insisted, pointing to a bank of ambulance units parked beyond the gate.

'Sure,' said Coupland. He headed towards them then turned at the last minute to follow a group of enforcement officers towards a set of stairs at the back of the house.

'You're going the wrong way, DS Coupland!' shouted Romain.

'Sorry, can't hear you, sir,' Coupland responded as he descended the stairs.

The lower floor consisted of several derelict rooms with bare concrete floors and exposed brick walls. There were rows of camp beds in one room beneath a solitary light bulb. Another was being used as a makeshift dressing room. Dresses hung on a clothes rail on one side of the room; a dressing table with a mirror and pots of makeup stood beside it.

Coupland caught sight of his reflection in the mirror. Used his sleeve to wipe the Dutchman's blood away. Two girls stood solemnly, dressed up and preened, ready to go upstairs and 'perform'. One held onto a teddy bear while she waited.

In another room a dozen young women and girls huddled together on the floor as enforcement officers explained they weren't in trouble, that they were to raise their hand if they could speak English. Several put their hands up. One woman explained it was her job to go up to the party first to put the men in good spirits. Later, when they were *really happy*, they'd send for the younger girls to join them.

A girl aged about twelve stumbled towards Coupland. Two trails of snot ran from her nostrils to her mouth. 'One minute they want us to call them daddy, the next minute they beat us.'

Coupland swiped his thumbs across his eyes. He looked at the ceiling. Muttered, 'Christ Almighty.'

Superintendent Romain descended the steps, heading towards Coupland.

'I'll get checked out later, sir,' Coupland told him, waiting for him to object.

'Never mind that,' said Romain. He held up a clear plastic evidence bag he'd been carrying. 'One of the NCA officers found these stuffed in a cupboard on the top floor.' The bag contained what looked like thirty or forty passports and two mobile phones.

'I'll take them, sir,' said Coupland, lifting the bag out of Romain's hands and tipping the contents onto one of the camp beds.

'What are you doing?'

'Looking to see if one of them belongs to Eliza Evans.'

'We can go through the contents back at Nexus House.'

'It'll take two minutes,' Coupland persisted, snapping on blue nitrile gloves. 'Here!' he said, his tone triumphant as he held up the newly qualified teacher's passport. He jabbed at the 'On' buttons on both phones but they were out of power. One of them was Eliza's, he could feel it. Was it possible that she was here too?

He threw the items back in the evidence bag and removed his gloves. Clutching it under his arm as he ran into each room, he called her name. 'ELIZA! IS ELIZA HERE? Is there anyone here called Eliza Evans? She's not in trouble. We just want to know she's safe.'

'We're not allowed to use our real names,' a malnourished girl of about six told him, as though he was an extremely stupid man.

Coupland watched as the girls were escorted outside and loaded onto vans to be processed. All would be checked over by the waiting paramedics before they were taken anywhere. Coupland ran over to where the ambulances waited. There was an occupant inside one of them, being attended to by a paramedic. 'Do you have a name for her?' he called out.

The paramedic shook her head.

Coupland climbed into the unit. He approached the young woman slowly so as not to frighten her. She had a black eye and a scraped cheek. There was a cut on her temple and a faint line around her neck as though something had been wrapped around it and pulled tight. To suffocate, but not to kill. Her mouth was swollen and raw. She sat hunched forward, the fight gone out of her.

She barely looked at Coupland.

'Are you Eliza?' he asked. 'Eliza Evans?'

She closed her eyes. Nodded.

'It's great to finally meet you, love,' he said, draping a blanket around her shoulders. In time, she'd be able to help them piece together the events leading up to her abduction, and what she'd been subjected to. Tell them who the main instigator had been. Dylan Breakwell, or Marek Novak. Not that it mattered in the grand scheme of things. Both were destined to a life behind bars. He hoped Eliza didn't become a prisoner too. 'You're safe now,' he told her. It was a start.

Coupland's phone started to vibrate. He stepped out

of the ambulance to answer it. Didn't bother looking at the screen. Barked his name.

It was DS Ashcroft. He sounded odd. *'Where are you?'*

Coupland observed the chaos around him. 'I'm in the middle of a job, mate.'

'Then listen to me. Listen up good.'

CHAPTER THIRTY-ONE

Coupland drew in a breath. Choked it back out.

His throat was dry, he was aware of someone touching his arm. He roared and stumbled backwards.

Sat in the passenger seat of an area car. Joe Edwards driving. Blue lights, siren.

Ashcroft at the entrance to A and E.

The corridor full of familiar faces. People Lynn had talked about over the years. Colleagues. Bosses. Friends. He couldn't remember getting here.

He walked beside Ashcroft. Kept pace with him. Ashcroft silent. Strong. Coupland felt like he'd been blown to smithereens. He was nothing. Particles. Mist.

A man in blue scrubs stood outside the relatives' room, beckoning Coupland in.

'Not here,' said Ashcroft, assertive. 'He's spent his career watching people's lives disintegrate in that room.'

The doctor nodded, asked them to follow him.

This wasn't supposed to happen. She was supposed to die of cancer. It was supposed to come back. Take her slowly. Give them time to say goodbye. He'd rehearsed it in his head. Knew what he'd need to do. Not this fucking way.

All those years of worry hadn't prevented it. Coupland pushed his anger away because he didn't have room for it. This wasn't how it was supposed to end.

He tried to do what he always did when the oncoming train in his head wouldn't stop. He thought of Lynn. This time it didn't work, it couldn't possibly work, because Lynn wasn't at home keeping his world together; she was in the resus room preparing to leave it.

He tried not to think about the possible outcomes. The number of different ways the day might pan out. Lynn's belongings folded into a clear plastic bag. Her engagement ring and wedding ring kept safe in a little paper envelope. There was only one acceptable option. Two, if her injuries were life altering. Just let her come home, he whispered. Let her live.

Move on. Think of something else. The first day he saw her. The end of a double shift in A and E. Scrubs and flat shoes. Carrying out obs on an officer who'd been given a pasting.

Her smile.

It had stopped him in his tracks. Still did.

Her voice.

The short shrift she'd given some layabout who asked for her number. The short shrift she'd given Coupland for telling the layabout to jog on. 'I can fight my own battles,' she'd told him. And that's what she'd done ever since.

Now, because of him she faced the biggest battle of her life. He pushed away other memories. Their wedding day. Amy's arrival. He remembered everything and nothing. As if she were already slipping from his grasp.

He wasn't ready to look back on the life they'd had. He wanted her in the here and now. Coupland's heart pumped queasily in his chest. He whispered her name, like a secret that could never be told.

Lynn.

*

In the staff room the doctor explained about the multiple fractures. He saved the most worrying injury, the bleed on her brain, until last. He talked about the emergency surgery she was undergoing. That as soon as they were able, they'd take Coupland to her. One of the nurses from her ward stepped in to see how he was bearing up.

'She always talked about you, Kevin. Said how special you made her feel.'

He glared at her. 'Stop talking about her like she's dead! She's not dead!'

Did they think he couldn't see the shifty looks they were giving him?

'She's not dead, yet,' he said, though more to himself this time.

Ashcroft pressed something into his hands. Tea. Sweet as fuck.

He tried to swallow. The boulder in his throat wouldn't budge. 'Tell me what happened.'

Ashcroft had already explained it, but he told it again, as though saying it for the first time:

'The car went straight for her as she reached the bus stop. Eyewitness claims it was deliberate. We're pulling out all the stops, Kevin. That's why the boss isn't here. Everyone's out, searching. Even if the order was given by someone in the network you're chasing, chances are it'll be a local face that's done the deed. You know how it works. We'll get the bastard.'

Coupland sipped at his tea. Went to the toilet. Threw up.

*

'*You* did this, Dad.'

He looked up to see Amy standing by the window. How long had she been here? Where was Lynn?

'This happened because of you.'

'Amy, I didn't know this was going to happen…'

'Didn't you? Really? It was beyond your worst nightmare?'

Coupland looked away.

'I hope it was worth it.'

'Please Ames, don't.'

Coupland looked around the room, confused.

'Where's Tonto?'

'He's with his Nana. I don't want him growing up thinking it's normal to spend so much time in A and E. What kind of life is that? You're to blame for this, Dad. You, not the network you've been chasing. I don't understand why you have to get so involved. Always be the big man. Why can't you ever leave things alone?'

'I wouldn't be much of a cop if I did that, Ames.'

'There you go again, calling me by the name you used when I was little. It's like there's only room for one decision maker around here and that's you. Why didn't you make her go somewhere safe?'

'She didn't want to go, Ames. *Amy*. I wasn't happy but I respected that. Are you now saying that I should be the sort of person who makes her do things against her wishes? You know she wouldn't stand for that.'

Not content with conceding his point, Amy changed tack. 'You take every case personally. You might think you leave everything at the front door but you don't. The number of times she's said over the years *Leave your dad be, he's had a hard day. Cut him some slack, his job's tougher than yo realise, Amy*. All these years she's been your number one fan. Even if she survives, how is this going to affect her? She's always been the ray of sunshine at home. What if she blames you too?'

It was more than he could think about. He visualised a box on its side, all his uncertainties tumbling out.

Coupland sat there, not moving long after Amy had walked away, her footsteps fading to silence along the corridor. Her words reverberating loud in his head. The twist and tug at his insides, sharp and real. He leaned against the wall and closed his eyes, waiting for his heart to return to its normal rhythm.

The medic appeared at the staff room door. 'You can see her now.'

Coupland stepped into Lynn's room, scared at what he might see. Amidst the quiet humming of machines she lay pale beneath white covers. He stooped to kiss her but she didn't wake. He pulled the chair beside the bed closer so that he could sit and hold her hand. He waited.

Kevin, she said after some time. She opened her eyes. *Kev.*

Then closed them again while Coupland cried.

CHAPTER THIRTY-TWO

Ashcroft remained at the hospital with Coupland. On hand to provide updates on the search for Lynn's attacker when there was something to report, offering moral support when there wasn't. Joe Edwards returned to Nexus House, with a similar promise to keep Coupland updated. They both knew he wouldn't. The investigation had become too personal. If someone in the network had given the order to harm Lynn it was hardly a line of enquiry Coupland could deal with objectively.

It was the next morning before the consultant was willing to use the word 'stable.' Lunchtime before Amy could bear to be in the same room as him. She was civil to him within earshot of Lynn, though her eyes told a different story.

For the last half hour Coupland had smoked back-to-back cigarettes in the smoking bay, enjoying none. A guy in a tracksuit with a beat-up face came towards him. It took a moment for him to place who he was. 'Why are you here?'

'I wanted to check on you,' Jay O'Neill explained. 'How's your wife?'

Coupland's chest tightened. 'The bastard left her for dead.'

'But she'll be OK?'

Lynn would need months of physiotherapy. Even

then she'd likely have a permanent limp. Christ knew how long she'd be able to get off work before they signed her off on medical grounds. She loved that job. He didn't want to think what losing it would do to her. To them. What did you do when the most positive force in your life was the thing that was damaged? 'She'll be OK,' he said, trying the words out for size, hoping to Christ they were possible.

Jay nodded. 'I had a girlfriend, when I first got into this lark. We'd been together a while. It was at that point in my life where I thought coming home to the same person every night would be a good thing. You know what I mean? Like you finally realise you're not missing anything playing the field, and you've started thinking that your mates who still do are sad sacks. You might not know what the question is, but the answer is right there the moment you get home and close the door behind you.'

Apart from Ashcroft, and a mate he'd lost touch with by the name of Flemish Joe, Coupland had no experience talking to men without the cover of banter. He wondered where this conversation was going.

'When I saw what this job had the potential to do, I broke up with her. I never told her the reason why. Just the usual lame excuse, *It's me not you* bullshit. I couldn't do this job properly if I kept looking over my shoulder all the time. There's always that fear that someone can come along and blow it all away.' He paused, a look flashing across his face that Coupland struggled to read.

'Spit it out, son. This isn't the day for keeping me waiting.'

Nodding, Jay reached into his tracksuit top and pulled out a manila file which he handed over. 'There's something in there I think you should see. I'm just worried about what you'll do once you've seen it.'

Coupland took the file and flicked it open. Photographs and surveillance reports. Something in one of the photos jumped out at him. It was a photo of the car eyewitnesses had described had ploughed into Lynn. The same car was in the next photo, along with a close-up image of the driver at the wheel.

'What is this?' Coupland asked, his brain already telling him that was a stupid question. He was staring at the car – and bastard – responsible for causing Lynn's injuries.

'I told you the intel I'd been sending upstairs wasn't being acted on?'

Coupland nodded.

Jay pointed to the driver of the car. 'This guy had started hanging around the place. He seemed to be everywhere I was. No one but Lino knew him but he went about with attitude, know what I'm saying? Then he rocks up in what was obviously a stolen car. I sent the photos to my handler. Asked whether another UC officer had been sent in without my knowledge. Like I told you before, it wouldn't be the first time.'

Breath caught in Coupland's throat. 'And?' he demanded, spit forming in the corners of this mouth.

'My handler comes back to me within the hour. "Leave well alone," she says.'

'That's not a fucking answer,' Coupland spat.

'That's what I told her when I picked up the phone and called her. I told her I didn't give a fuck what time it was, I'm out here putting my bollocks on the line and some guy's started showing his face like he's king fucking dick. She told me bigger fish were watching him. That she'd checked with her boss and been given strict instructions I wasn't to go near him. His presence was known but we were to leave him be.'

'Your handler's boss,' Coupland demanded, trying to keep his breathing under control. The person who had played silly buggers at the outset when he'd tried arranging a meeting with Jay. He'd never found out who the jobsworth was. 'Do they have a name?'

Jay told him.

*

Coupland parked in front of the double fronted Victorian semi. Banged on the front door. Might as well make it clear this wasn't a social call. She must have checked who it was through the spyhole, his murderous face hadn't deterred her from opening the door.

Superintendent Lara Cole took one look at him. 'Kevin!' she began, the rest of her sentence muffled as he pushed his way inside.

Coupland backed her against the wall. He'd never raised his hand to a woman, but Lynn was damaged because of her. Was he prepared to make an exception? He shoved his hands deep into his pockets, reducing the temptation to lash out. He wanted to maim. Kill. But he wanted to be sure he maimed, killed, the right person. He'd never been more aware of his feelings, his thoughts. In that moment nothing separated him from Kieran Tunny, from any murdering gangster. He wanted to tear the person who'd wreaked havoc on his family limb from limb. He wanted to hurt them. Decimate them. Jesus, fuck, he was the wrong side of crazy to think of the consequences but he didn't care. His body trembled with adrenaline.

He let her push him away. He wanted her to talk, not to cower. 'It was you! You gave the order on Lynn!'

'*No!*' Her face twisted as she spat out the word. 'But I knew what would happen,' she admitted, then, seeing the look that flashed across Coupland's face, 'N-Not like that!' she stammered, 'I didn't know that they were going to do that! I just thought they were going to warn you off by scaring her a little, frighten you off that way. I did ask you to take your rest days.'

'Oh, so it's my fault! You had no choice but to up the ante to make me back off!'

'You make it sound worse than it is.'

'No! I don't! She nearly died because of you.'

Coupland took a breath.

'When Jay O'Neill sent a photograph of a jumped-up joy rider who'd showed up on his patch, asking for intel, you were the one that quashed it.' It wasn't a question.

Lara Cole nodded. 'They – the people who made me do it - didn't want him getting the wrong sort of attention. That's all.'

Coupland shook his head. 'It was easy to discredit anything Jay sent through since you'd done such a good job of badmouthing him.' The rumours that Jay had gone rogue started on Coupland's first day in the job. He'd never got to the bottom of where those rumours had come from. Now it was obvious. He wouldn't put it past her to have arranged his beating at the lock-up.

'They asked you to find out where Lynn worked, didn't they?'

She looked at the floor.

He remembered their conversation. Her faux concern when he'd confided that a hit had been put out on him

How he'd fallen for it. Answering her questions like an obedient child. 'And you passed that information on, knowing that her life would be in danger.'

'I had no choice!'

'There's always a choice!'

'Please, let me explain…'

Coupland's eyes widened. 'You seriously think you can come up with anything that will make me say "Aw, how awful, well in that case maiming my wife was the only fucking answer"?'

'Please…'

'Save it!'

'They were threatening my son.'

'I DON'T GIVE A FUCK!'

'You would if it was your family that was threatened.'

Coupland cupped his hands over his mouth. Breathed in and out slowly.

'He's in jail,' she said carefully, as though she was putting the facts right in her head. 'For dealing drugs. No one knows. Obviously. I mean, how would that work? I'd have lost my job. The only reason I managed to keep it secret was because I've never used my married name. The kids stayed with their dad when we divorced, moved down to London to be near his parents.'

Coupland looked on, impassive.

'These people are clever. You said as much right from the beginning. They find every weakness. When they found out our connection they planted someone in the jail. On his actual bloody wing. Told me what they'd do to him if I didn't cooperate. The camera blind spots where he could be cornered. The places where even the prison officers don't linger. They made him phone me and put them on the line. Can you imagine what that's like? I've been a crap mother to him, this was something I had the power to stop.'

'How did they find out about your son?'

'I transfer money every week into his prison account so he can buy things he needs, like shaving foam or pot noodles, the odd bar of chocolate. The name of the prison is on the account reference number along with his name and date of birth. Hardly rocket science.'

They already knew the Dutchman's network included people like Andrew Chadderton who paid bank employees cash for personal customer data. Anyone who'd seen the weekly prison payments and checked what Lara Cole did for a living must have thought they'd hit the jackpot.

Coupland stood motionless. He was unable to look at her without feeling sick to his stomach. He stared at the wall. Thinking.

According to Jay this boy racer was known to local enforcer Lino Pavel. Pavel took his orders from Graham Prentice. It would be easy enough for the ex-con to get his cronies to put the frighteners on a daft lad in jail – and use the threat of that to control his mother, a high-ranking police officer attached to the taskforce hunting down members of the network that he worked for.

'Was it you that leaked that photo to the press? The one where Romain and me were in that restaurant?'

Cole nodded. 'They wanted to discredit the operation. I paid a waitress to take a photograph while you were there. I sent it onto them and they took it to the newspaper.'

'Who did you send it onto? Was it Lino Pavel?'

'I was given the number of a burner phone – I suppose

it could have been him that answered.'

'He was the one paid to kill me. But then you know that,' he said, sending her a look of contempt. 'I'm guessing you put my name forward as a target. And there was me thinking I didn't live up to your expectations.'

'I had no choice! They just kept piling the pressure on. I had to give them something.'

'Someone. You had to give them *someone*.'

Coupland remembered what Jay had told him the night he thought he was being followed. That Lino Pavel had murdered Andrew Chadderton. 'You passed on the address of Andrew Chadderton's safe house, didn't you?'

Lara Cole nodded. 'What are you going to do? With me, I mean?'

'I'm going to give you until the end of the day to hand yourself in. I'd drag you in myself but there's somewhere I need to be. Oh, and don't think about doing a runner because I will come for you, and I won't stop until I find you. You understand?'

'What about my son?'

'If you're lucky, the Commander might get him transferred somewhere else, but I really don't give a shit.'

*

Coupland sat in his car. The manila file Jay had given him open on the passenger seat. He grasped the photo of Lynn's would-be killer, his hands shaking as he imagined the feel of them around the bastard's neck. Squeezing, squeezing. He placed the photo on the dashboard so he could study it while he lit a cigarette, remembering too late that he wasn't supposed to smoke in the car anymore.

Something else he'd failed at.

He recognised the driver's face. His coat hanger smile that had mocked him the first time they'd crossed paths. Granted, he hadn't looked quite so pleased with himself when Coupland had put him away for James McMahon's hit and run. The irony of it. That it was his sentence, along with Kieran Tunny's, that had been quashed on appeal due to the failings of the forensic lab. Coupland had been apoplectic when Chief Superintendent Curtis had broken the news at his leaving do. If he'd had any inkling what the consequences would be…

Tunny would deal with him if he asked him to. He might have been his apprentice back in the day but what he'd done to Lynn would bring shame. One word from Coupland and this time tomorrow he'd be in the bottom of the ship canal or under the foundations of some tower block development. Coupland wasn't sure of the satisfaction he'd get if it wasn't his own knuckles that bled from the graft of it. If his own face wasn't the last one the bastard saw.

If there was ever a time he felt compelled to cross the line, to tread in the shoes of the monsters he'd put away over the years, this was it. He swiped the photo onto the floor of the car and started the engine.

He knew what he had to do.

*

Sean Bell was arrested at 4pm for the attempted murder of Lynn Coupland. Residents nearby the halfway house he'd been placed in since his release from prison could be forgiven for thinking they were in the middle of a full-blown Armageddon. Armed police, dog handlers and the division helicopter were deployed to bring him in. Some thought the amount of force used was unnecessary, as though a point was being made, though if there was, no one knew what it was.

Thanks to the diligence of local youths, the burnt-out car was located and impounded for testing by a newly appointed forensic laboratory. Even so, the most damning evidence, the one that would nail Sean Bell to the cross, was the photograph of him at the wheel of the car, taken by an undercover officer referred to in the CPS file as UCO592.

EPILOGUE

Lynn stayed in hospital for ten days before returning home. She had a calendar full of physio appointments. She was fit and given time her body would mend. Coupland, granted a leave of absence from work, fetched and carried and learned how to make soup. Lynn's inability to blame him, compounding his guilt all the more.

They were in the front room. She was propped up on the sofa, a book she'd been meaning to get into open on the table beside her. Coupland stood by the fireplace, reading the card that came with flowers sent from the team at Nexus House. Everyone had signed it. Apart from Lara Cole, who'd been suspended from duty and faced a gross misconduct hearing. A criminal investigation against her was also underway. A jail term was still possible.

It would take several months for work to be complete on Operation Maple's CPS file, though Coupland would no longer be involved. DCI Swain and Joe Edwards had their placements extended so that they could help the Super get it over the line. Ben Taylor, Noah Rainey and Jared Ozin were to return to their teams over the next couple of weeks.

Coupland had been in the office once since Lynn was injured. To give his account of his part in the raid on Grafton Manor, followed by a celebratory meal with the team which Lynn had insisted he attend. It was a low brow affair at a Mexican restaurant. They'd all worn sombreros and Coupland had tried explaining the concept of a kitty to Superintendent Romain only for him to go one better and pick up the bill for the table. 'Some people jusssht ooze classss,' Coupland had hiccupped, appreciatively.

Even so, he spent too much time hovering around her. Trying too hard. He'd dragged the Christmas decorations down from the loft, made a ham-fisted job of making the place look festive though none of them were feeling it.

Lynn'd had enough.

'It wasn't your fault, Kev,' she said in a rare moment when they were alone. Tonto was hitting a swing ball with Amy in the garden.

'Yes, it was,' he said, stubborn as ever.

'You weren't driving that car.'

'He went for you because of me.'

'You were doing your job, that's all.'

Coupland stared out of the window. He caught the eye of a neighbour lifting shopping bags out of his car across the road. The man raised his hand in greeting. Coupland rewarded him with a half nod. If he hadn't joined the task force Lynn wouldn't be hurt. The taskforce's mission had been successful, but Amy was right. He shouldn't let the job consume him. Behind him, Lynn's sigh was long and low, making him turn.

'I need to put all my energy into getting better, Kev. I can't keep propping you up anymore, being the go-between for you and Amy. You did nothing wrong, but the way you are handling this isn't right. You need to build bridges with your daughter, and I can't help you with that.'

Coupland walked over to the sofa, leaned down to kiss

her cheek. An apology? In gratitude? He wasn't sure. All he was sure of was that she was right.

Straightening himself, he headed out to the garden.

THE END

ENJOYED THE DS COUPLAND SERIES? READ ON FOR THE FIRST BOOK IN EMMA'S EDINBURGH GANGLAND SERIES...

TRUTH LIES WAITING

Chapter 1

It's funny how the do-gooding public think prison is the answer, like a magic wand that wipes your criminal scorecard clean. Only it isn't like that, the problems you leave behind are still waiting for you when you step back out into the daylight, except now they're much bigger, and this time you don't have as many choices. I was one of the lucky ones, moved back into my family home and into a job that paid decent money. I should send a shout out to my probation officer; she came up trumps, getting me in at Swanson's rather than pretend work on a poxy job creation scheme. OK, packing cardboard boxes is boring as Hell, but you can have a laugh with the guys on the shop floor and turn the radio up when you run out of things to say.

Even so, only one day in the job and already things started going pear-shaped. I was heading towards the bus-stop at the end of my shift when a small boy riding a BMX bike mounted the pavement, circling round me a couple of times like a playground bully eyeing his victim. Close up he was older than I'd first thought, maybe thirteen or so, with shaved blond hair and a forehead that was way too wide for the rest of his face. His eyes were sunken and further apart than was right and a mouth that hung open as though his lips were too heavy for his jaw.

'You Davy?' It came out as a statement rather than a question, but I nodded anyway.

'Gotta message f'ya.' The kid had a nasal whine, the kind that'd get on your nerves if you had to listen to it all the time. I wasn't worried by the sight of him though; a boy on a bike makes a bee-line for you and says they've got a message; it's not that big a deal round here. As far as I know, Hallmark and Interflora don't stock '*Glad you're out of chokey*' gifts and where I'm from your first stretch inside is a rite of passage. News of my release is bound to have got around.

'Mickey's givin' ye till the end o' the week to make your first payment.'

I nodded in agreement, his terms seemed reasonable; he was hardly going to write off my loan because of my spell inside.

'Said to tell ye he's adjusted the figures.'

Ah. Bike Boy's voice was beginning to grate but he had my full attention. 'Said something 'bout the credit crunch an' compound interest, or was it compound fractures?' the boy stated maliciously. 'Either way he said I wasn't tae worry if I forgot the gist, so long as I told ye how much yer payment has gone up tae.'

I had a feeling I wasn't going to like this. Bike Boy paused for effect, as though I was an X Factor contestant about to learn my fate: whether I was to stay in the competition or return to the life I'd been badmouthing every week.

'Two hundred quid,' he said firmly.

I was confused. That was the amount of my original loan. I'd been due to pay it off fifty pounds a week until

Mickey got bored but now he seemed to be giving me the chance to pay off the debt in full. It'd be a stretch, after tax I'll be clearing two fifty a week, but it'd be worth it. Bike Boy smiled, not altogether unkindly but there was a glimmer of pleasure there, even so.

'Two hundred a week until further notice,' he clarified matter of factly.

'Yer havin' a laugh!' I began to object but the kid was already peddling away, job done. I know my spell inside meant Mickey'd had to wait for his money but this was some penalty. After bus fares and board I'd be working for nothing.

And so this morning I'm trying to manage my expectations. To start my day as I mean to go on. Good things don't happen to Davy Johnson, never have done, never will. I'm your original walking talking magnet for bucket loads of shit but today I'm going to look on the bright side; the sun is shining, I have a pack of smokes in my pocket and I have a job. I take a cigarette from the pack and light it, drawing down hard, enjoying the sensation of the nicotine inflating my lungs. Is it so wrong to be drawn to something that really isn't good for you?

The sun's rays beam down steadily and I roll my overalls to my waist before lying back on the wooden bench, savouring each lungful of smoke. My upper body tingles; already the skin on my chest is beginning to turn pink. Be good to get some colour, get rid of the grey pallor that is the trademark of a stretch inside. I close my eyes, lifting my cigarette for a final drag before returning to the pallet of cartons waiting for me. All I need to top the day off is a nice cold beer and I promise myself one at the end of the shift with a couple of guys from the shop floor if they're up for it.

A cold chill across my stomach makes my eye lids snap open. There, in my eye line, blocking out the sun like a spiteful raincloud stands a familiar but unfriendly face. Police Constable MacIntyre arrested me six months ago and here he is larger than life staring down at me as though I'm a giant turd. I look past MacIntyre to the squad car parked by the factory gates and the officer in the passenger seat picking his nose while scrolling through messages on a mobile. I don't think they're supposed to use their phones on duty but I know better than to air unasked for views. Instead, I push myself to a sitting position, pulling my overalls up over my shoulders whilst checking across the factory yard to see if my visitors can be seen from the main building. Candy Staton, the boss's PA, has her back to the canteen window while she busies herself getting drinks for the managers. Petite with long shiny hair tied back in a ponytail, she is the prettiest girl I've set eyes on in a long while. She smiled at me on my first day here even though she must have seen my personnel file. I wonder what she'll make of the new guy not yet a week in and bringing police to the door.

'Heard they'd let ye oot.' PC MacIntyre is a prize prick with eyes that tell you he likes a drink almost as much as he loves a ruck. Thick-set arms protruding from a dumpy body, his Kevlar vest provides an illusion of muscle. 'Thought I'd come see for myself.'

I say nothing. I learned long ago not to rise to the bait; that smart mouth answers got me locked up for the night. Instead, I stare at the man's forehead as though looking for his third eye.

'What's this… fancy dress?' MacIntyre smirks at my

overalls and work boots while at the same time taking a step closer, all the better to intimidate. Slowly I push myself up from the bench, making us equal in height though we both knew which man has the upper hand. Over the officer's shoulder I can see Candy pause by the window, watching us.

'Look,' I reason, arms outstretched to let MacIntyre know he'll get no trouble from me, 'I need to get back, we only get ten minutes for a break.'

The officer sniggers as though this is the funniest thing he's heard in ages. '"We only get ten minutes for a break!"' he mimics. 'Who ye trying tae kid, son? Work's no' good enough fe the likes o' you,' he snipes, 'I know for a fact ye'll no' last the shift.'

Not for the first time I wonder whether there is a section in the police training manual called *Easy steps to Provoking and Needling;* only this is a skill MacIntyre really works hard at. Each meeting is like an Olympic pissing contest except there can only ever be one winner. I stay silent, yet still there's only a slim chance of me coming through unscathed.

'What they got ye doing then, sweeping the floor?' MacIntyre smiles but his eyes are cold and hard.

'Packing boxes,' I mutter, wondering if this simple answer can incriminate me in some way, although for what, I can't imagine.

MacIntyre nods as though he already knows this answer and I've merely been sitting some kind of test. 'Ye don't have to be Einstein then, eh?' he smirks. I shrug, I've been told I was thick by every teacher in school, if this insult is intended to wind me up he's way off beam; you can't be offended by a fact.

'Then again, with your pedigree…' MacIntyre taunts. Here it comes, the bit about my Dad being an alkie and handy with his fists, especially where Mum was concerned. How come his jibes always end up with my Dad? He was a wrong 'un so I'm destined to be one too, is that it?

'I mean,' MacIntyre grins as though he's second guessed my thoughts and has deliberately chosen to change tack, 'what with ye mum being on the game and all, not exactly going tae come across many great male role models are ye?'

I keep my mouth clamped shut but it's getting really hard not to rise to his bait. Digs about me or my old man I can cope with, but there's not a soul on this earth who'll get away with saying anything bad about Mum. She put food on the table every day of my childhood, made sure I had decent clothes and a roof over our heads. In fact life improved once Dad was no longer around and Mum was grateful to have a job that meant she was there for me when I'd been small. *Ye gotta roll with the punches, Son,* was the way she explained it, *ye have to deal with the hand ye've been dealt.* It wasn't her fault I'd got in with a bad crowd. Yes, my bravado cost me a stint inside, but it was a mistake I had no intention of repeating.

'Cat got your tongue?' MacIntyre's sly little eyes follow my gaze toward the office window and Candy, a knowing look flitting across his face. 'Way out of your league, Sunshine,' he smirks, nodding in her direction. 'Especially when she hears about your pedigree.'

'Go fuck yersel'.' The words shoot out before I can stop them and in that moment I know how the rest of the day will pan out. Even at that point, there is little I can do to change the pattern of events.

PC MacIntyre's eyes light up like a child on Christmas morning, 'What did ye say, ye lanky streak o' piss?'

'Ye heard me,' I say, in for a penny, in for a pound. I pull myself up to my full height, which I know will look to the copper in the car like I'm squaring up but by now I no longer give a shit. I turn towards the wedged open fire exit I'd emerged from fifteen minutes earlier. The prefab building which has been my place of work for two whole days had offered endless possibilities; even the vain hope that Candy Staton would notice my existence. I look back to the canteen window; she's noticed me now, right enough, but for all the wrong reasons.

I turn to MacIntyre. 'They're expecting me,' I say simply.

'They're expecting ye to fuck up,' he says scornfully. 'Why don't you do everyone a favour and crawl back under your stone?'

Ignoring him, I walk towards the open factory door; I figure putting some space between us might stop him feeling the need to intimidate.

'Not so fast, Pal,' he warns, putting his hand on my chest to prevent me from moving but I brush it aside; the sooner I get back indoors the better. A crowd has gathered beside Candy at the canteen window, watching as MacIntyre's bulk blocks the entrance into the building, a smile plastered across his face.

Want to read the rest? Use the link below to download from Amazon today:

http://amzn.to/1KIrodZ

NEWSLETTER

Want to keep informed about new releases?

Find out more about the author and her other books at **https://www.emmasalisbury.com**, where you can sign up for her newsletter to receive all the latest updates.

AUTHOR NOTES:

Two books that helped me get a better understanding of undercover work was Shay Doyle & Scott Hesketh's *Deep Cover* published by Ebury Press, and Rob Evans & Paul Lewis' *Undercover – The True Story Of Britain's Secret Police*, published by Faber and Faber Ltd.

Wensley Clarkson's *The Crossing – The Shocking Truth About Gang Wars in Brexit Britain*, illustrated the extent to which organised crime and trafficking has become part of everyday culture in many cities.

ABOUT THE AUTHOR

Emma writes gritty crime fiction that focuses on the 'why'dunnit as well as the 'who'. Her previous job working with socially excluded men and ex-offenders provided her with a lot of inspiration.

When she's not writing she has been known to frequent bars of ill repute, where many a loose lip has provided the nugget of a storyline.

Find out more about the author and her other books at **https://www.emmasalisbury.com**

Printed in Great Britain
by Amazon